IMAGE COMICS, INC. — Robert Kirkman: Chief Operating Officer / Erik Larsen: Chief Financial Officer / Todd McFarlane: President / Marc Silvestri: Chief Executive Officer / Jim Valentino: Vice President / Eric Stephenson: Publisher / Corey Murphy: Director of Sales / Jeff Boison: Director of Publishing Planning & Book Trade Sales / Chris Ross: Director of Digital Sales / Jeff Stang: Director of Specialty Sales / Kat Salazar: Director of PR & Marketing / Branwyn Bigglestone: Controller / Kali Dugan: Senior Accounting Manager / Sue Korpela: Accounting & HR Manager / Drew Gill: Art Director / Heather Doornink: Production Director / Leigh Thomas: Print Manager / Tricia Ramos: Traffic Manager / Briah Skelly: Publicist / Aly Hoffman: Events & Conventions Coordinator / Sasha Head: Sales & Marketing Production Designer / David Brothers: Branding Manager / Melissa Gifford: Content Manager / Drew Fitzgerald: Publicity Assistant / Vincent Kukua: Production Artist / Erika Schnatz: Production Artist / Ryan Brewer: Production Artist / Shanna Matuszak: Production Artist / Carey Hall: Production Artist / Esther Kim: Direct Market Sales Representative / Emilio Bautista: Digital Sales Representative / Leanna Caunter: Accounting Analyst / Chloe Ramos-Peterson: Library Market Sales Representative / Marla Eizik: Administrative Assistant — IMAGECOMICS.COM

WINNEBAGO GRAVEYARD

script
STEVE NILES

art & design
ALISON SAMPSON

color art
**STEPHANE PAITREAU
EIKO TAKAYAMA**

letters
ADITYA BIDIKAR

cover colors
JORDIE BELLAIRE

essays
**SARAH HORROCKS
CASEY GILLY
CLAIRE NAPIER
ANNA TAMBOUR**

guest art
**MINGJUE HELEN CHEN, JEN BARTEL,
DAVID RUBIN, KATIE SKELLY,
PAULINA GANUCHEAU, DOUGLAS NOBLE,
CAITLIN ROSE BOYLE, HANNAH CHRISTENSON,
EMI LENOX, IRENE STRYCHALSKI,
DONYA TODD, ANNIE WU, AUD KOCH,
DAMIEN WORM, DAVE TAYLOR**

for monica, alastair, viv, jes, olivier & shayla

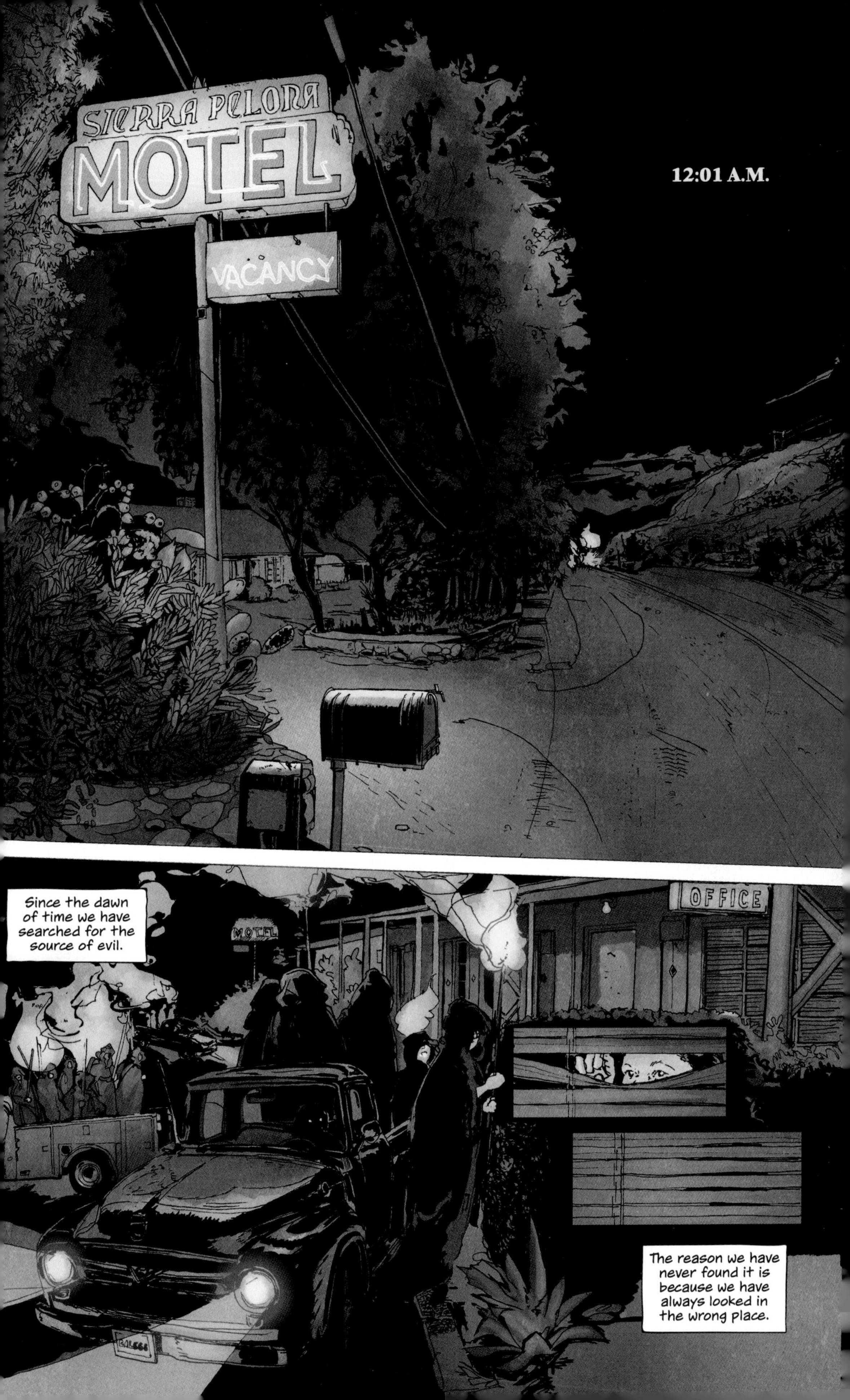
SIERRA PELONA
MOTEL
VACANCY
12:01 A.M.
Since the dawn of time we have searched for the source of evil.
MOTEL
OFFICE
The reason we have never found it is because we have always looked in the wrong place.

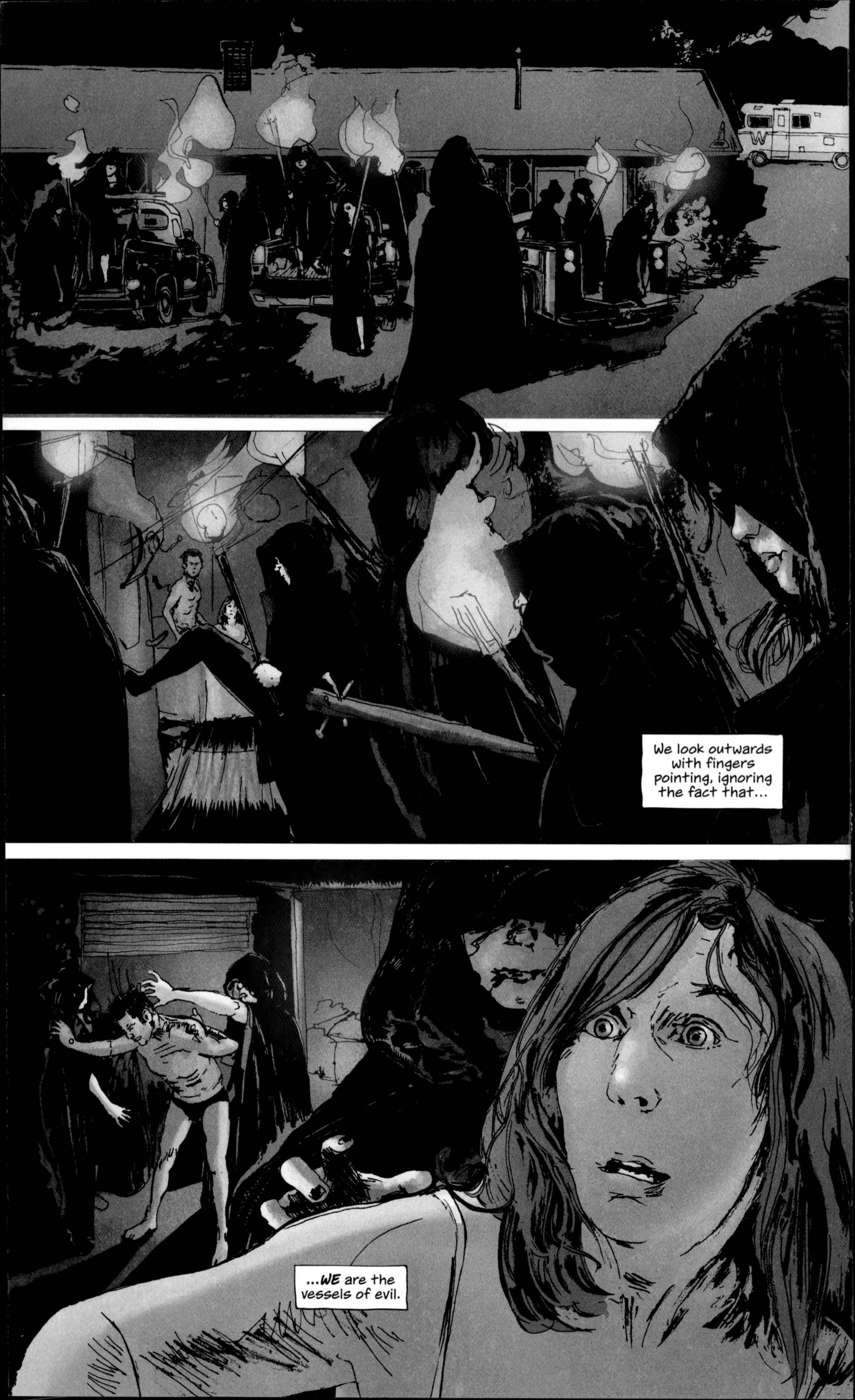
We look outwards with fingers pointing, ignoring the fact that...
...WE are the vessels of evil.

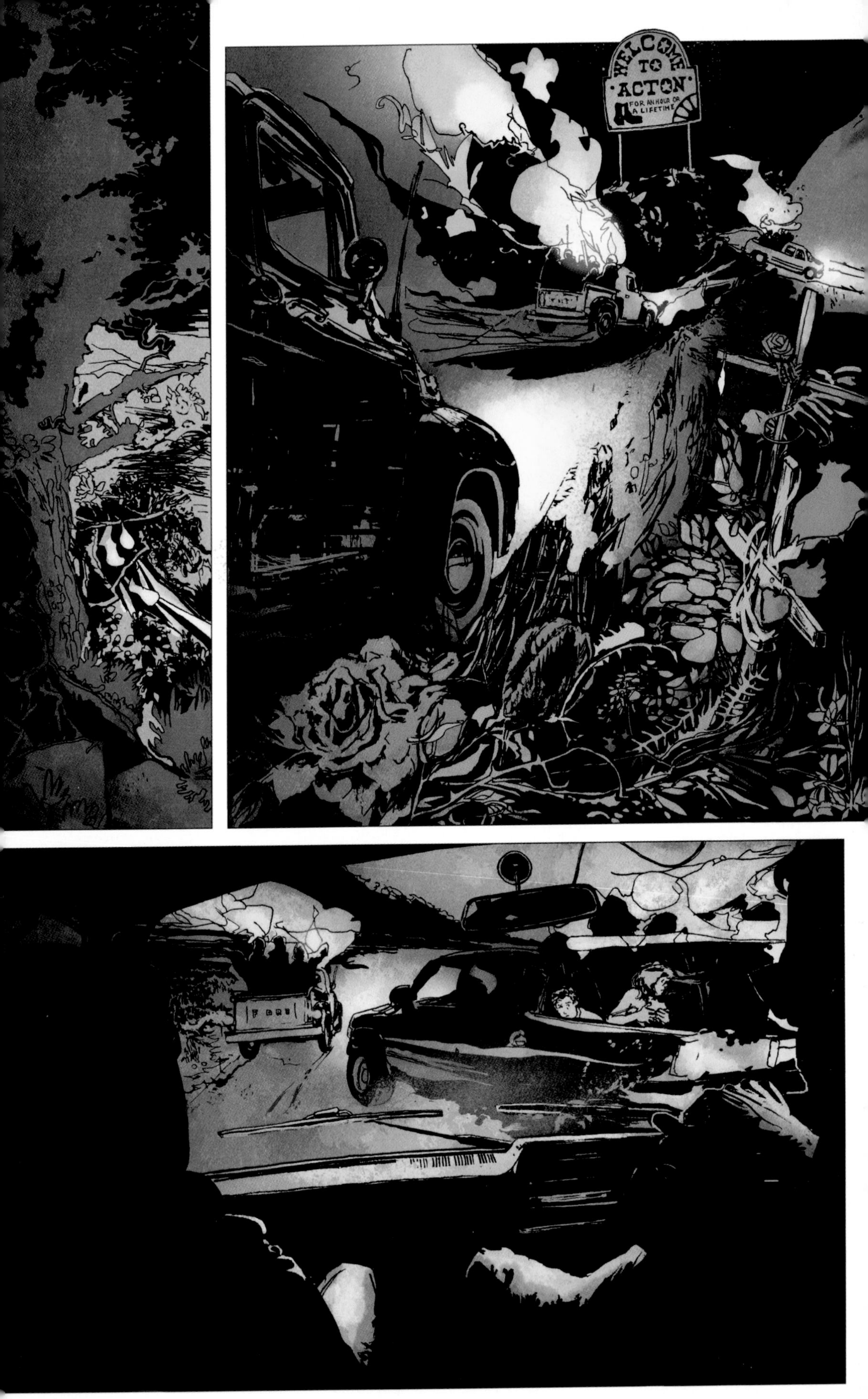
WELCOME TO ACTON
FOR AN HOUR OR A LIFETIME

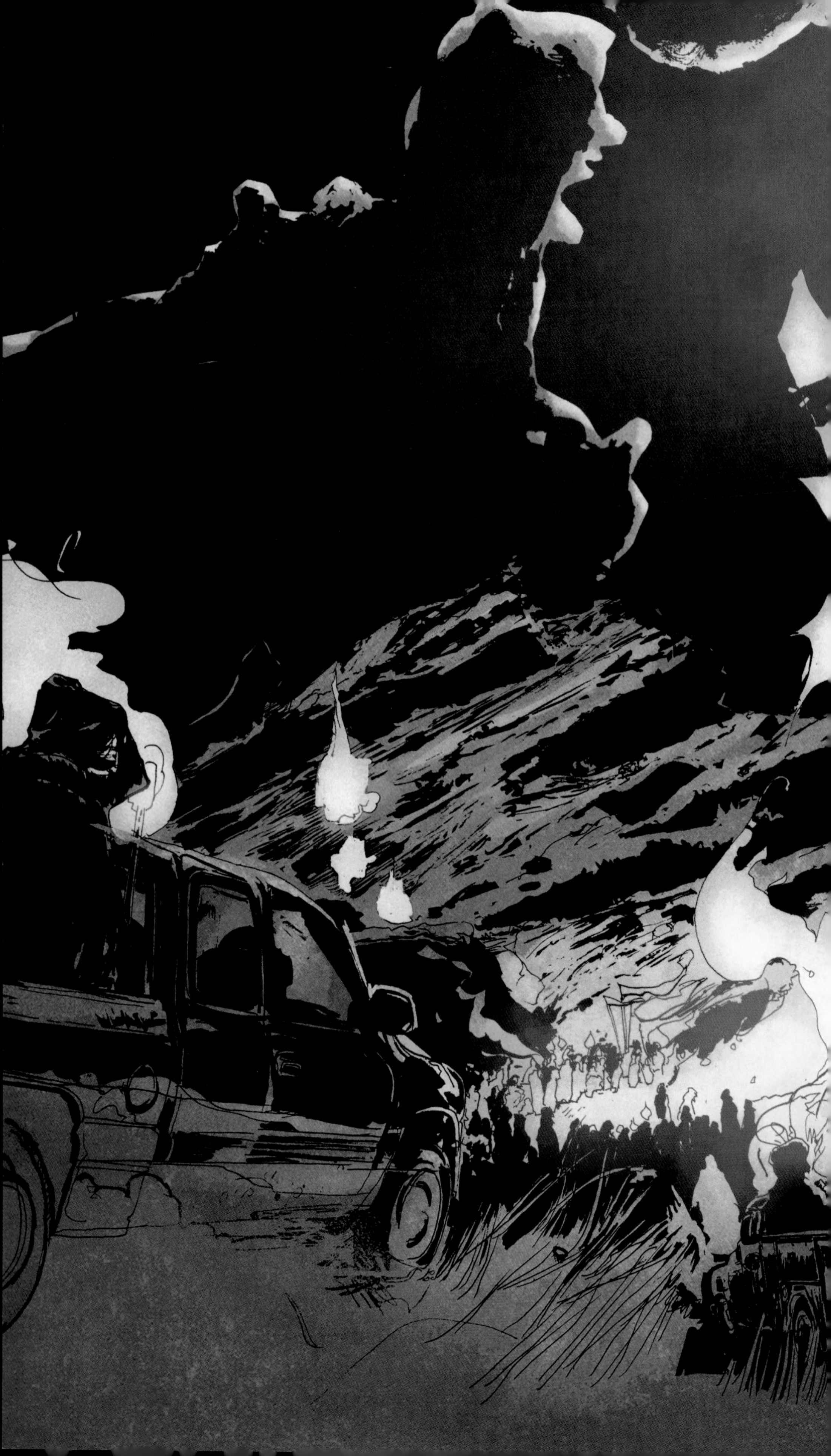

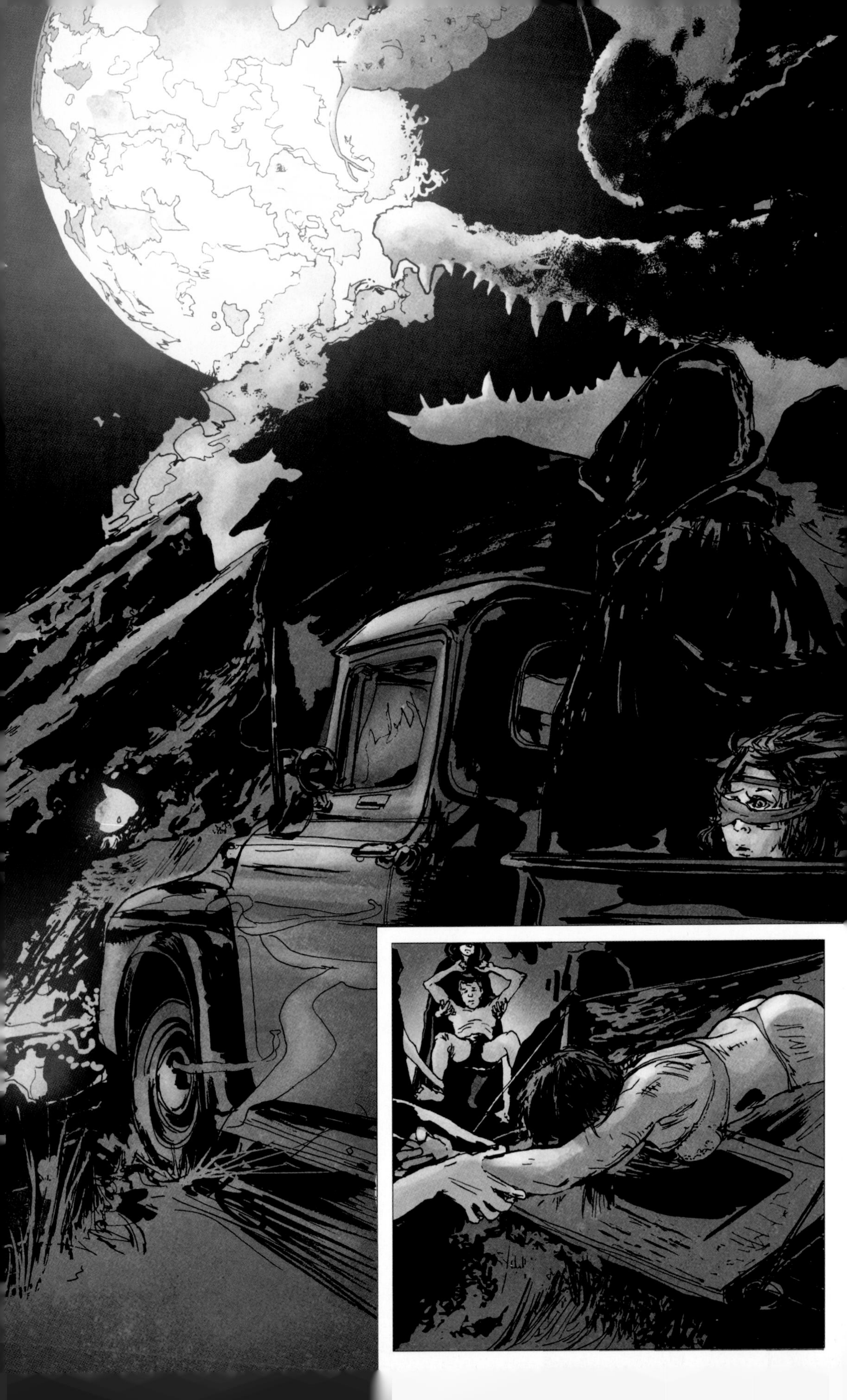

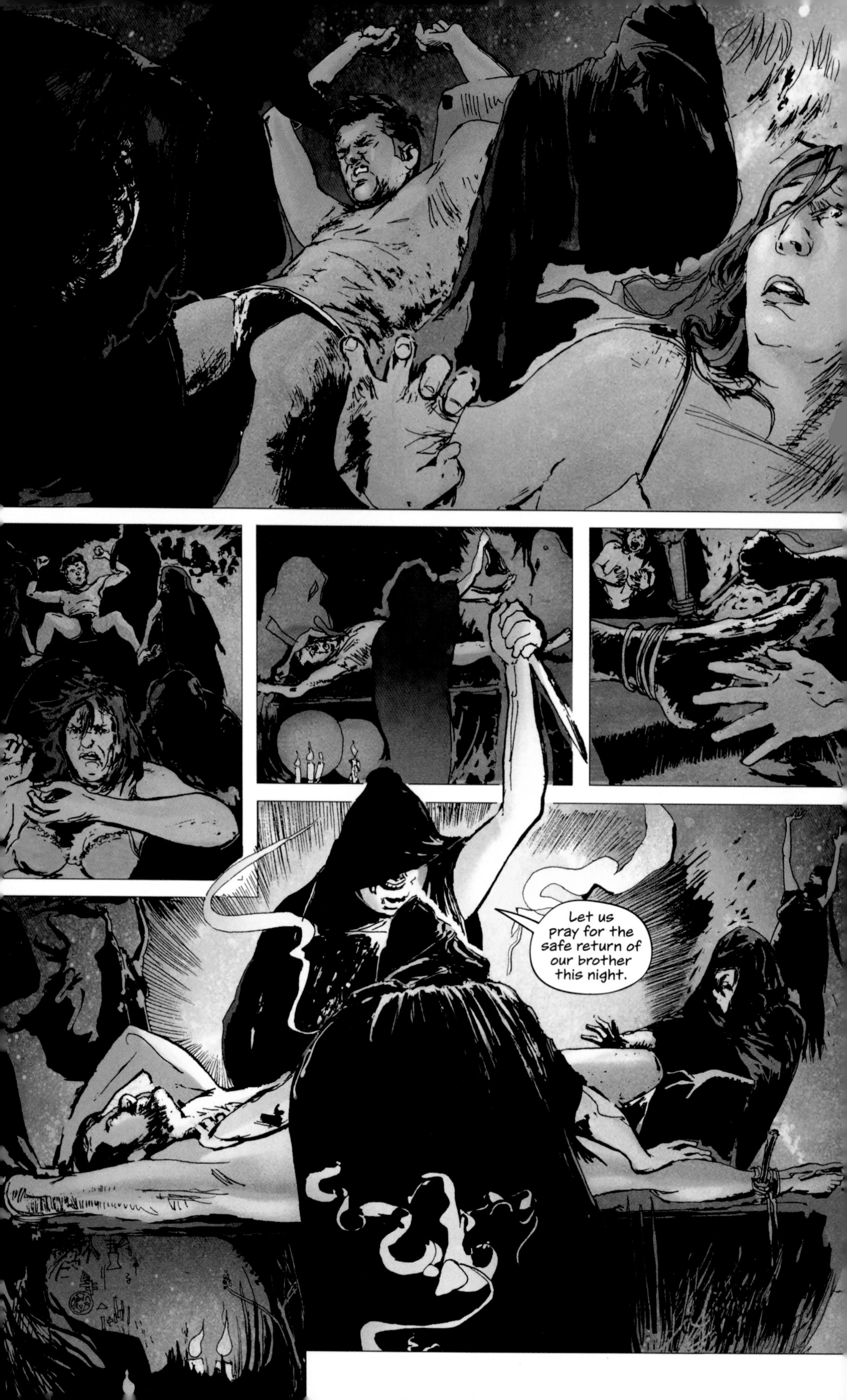
Let us pray for the safe return of our brother this night.

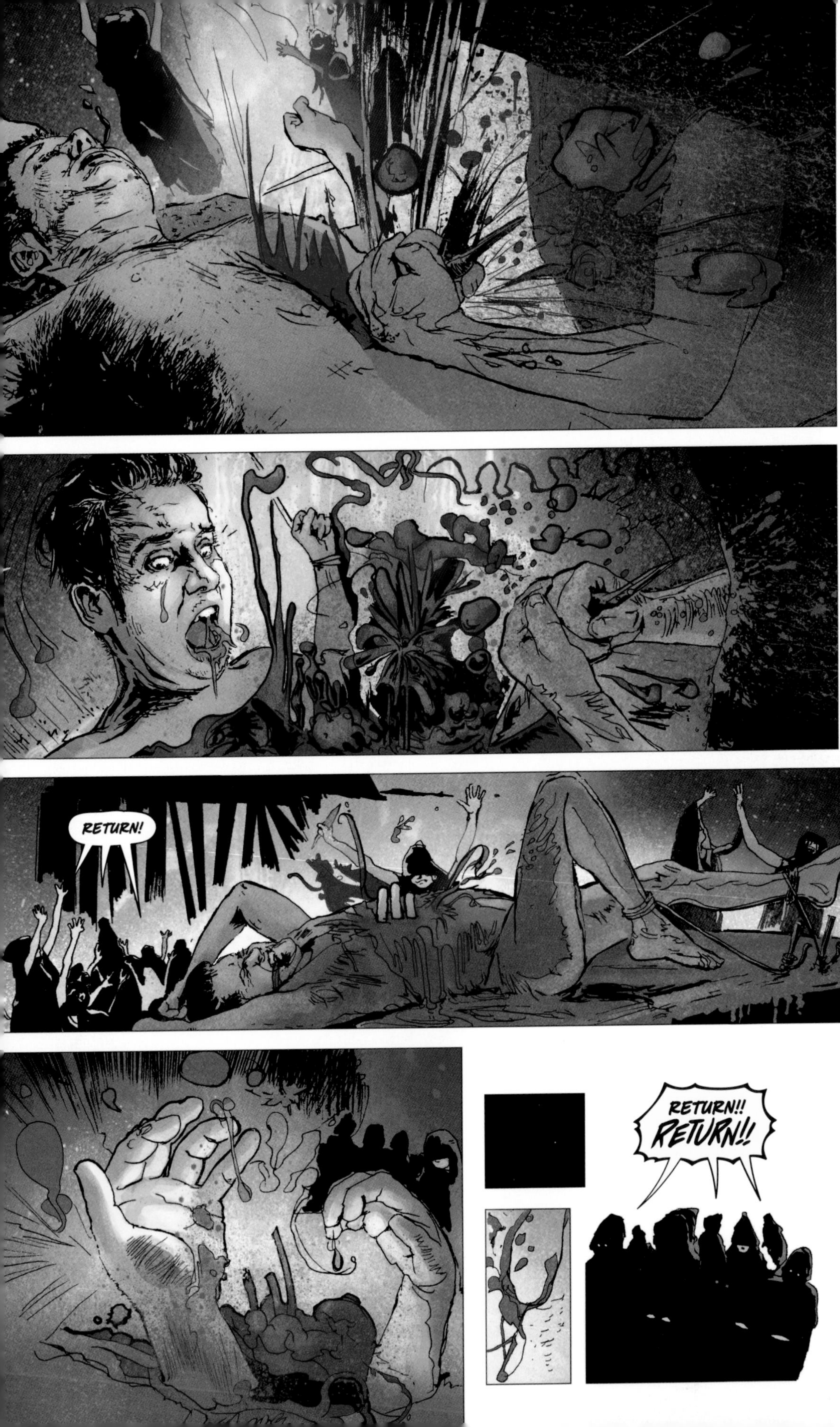
RETURN!
RETURN!! RETURN!!

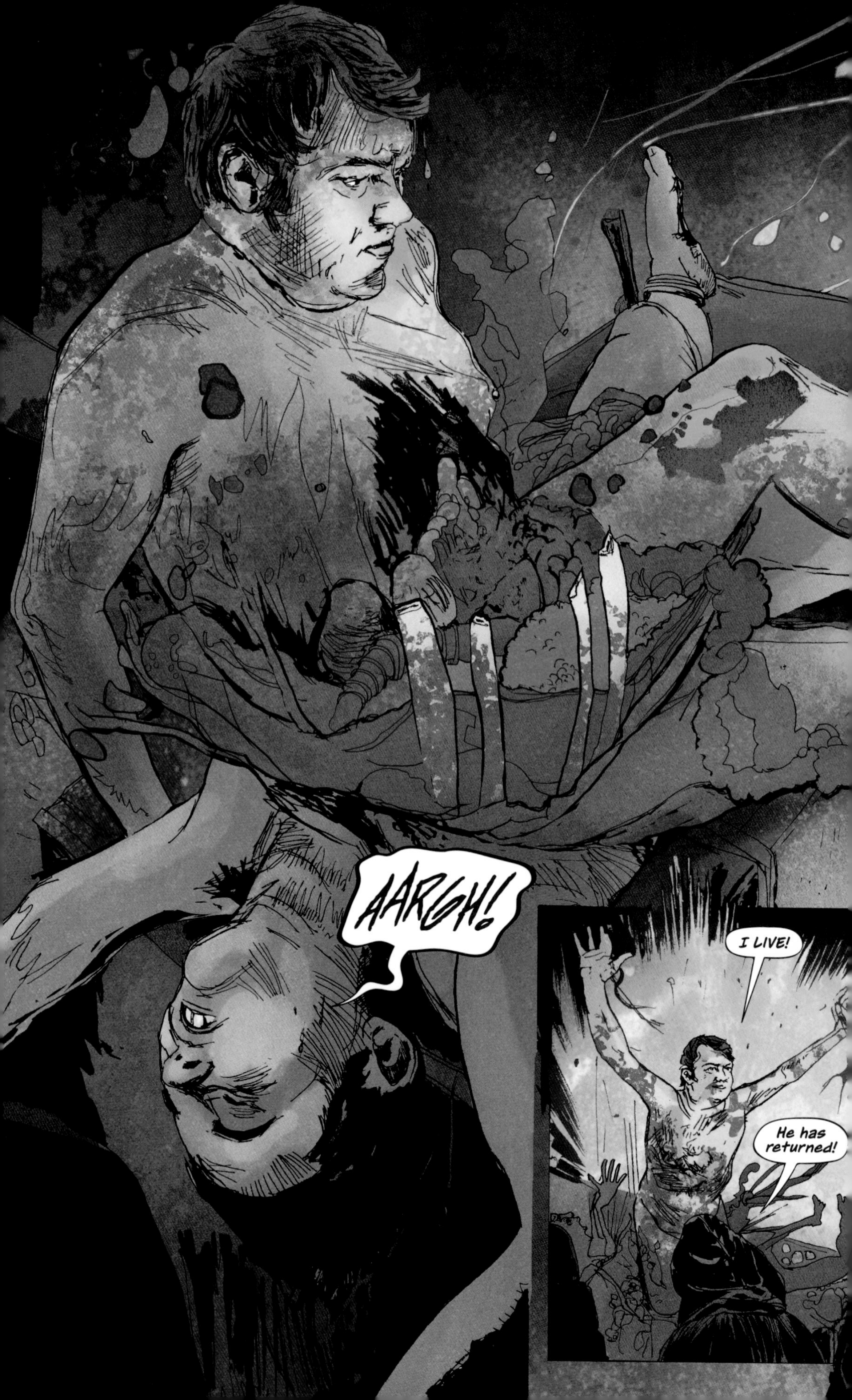
AARGH!
I LIVE!
He has returned!

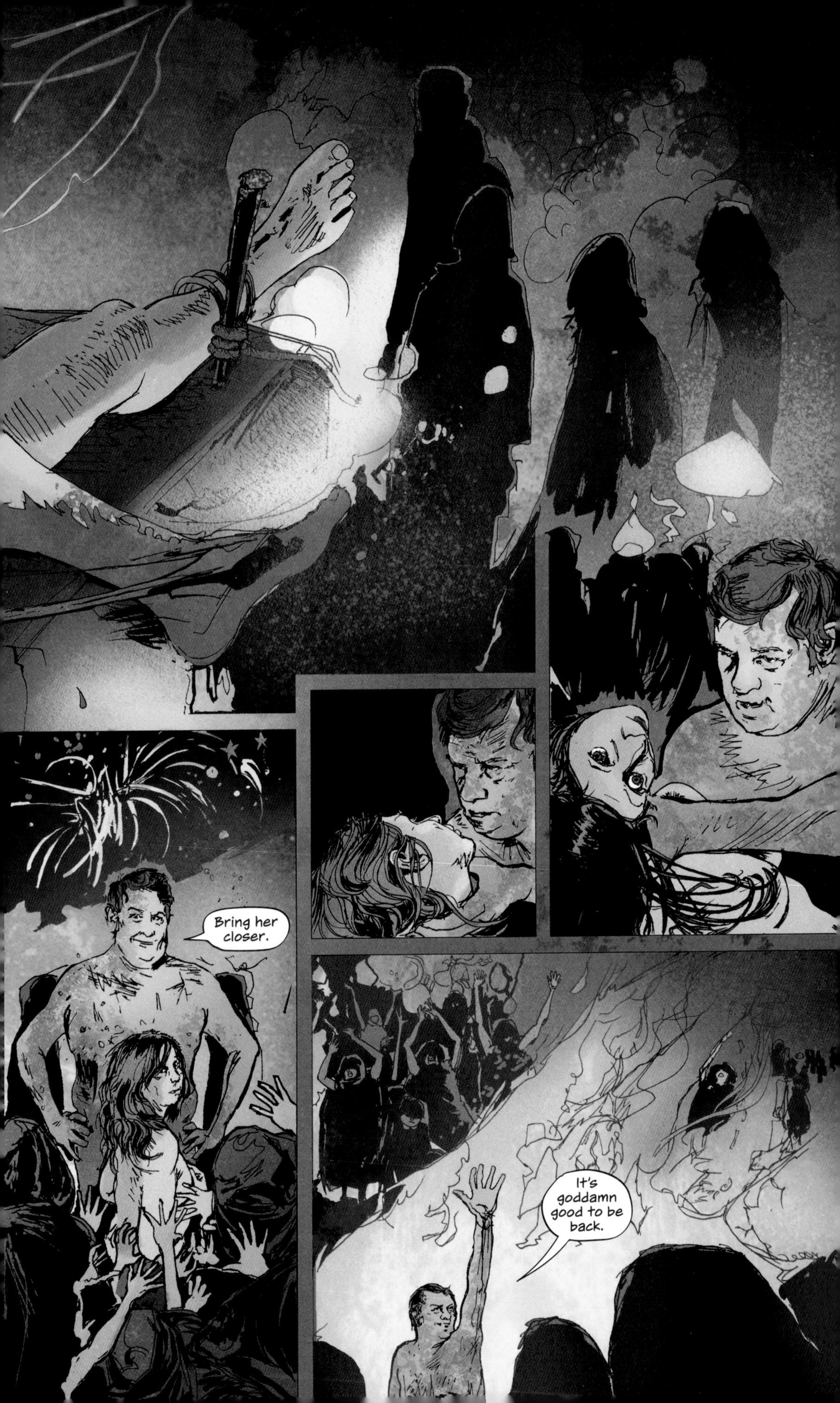
Bring her closer.
It's goddamn good to be back.

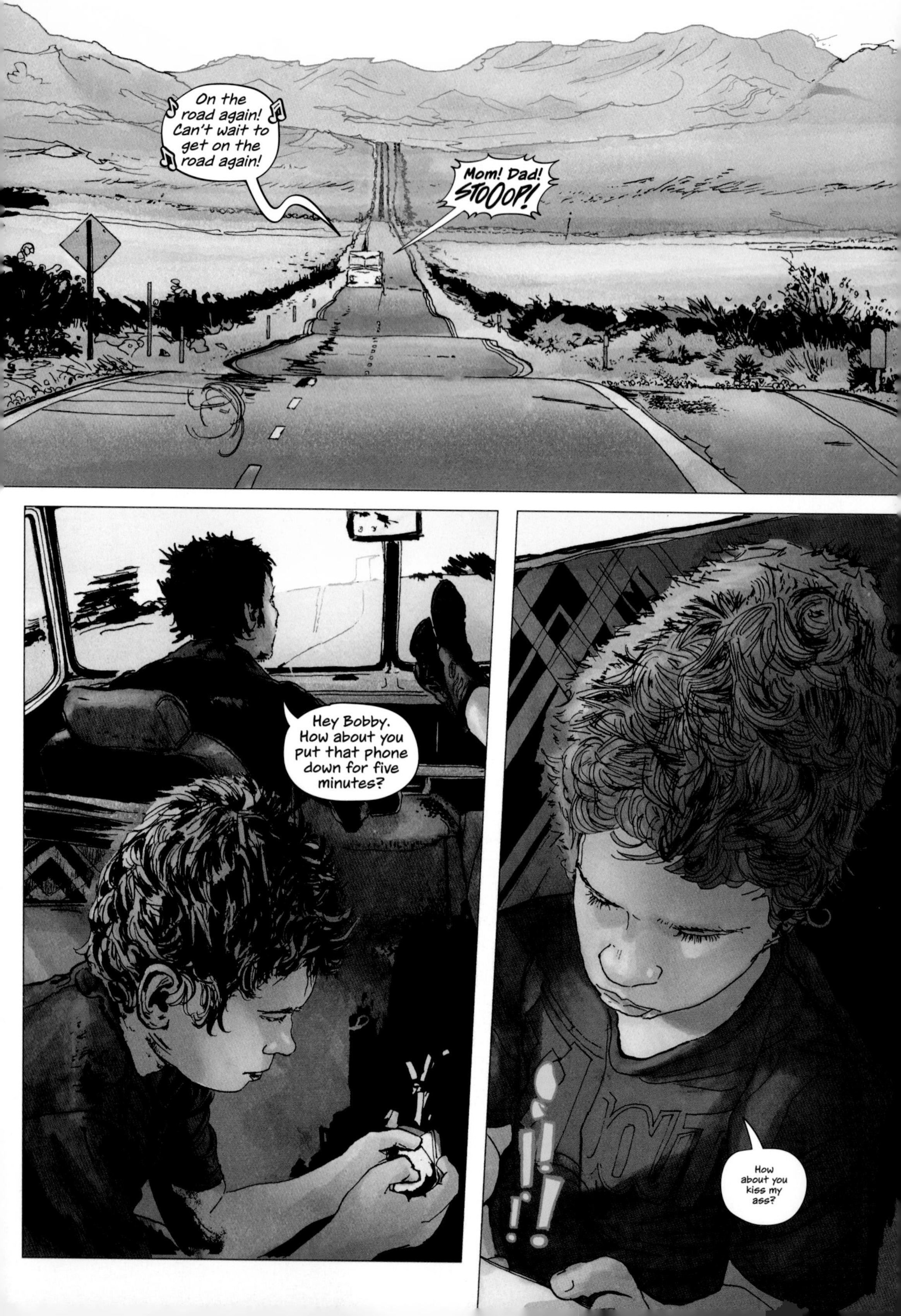

On the road again! Can't wait to get on the road again!
Mom! Dad! STOOOP!
Hey Bobby. How about you put that phone down for five minutes?
How about you kiss my ass?

ROADSIDE
CORBIS
CARNIVAL

SKREEEE

What did you say?!

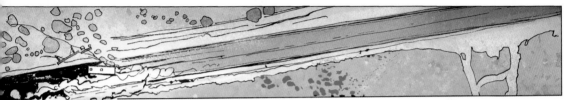

Dan...don't. It's what he wants. Come out and talk to me. Come on.

You have to calm down. He wants to get you fired up.

This is our first trip as a family, Christie. He could at least try.

He's thirteen. In his way he is trying. You have to give him some slack.

He thought he'd be spending the summer with his dad so he's bound to act out.

I know you're right but...I've had enough of his shit.

You need to be the cooler head here, the adult even.

Or we could all act like kids. Let's go to the carnival!

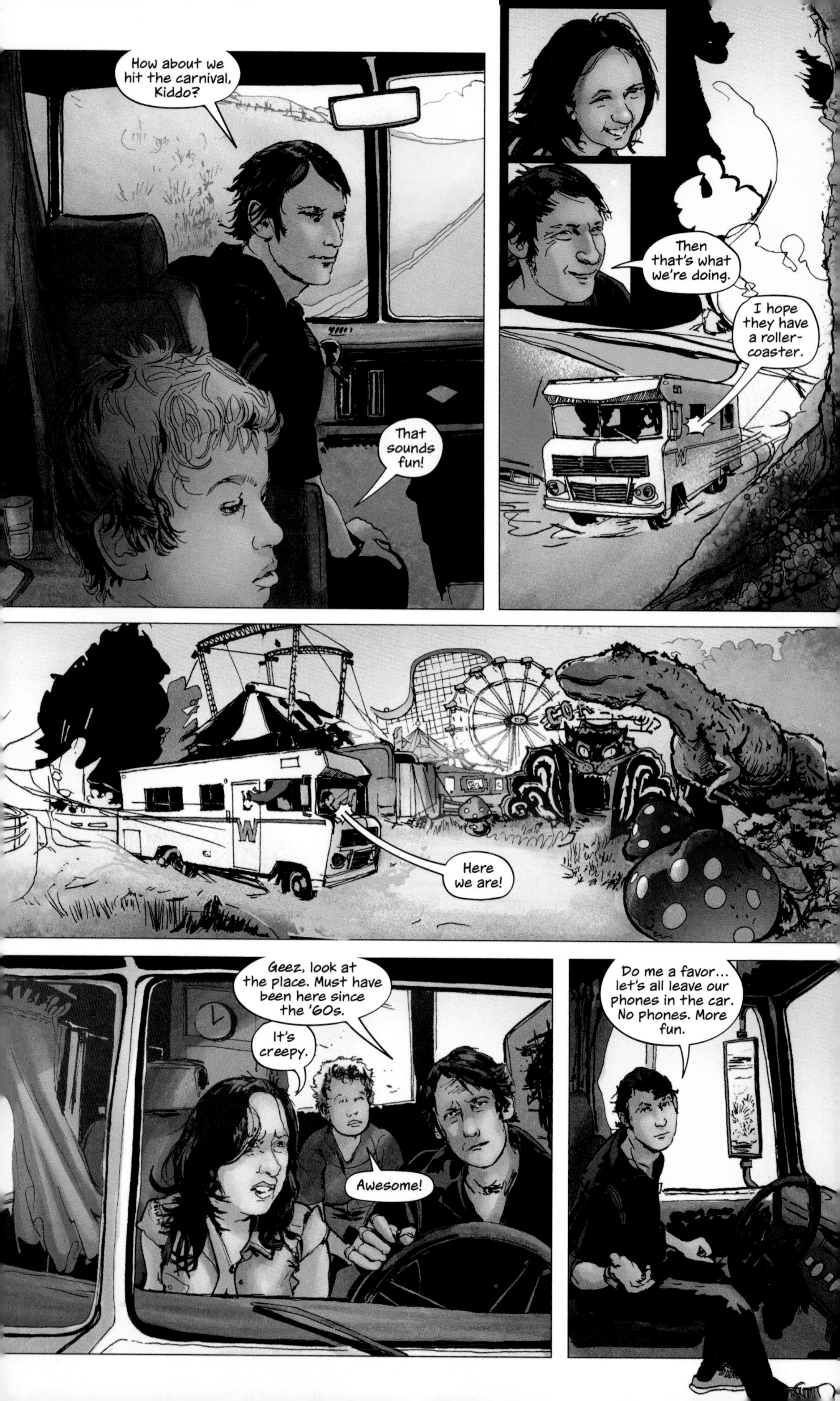
How about we hit the carnival, Kiddo?
That sounds fun!
Then that's what we're doing.
I hope they have a roller-coaster.
Here we are!
Geez, look at the place. Must have been here since the '60s.
It's creepy.
Awesome!
Do me a favor... let's all leave our phones in the car. No phones. More fun.

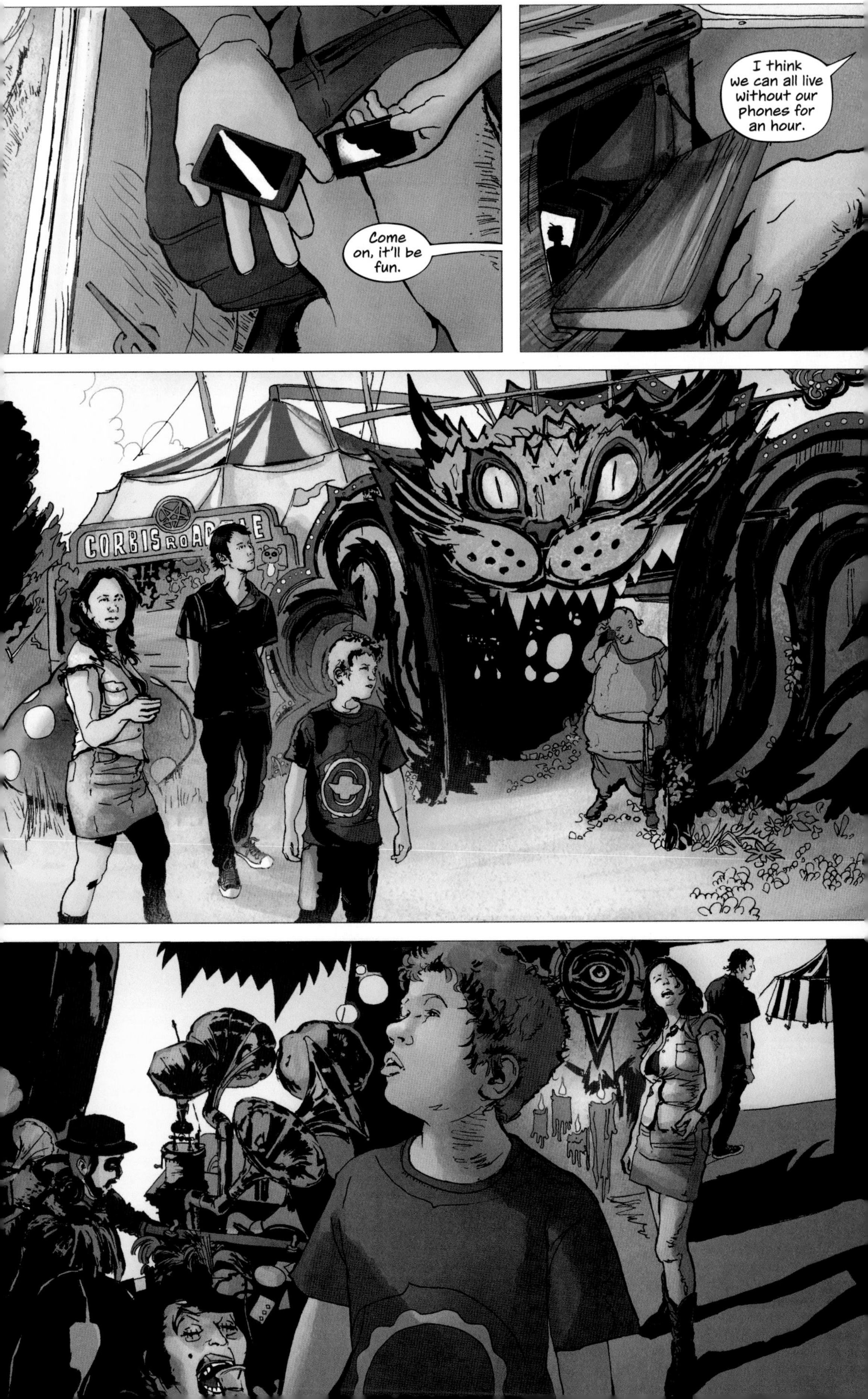
Come on, it'll be fun.
I think we can all live without our phones for an hour.
CORBIS

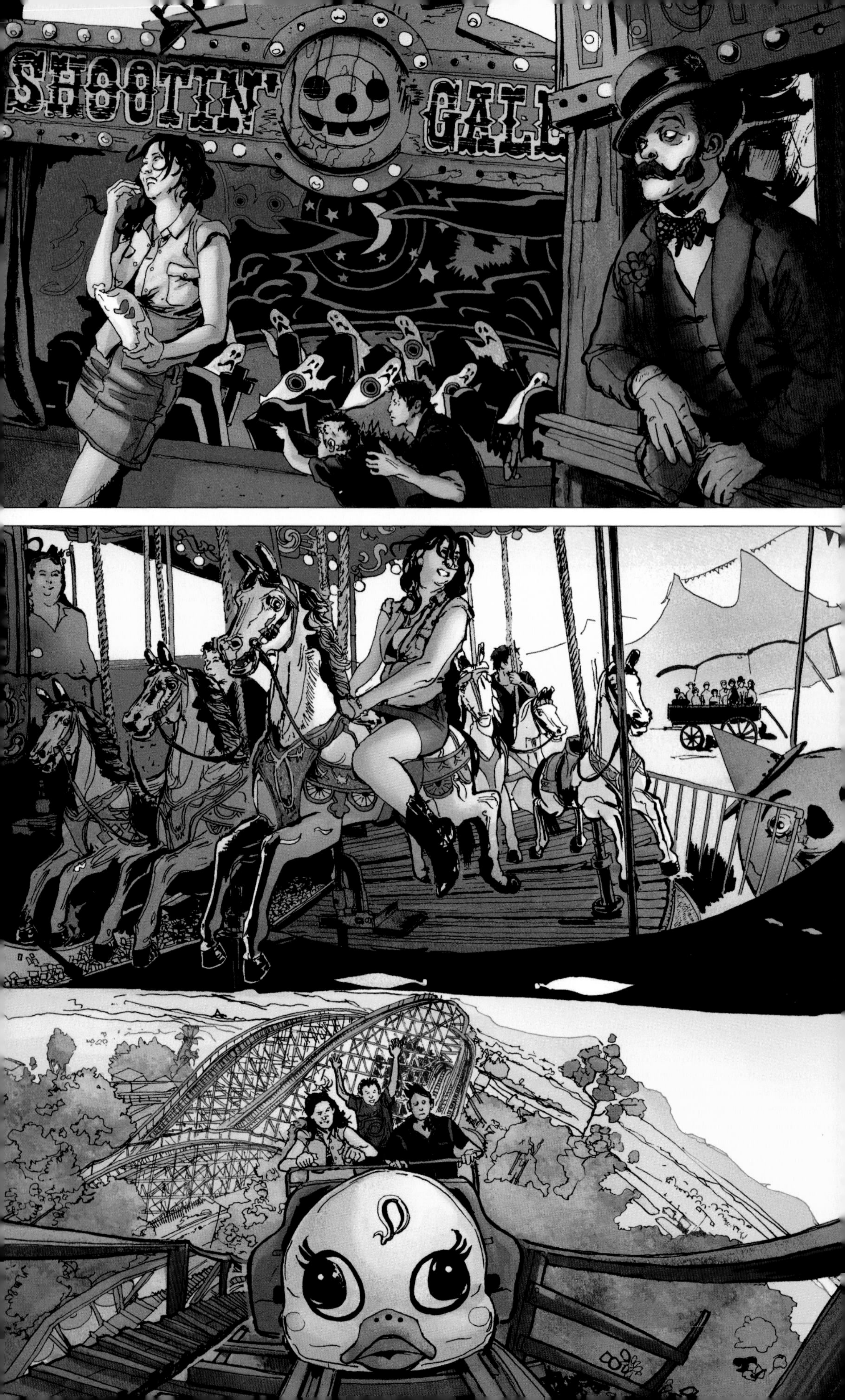
SHOOTIN' GALL

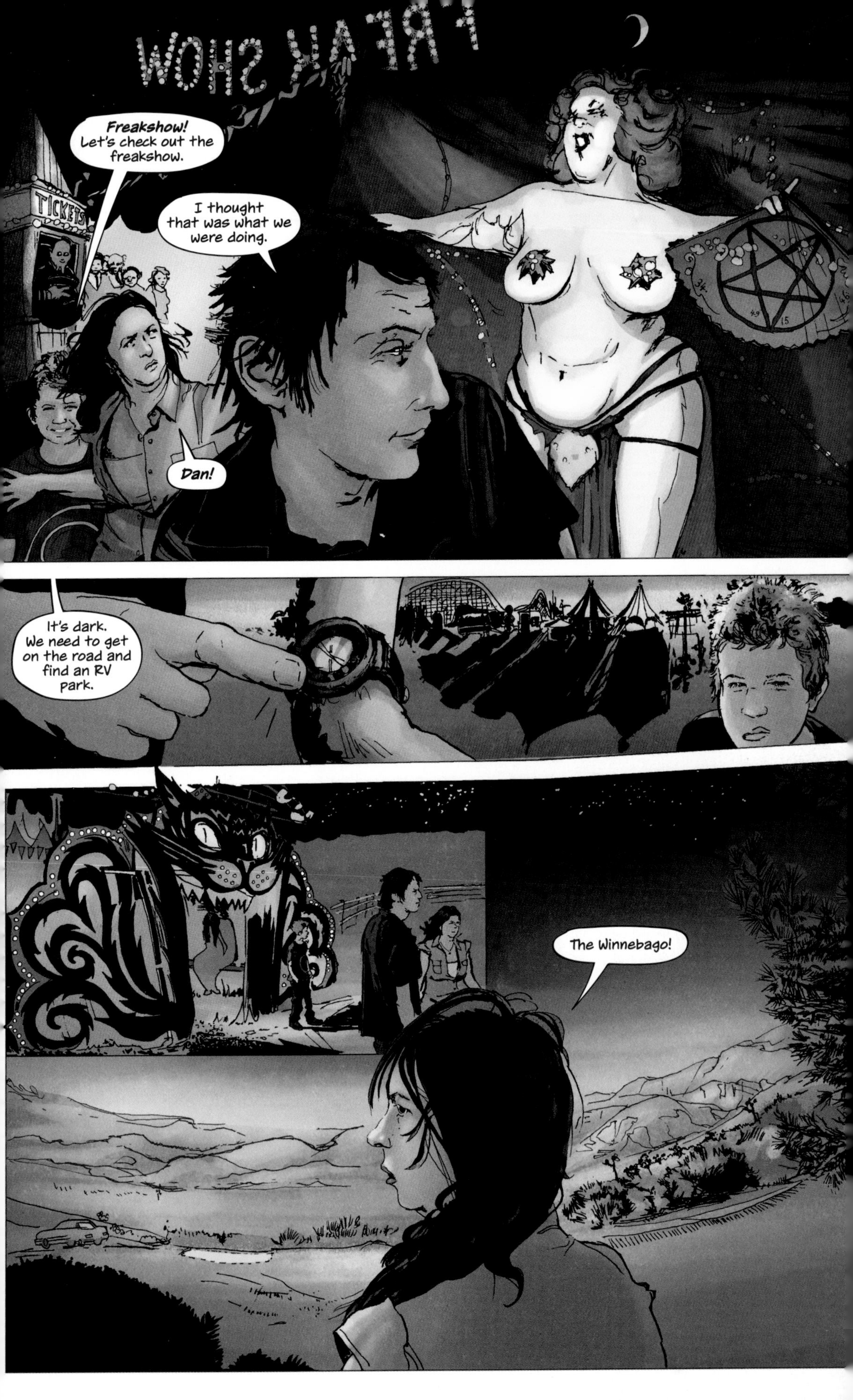

Freakshow! Let's check out the freakshow.
I thought that was what we were doing.
Dan!
TICKETS
It's dark. We need to get on the road and find an RV park.
The Winnebago!

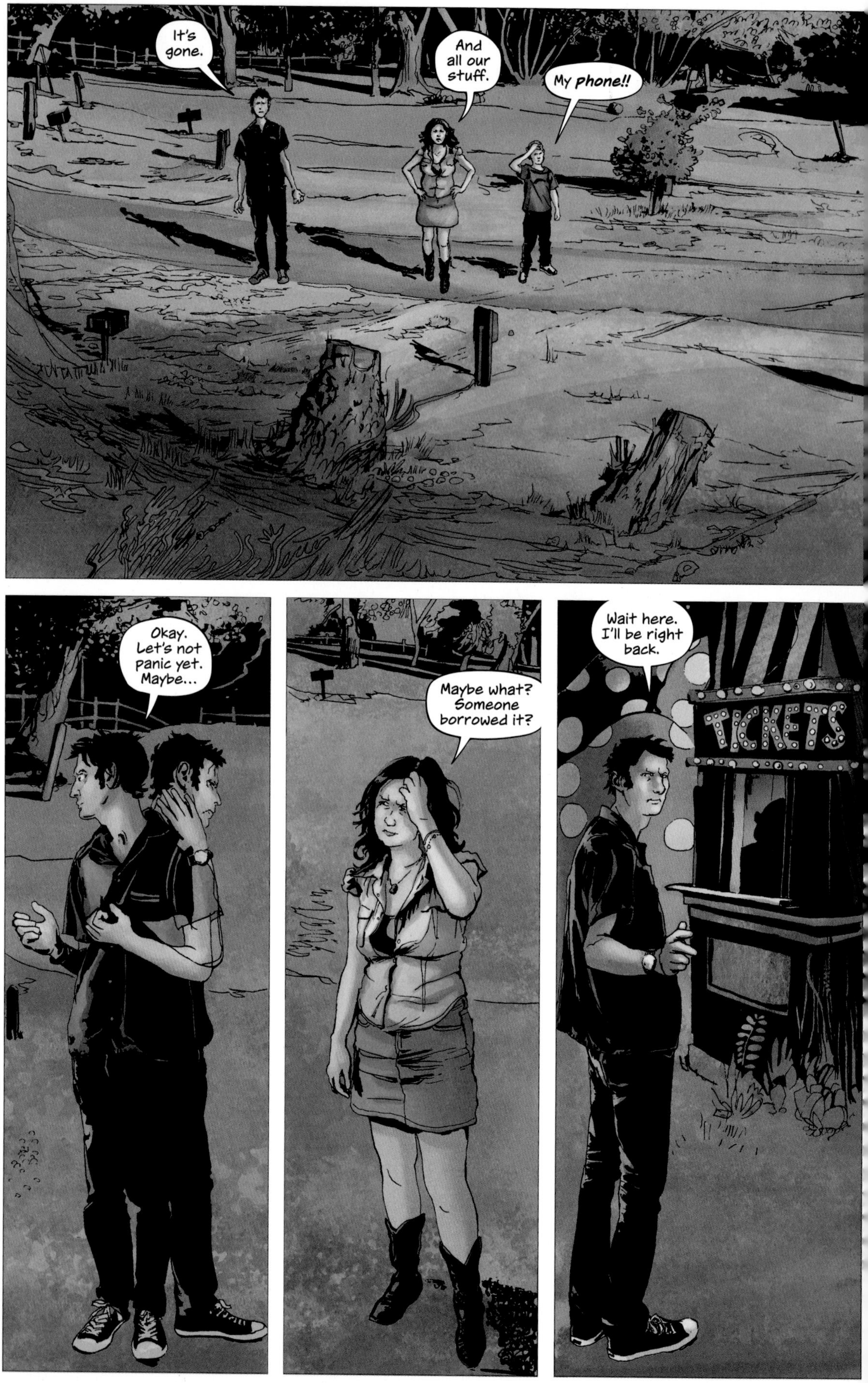
It's gone.
And all our stuff.
My phone!!
Okay. Let's not panic yet. Maybe...
Maybe what? Someone borrowed it?
Wait here. I'll be right back.
TICKETS

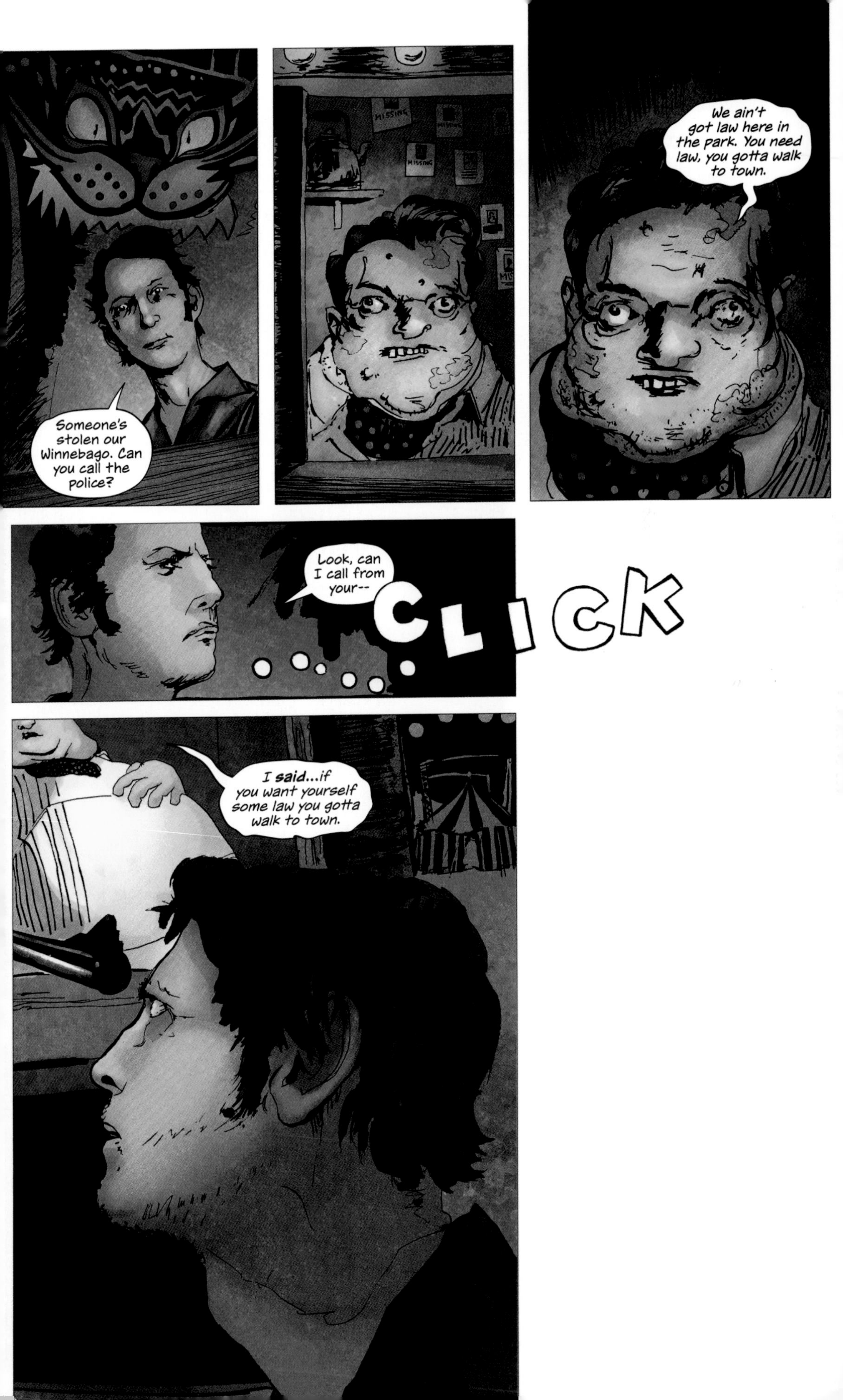
Someone's stolen our Winnebago. Can you call the police?
We ain't got law here in the park. You need law, you gotta walk to town.
MISSING
MISSING
Look, can I call from your--
CLICK
I **said**...if you want yourself some law you gotta walk to town.

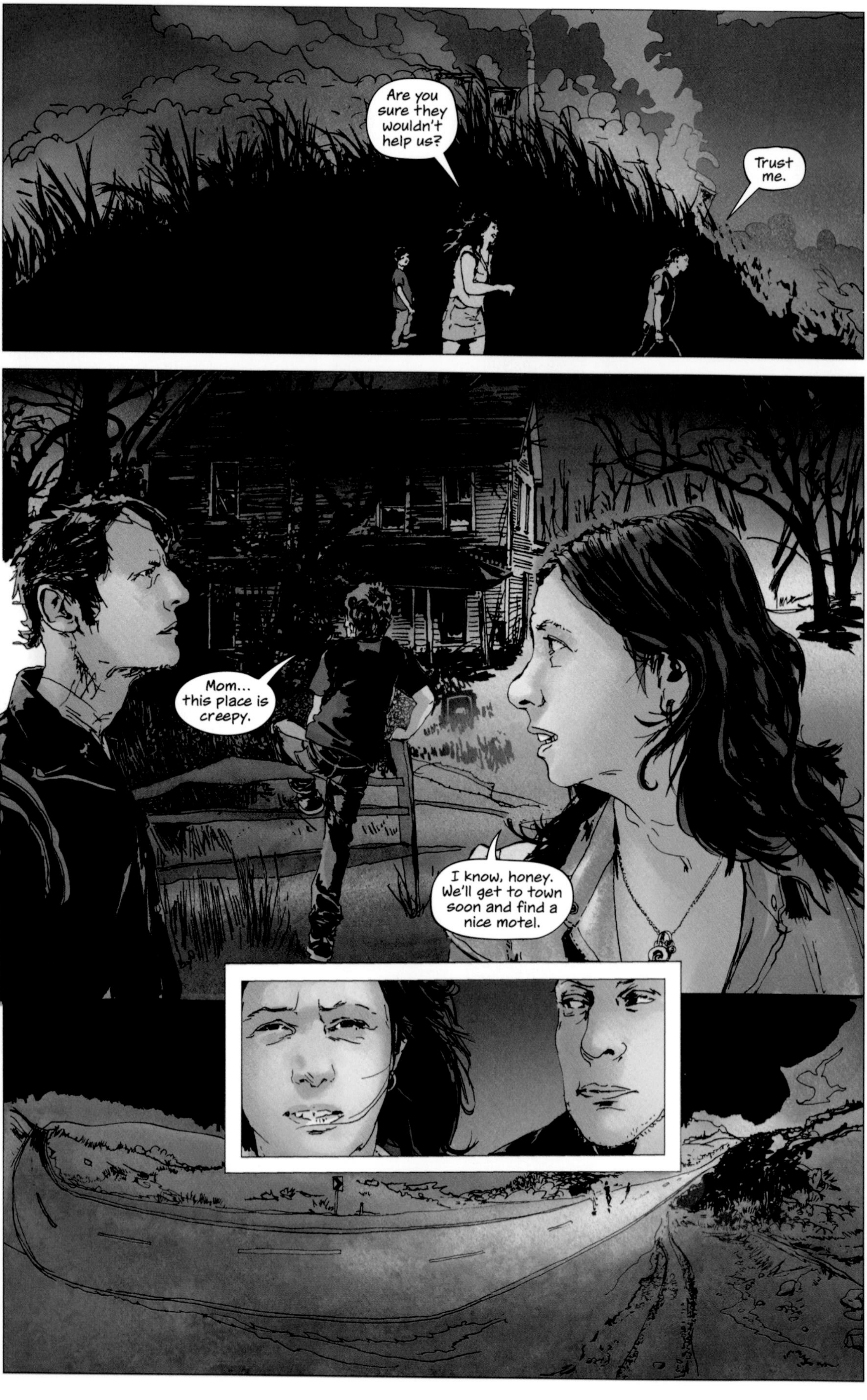
Are you sure they wouldn't help us?
Trust me.
Mom... this place is creepy.
I know, honey. We'll get to town soon and find a nice motel.

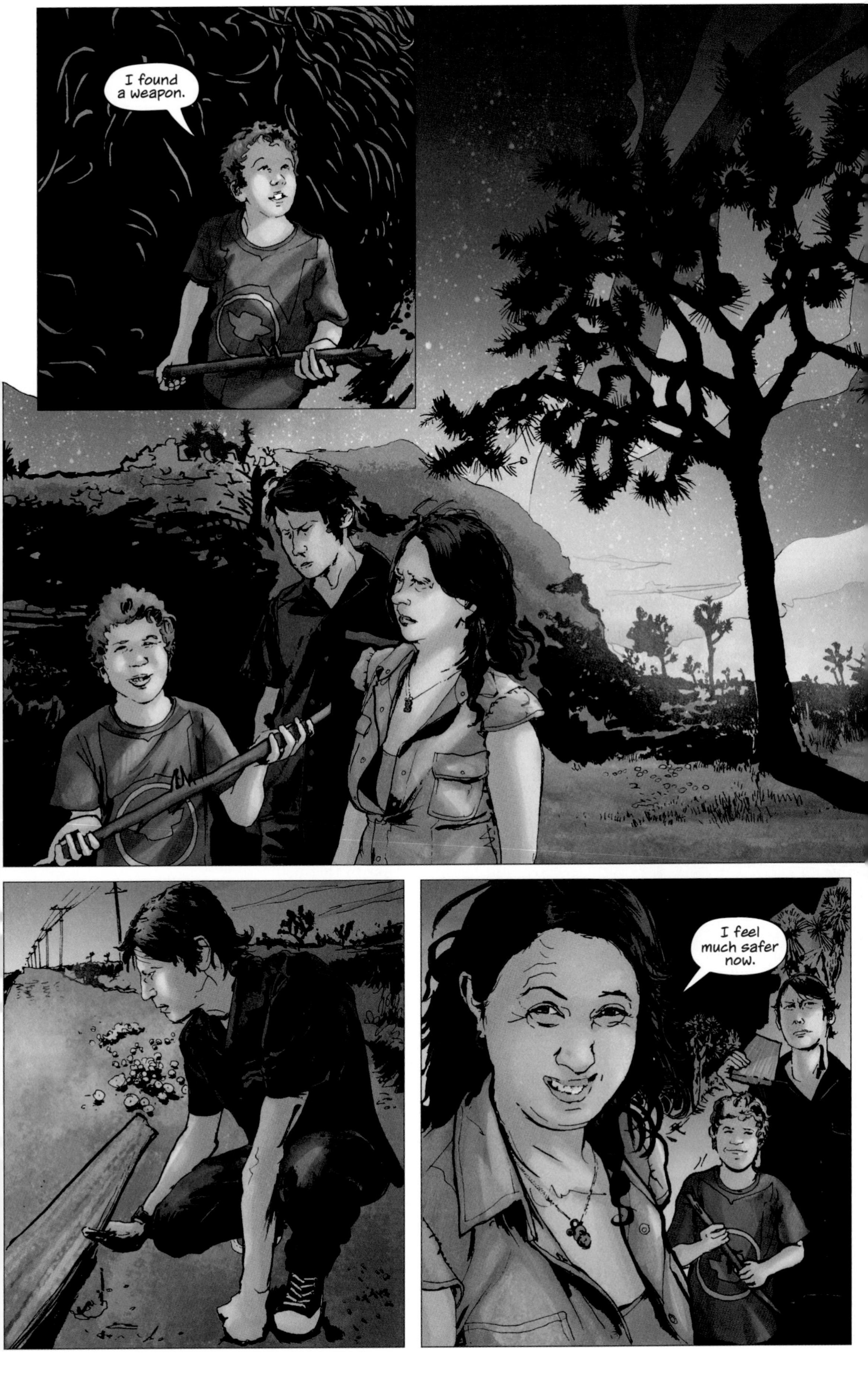
I found a weapon.
I feel much safer now.

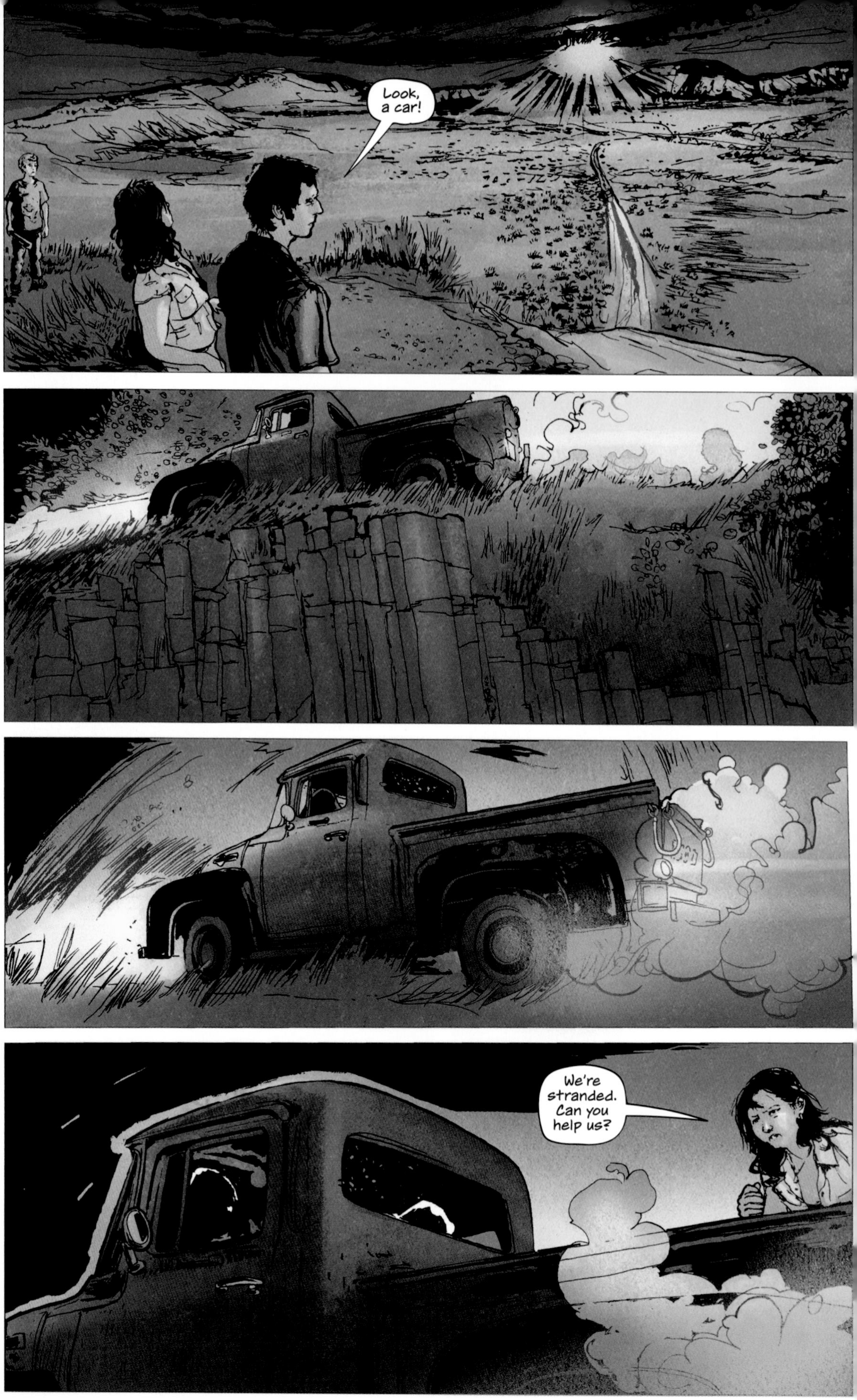
Look, a car!
We're stranded. Can you help us?

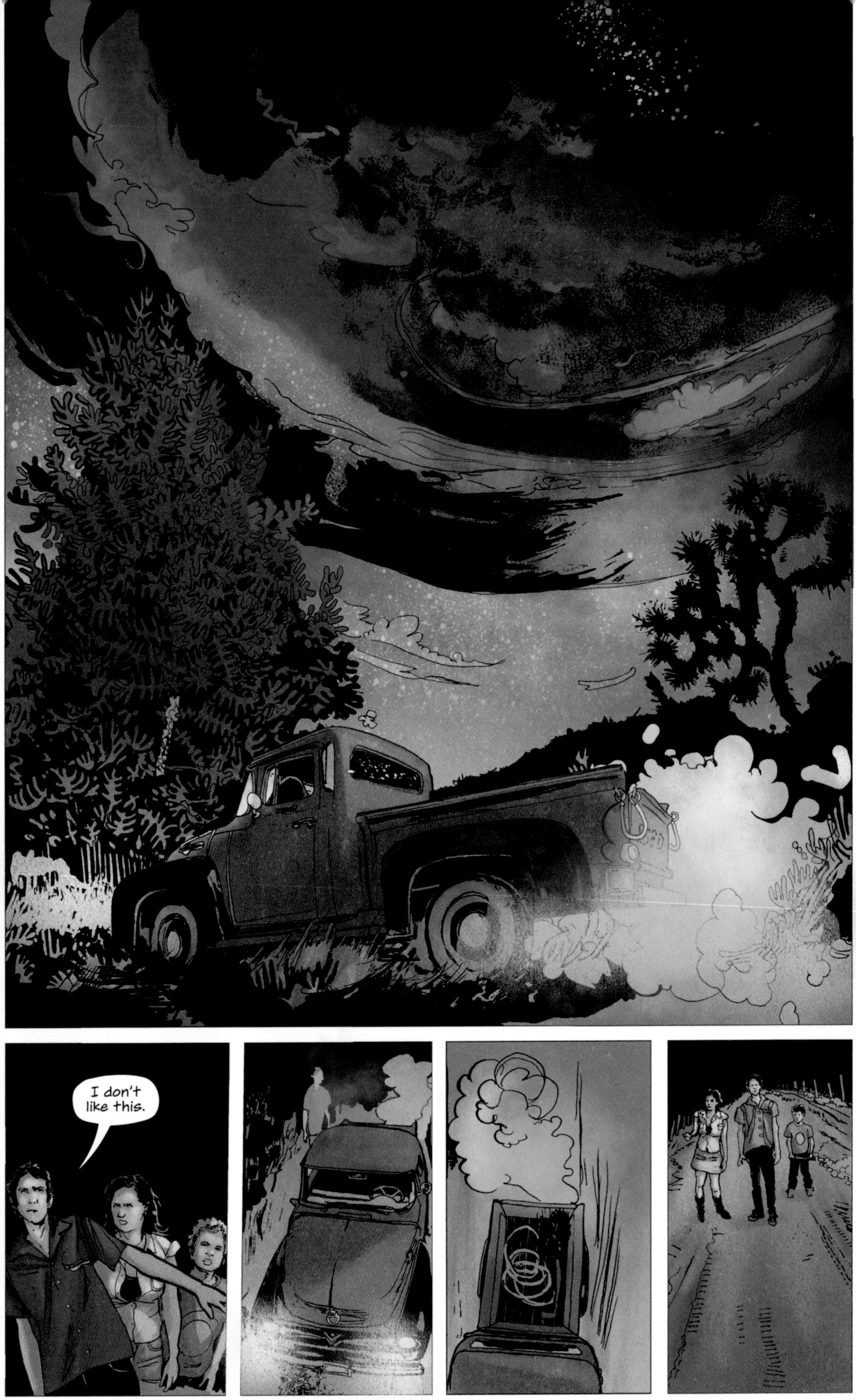
I don't like this.

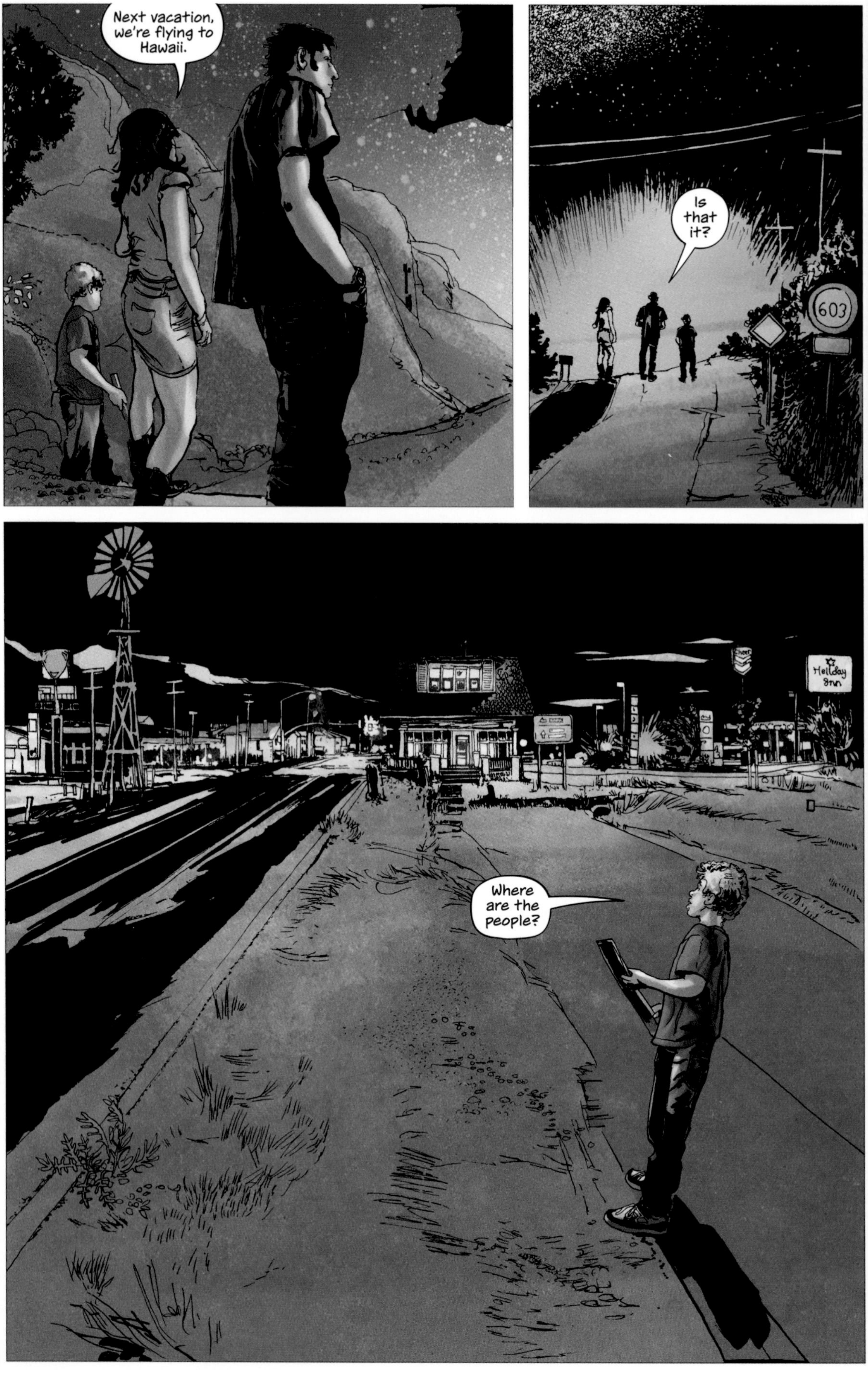

Next vacation, we're flying to Hawaii.
Is that it?
603
Where are the people?

CHAPTER 2

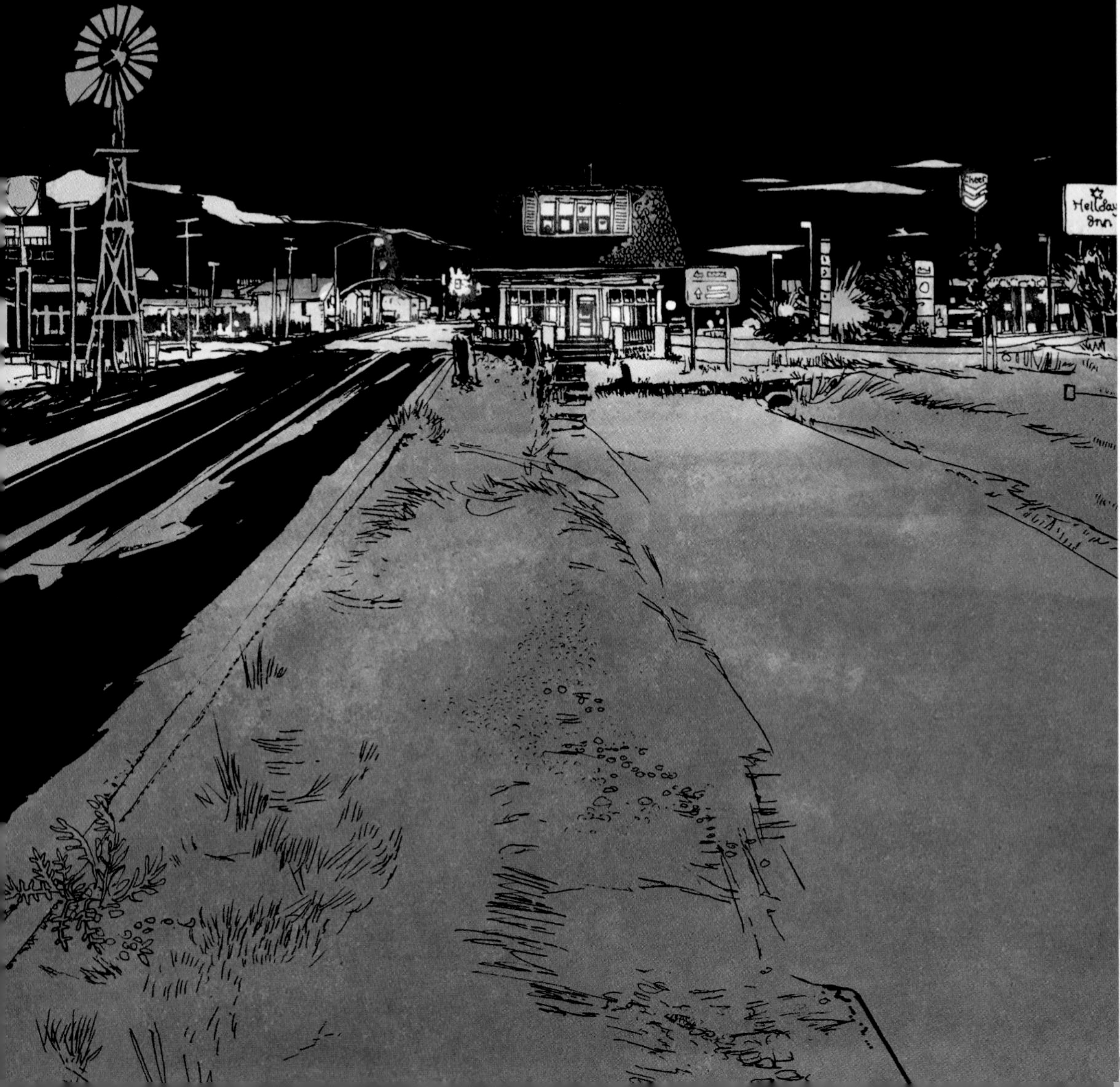

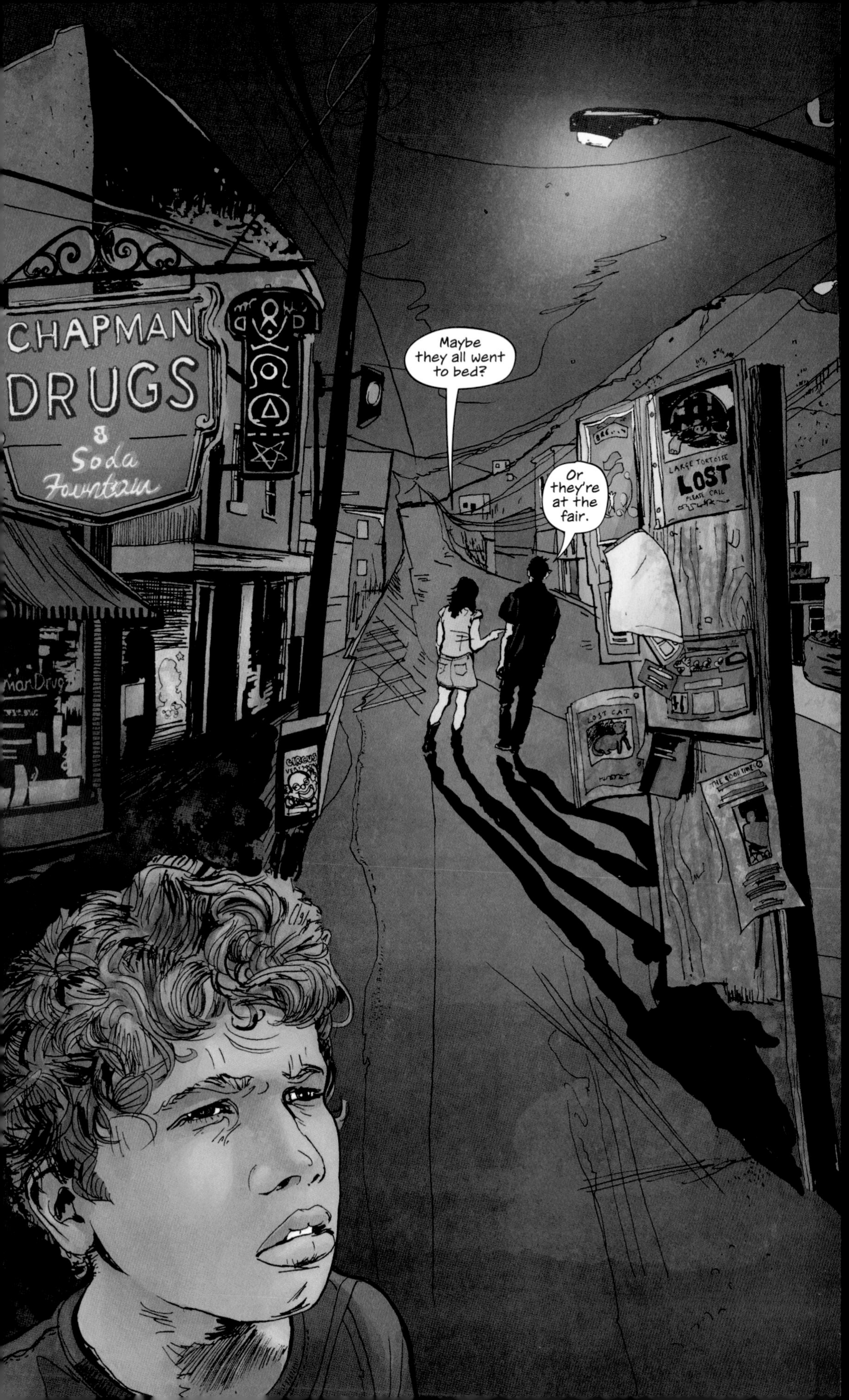
CHAPMAN DRUGS
&
Soda Fountain
Maybe they all went to bed?
Or they're at the fair.
LARGE TORTOISE
LOST
PLEASE CALL
LOST CAT
CIRCUS

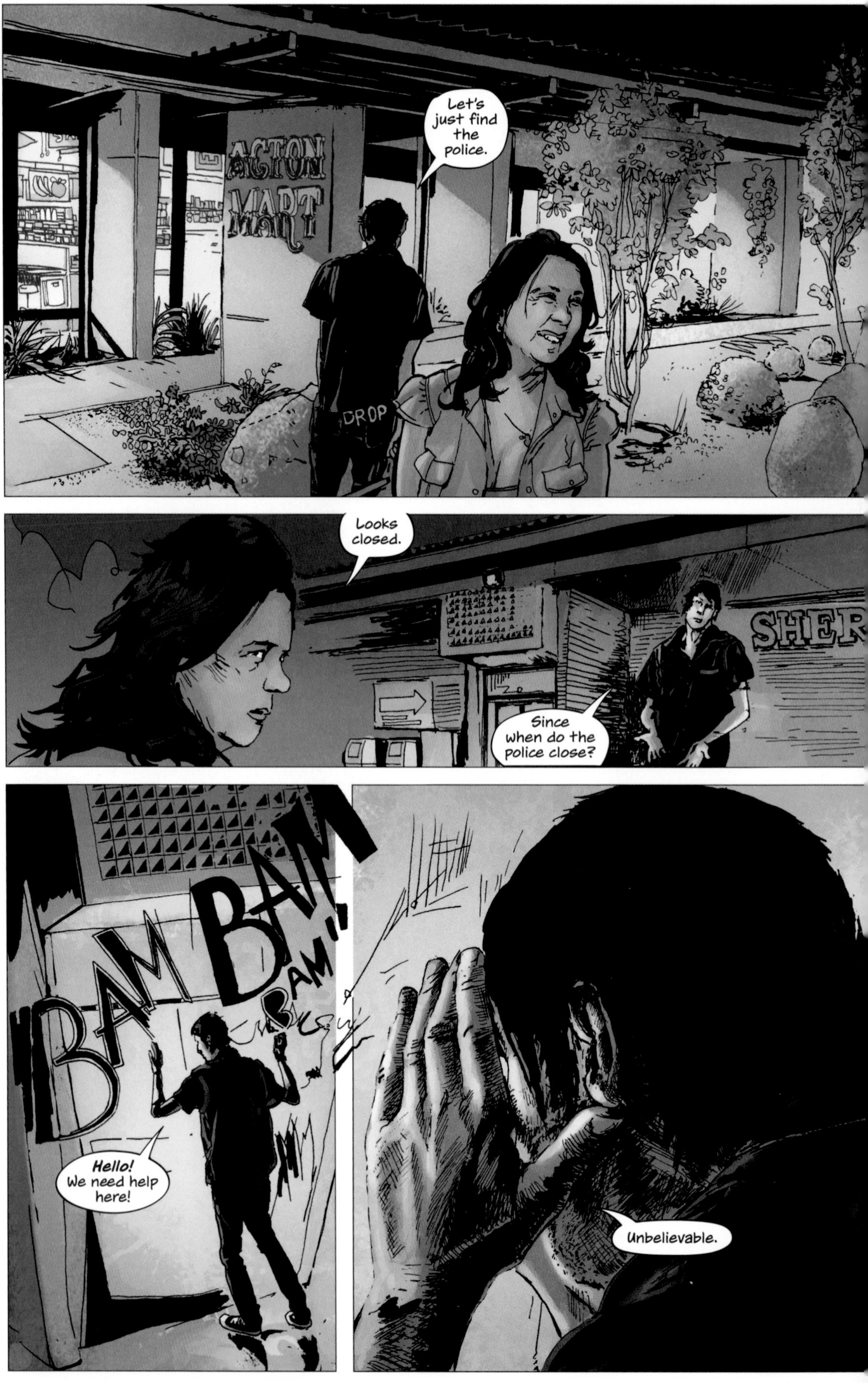
ACTON MART
Let's just find the police.
DROP
Looks closed.
SHER
Since when do the police close?
BAM
BAM
BAM
Hello! We need help here!
Unbelievable.

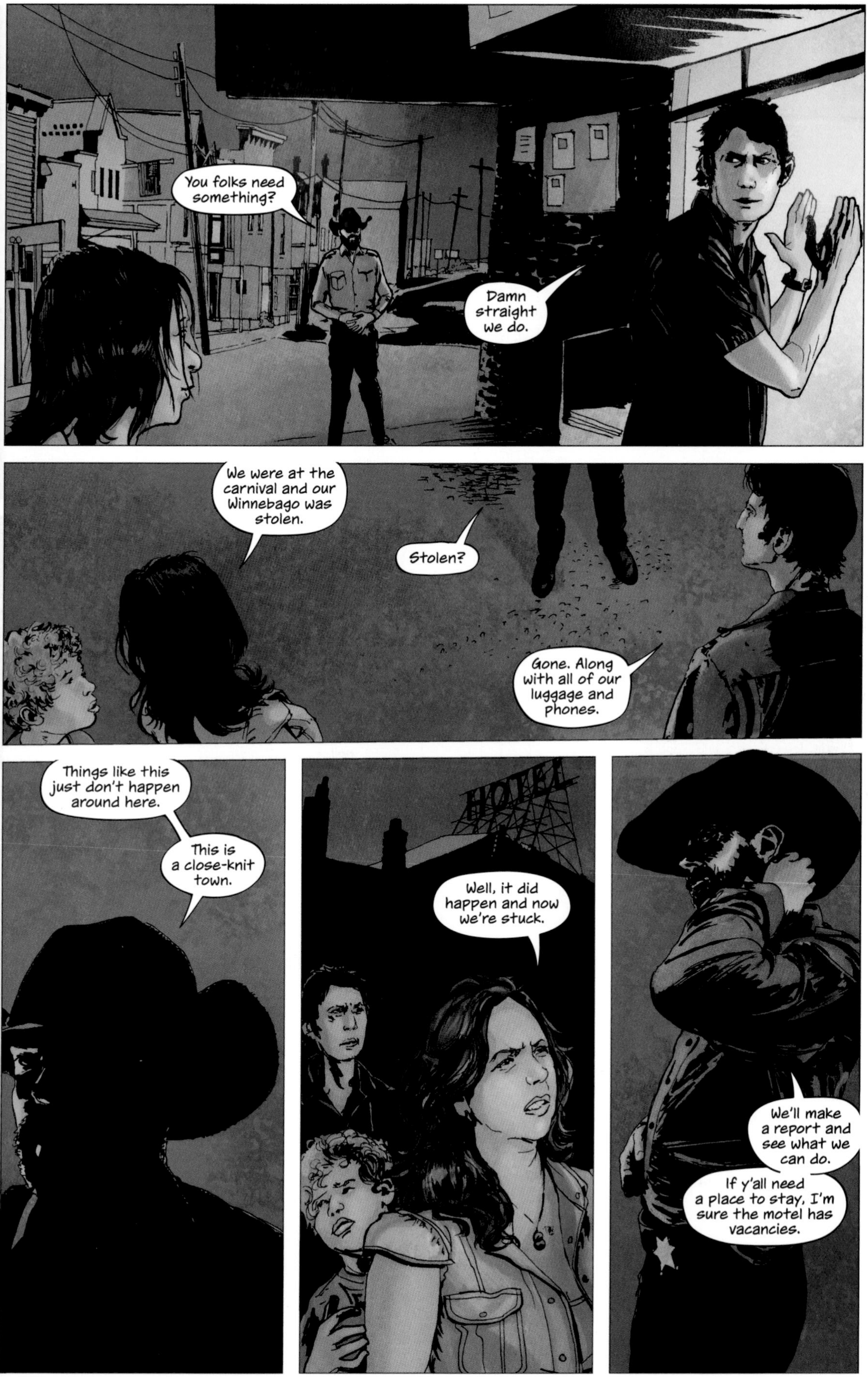
You folks need something?
Damn straight we do.
We were at the carnival and our Winnebago was stolen.
Stolen?
Gone. Along with all of our luggage and phones.
Things like this just don't happen around here.
This is a close-knit town.
HOTEL
Well, it did happen and now we're stuck.
We'll make a report and see what we can do.
If y'all need a place to stay, I'm sure the motel has vacancies.

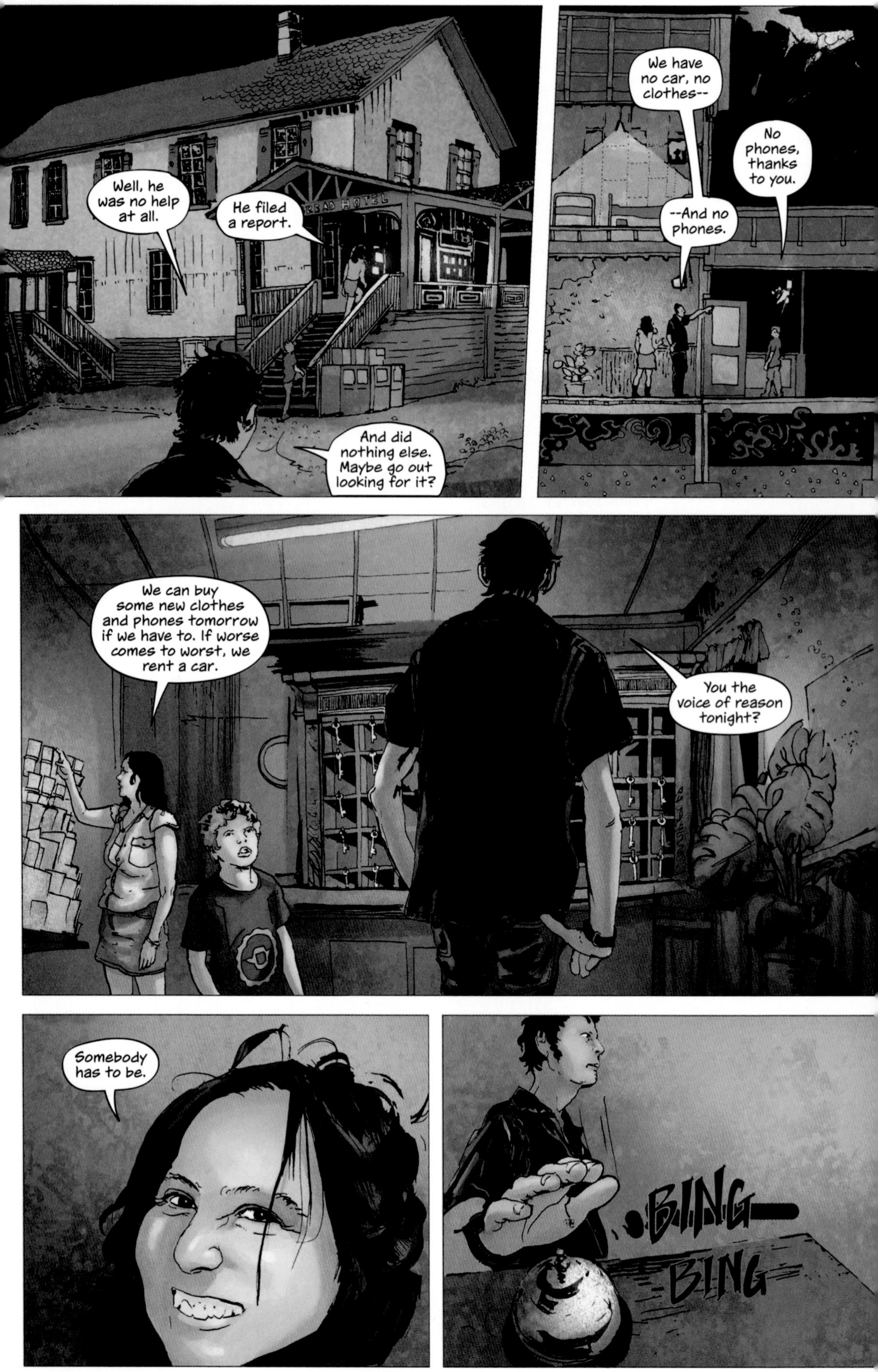
Well, he was no help at all.
He filed a report.
And did nothing else. Maybe go out looking for it?
We have no car, no clothes--
--And no phones.
No phones, thanks to you.
We can buy some new clothes and phones tomorrow if we have to. If worse comes to worst, we rent a car.
You the voice of reason tonight?
Somebody has to be.
BING-
BING

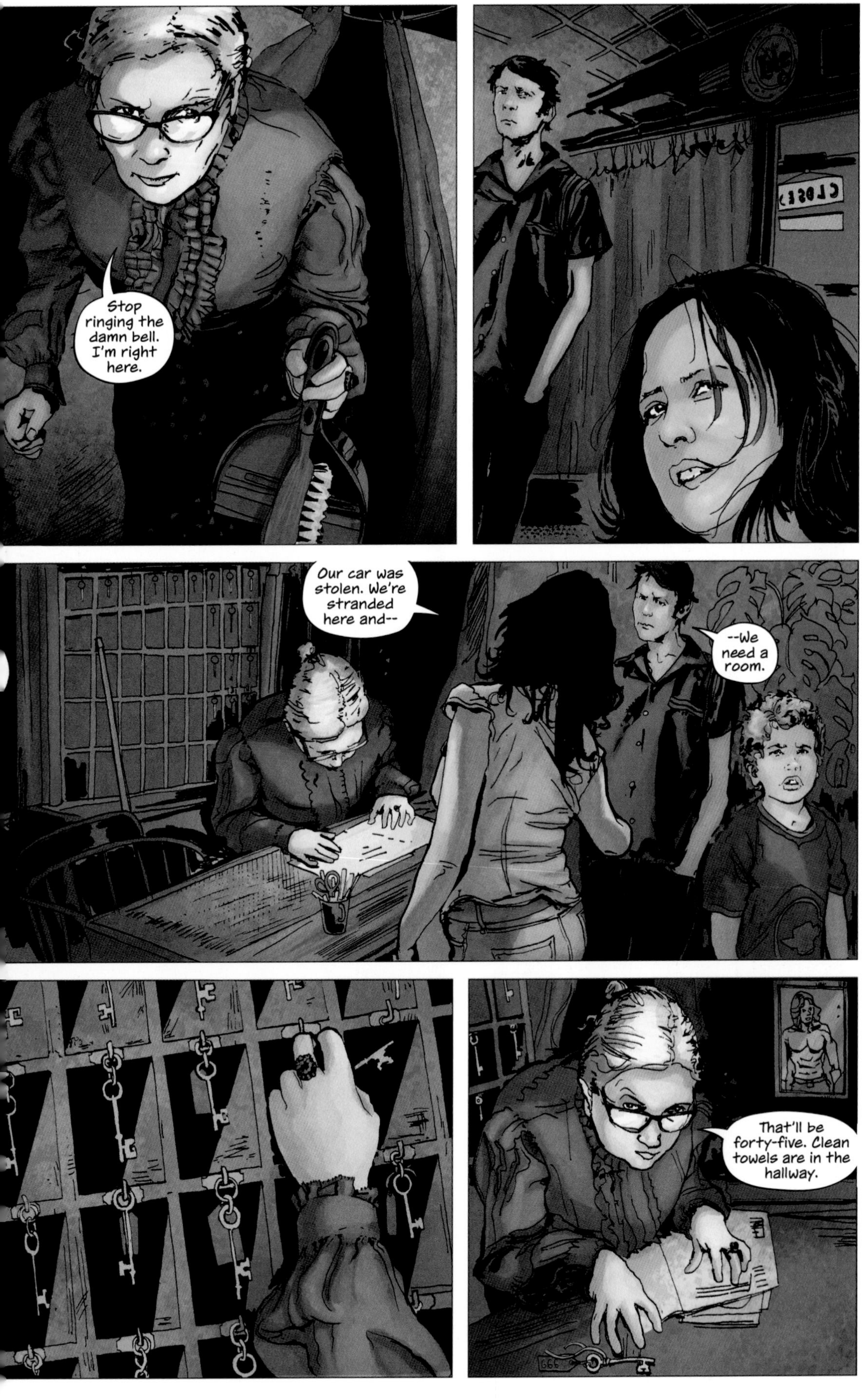
Stop ringing the damn bell. I'm right here.
Our car was stolen. We're stranded here and--
--We need a room.
That'll be forty-five. Clean towels are in the hallway.

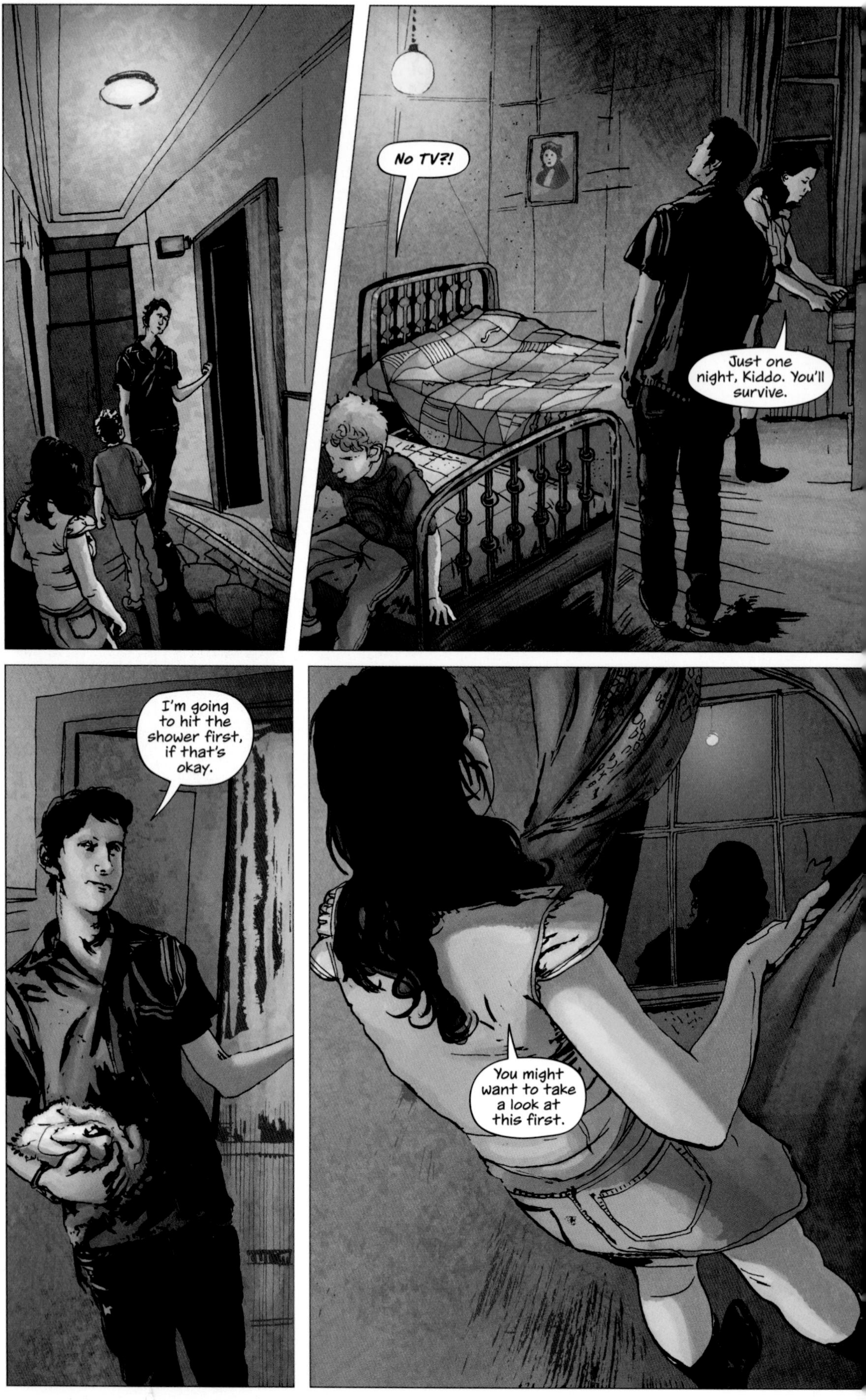
No TV?!
Just one night, Kiddo. You'll survive.
I'm going to hit the shower first, if that's okay.
You might want to take a look at this first.

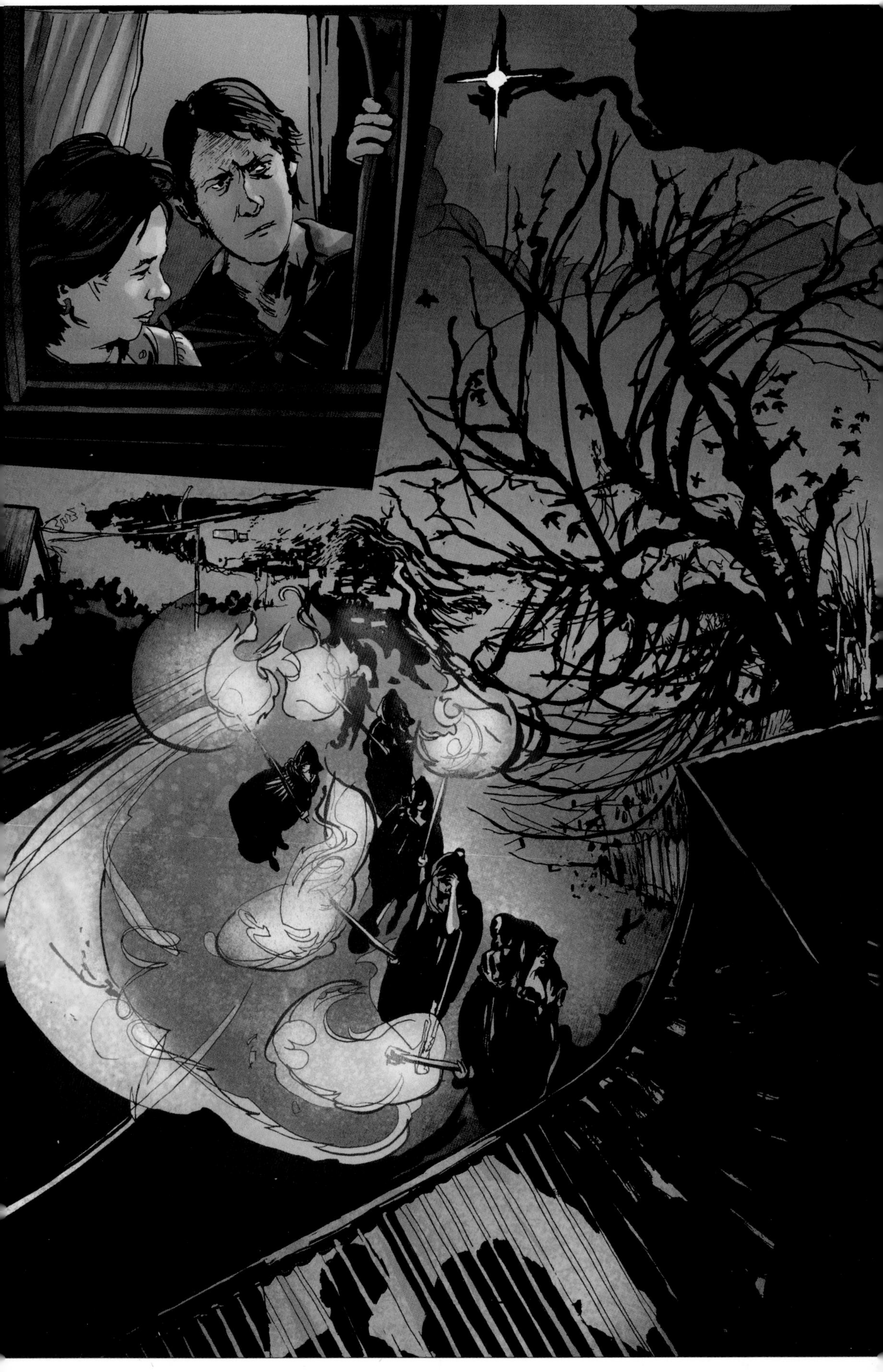

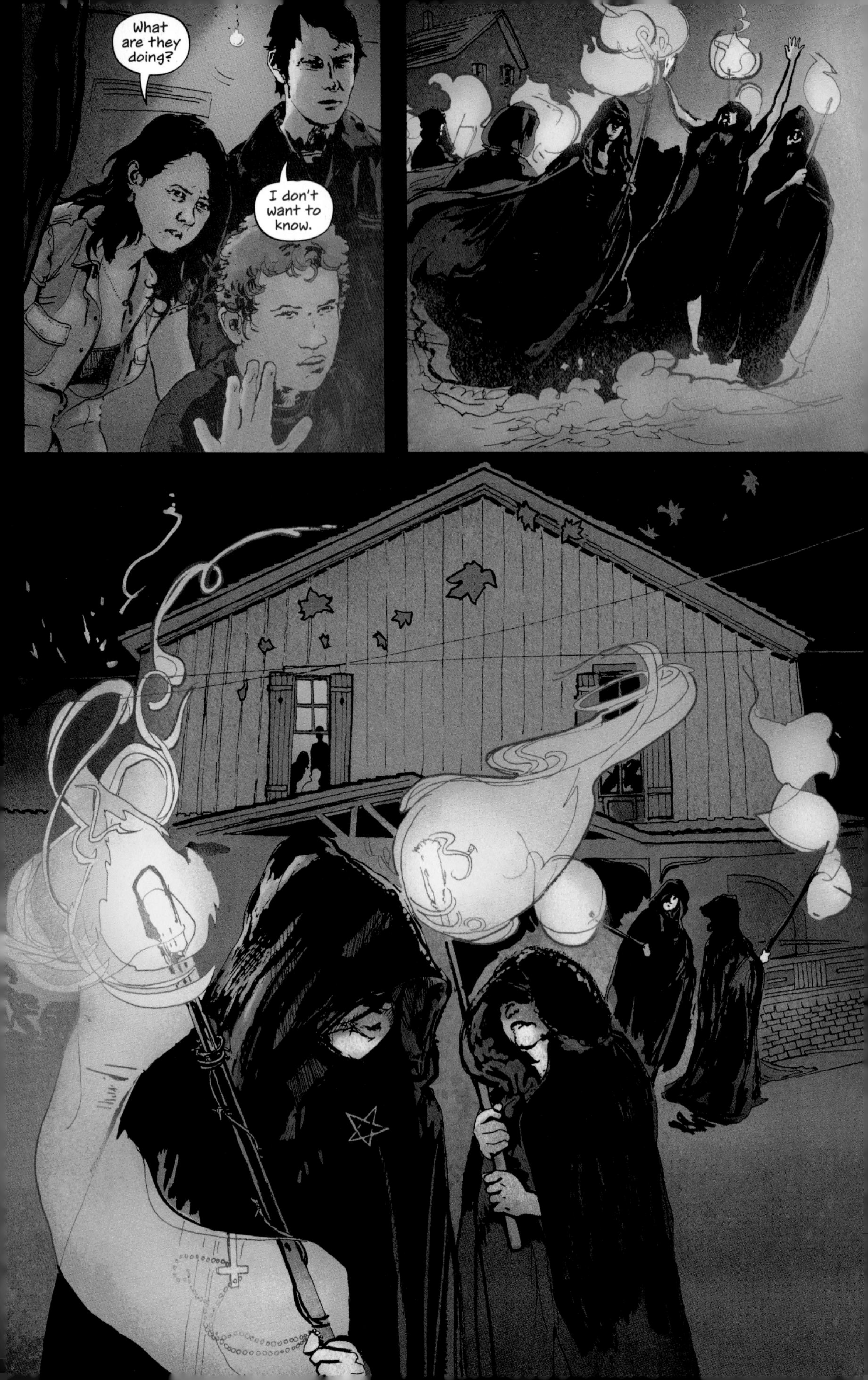
What are they doing?
I don't want to know.

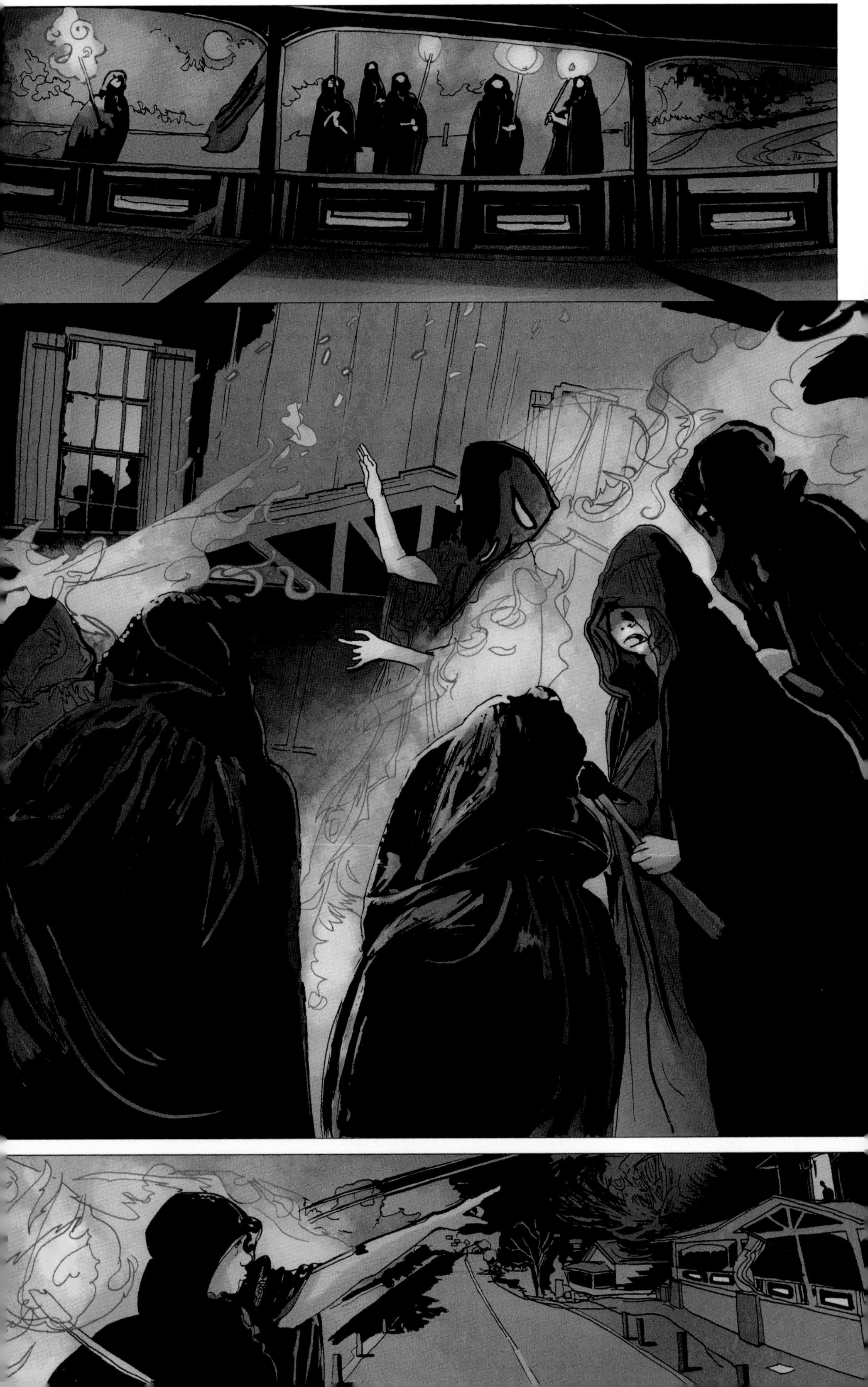

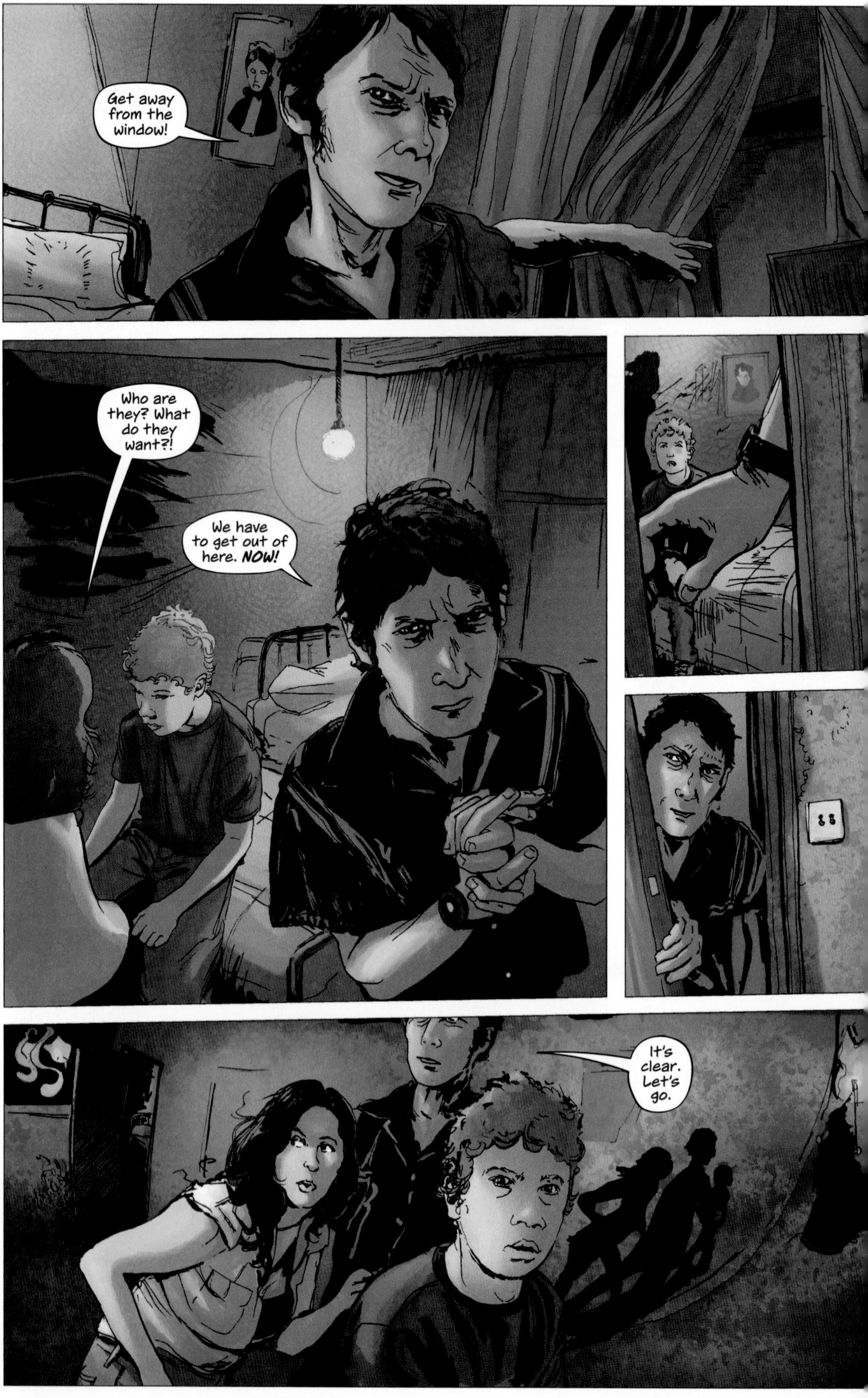
Get away from the window!
Who are they? What do they want?!
We have to get out of here. **NOW!**
It's clear. Let's go.

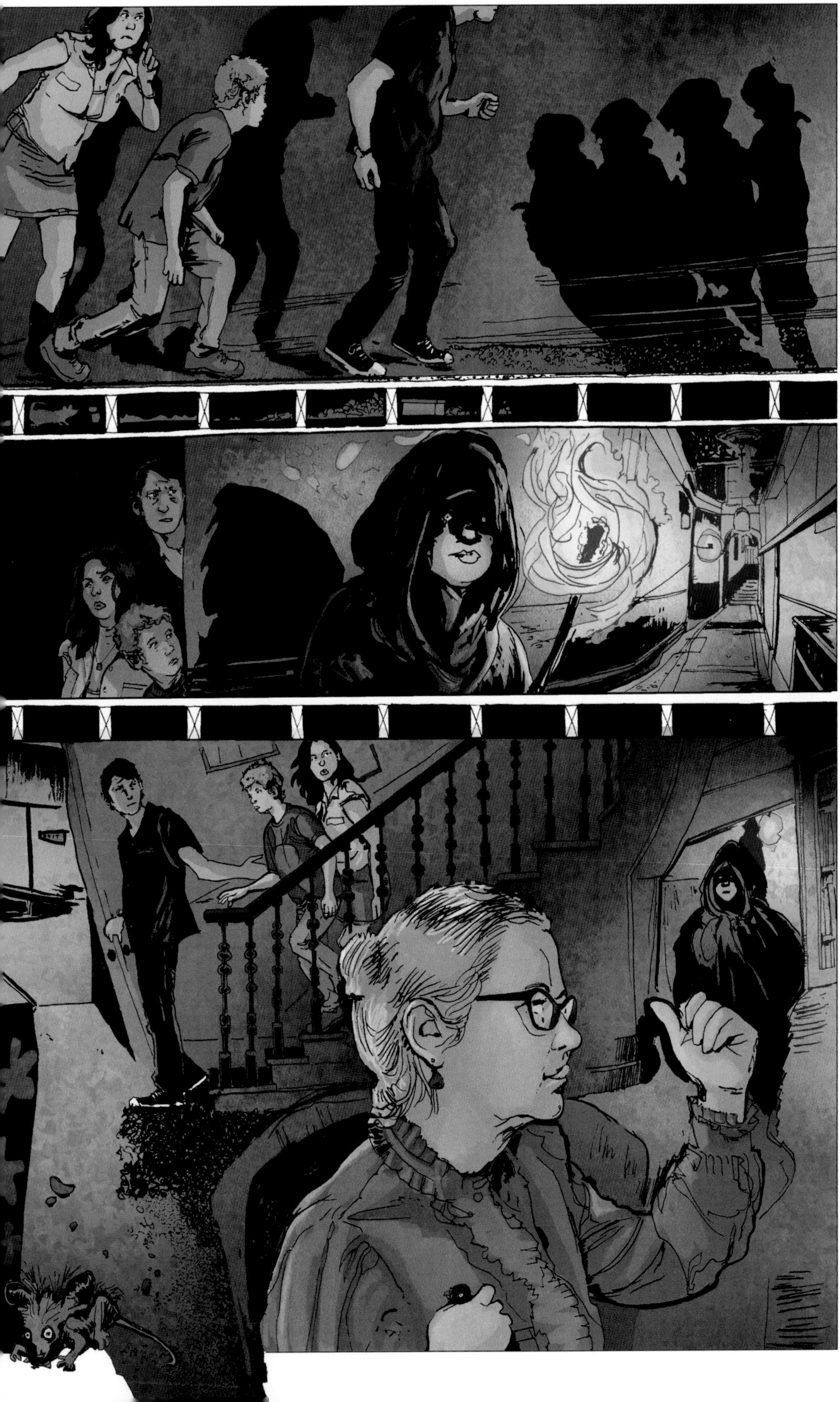

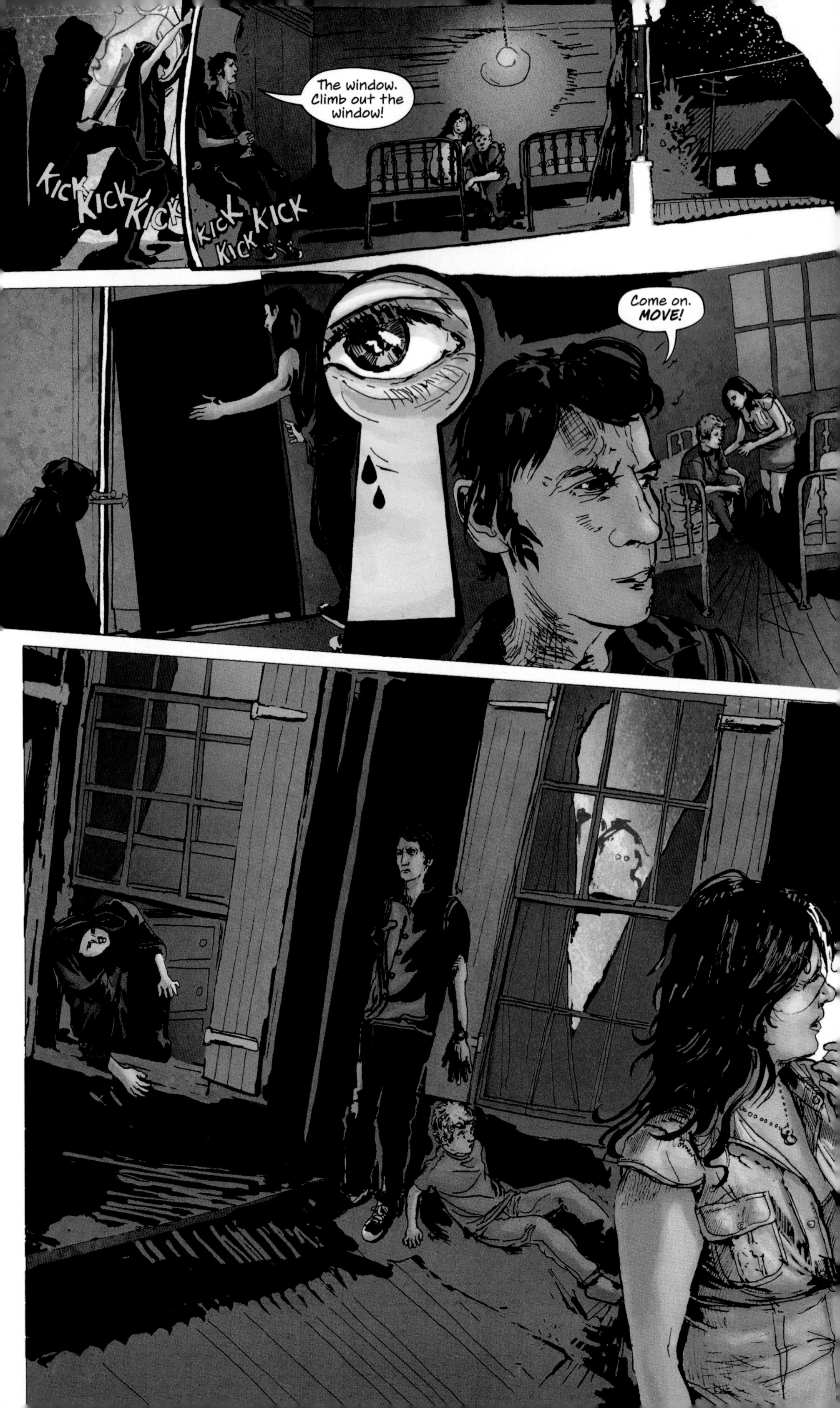
KICK KICK KICK
KICK KICK
KICK
The window. Climb out the window!
Come on. MOVE!

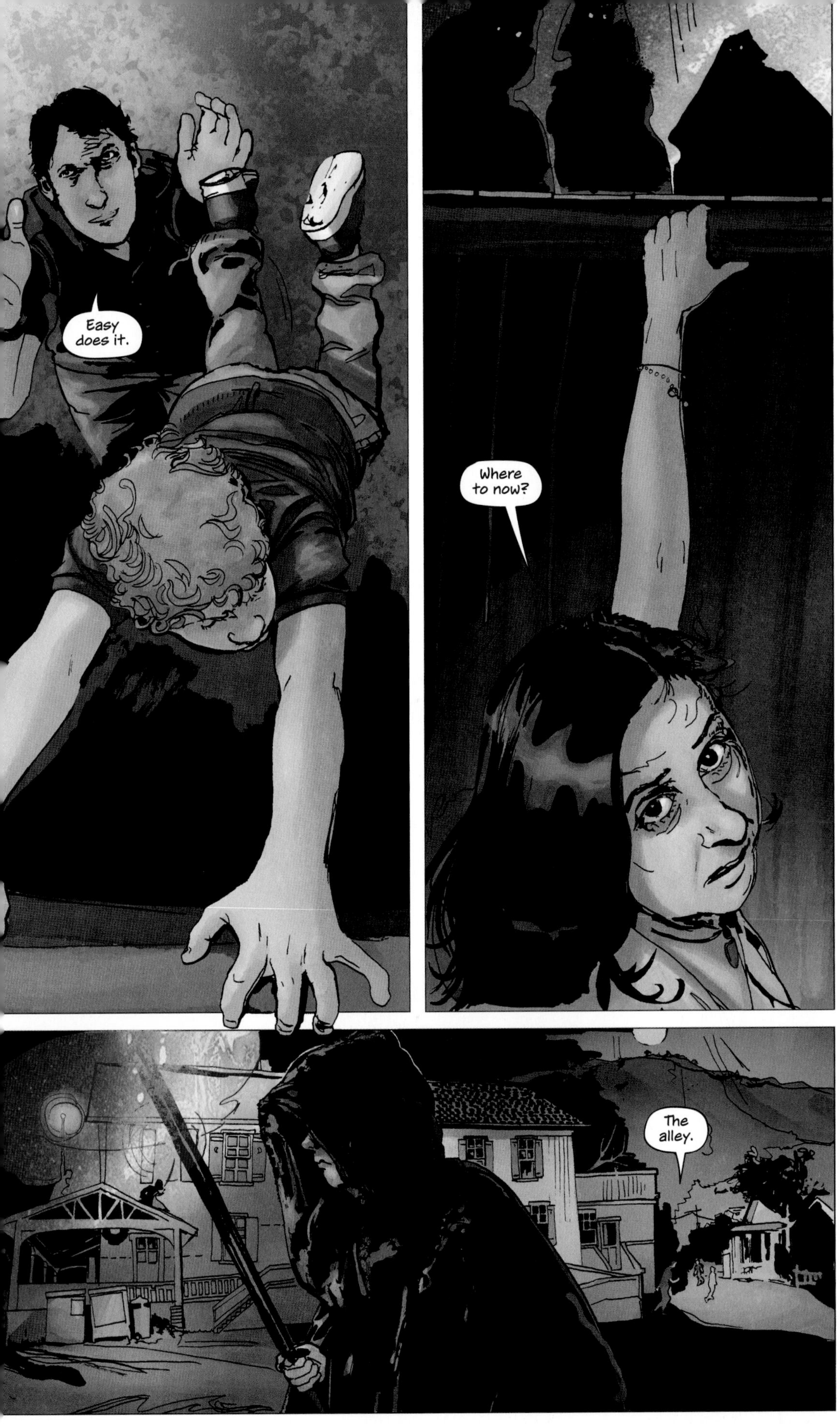
Easy does it.
Where to now?
The alley.

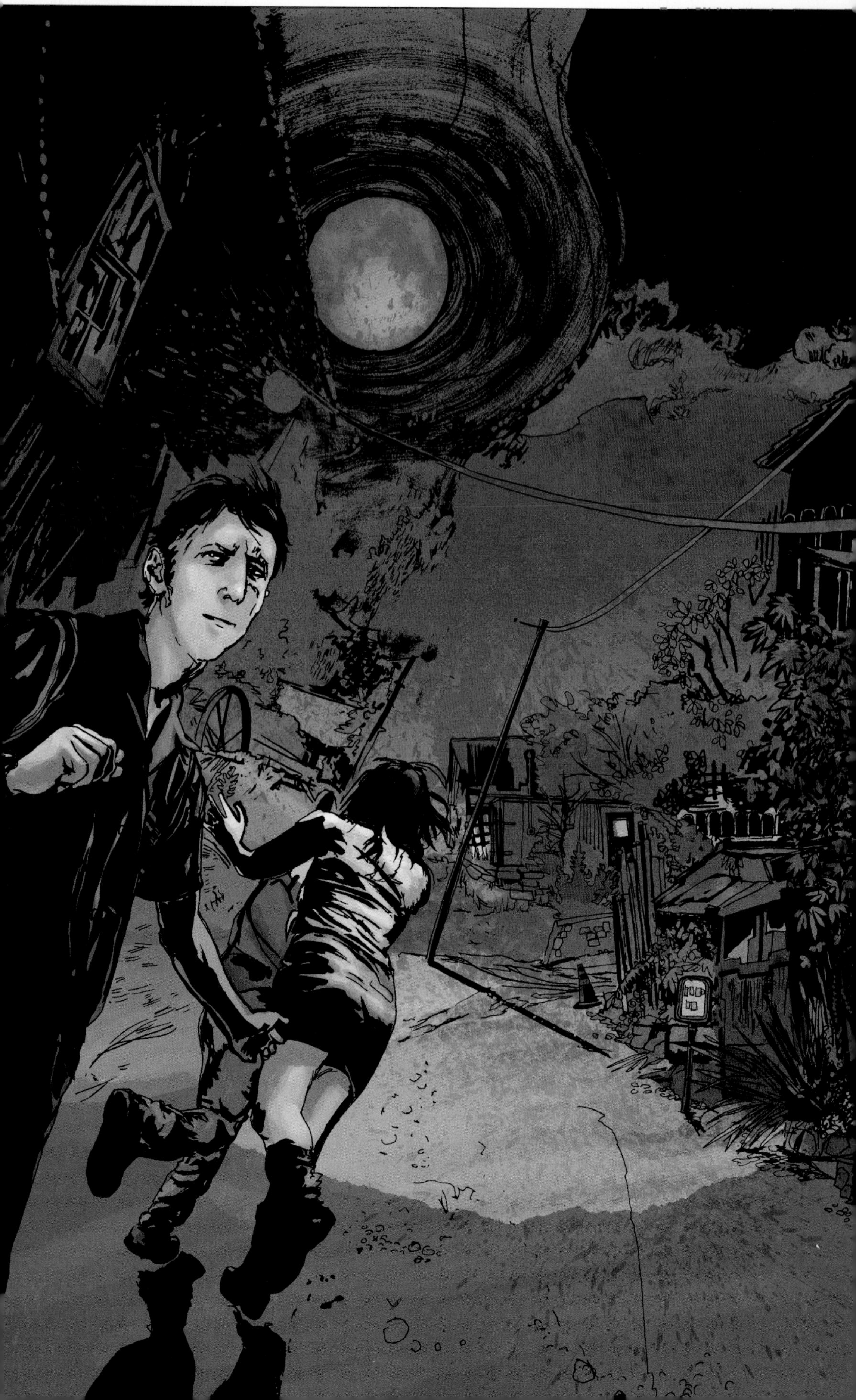

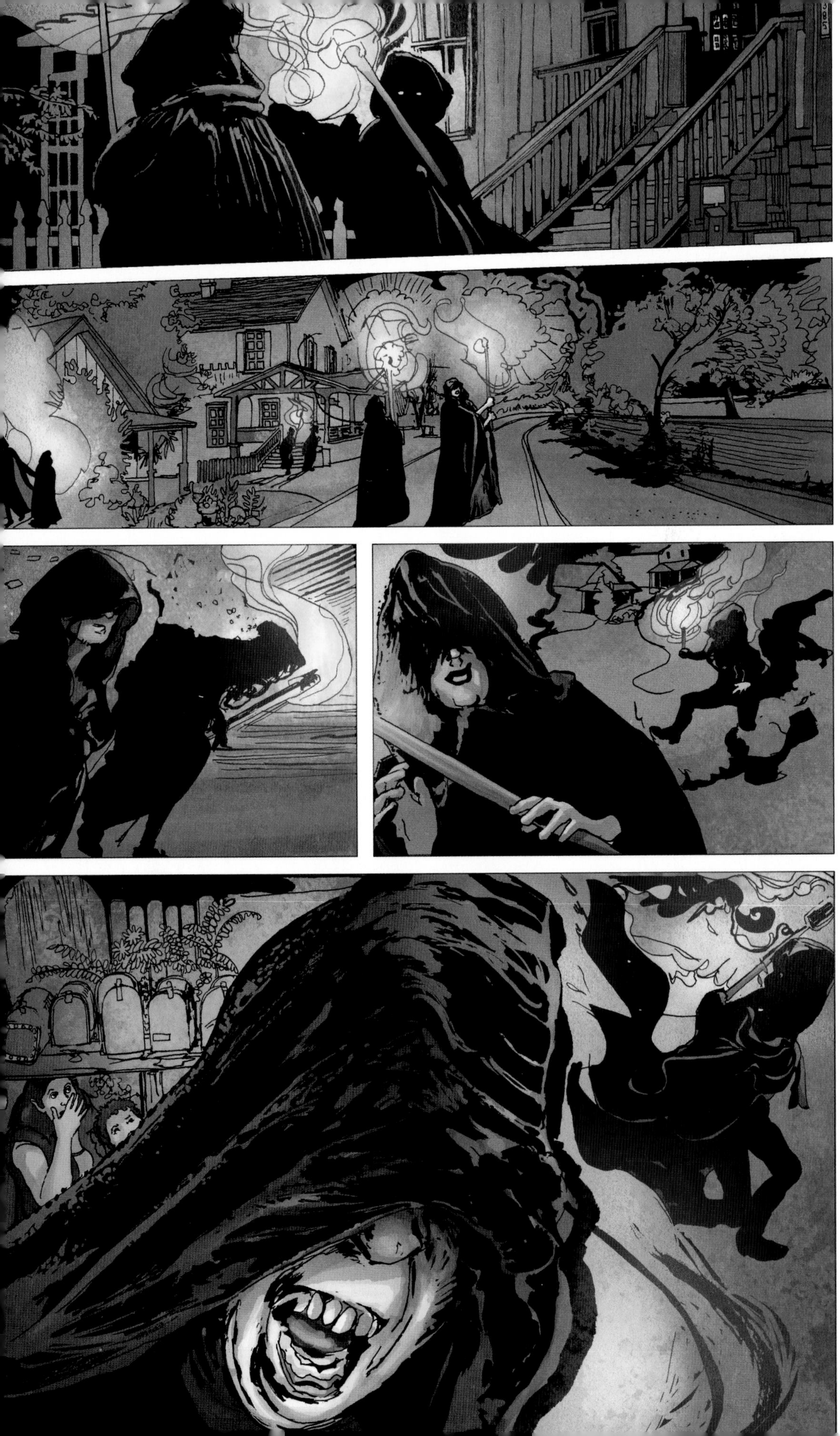

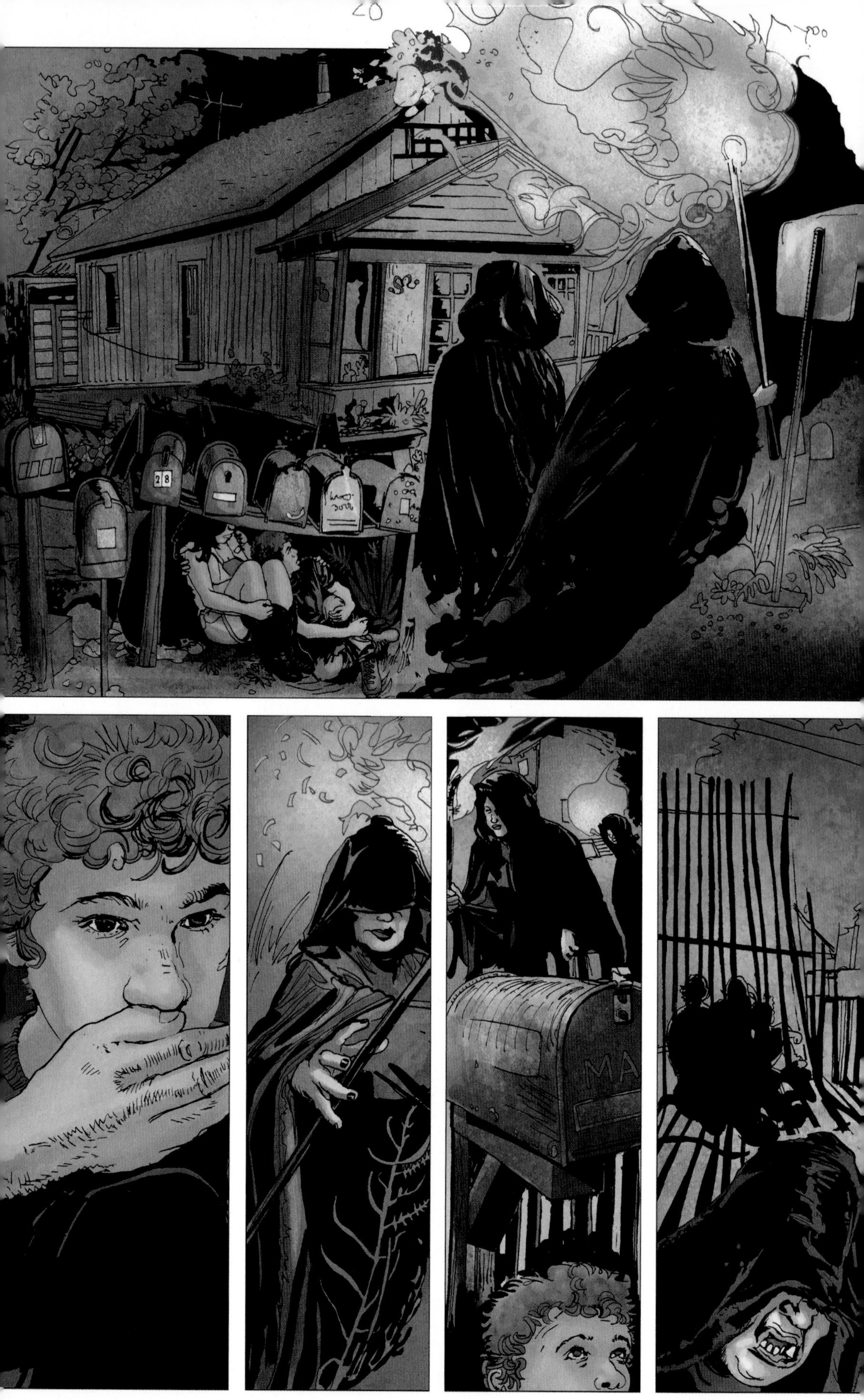
28

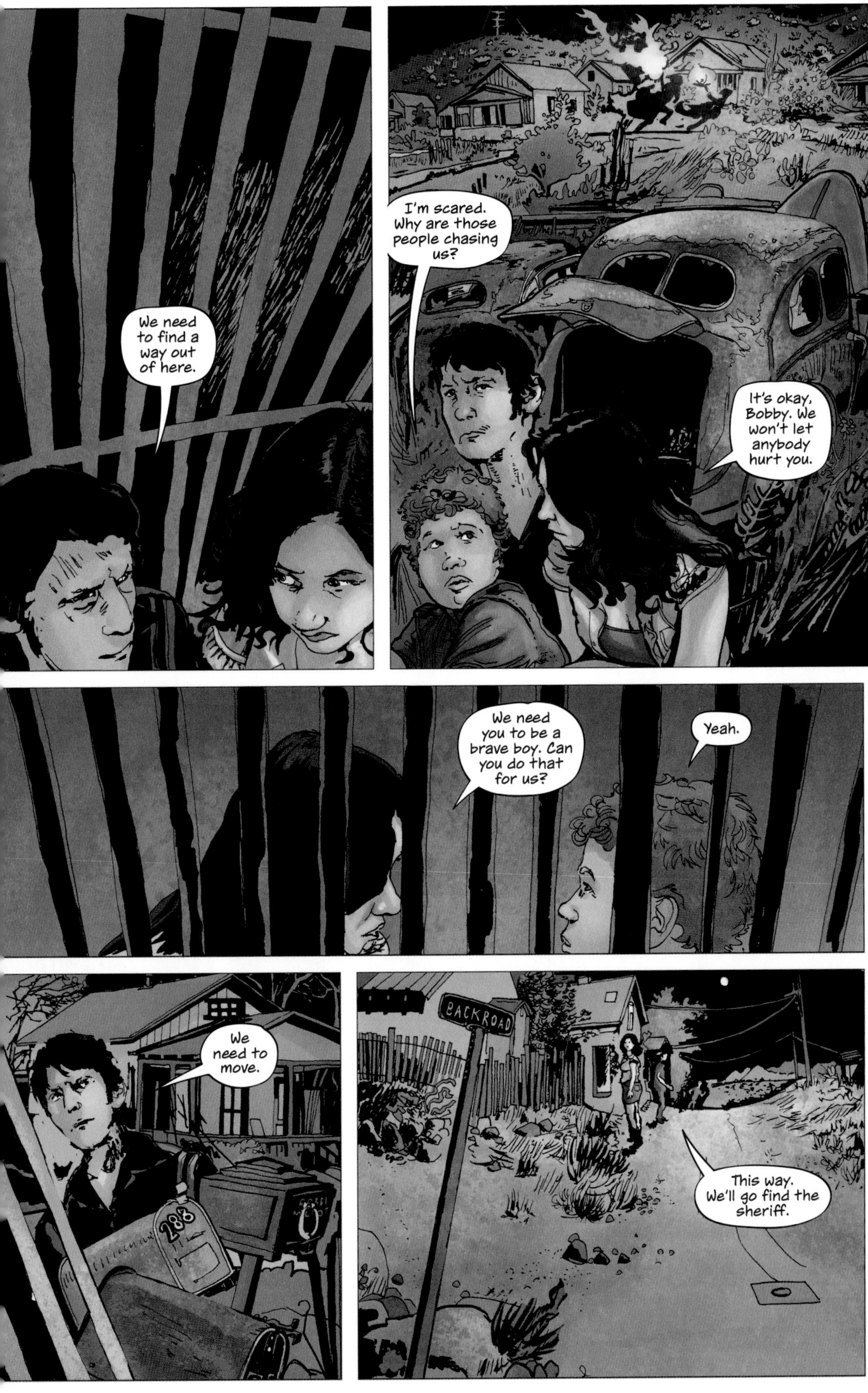
We need to find a way out of here.
I'm scared. Why are those people chasing us?
It's okay, Bobby. We won't let anybody hurt you.
We need you to be a brave boy. Can you do that for us?
Yeah.
We need to move.
288
BACKROAD
This way. We'll go find the sheriff.

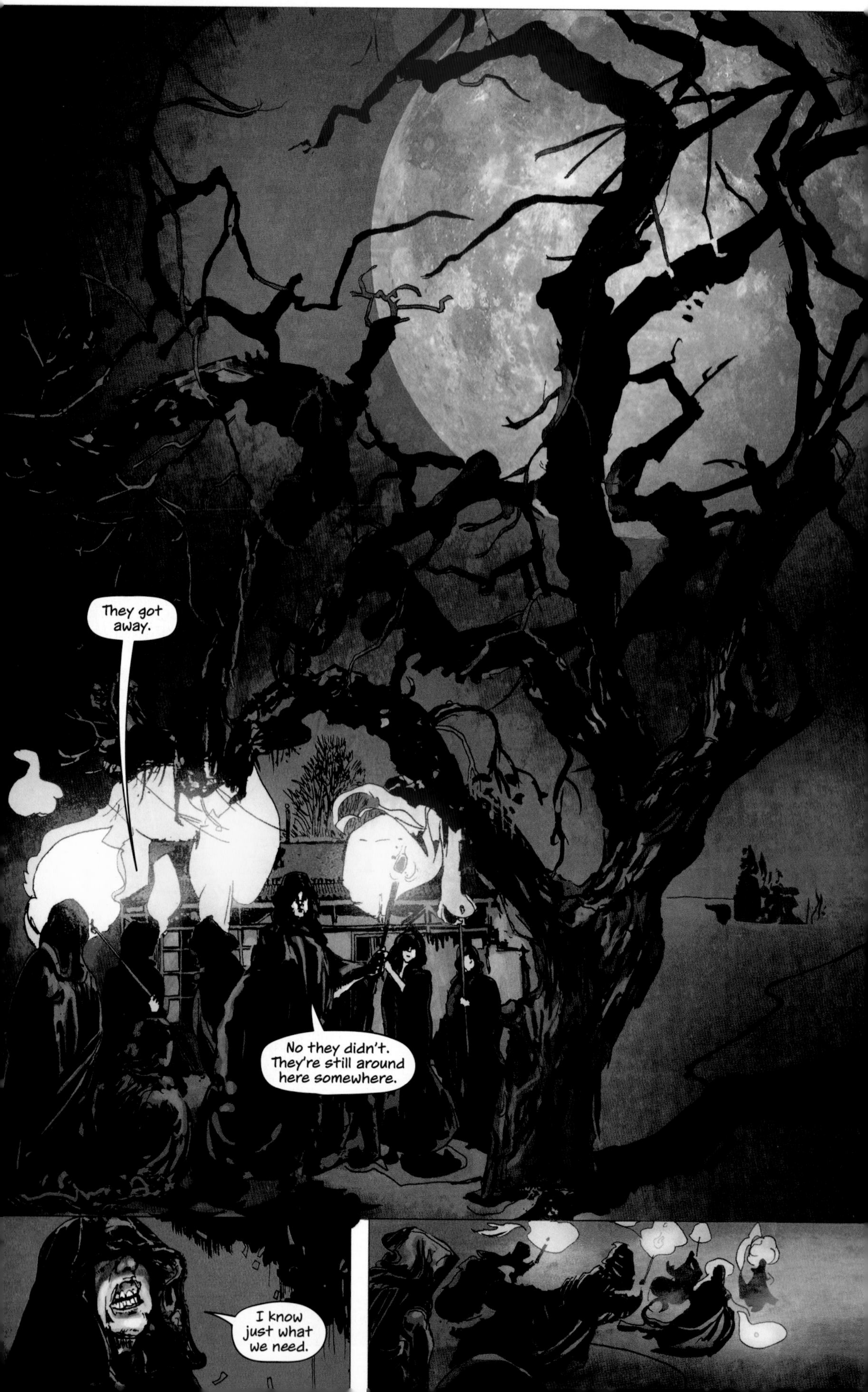
They got away.
No they didn't. They're still around here somewhere.
I know just what we need.

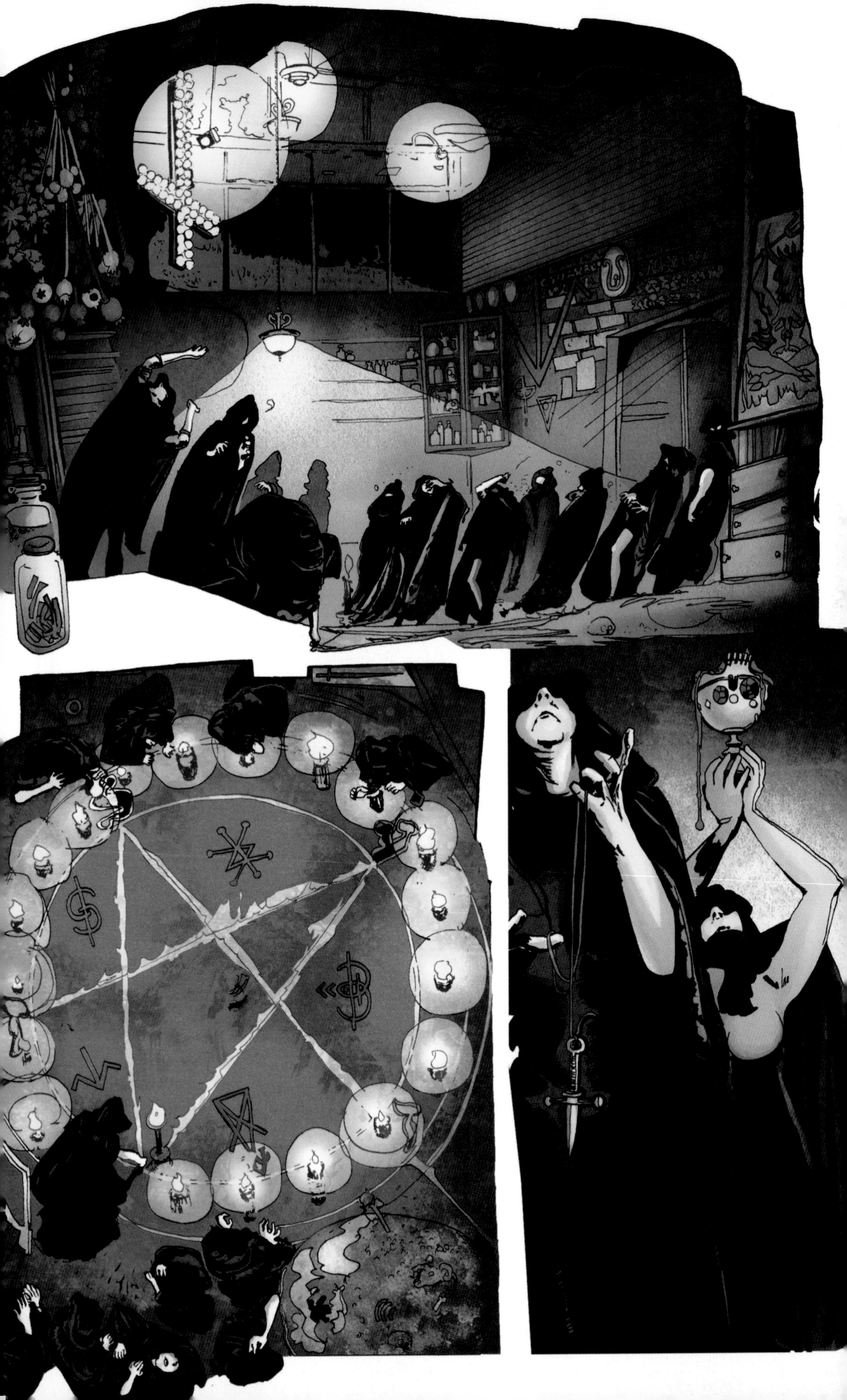

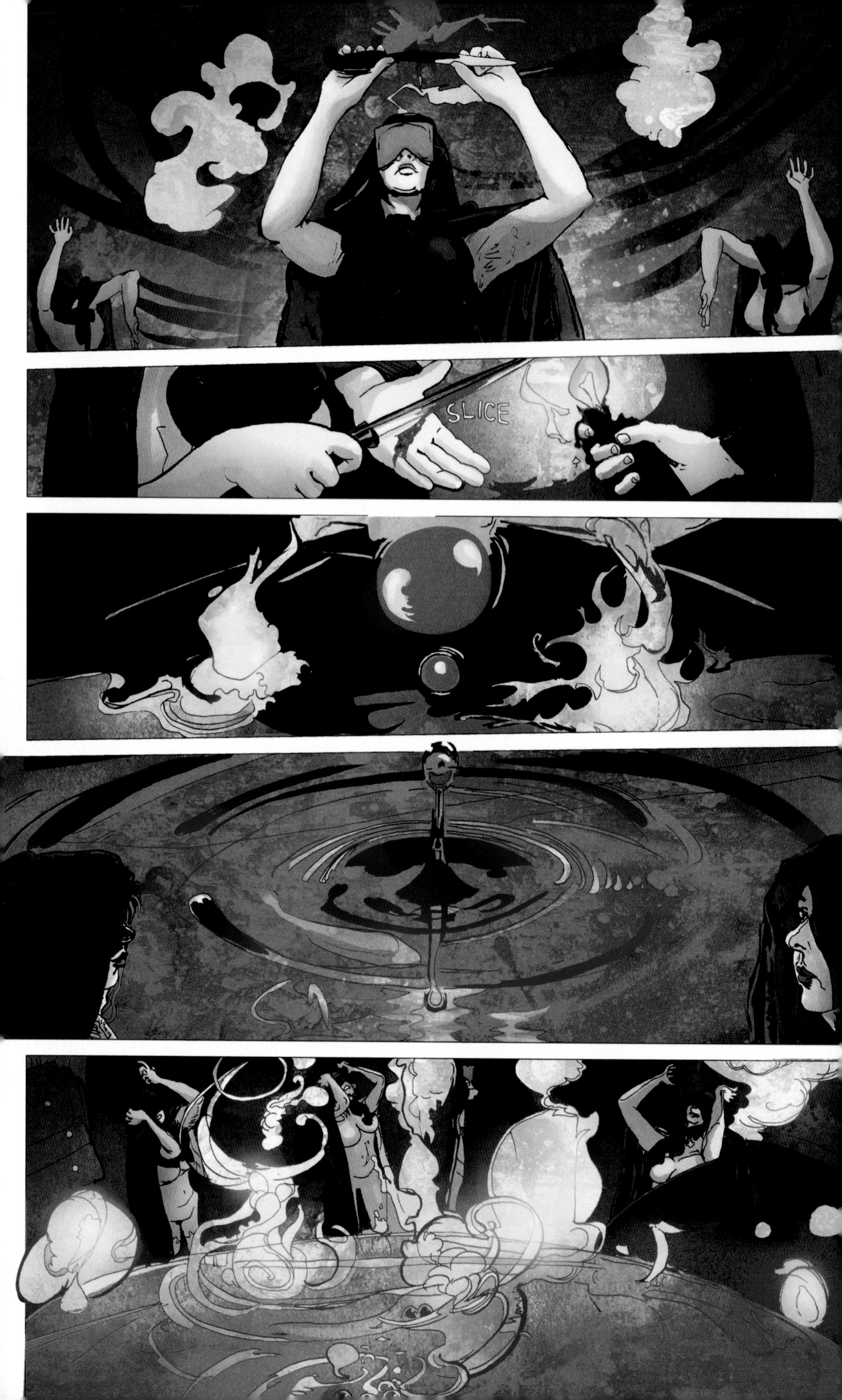
SLICE

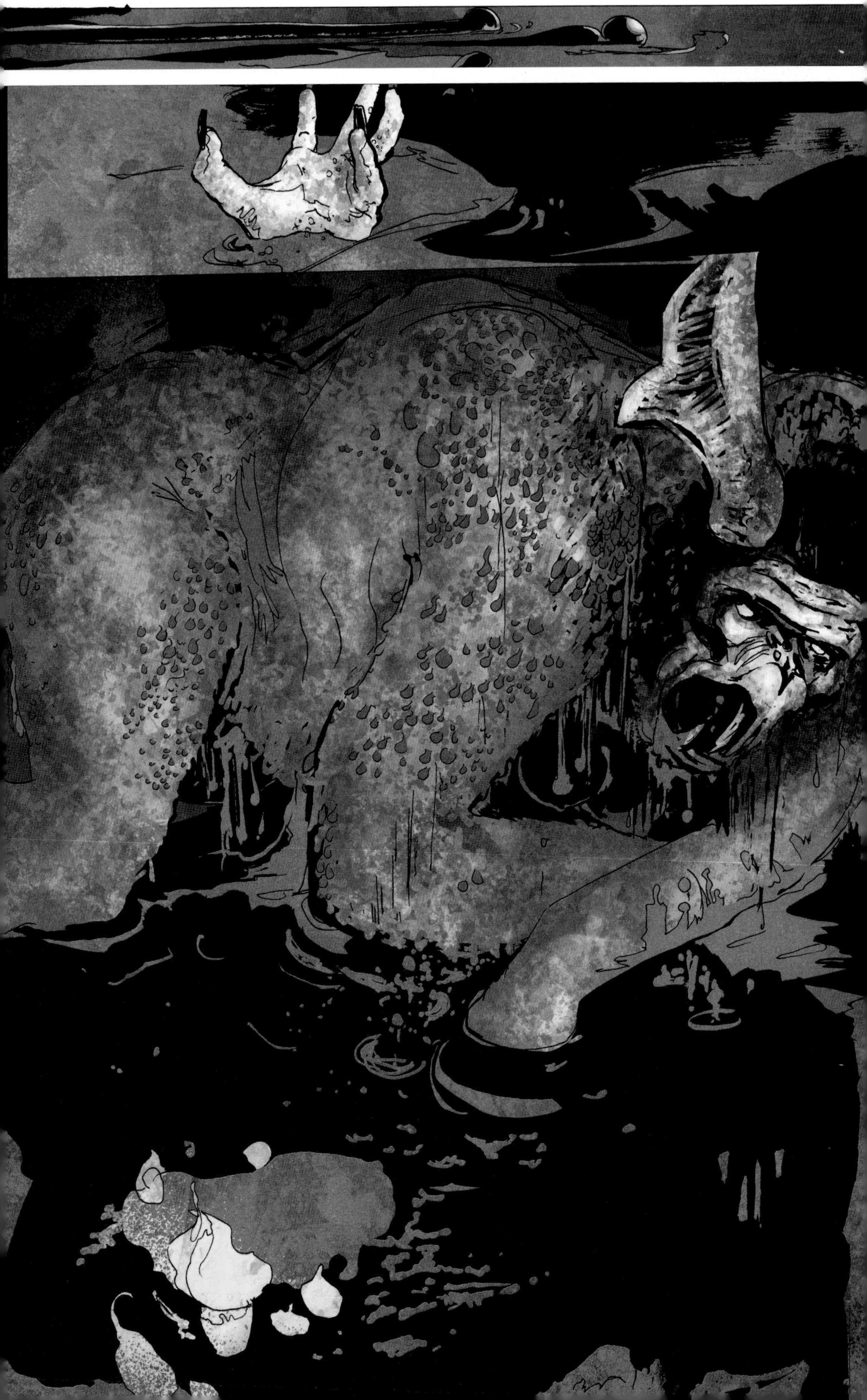

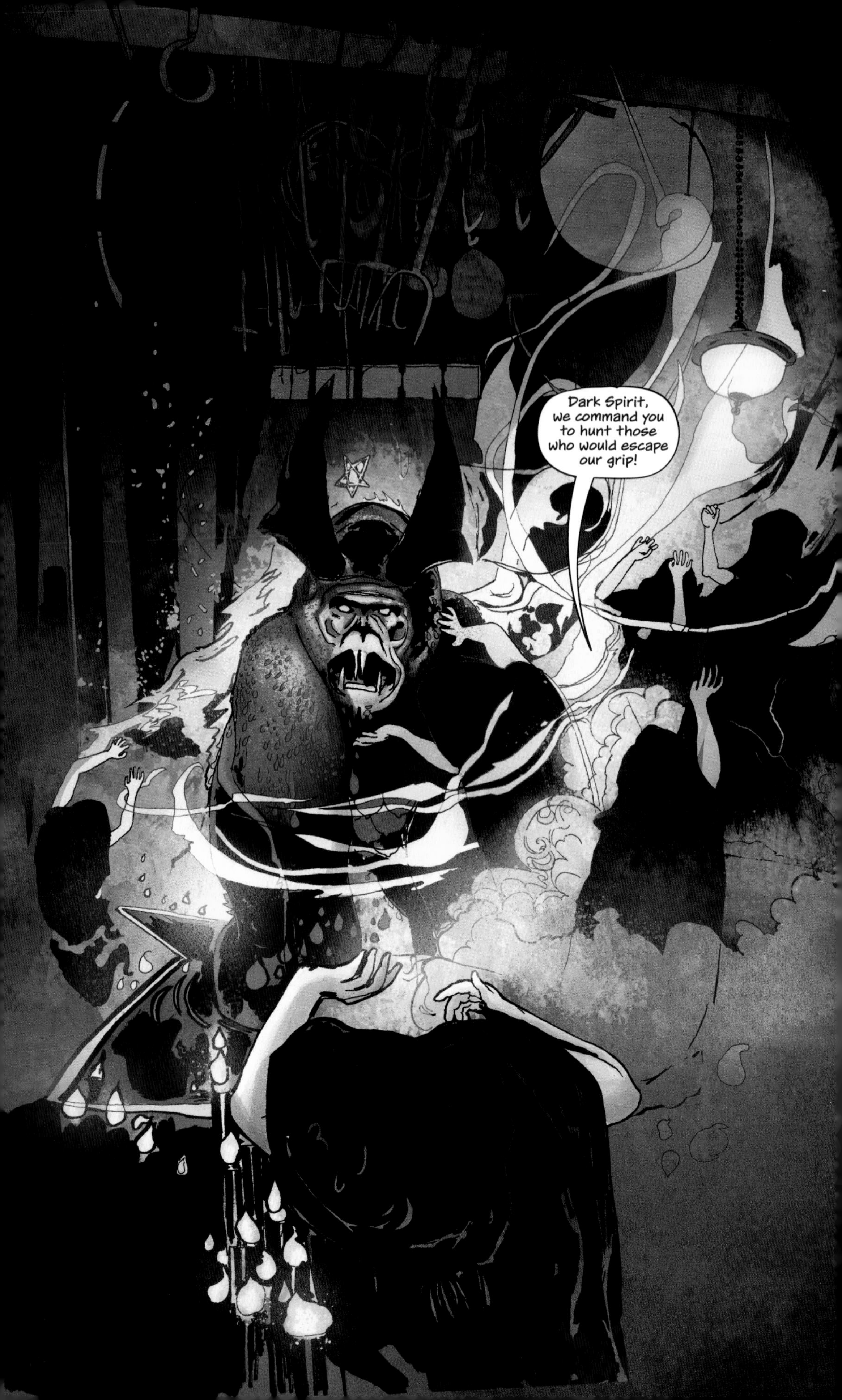
Dark Spirit, we command you to hunt those who would escape our grip!

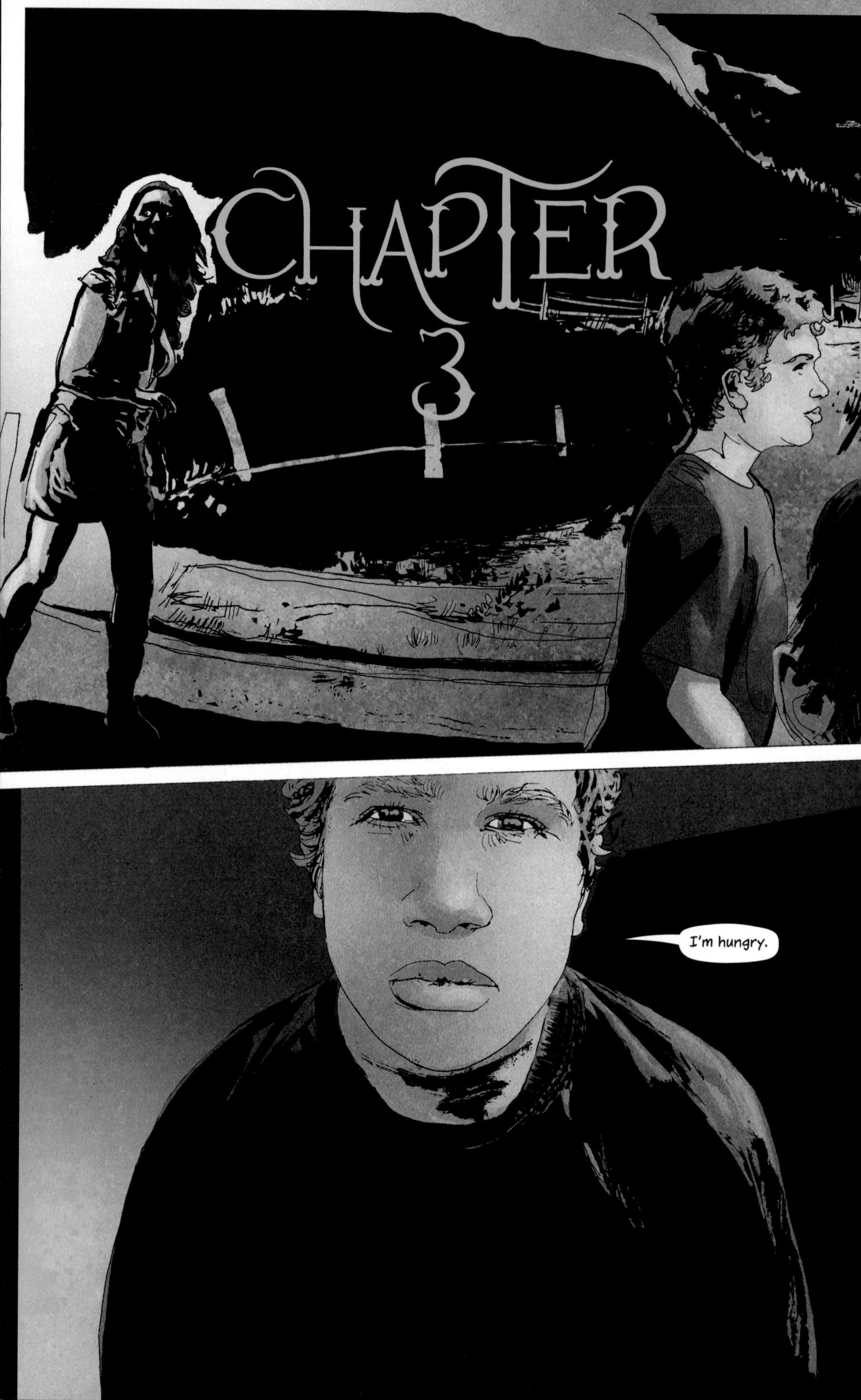
CHAPTER
3
I'm hungry.

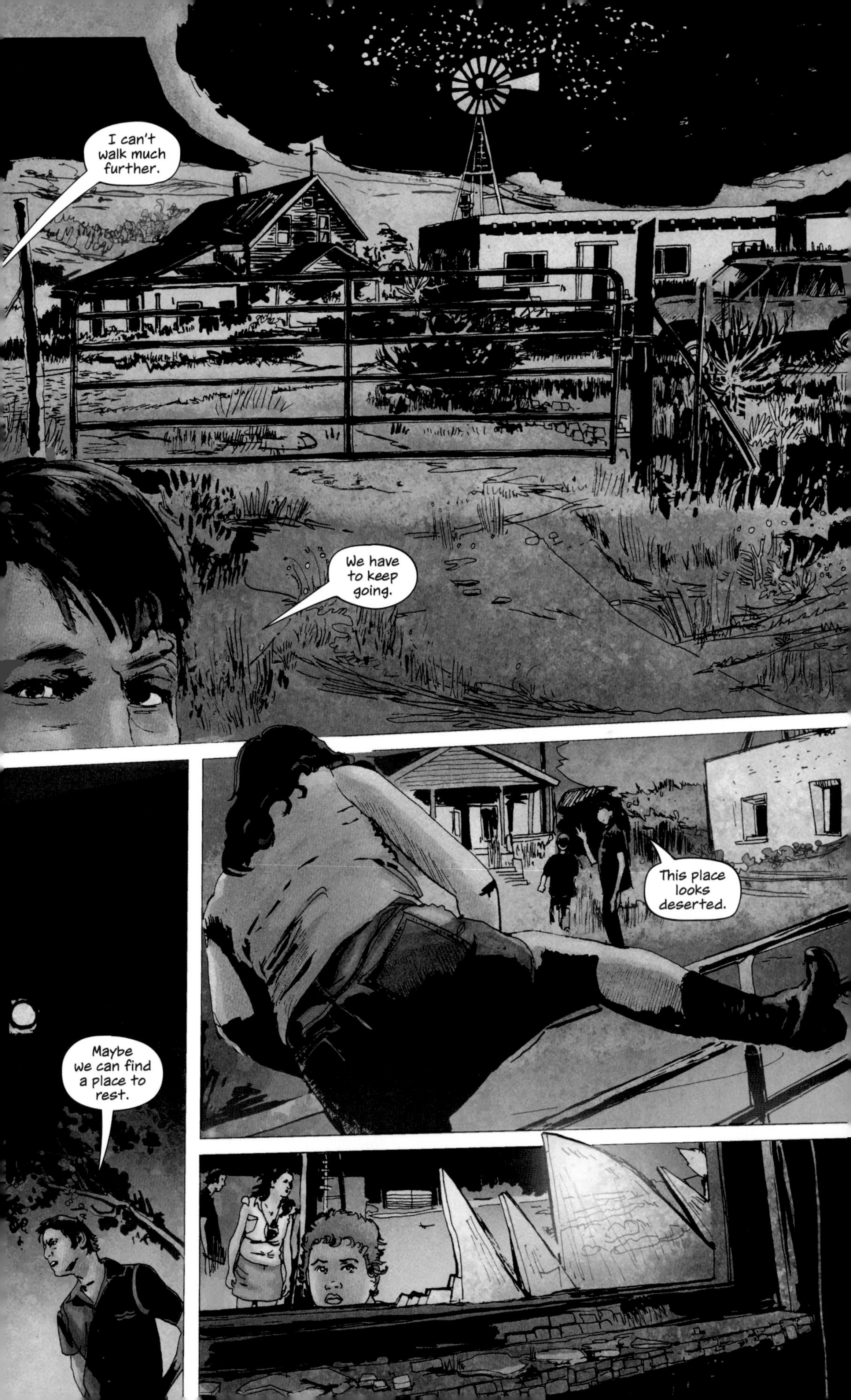
I can't walk much further.
We have to keep going.
Maybe we can find a place to rest.
This place looks deserted.

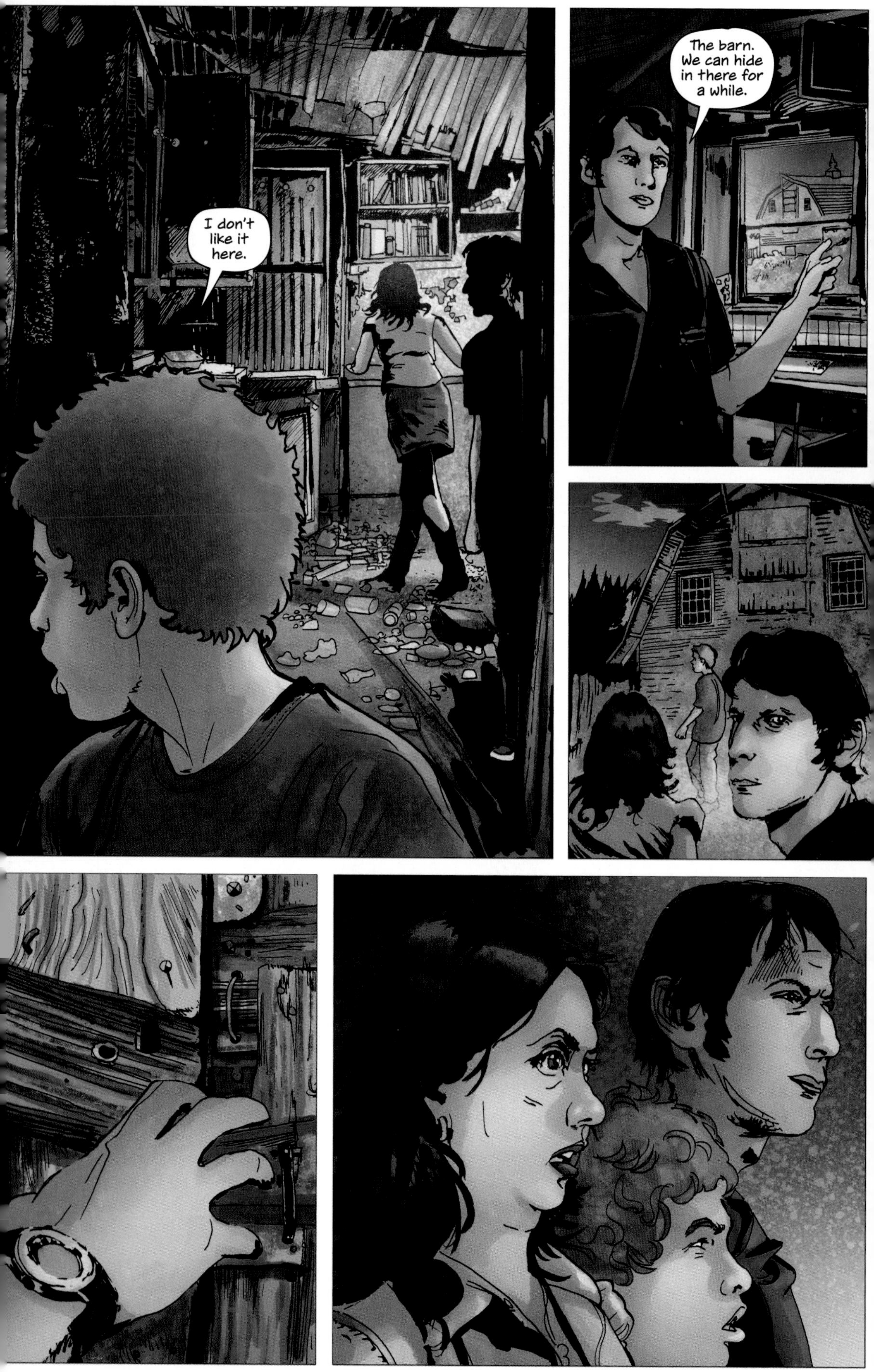
I don't like it here.
The barn. We can hide in there for a while.

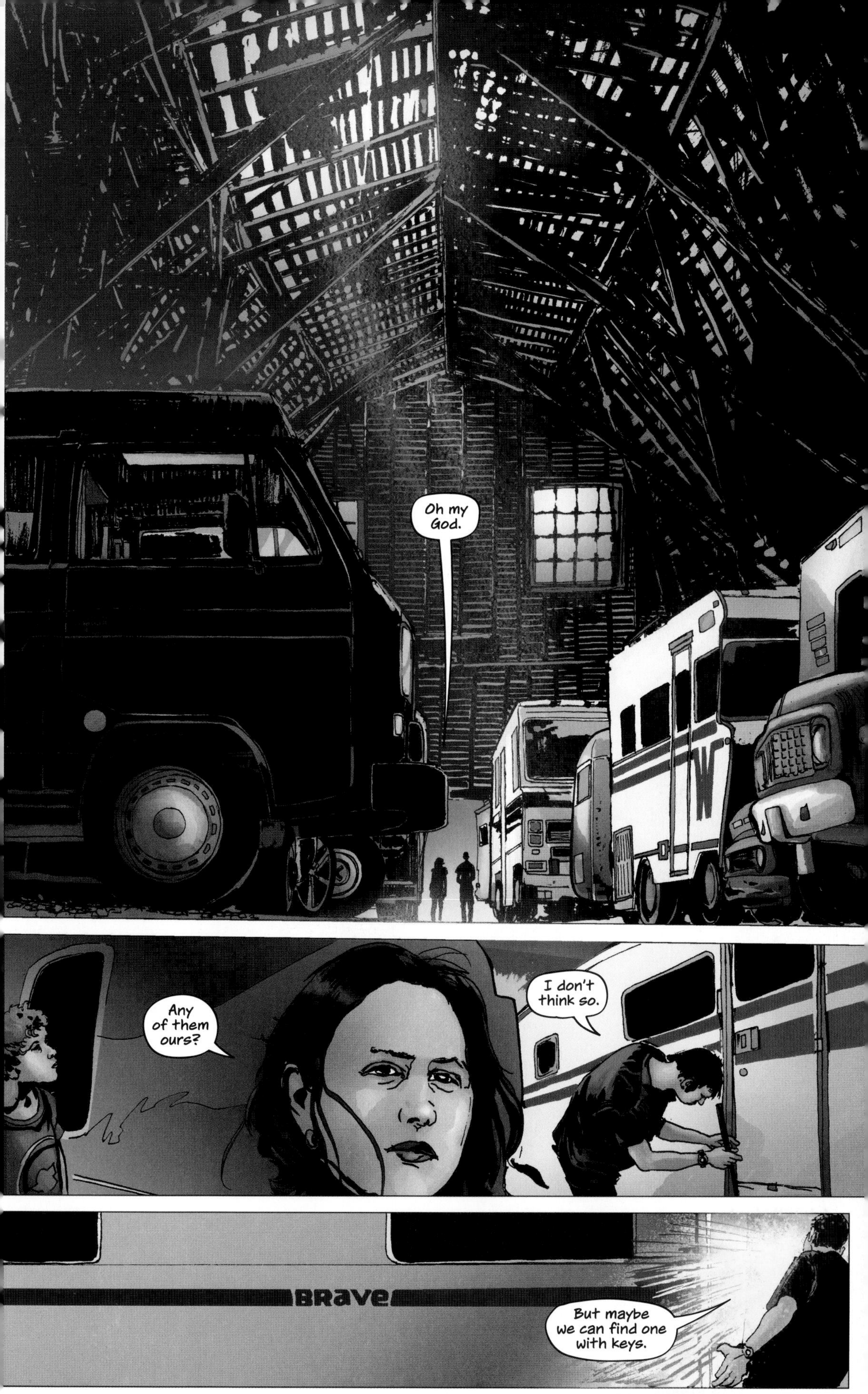
Oh my God.
Any of them ours?
I don't think so.
BRAVE
But maybe we can find one with keys.

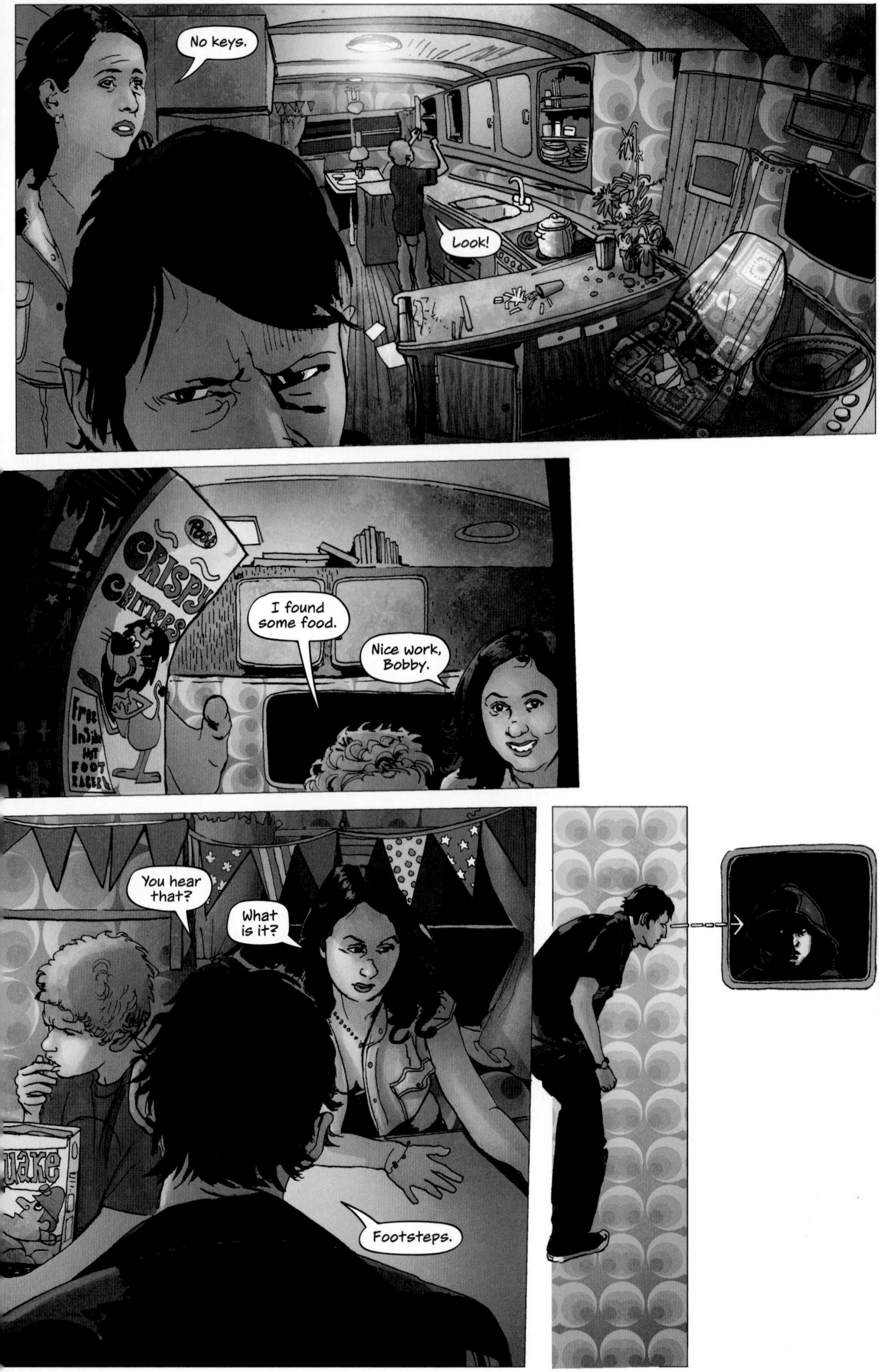
No keys.
Look!
Crispy Critters
I found some food.
Nice work, Bobby.
You hear that?
What is it?
Footsteps.

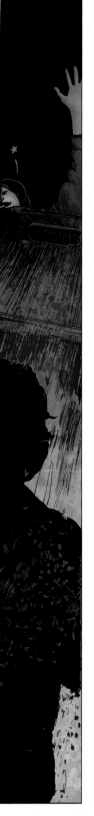

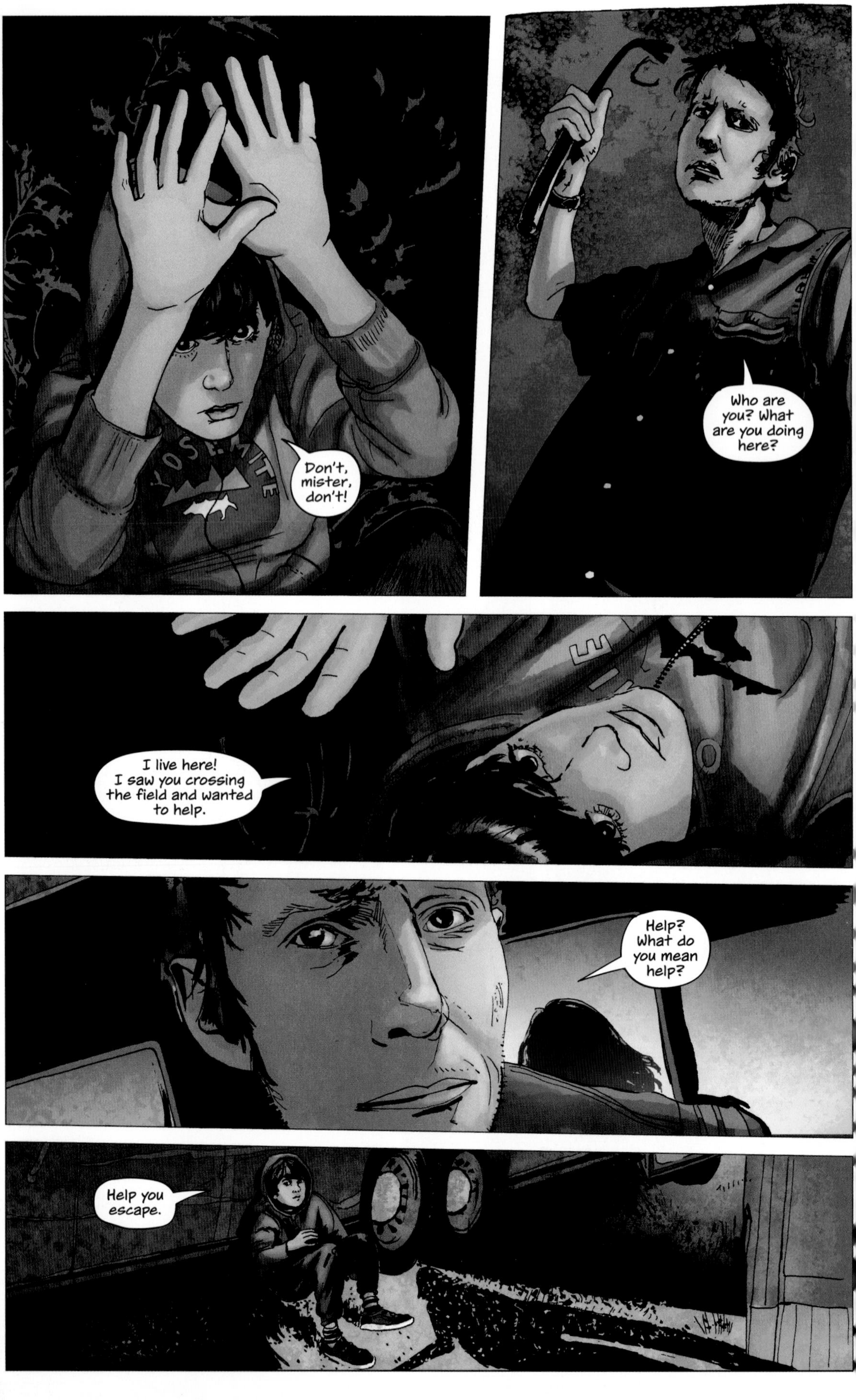
Don't, mister, don't!
Who are you? What are you doing here?
I live here! I saw you crossing the field and wanted to help.
Help? What do you mean help?
Help you escape.

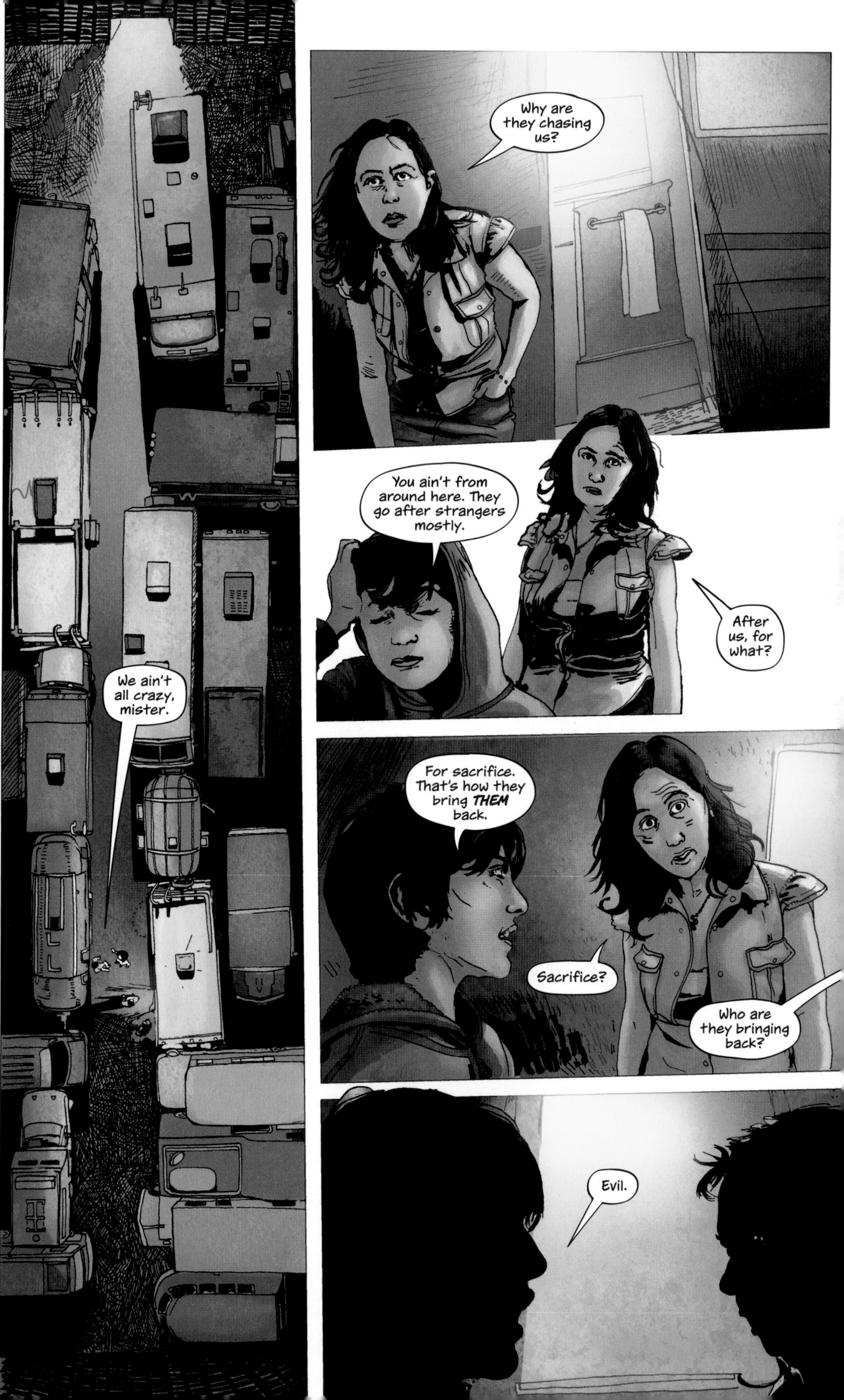
We ain't all crazy, mister.
Why are they chasing us?
You ain't from around here. They go after strangers mostly.
After us, for what?
For sacrifice. That's how they bring THEM back.
Sacrifice?
Who are they bringing back?
Evil.

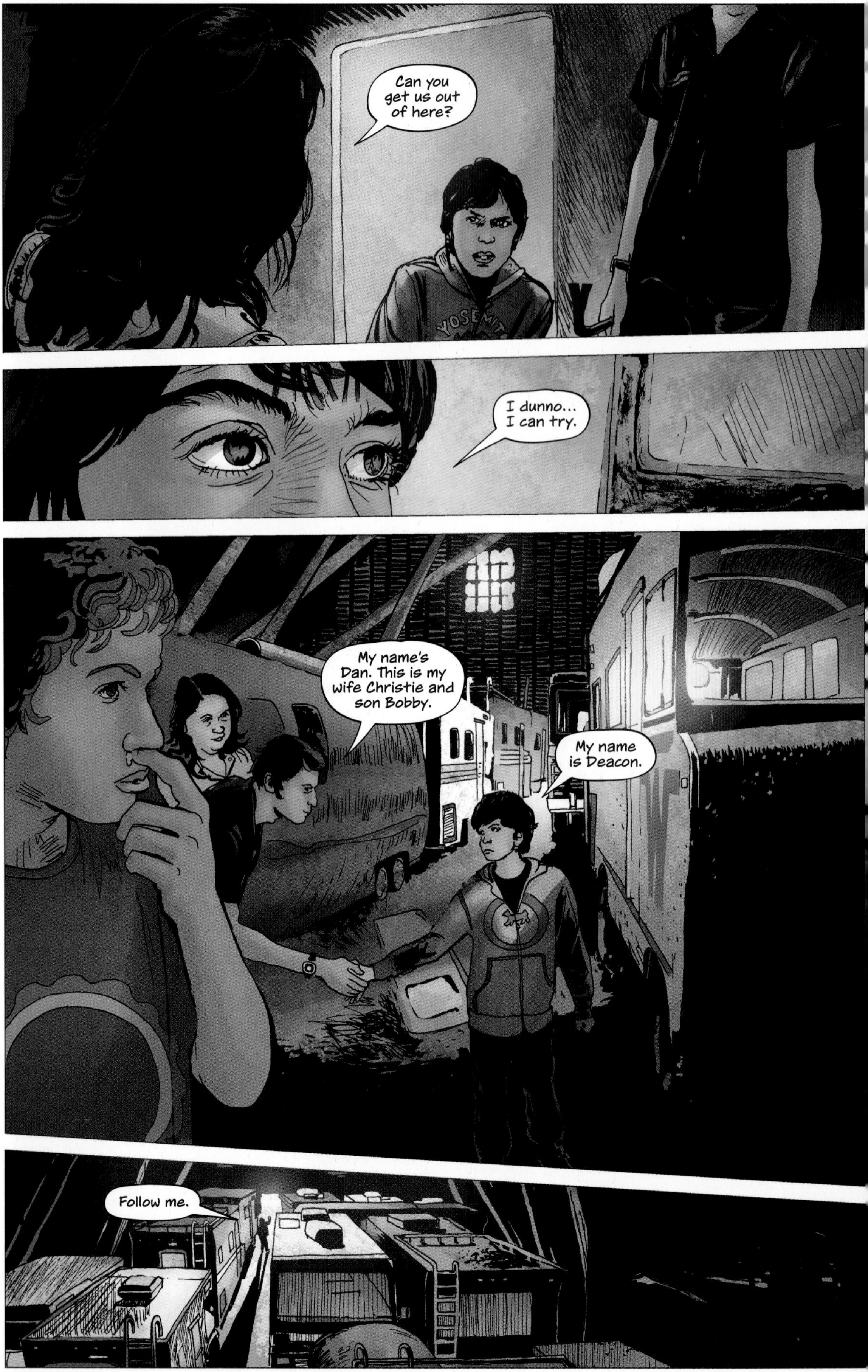
Can you get us out of here?
I dunno... I can try.
My name's Dan. This is my wife Christie and son Bobby.
My name is Deacon.
Follow me.

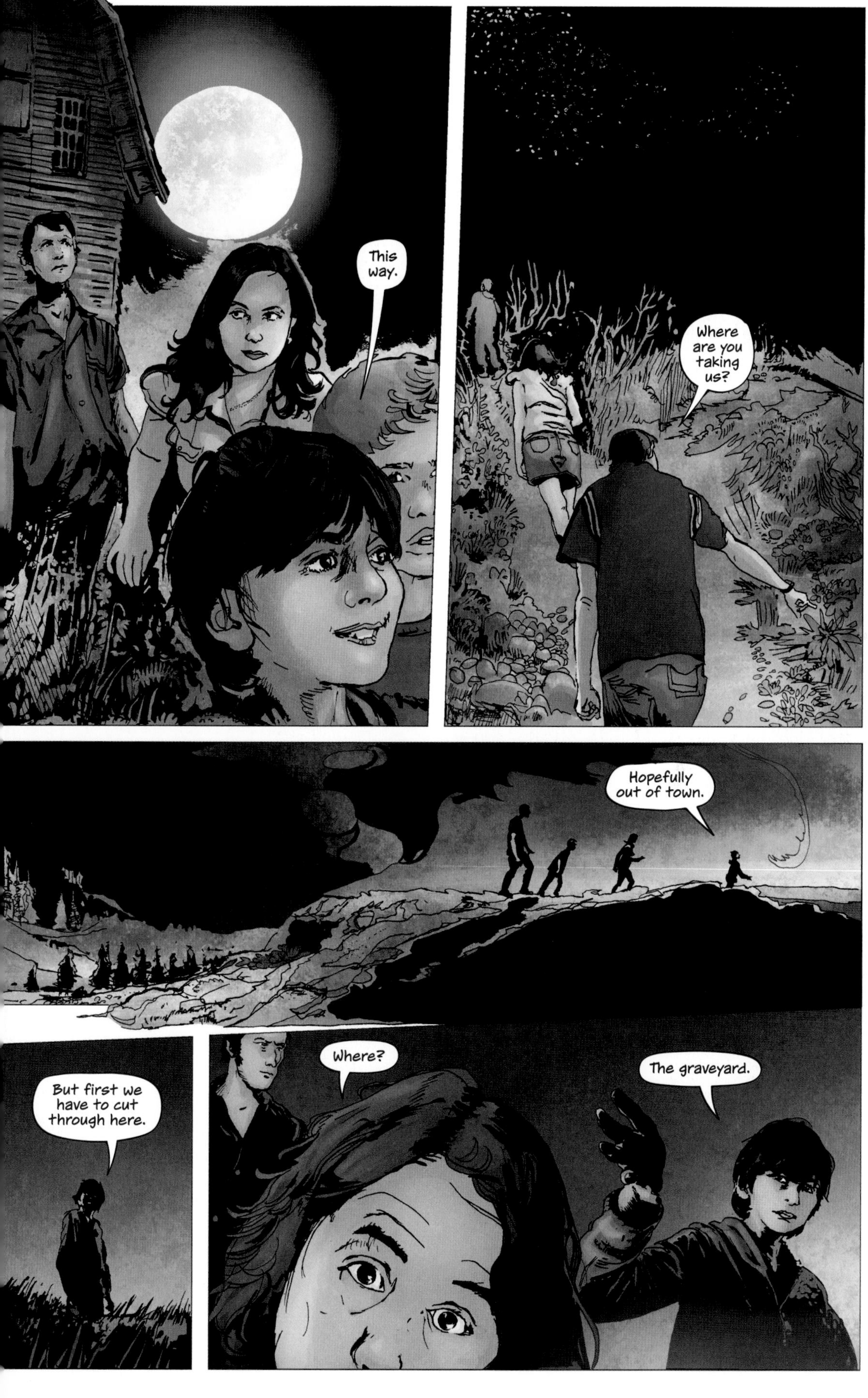
This way.
Where are you taking us?
Hopefully out of town.
But first we have to cut through here.
Where?
The graveyard.

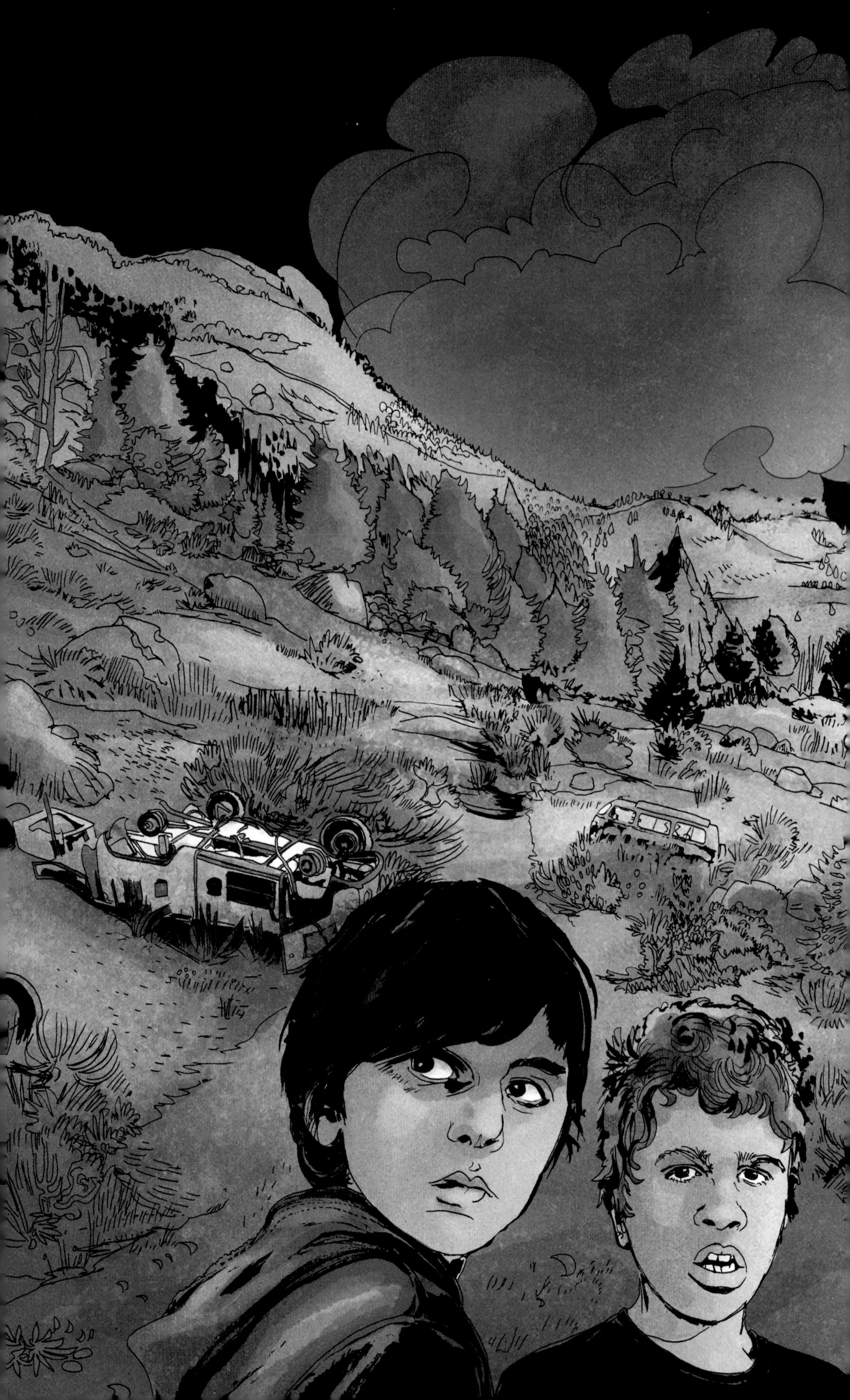

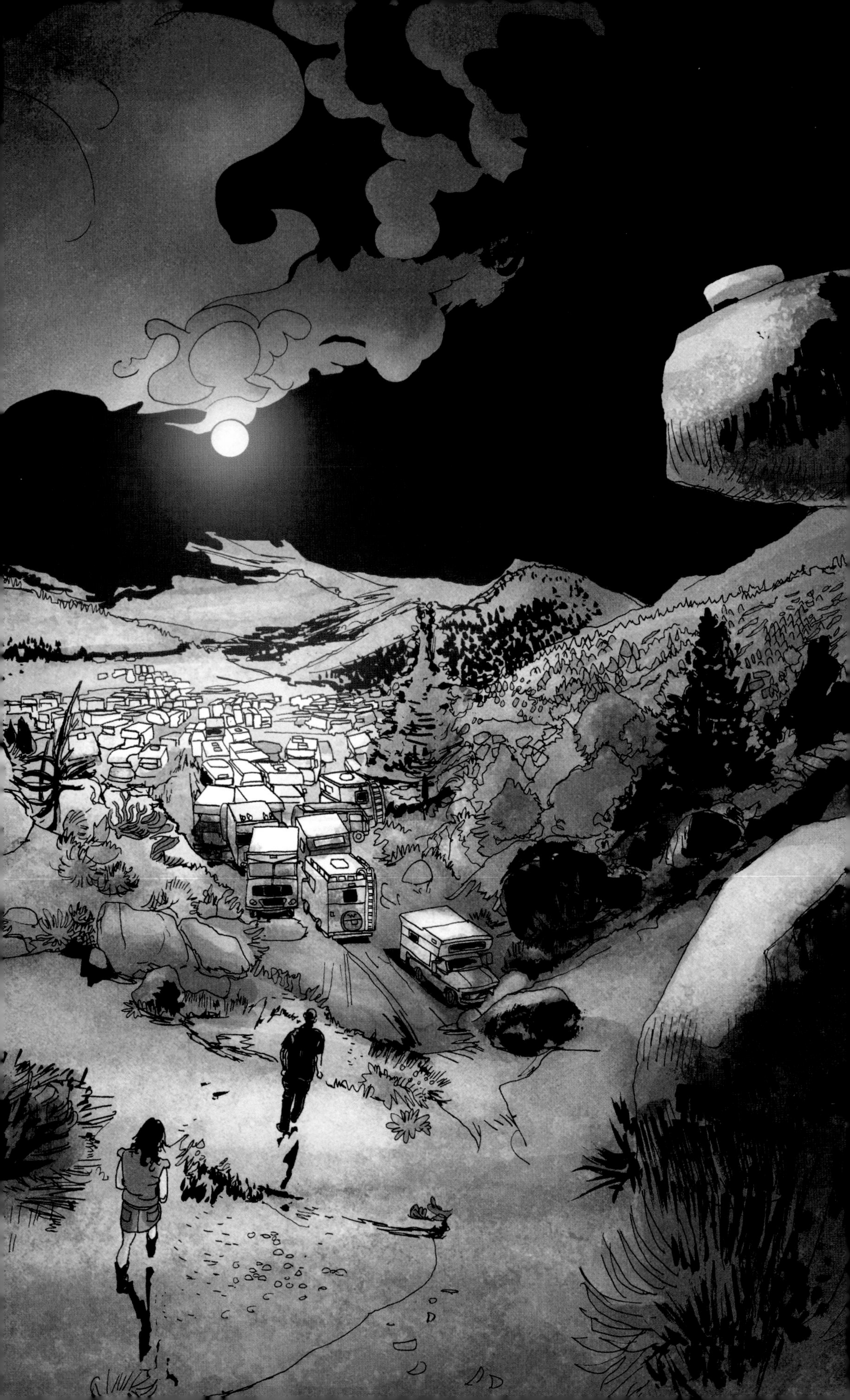

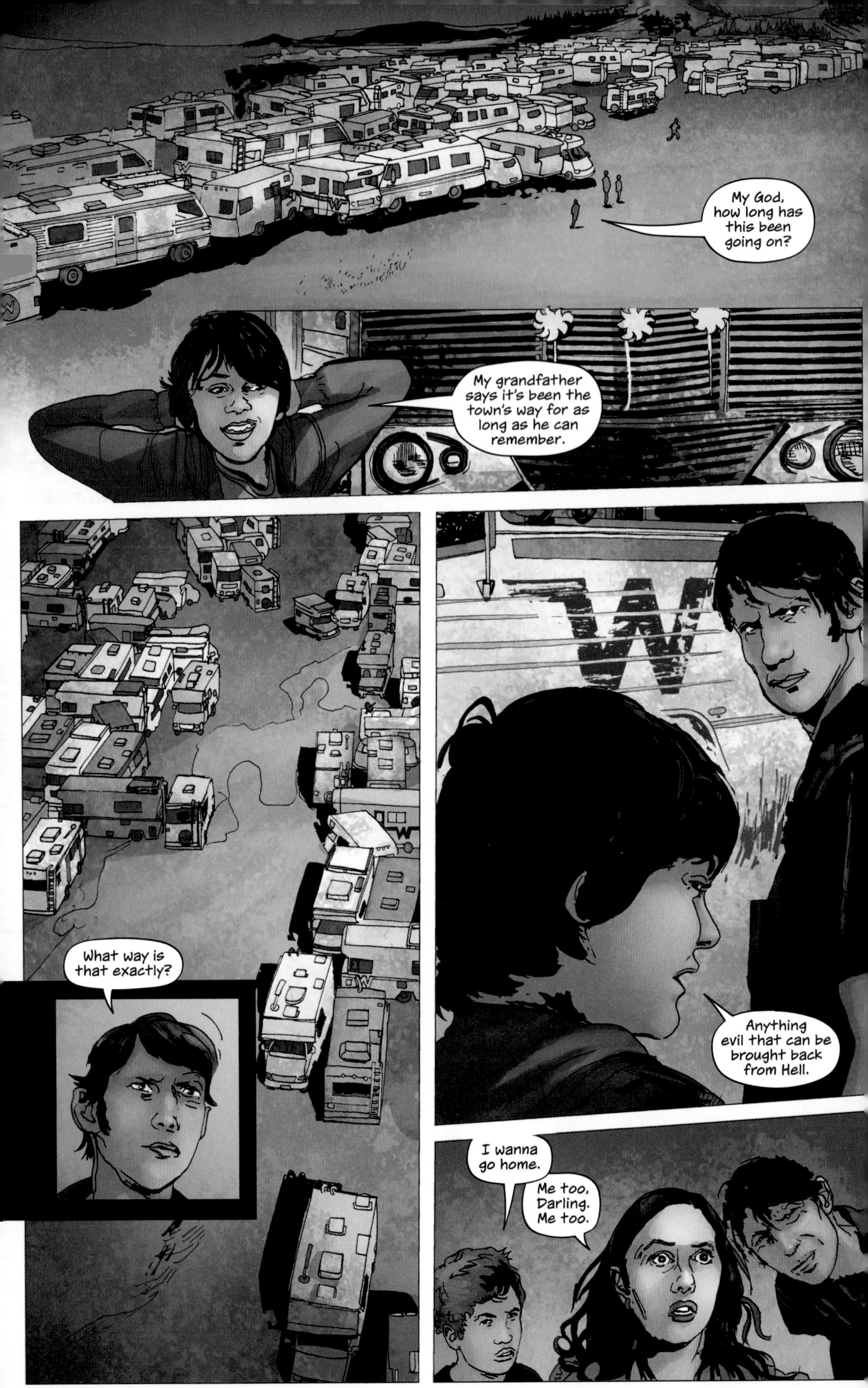
My God, how long has this been going on?
My grandfather says it's been the town's way for as long as he can remember.
What way is that exactly?
Anything evil that can be brought back from Hell.
I wanna go home.
Me too, Darling. Me too.

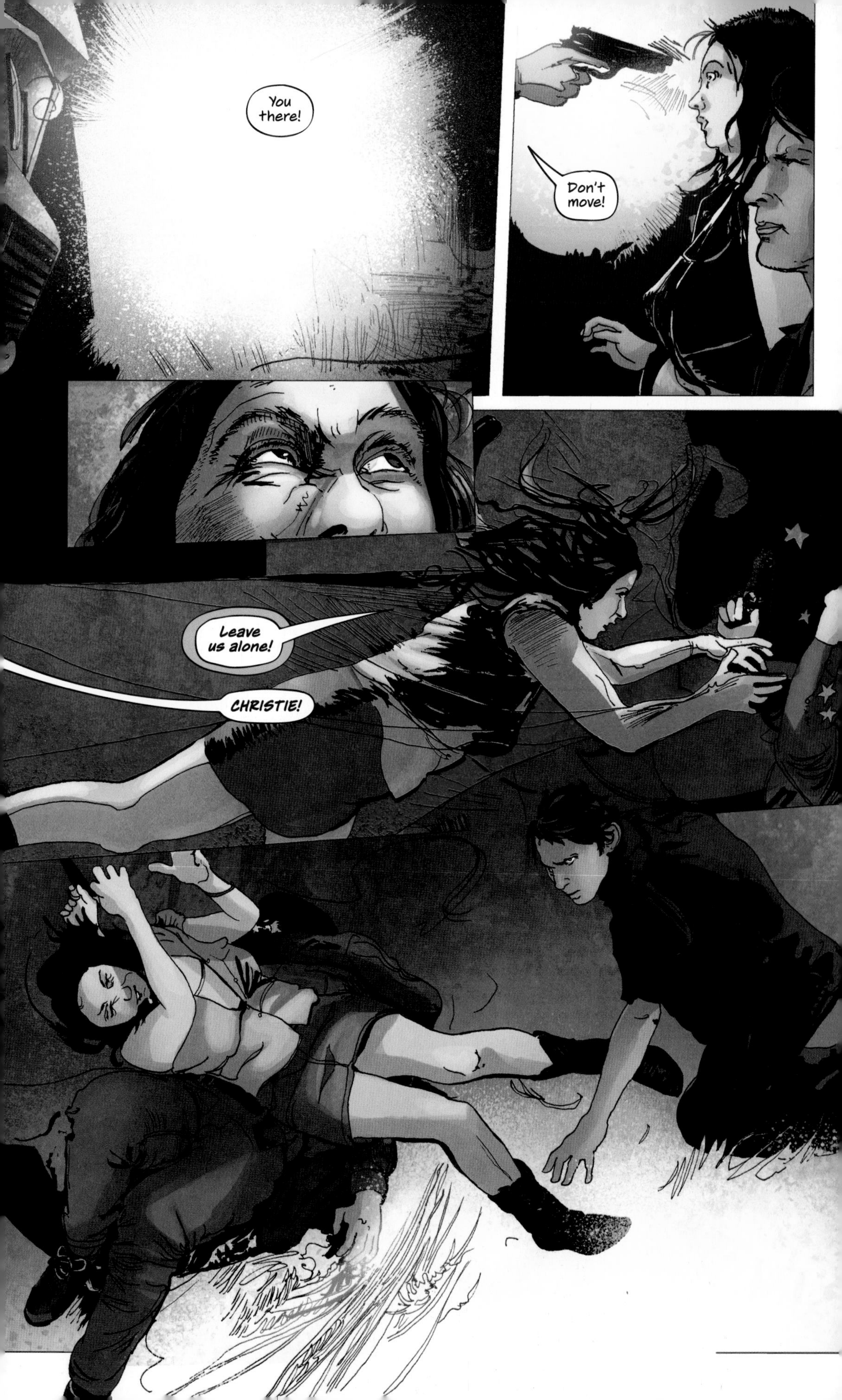

You there!
Don't move!
Leave us alone!
CHRISTIE!

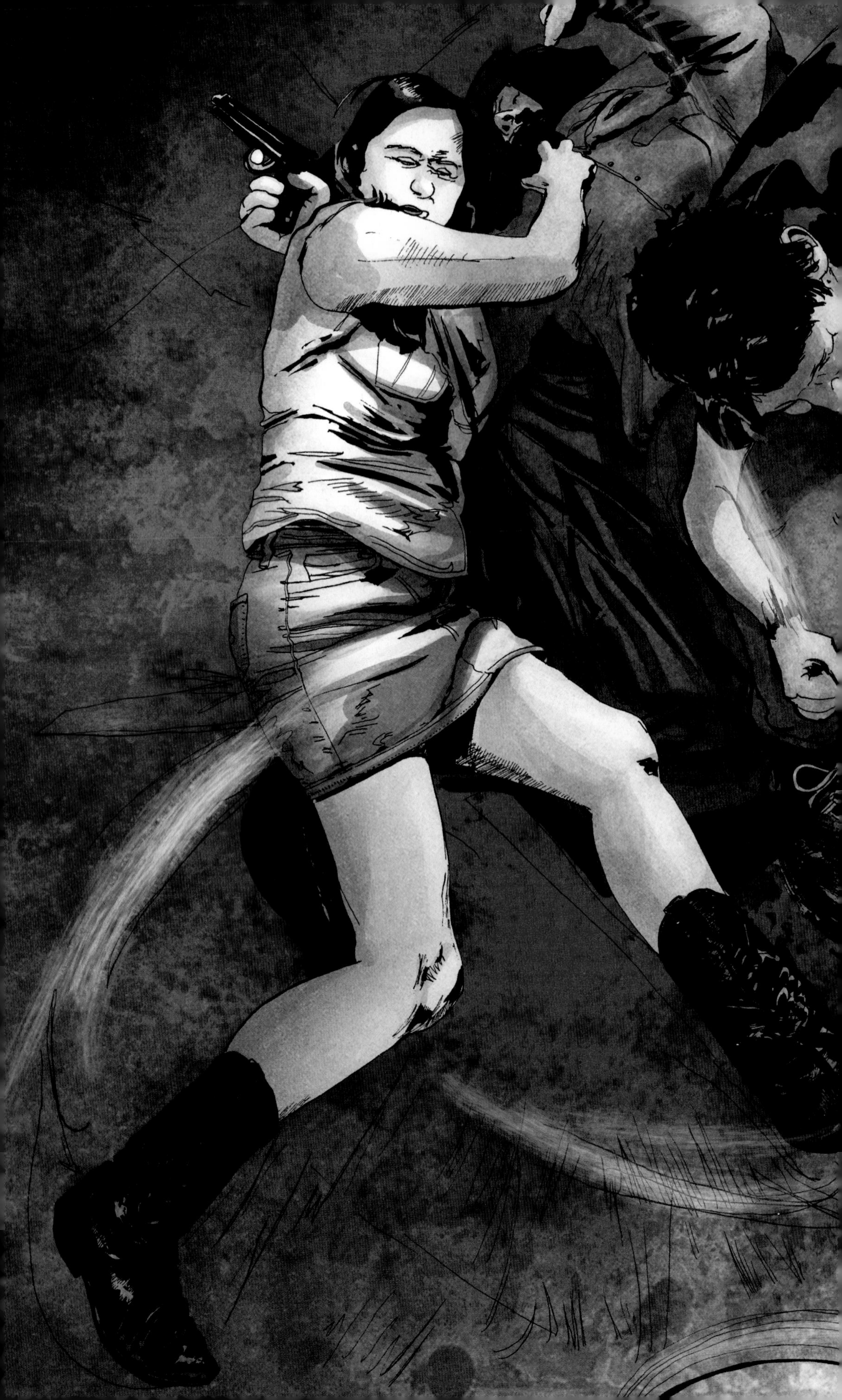

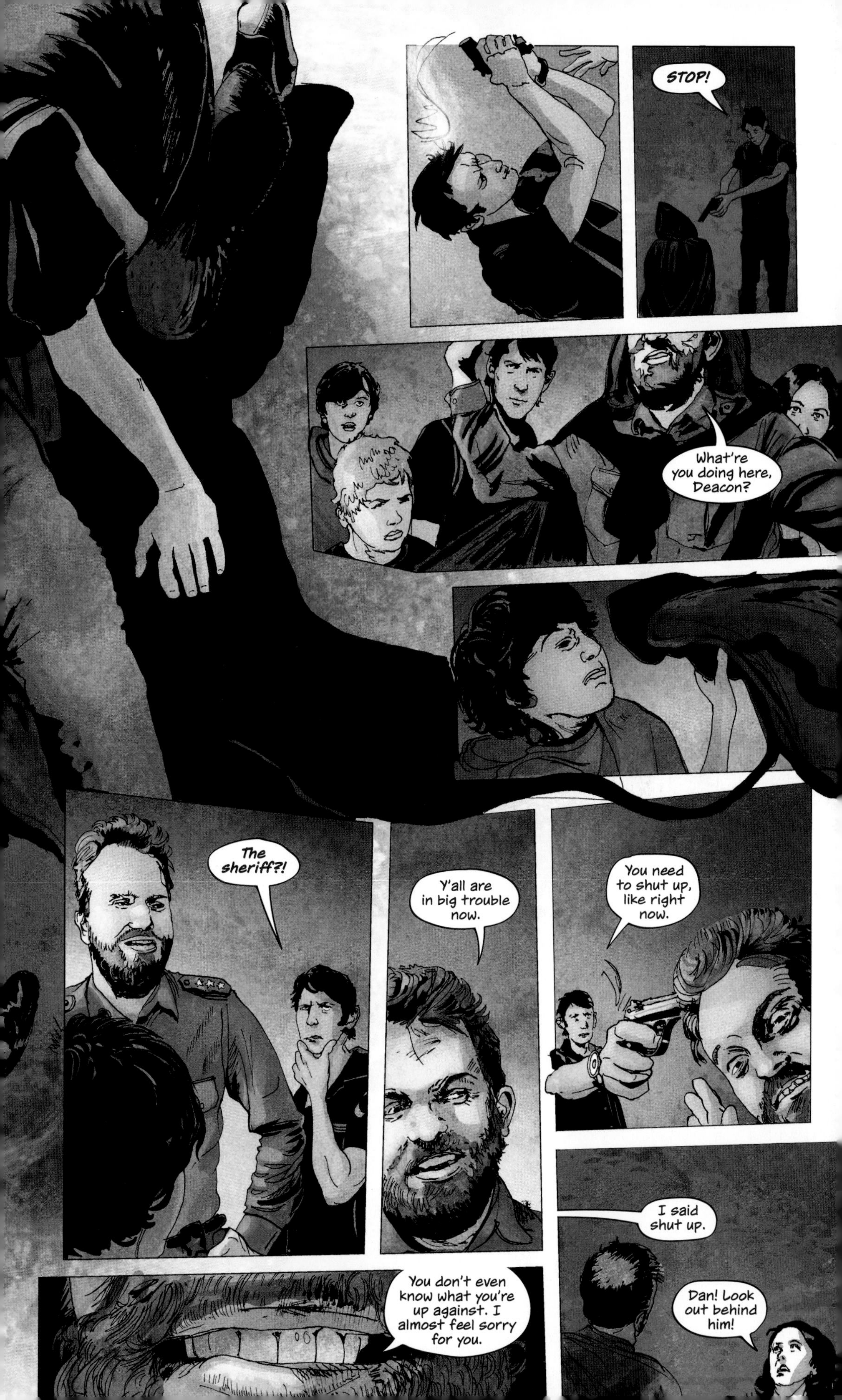
STOP!
What're you doing here, Deacon?
The sheriff?!
Y'all are in big trouble now.
You need to shut up, like right now.
I said shut up.
You don't even know what you're up against. I almost feel sorry for you.
Dan! Look out behind him!

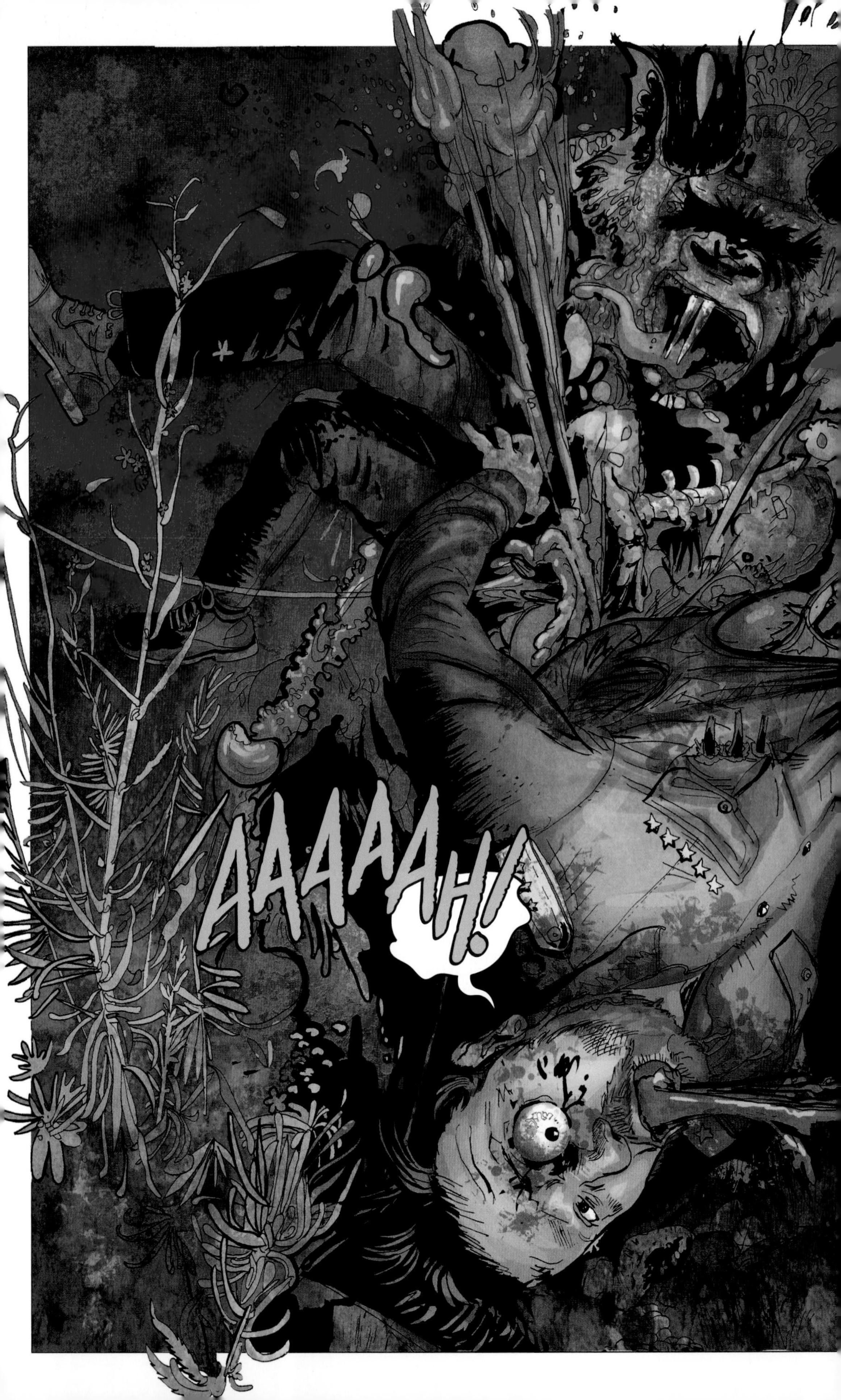
AAAAAH!

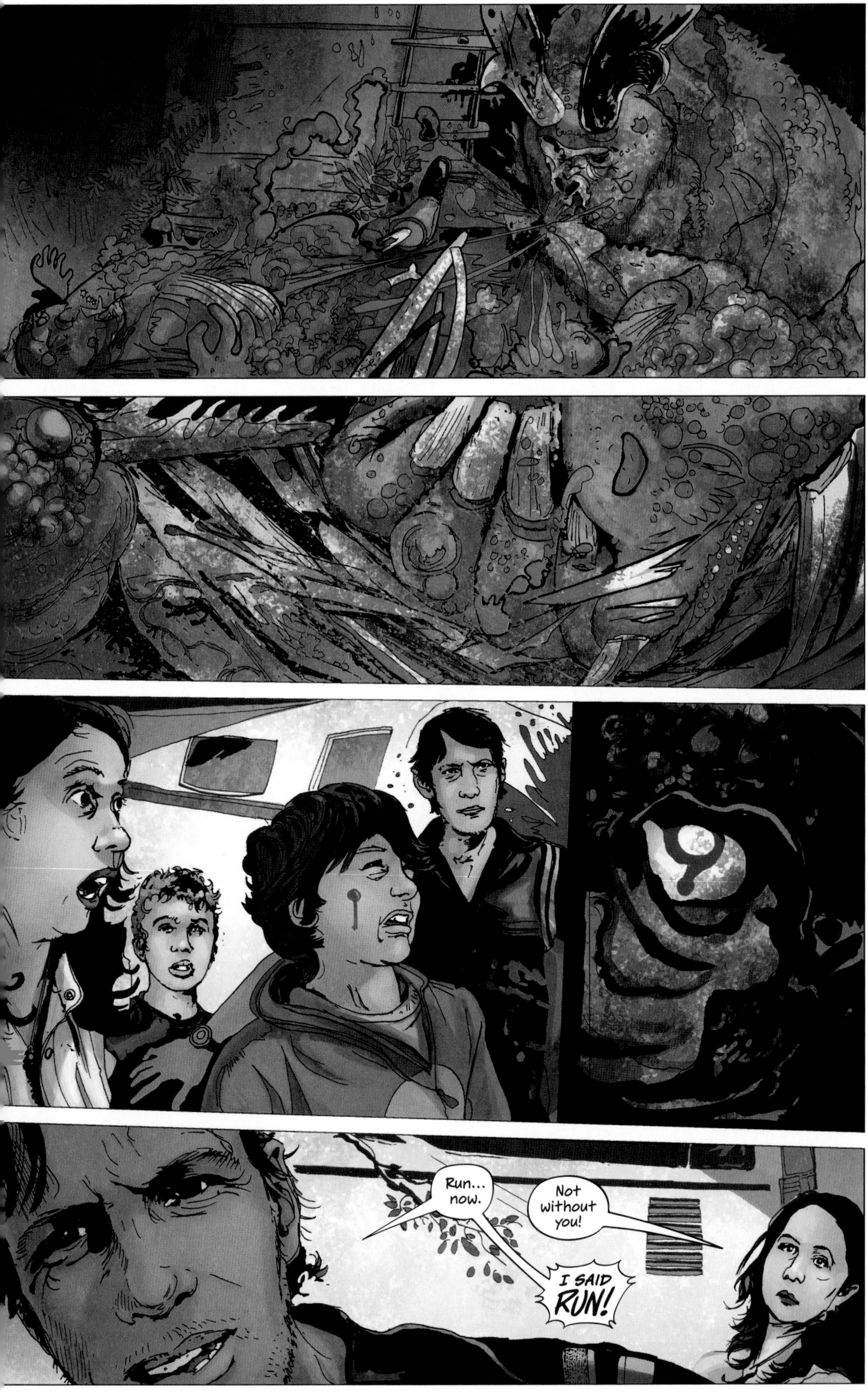
Run... now.
Not without you!
I SAID RUN!

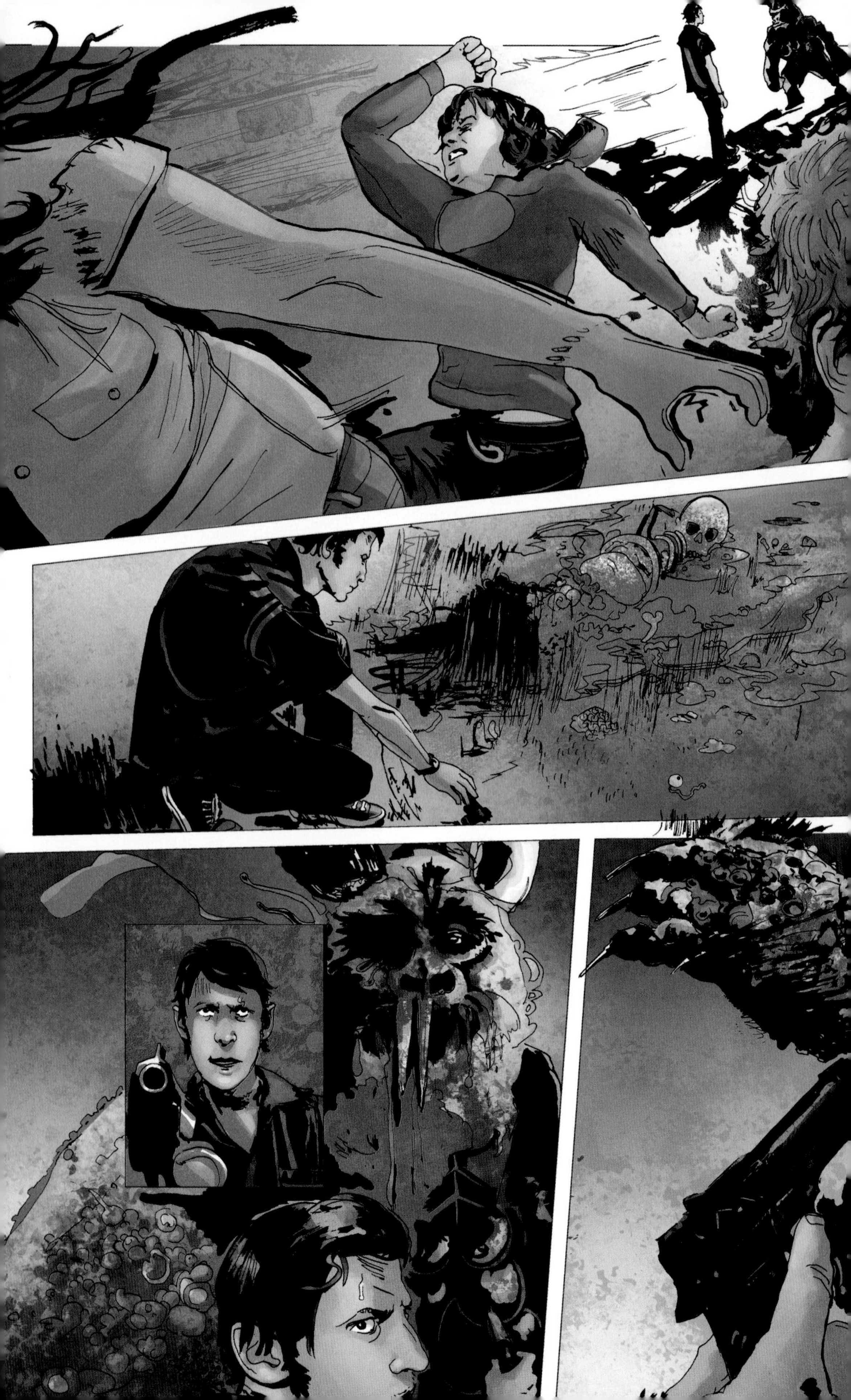

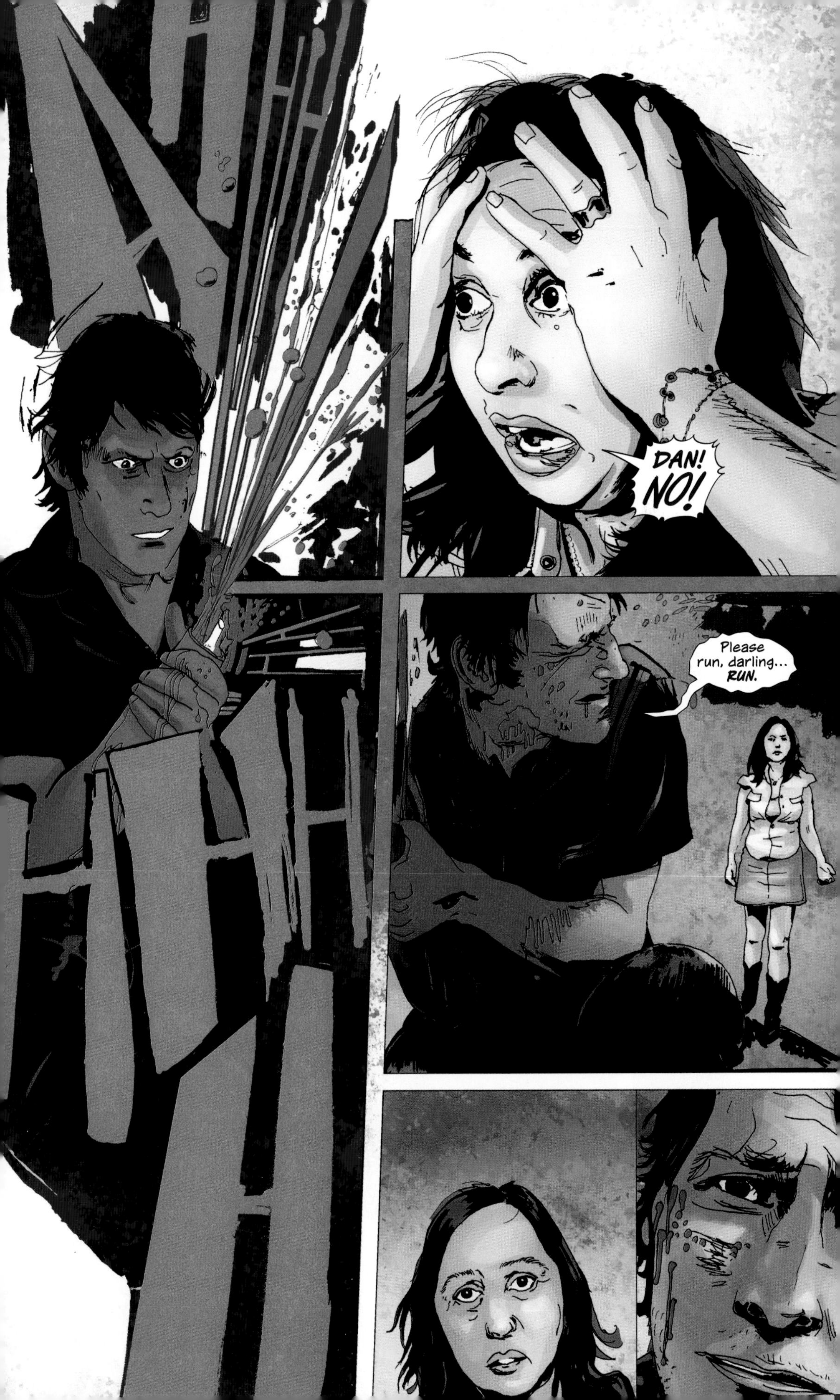
DAN! NO!
Please run, darling... RUN.

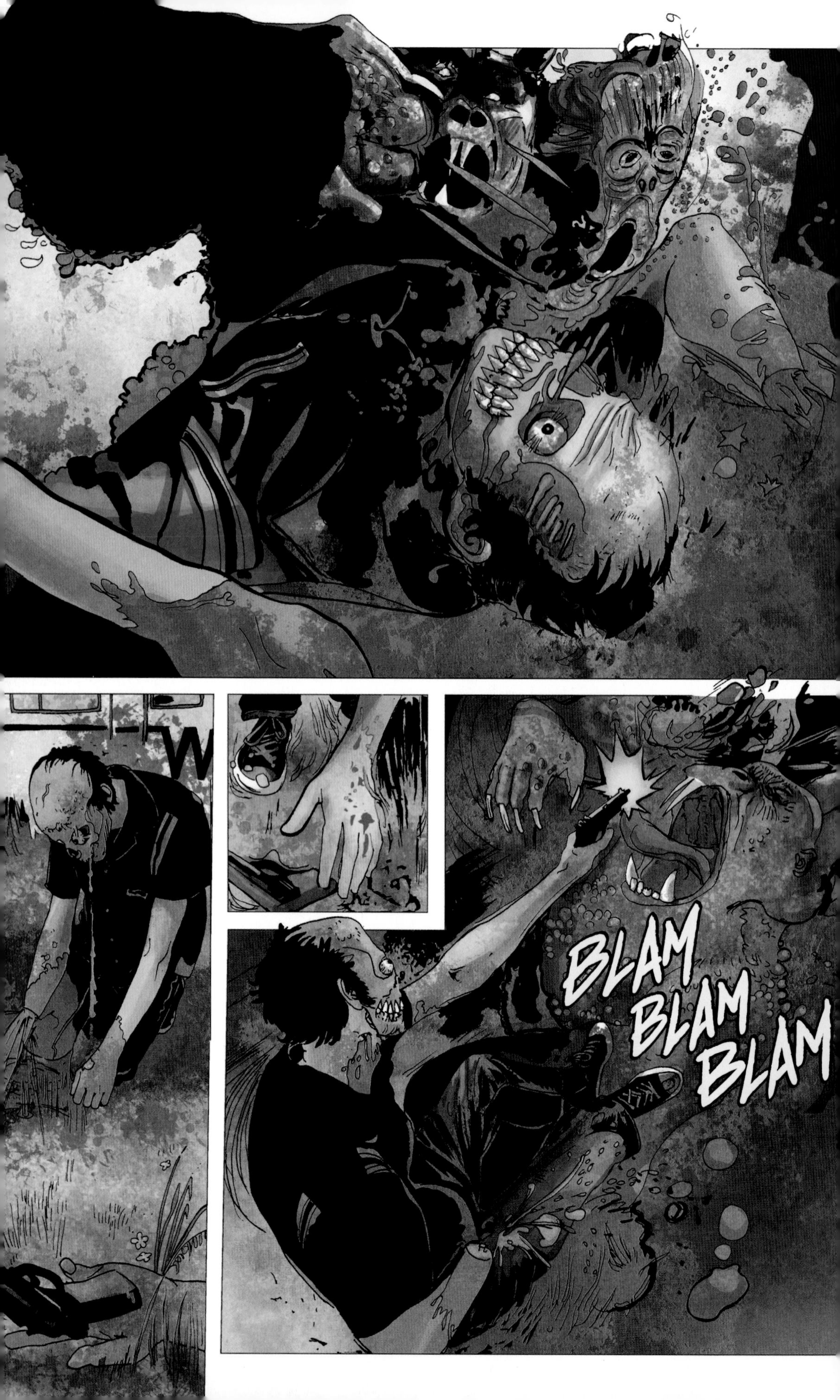
BLAM
BLAM
BLAM

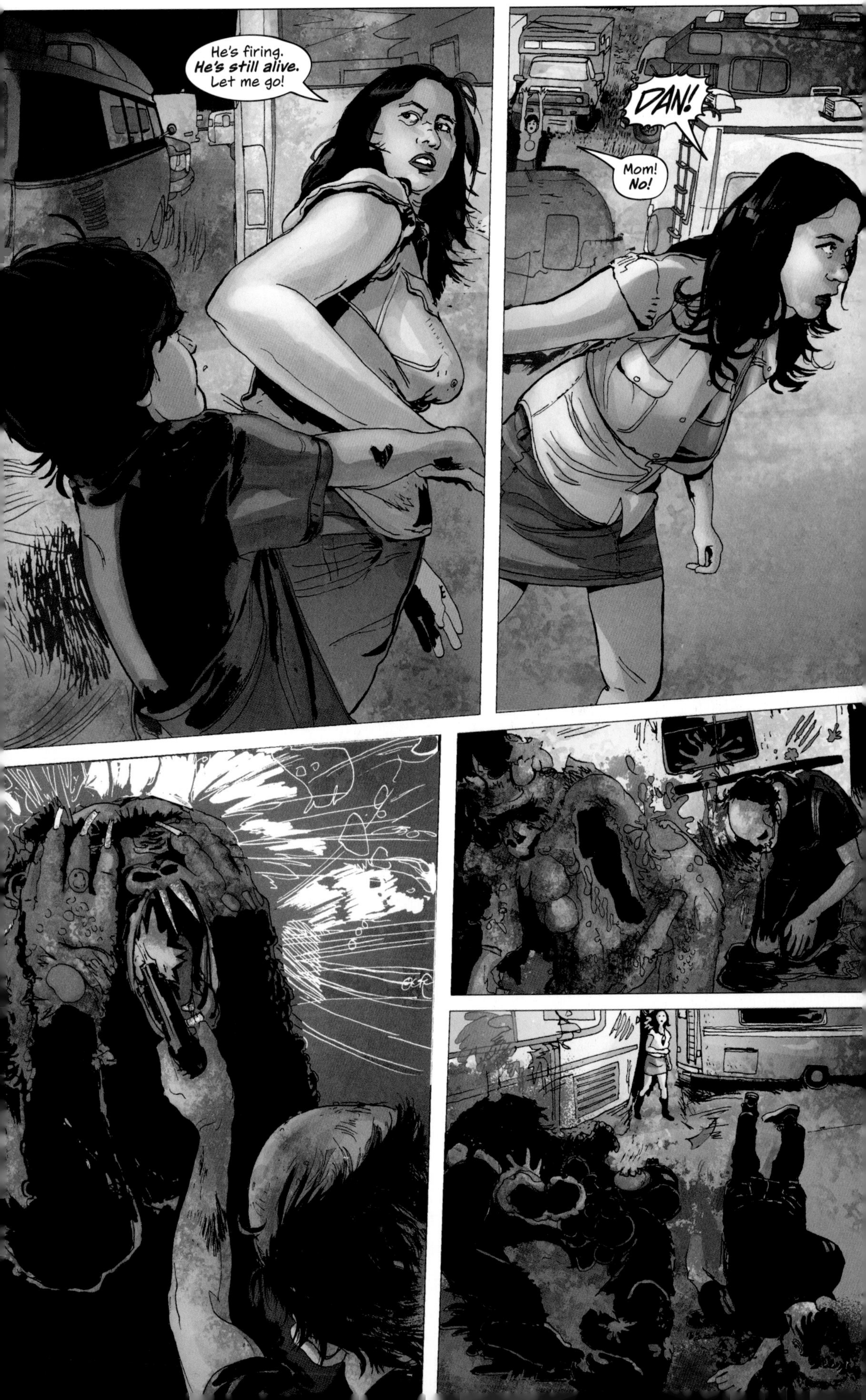
He's firing. **He's still alive.** Let me go!
DAN!
Mom! **No!**

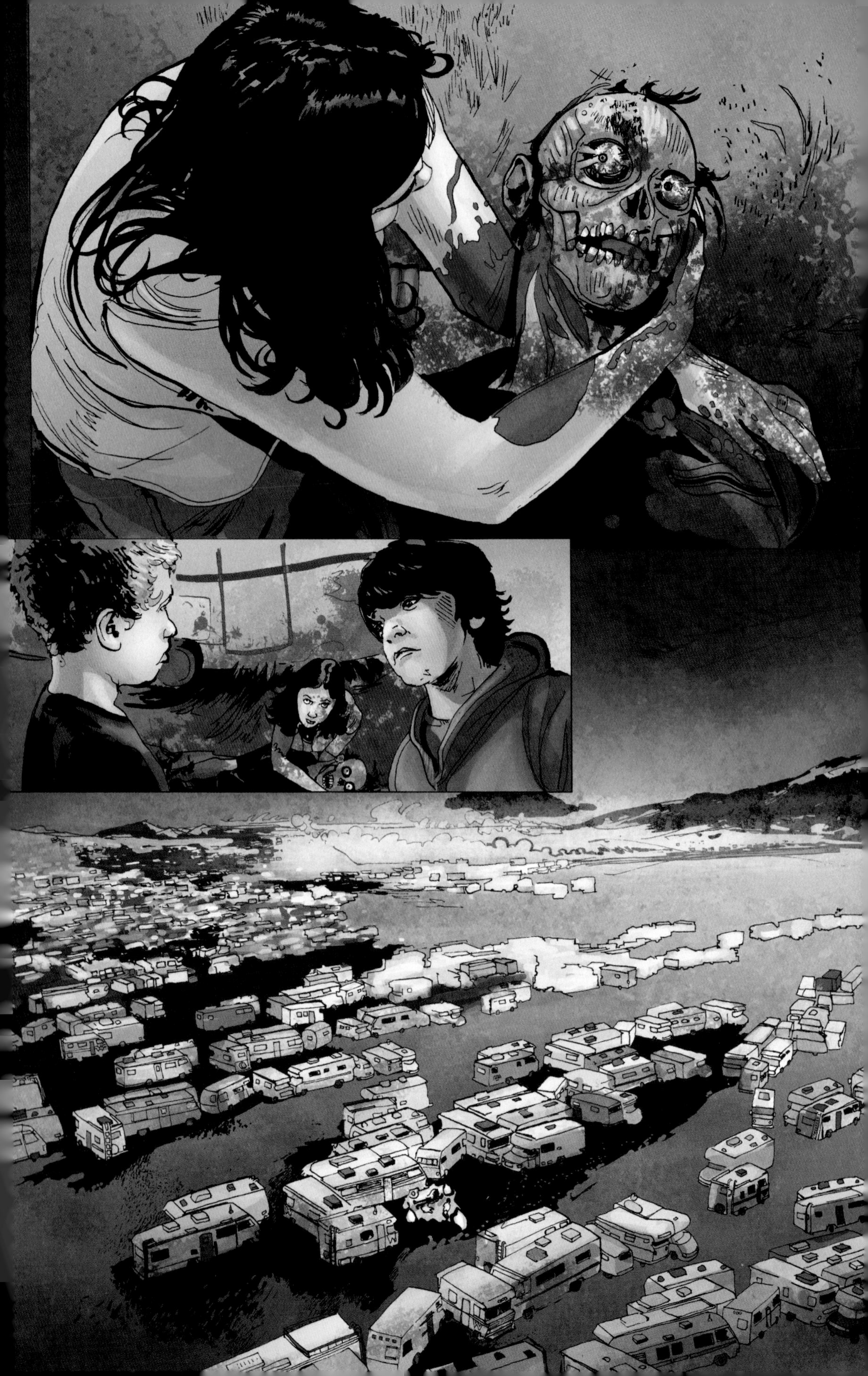

CHAPTER 4

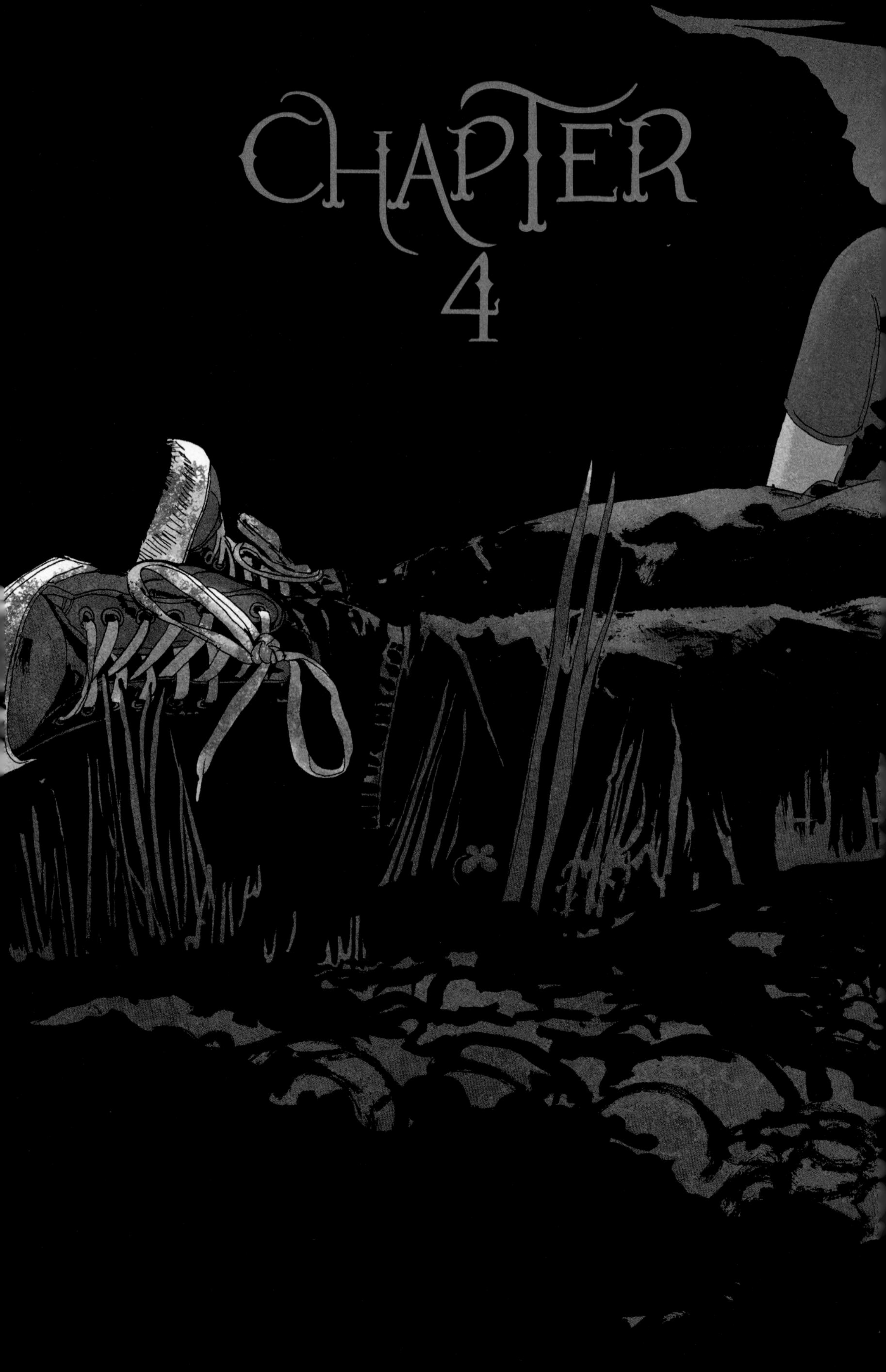

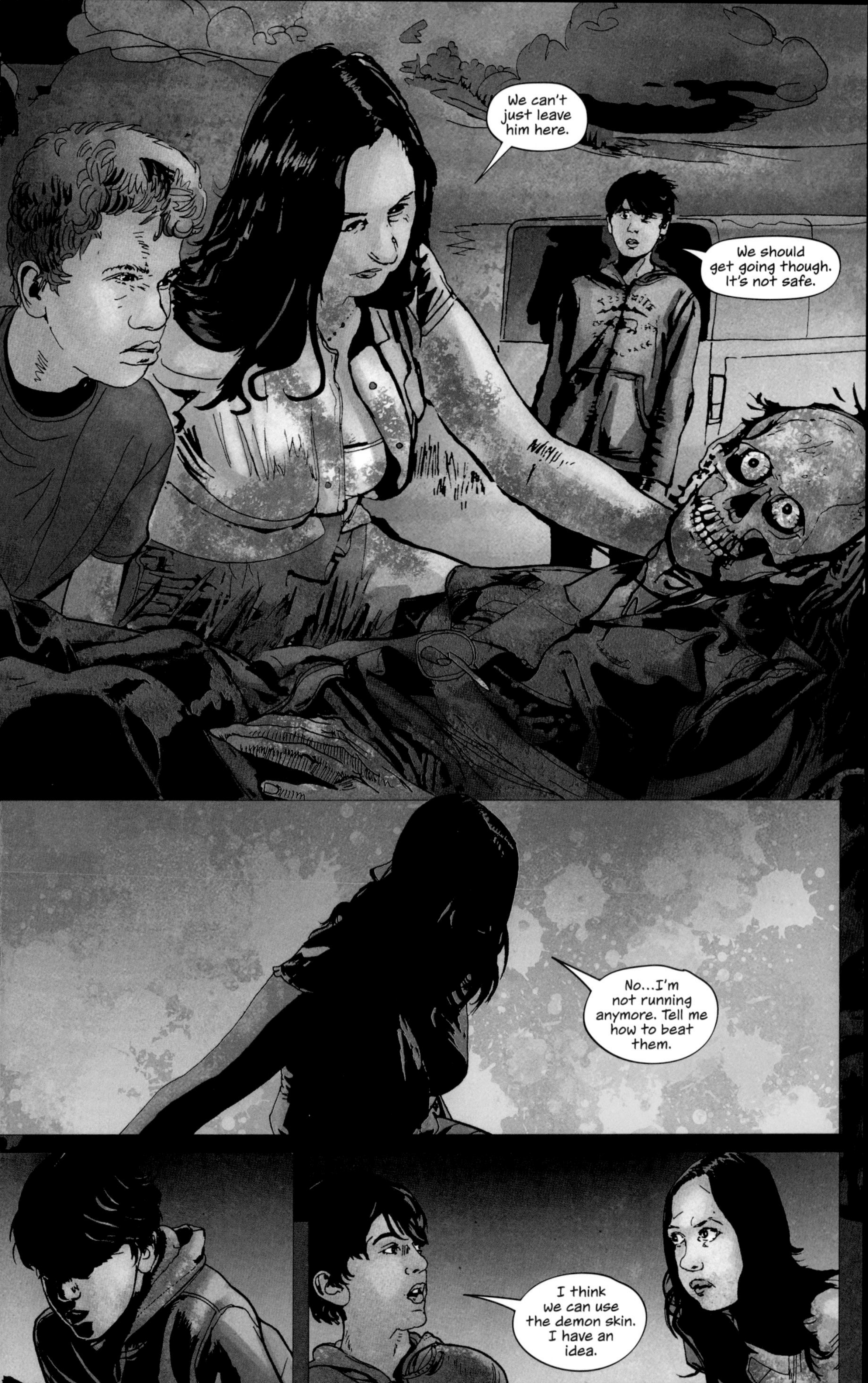
We can't just leave him here.
We should get going though. It's not safe.
No...I'm not running anymore. Tell me how to beat them.
I think we can use the demon skin. I have an idea.

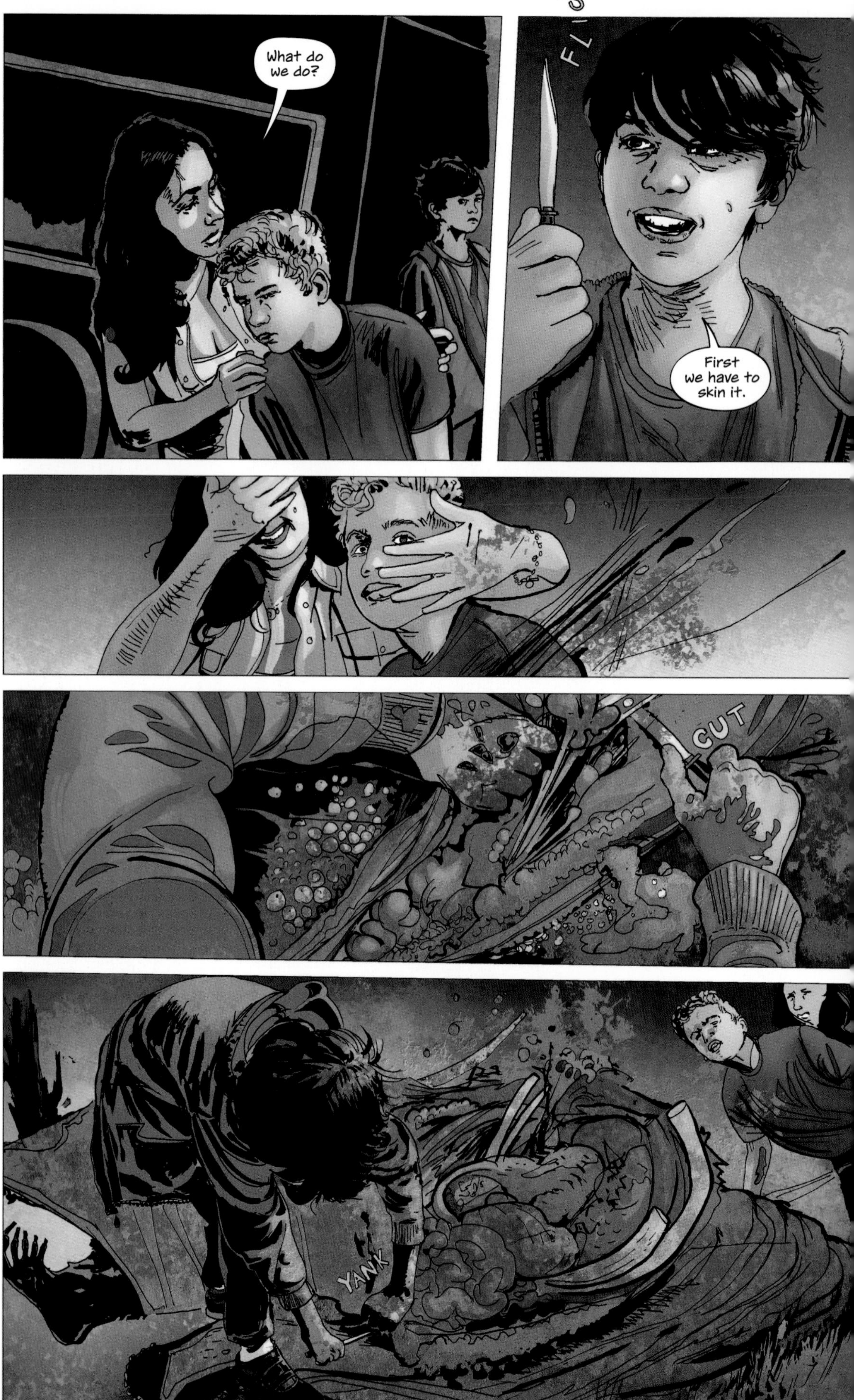
What do we do?
FLICK
First we have to skin it.
CUT
YANK

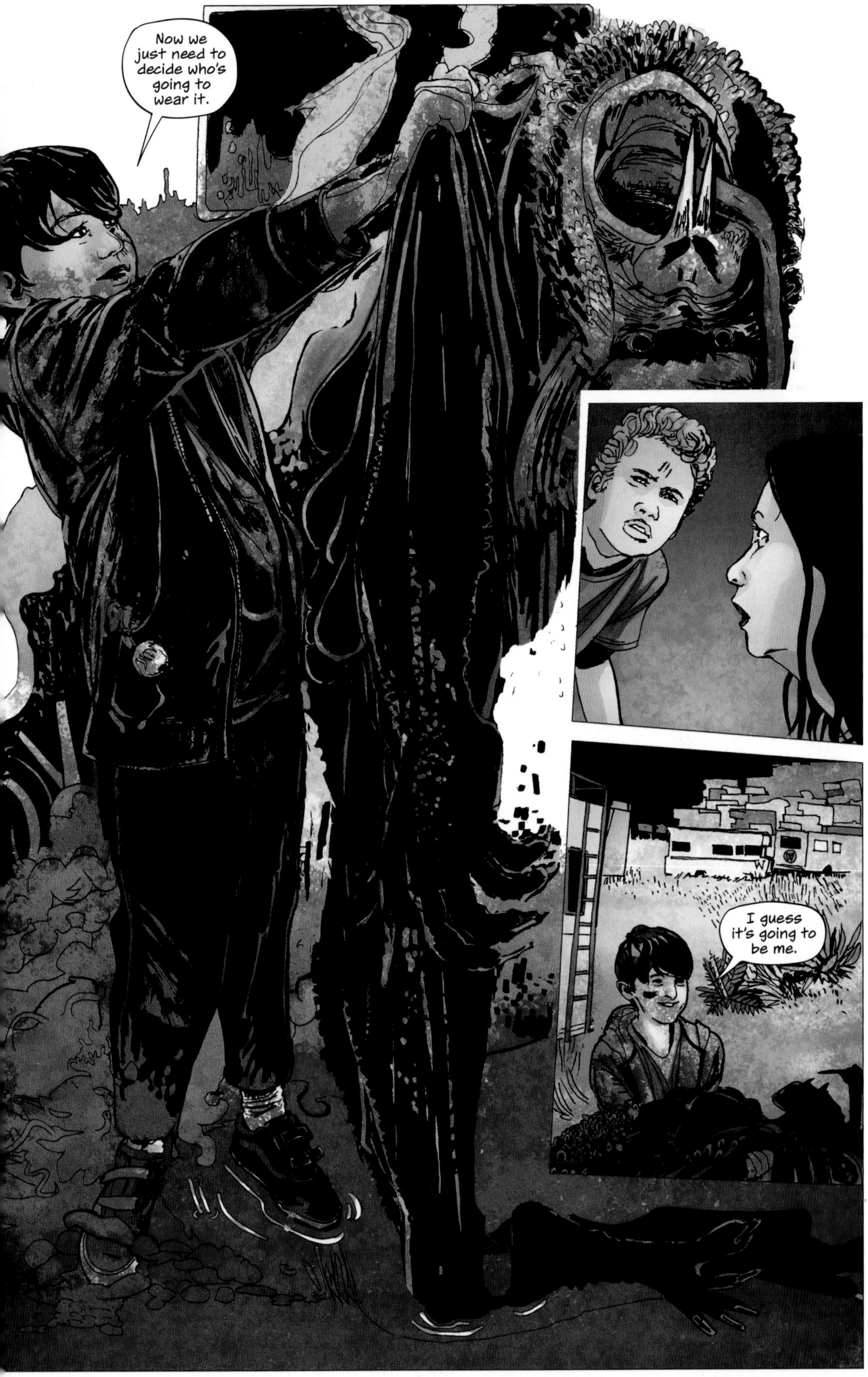
Now we just need to decide who's going to wear it.
I guess it's going to be me.

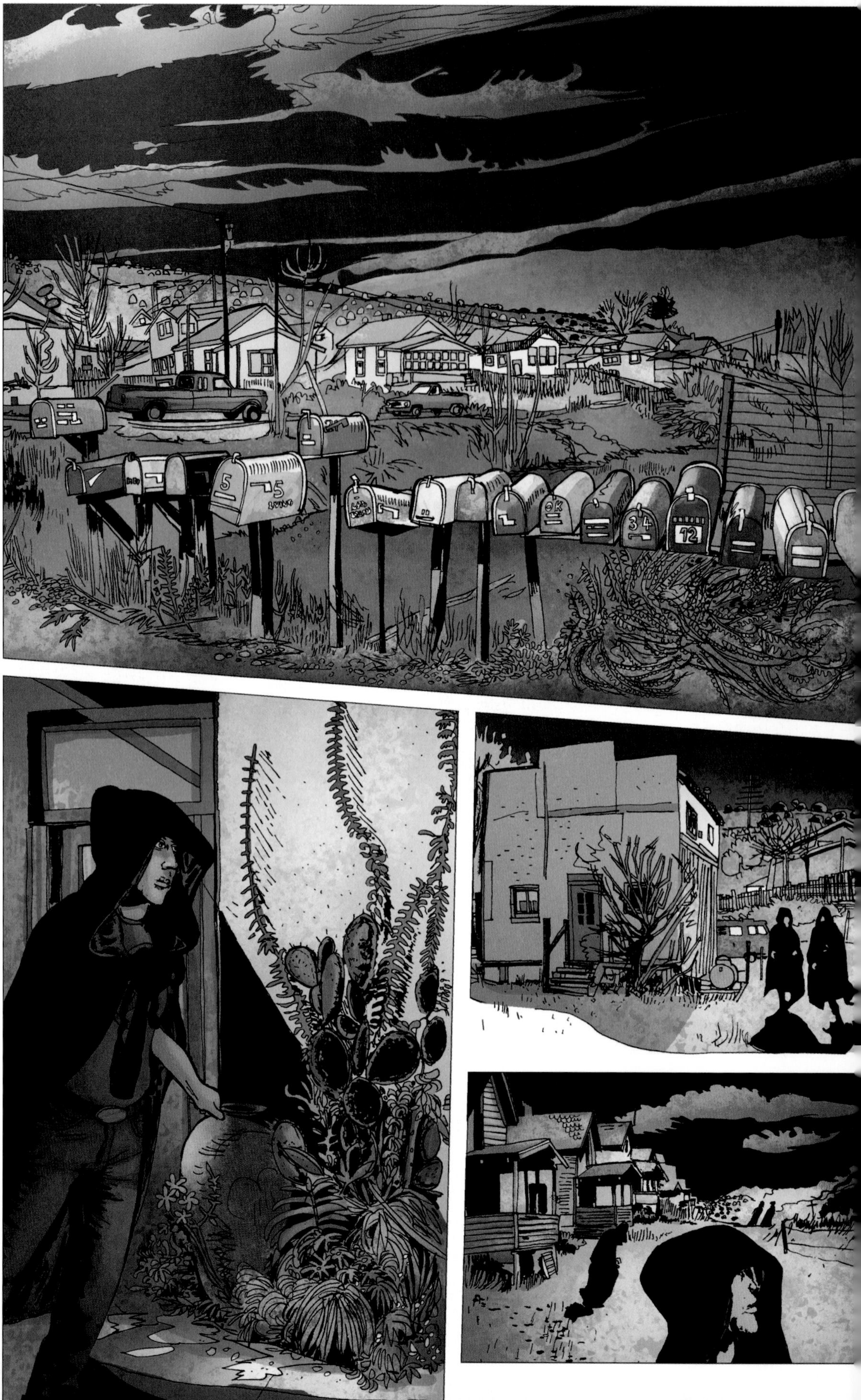
5
5
34
12

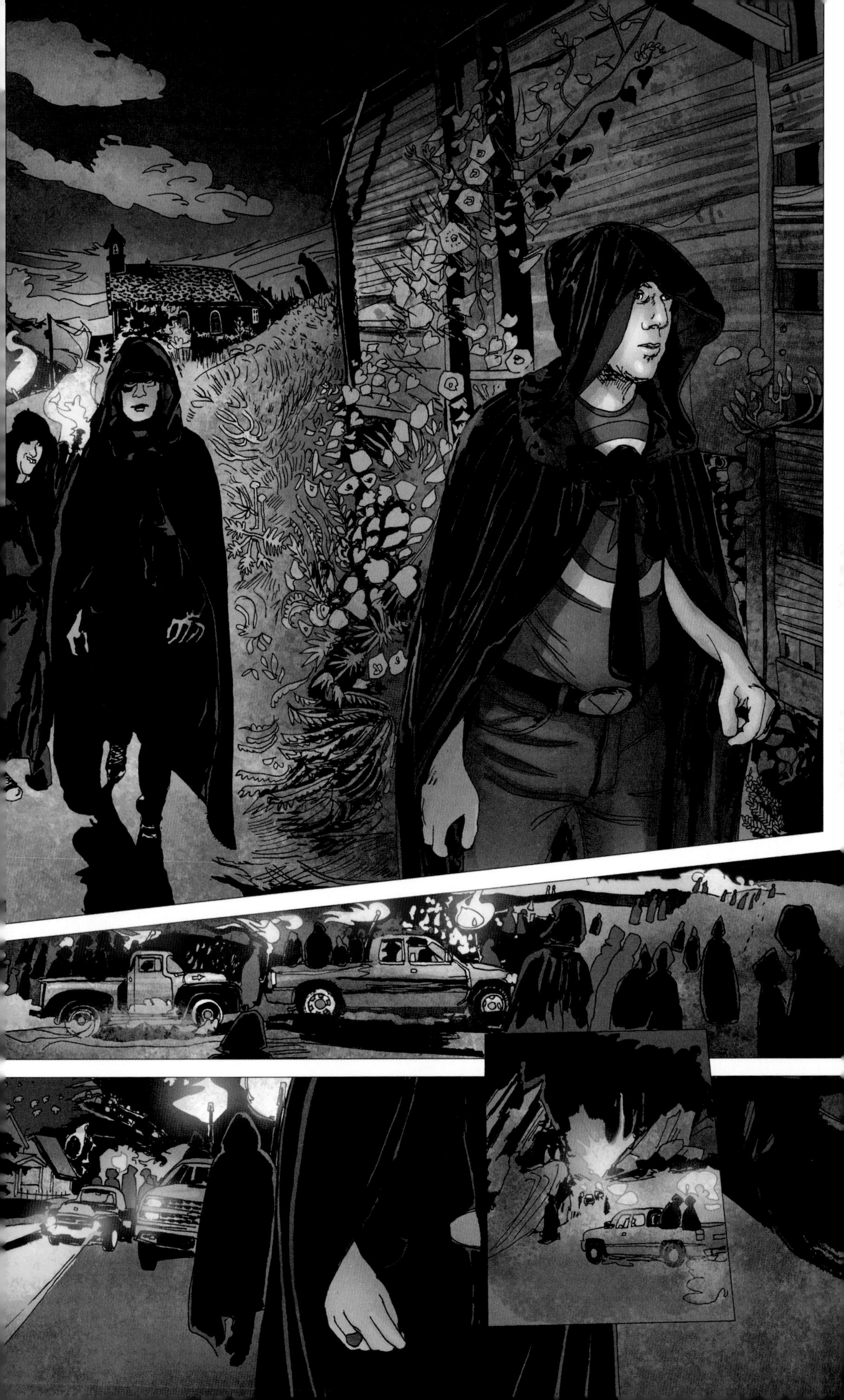

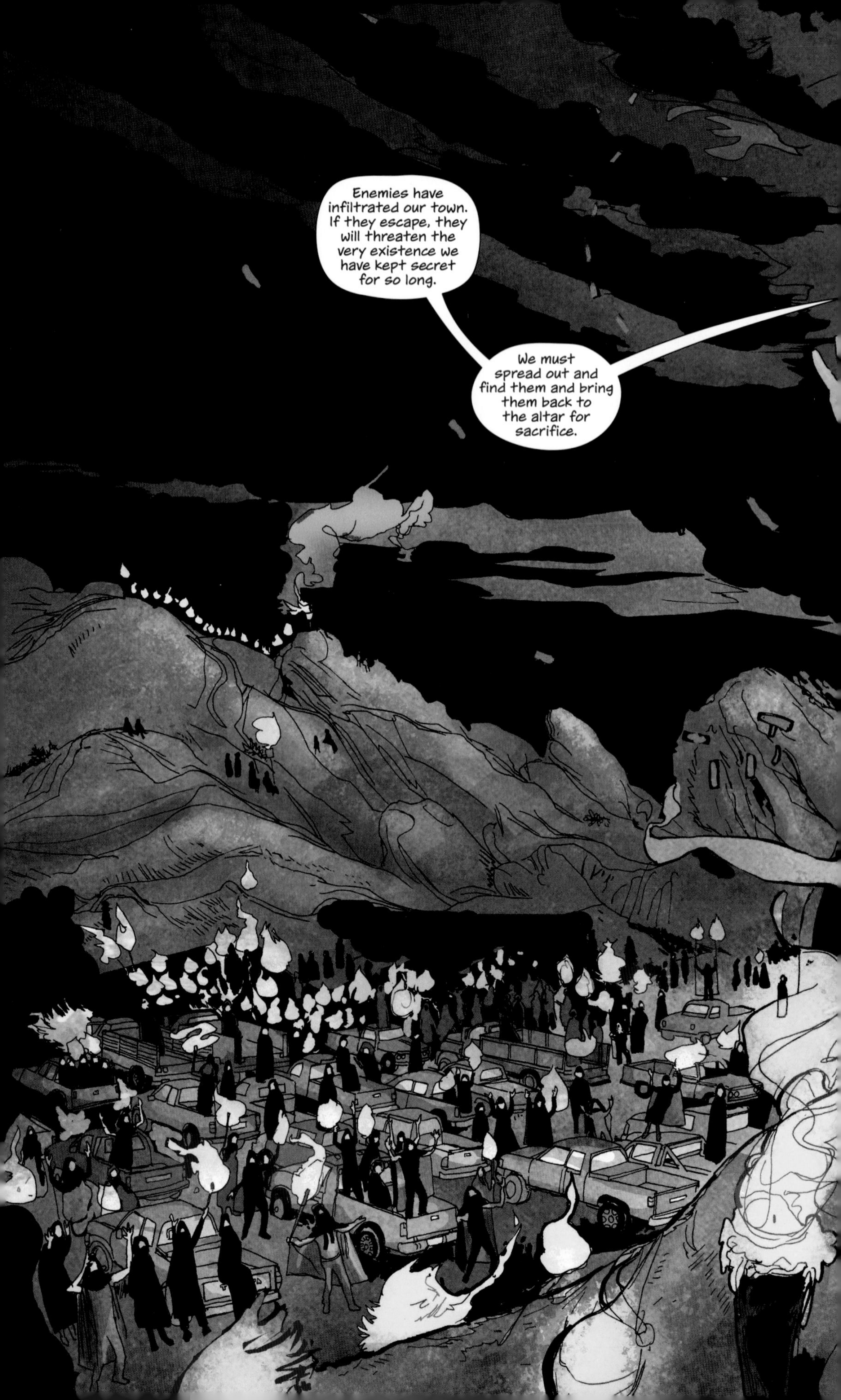
Enemies have infiltrated our town. If they escape, they will threaten the very existence we have kept secret for so long.
We must spread out and find them and bring them back to the altar for sacrifice.

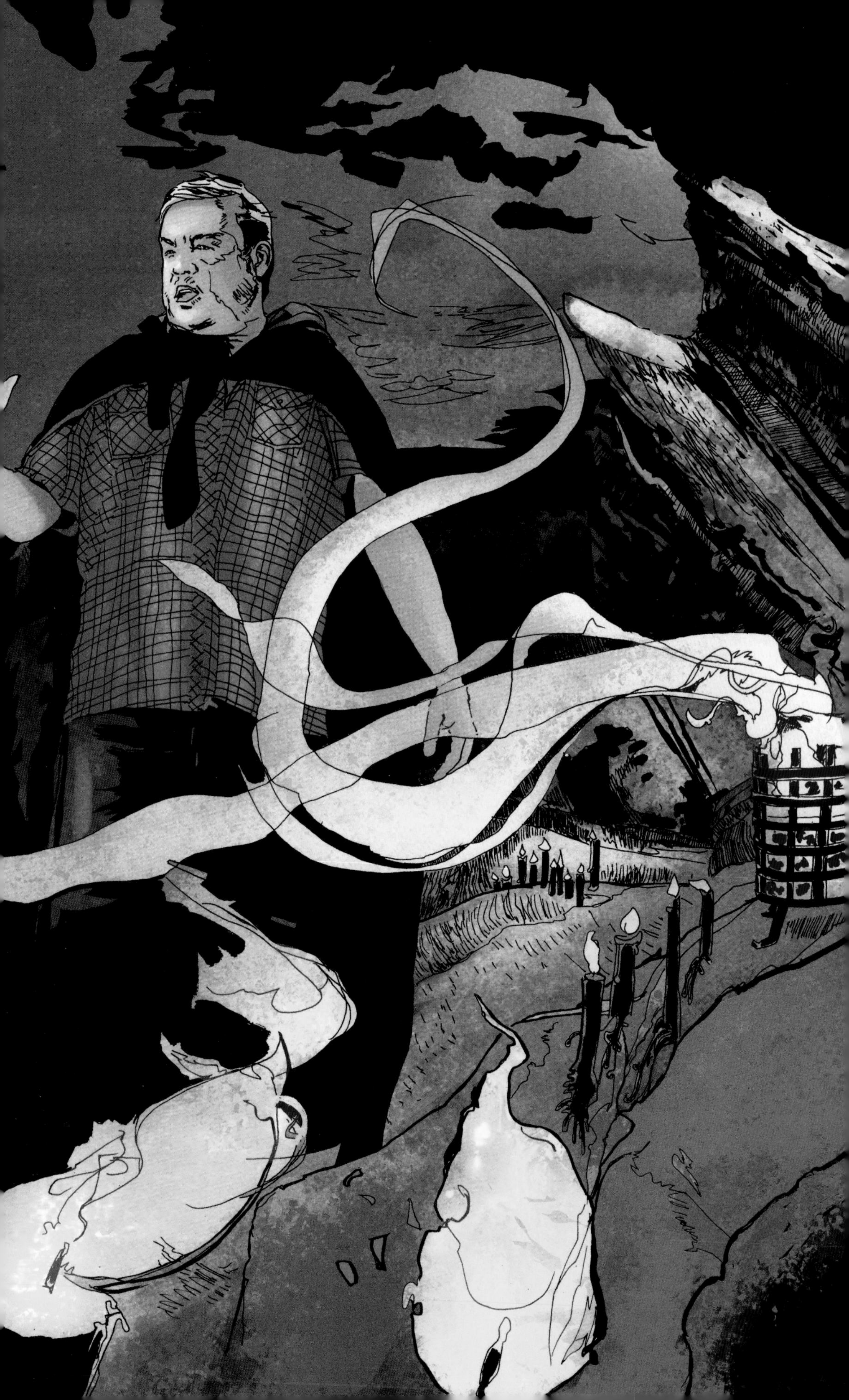

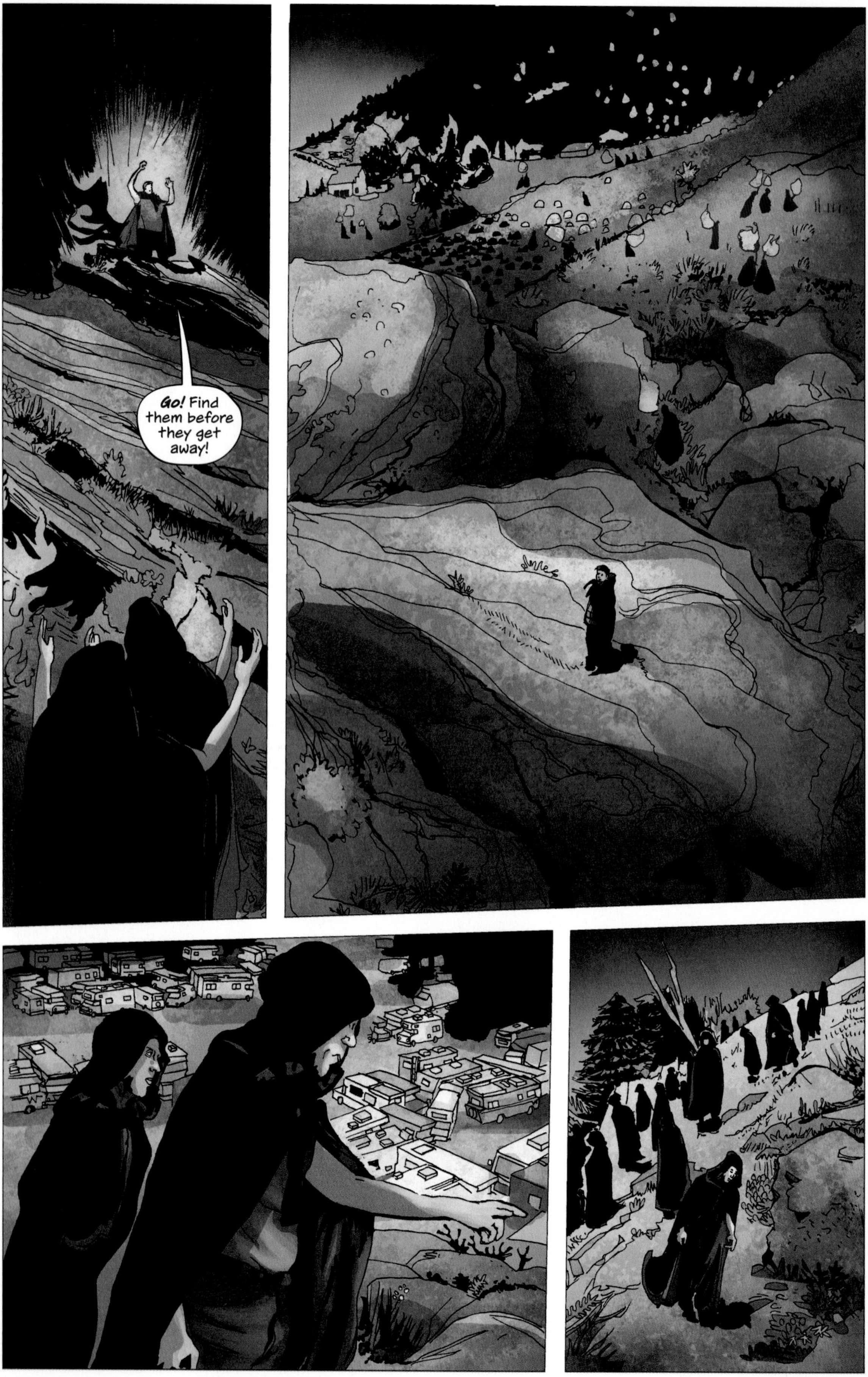
Go! Find them before they get away!

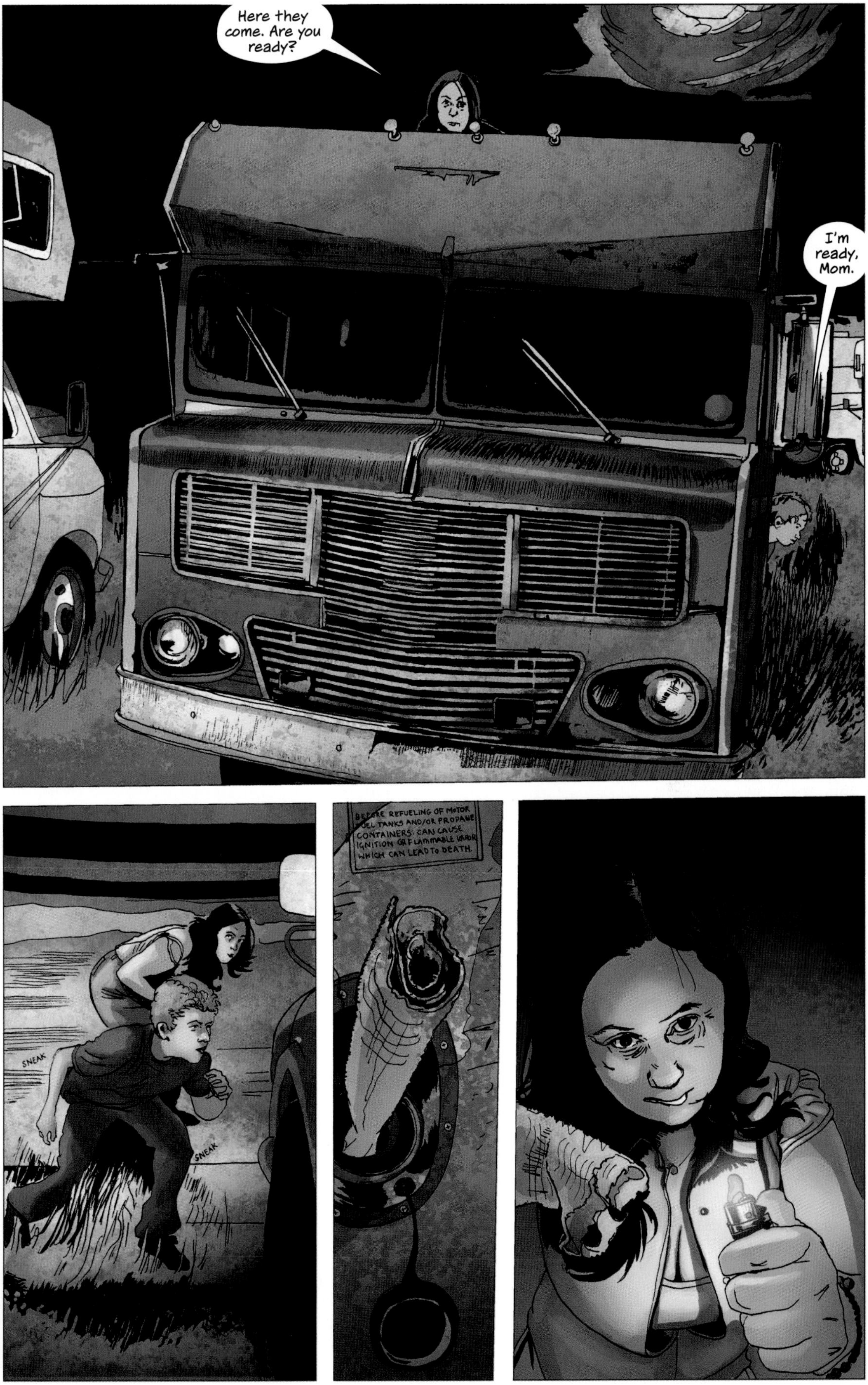
Here they come. Are you ready?
I'm ready, Mom.
SNEAK
SNEAK
BEFORE REFUELING OF MOTOR
UEL TANKS AND/OR PROPANE
CONTAINERS. CAN CAUSE
IGNITION OR FLAMMABLE VAPOR
WHICH CAN LEAD TO DEATH.

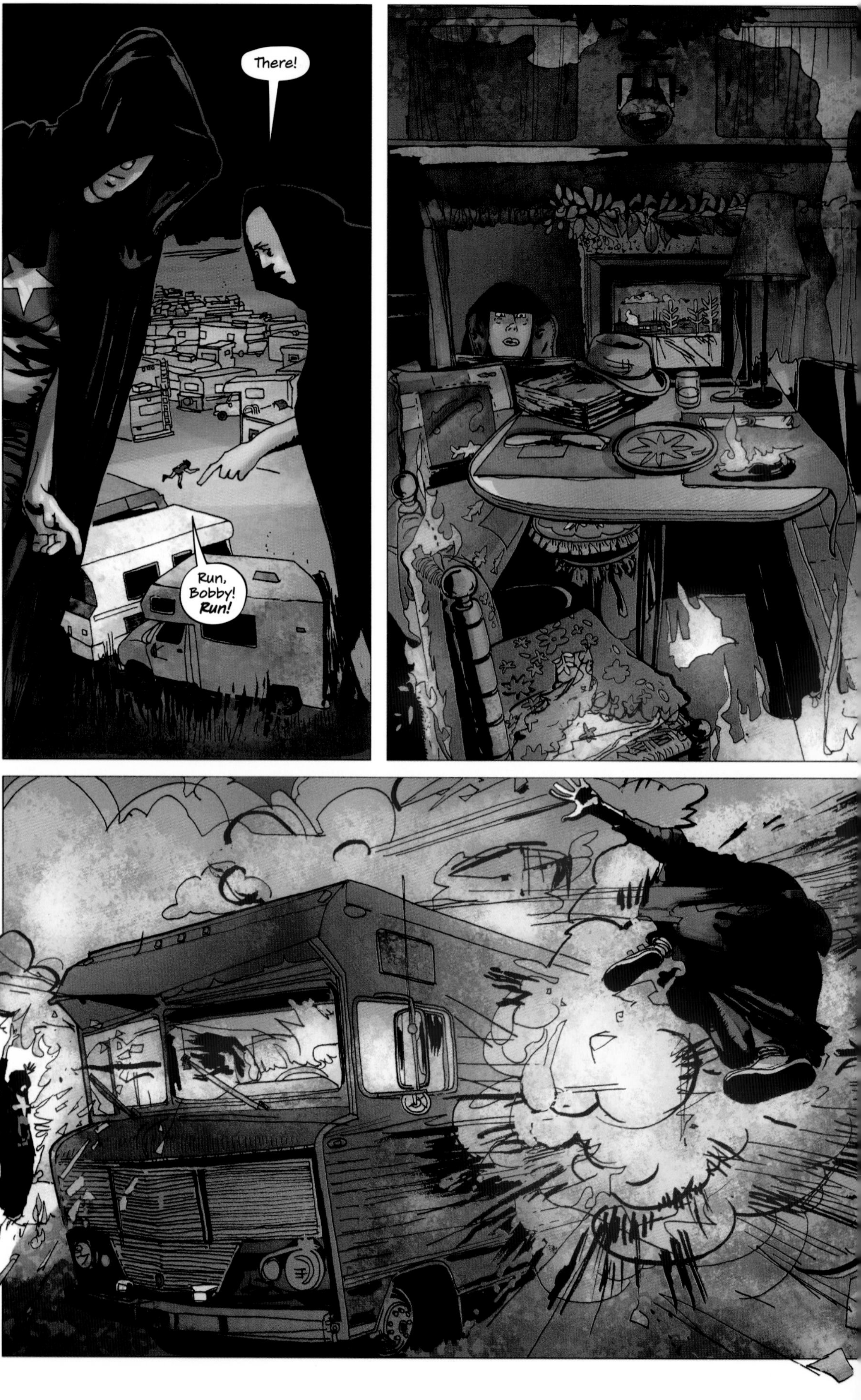
There!
Run, Bobby! Run!

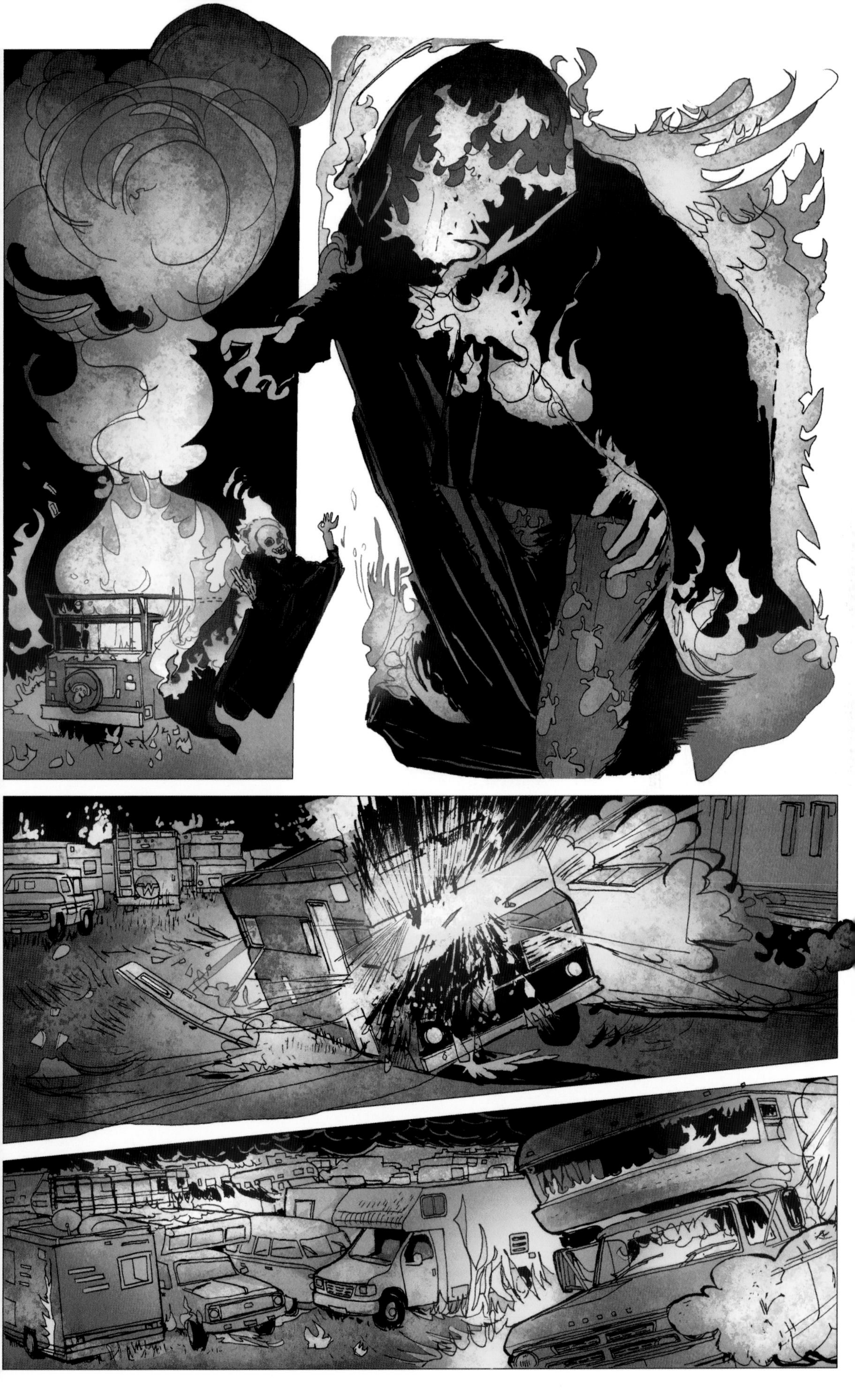

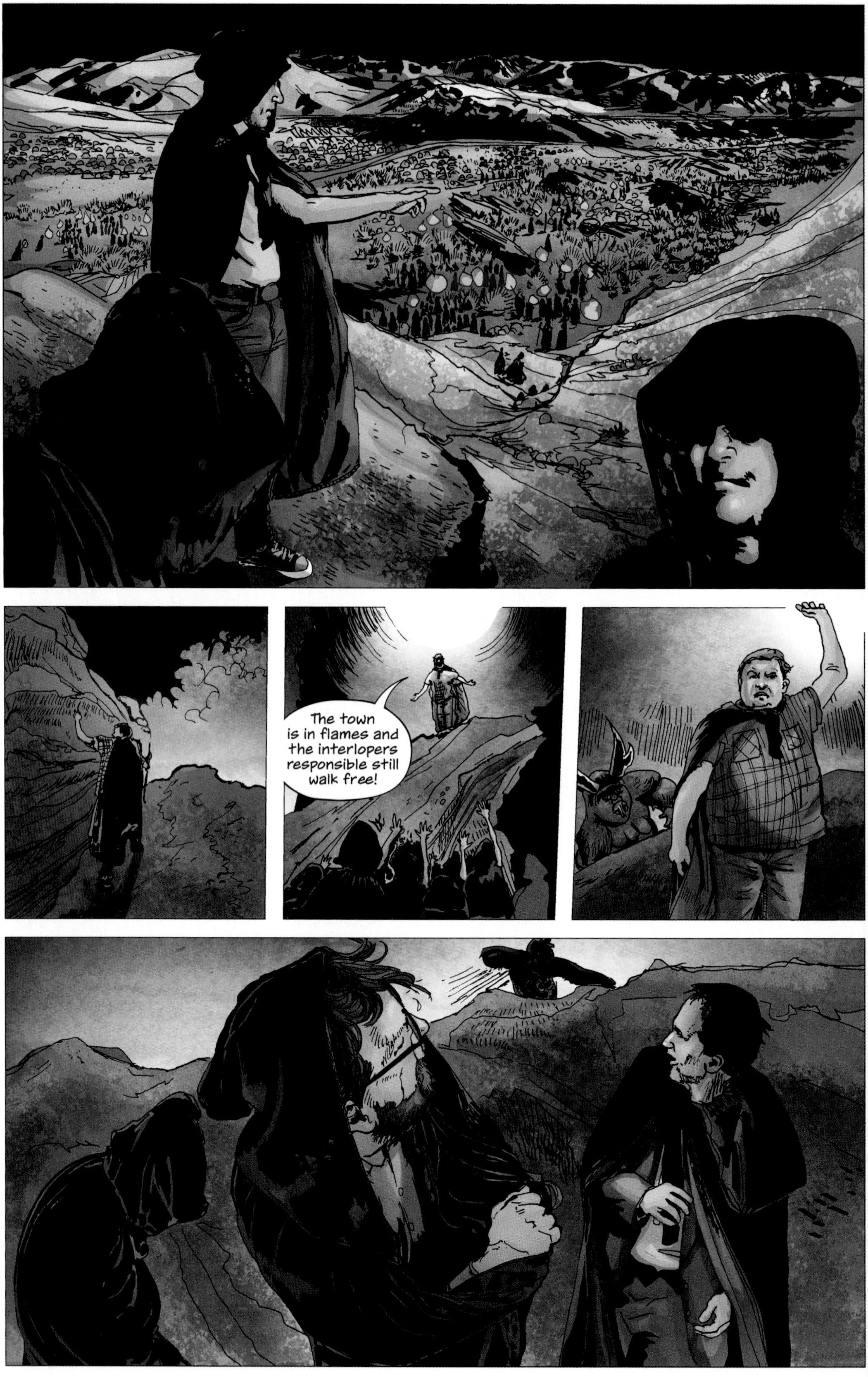
The town is in flames and the interlopers responsible still walk free!

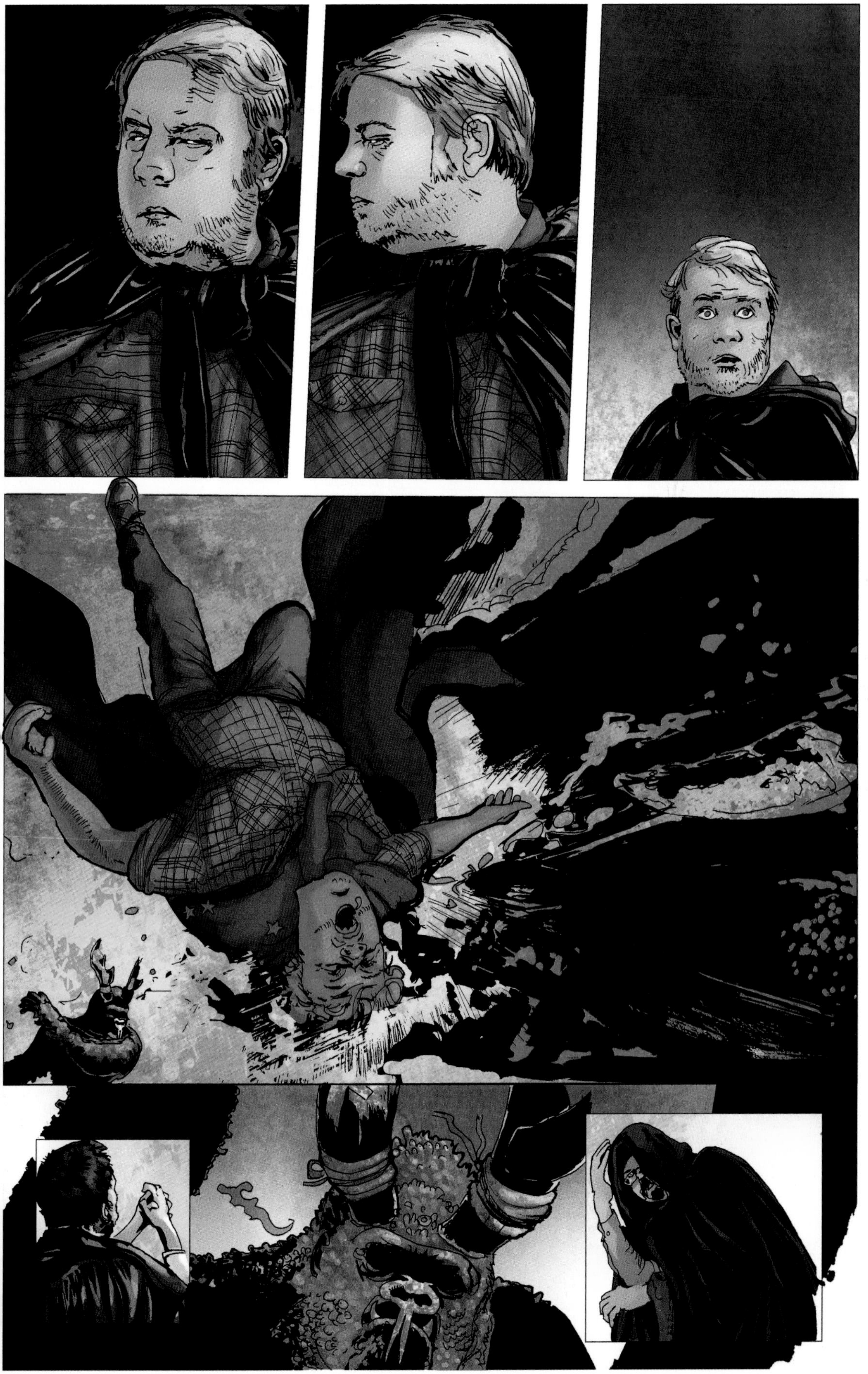

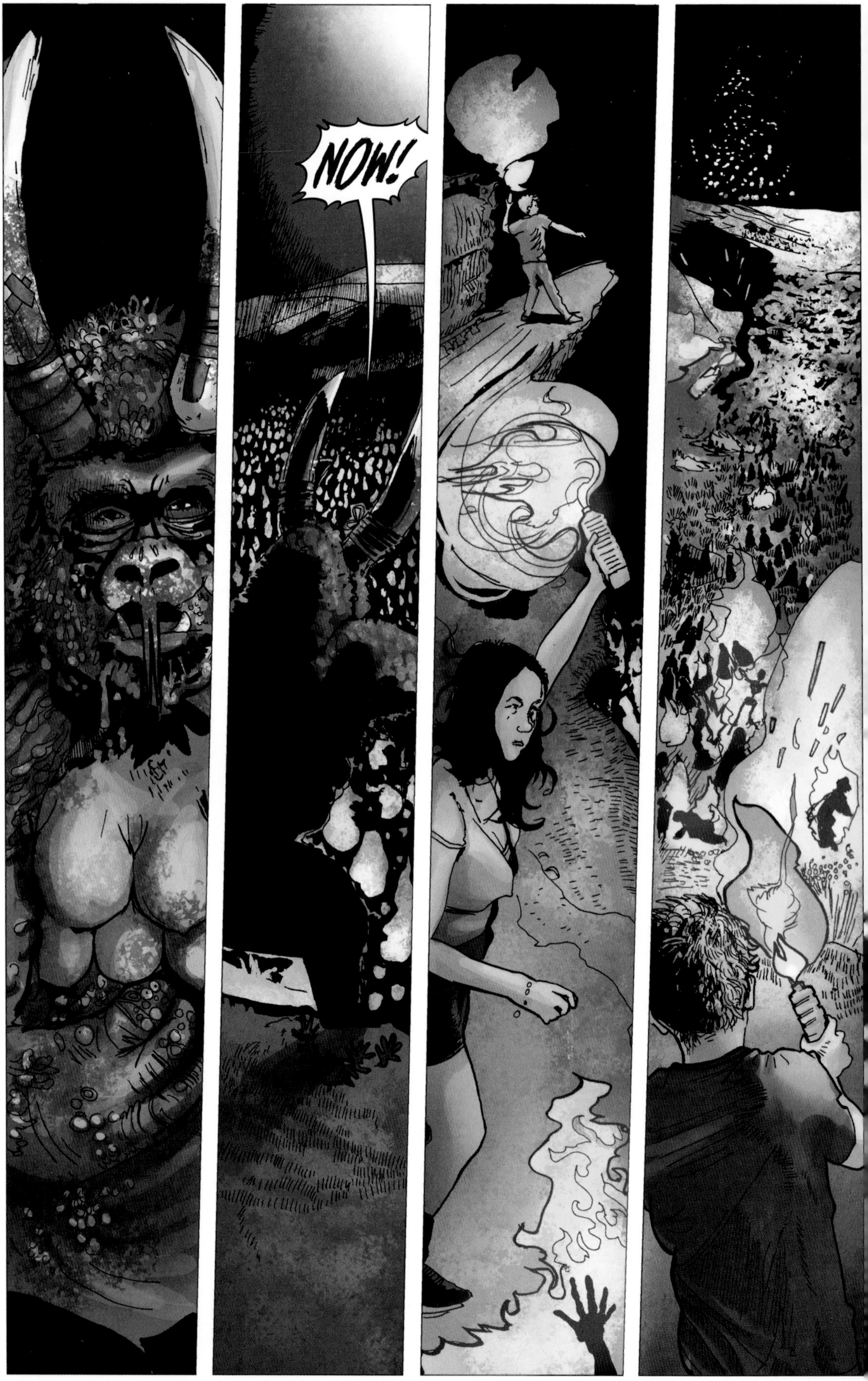
NOW!

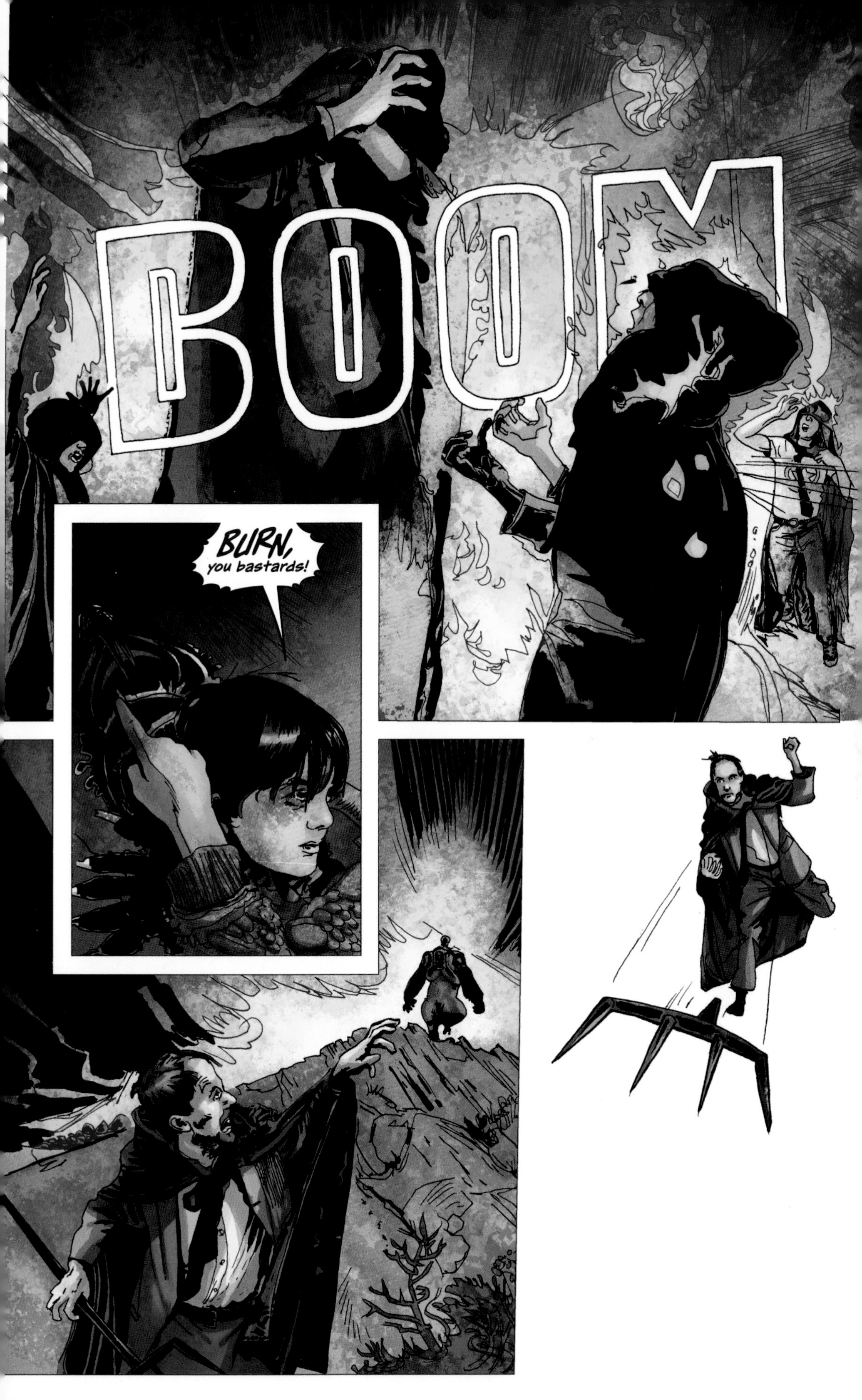
BOOM
BURN, you bastards!

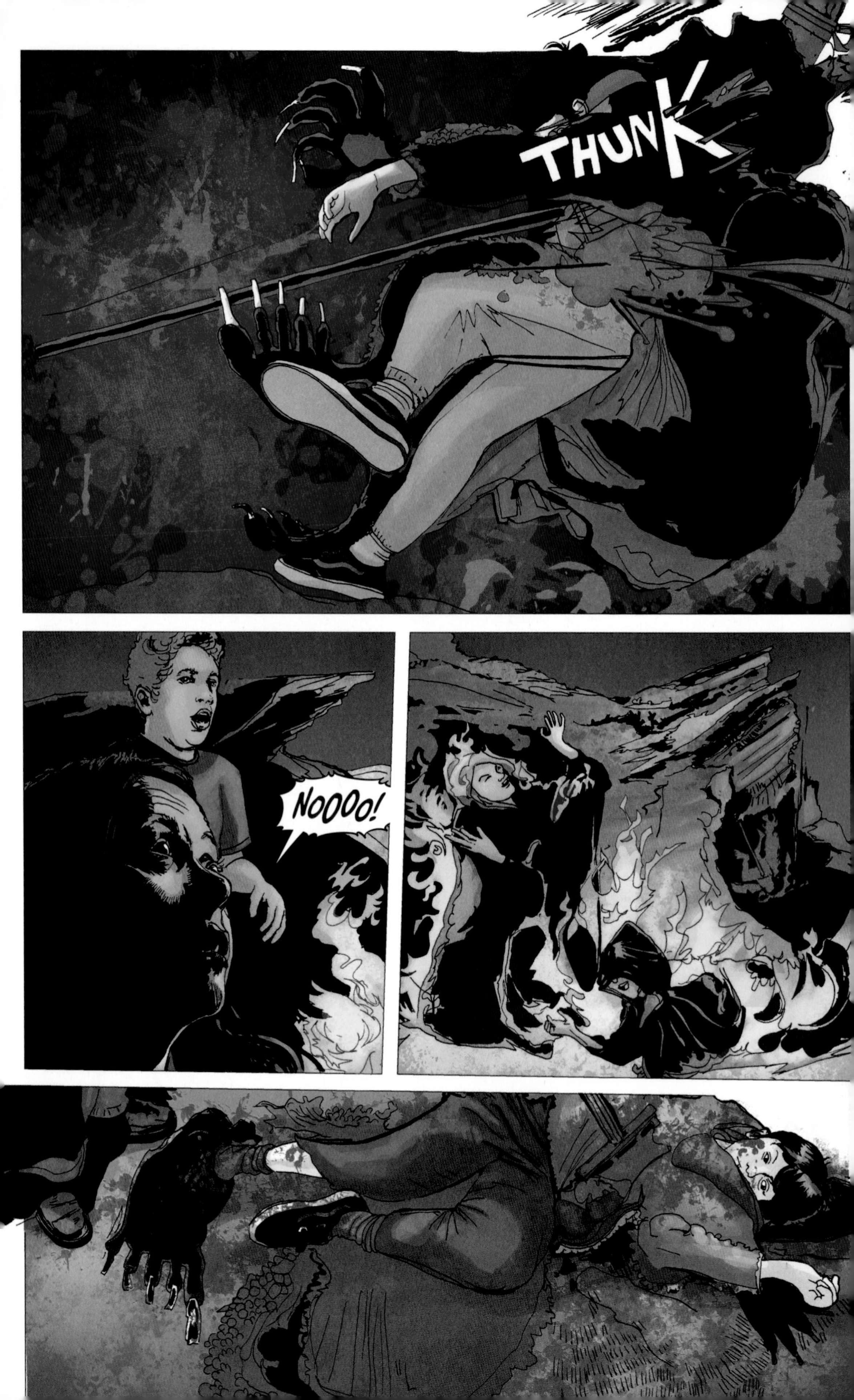
THUNK
NOOOO!

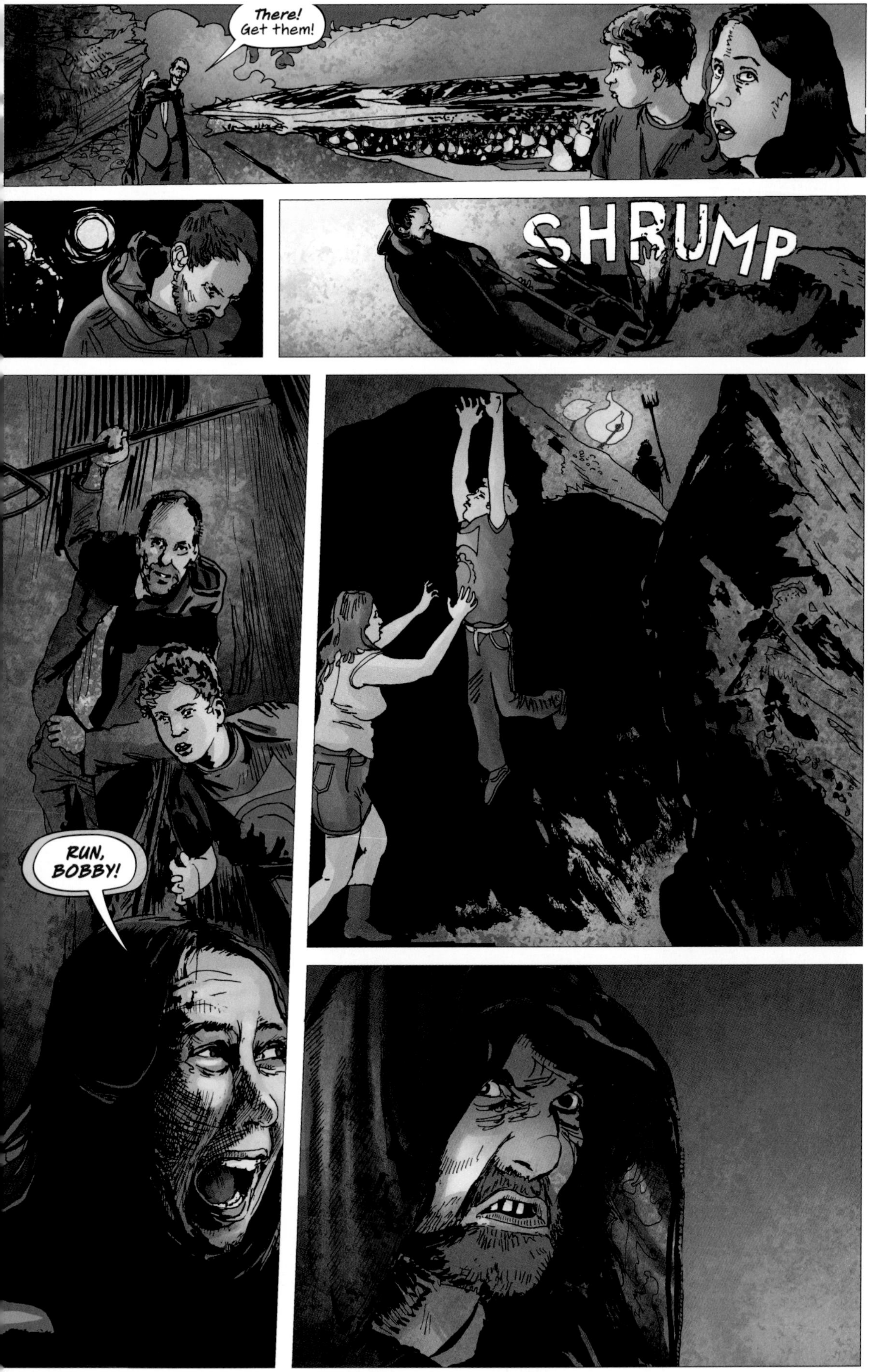
There! Get them!
SHRUMP
RUN, BOBBY!

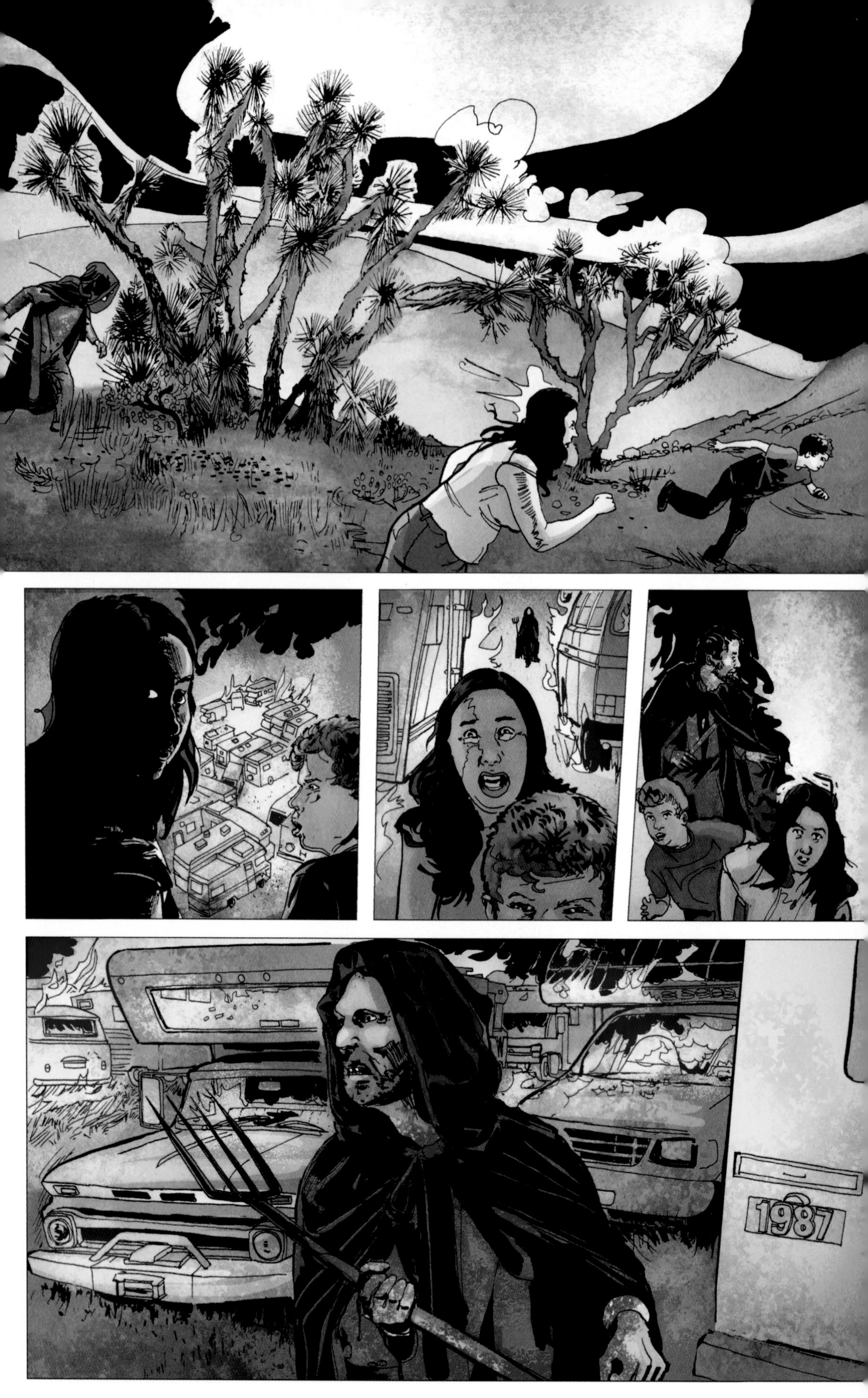
1987

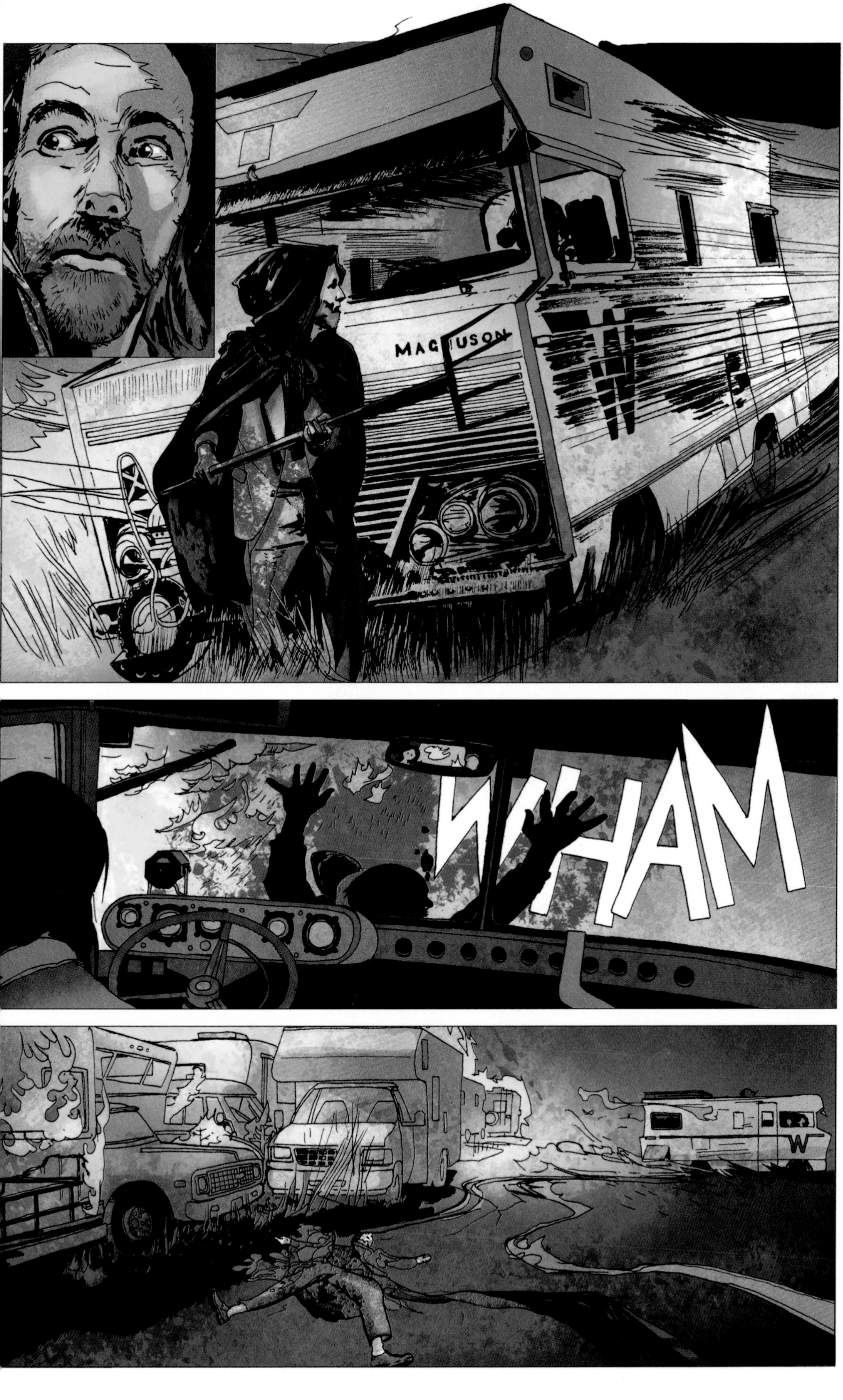
WHAM

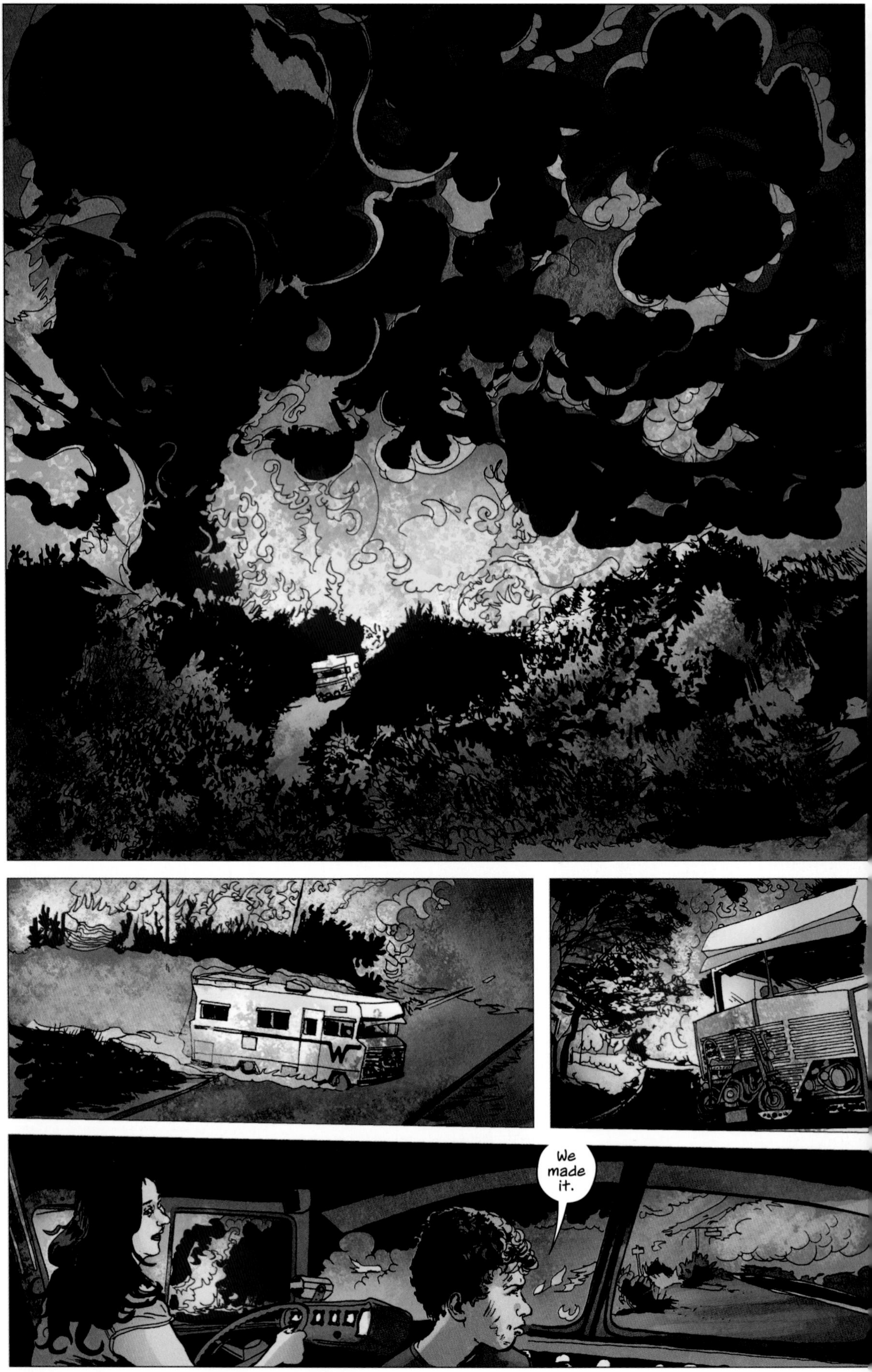
We made it.

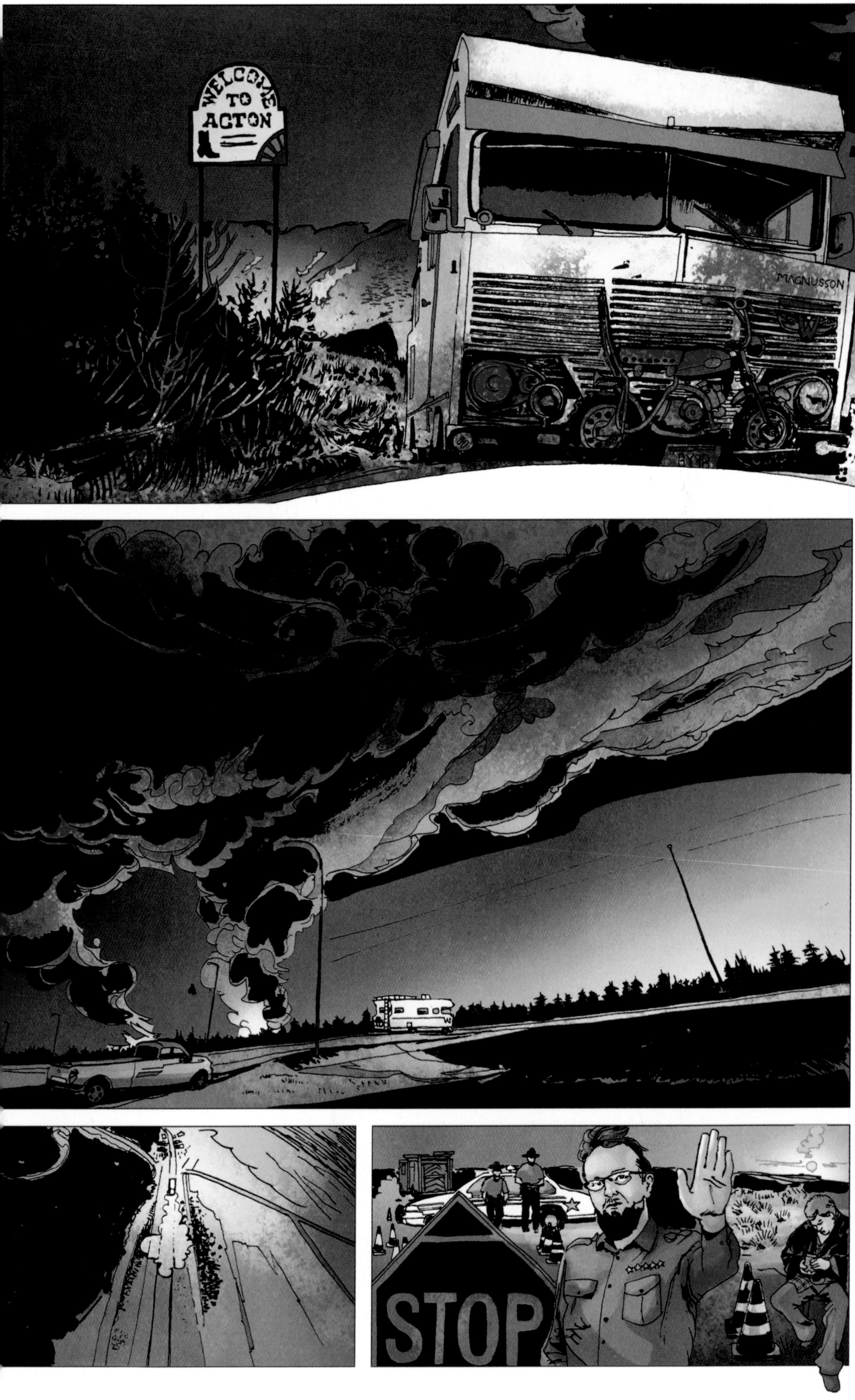
WELCOME TO ACTON
MAGNUSSON
STOP

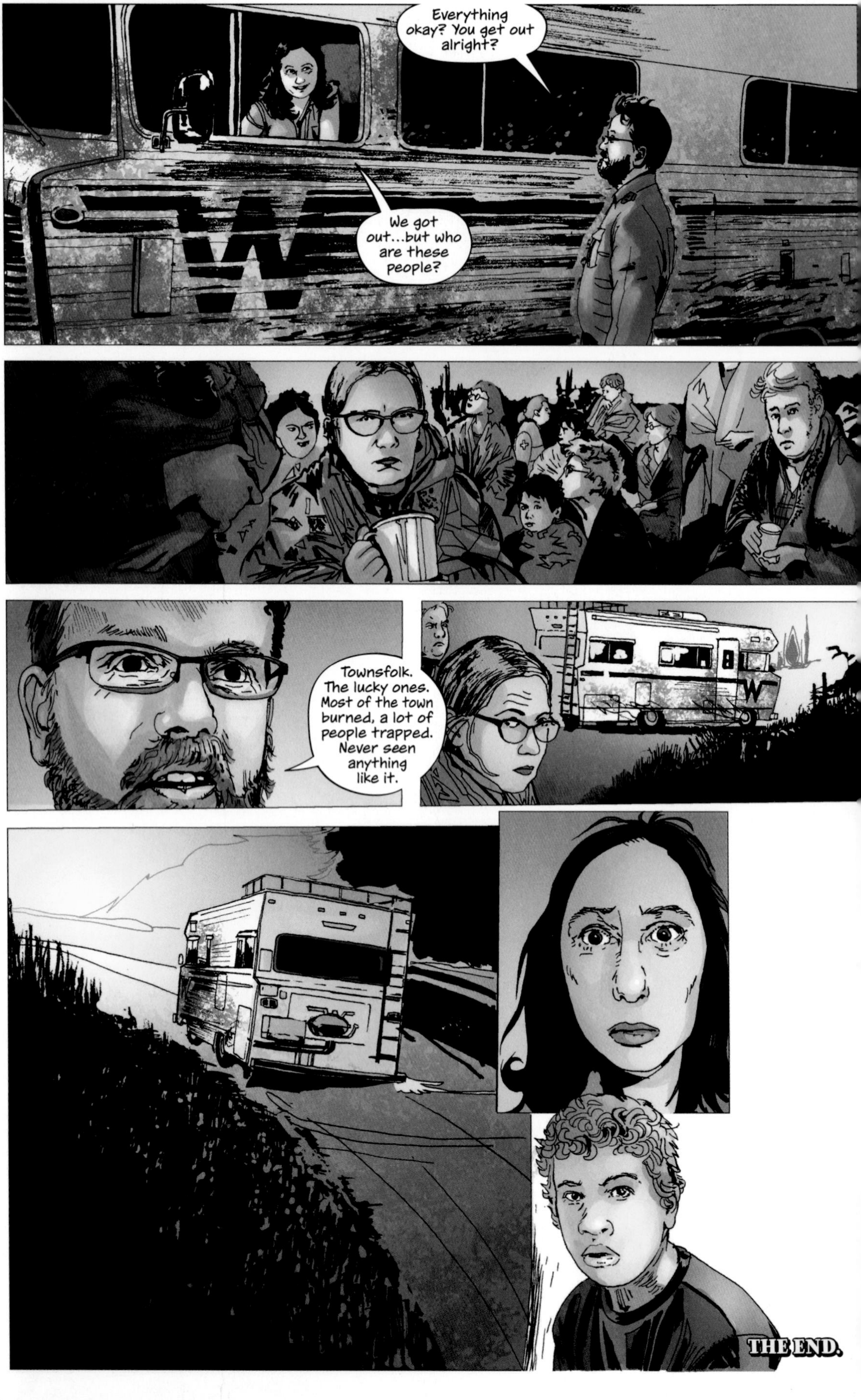
Everything okay? You get out alright?
We got out...but who are these people?
Townsfolk. The lucky ones. Most of the town burned, a lot of people trapped. Never seen anything like it.
THE END.

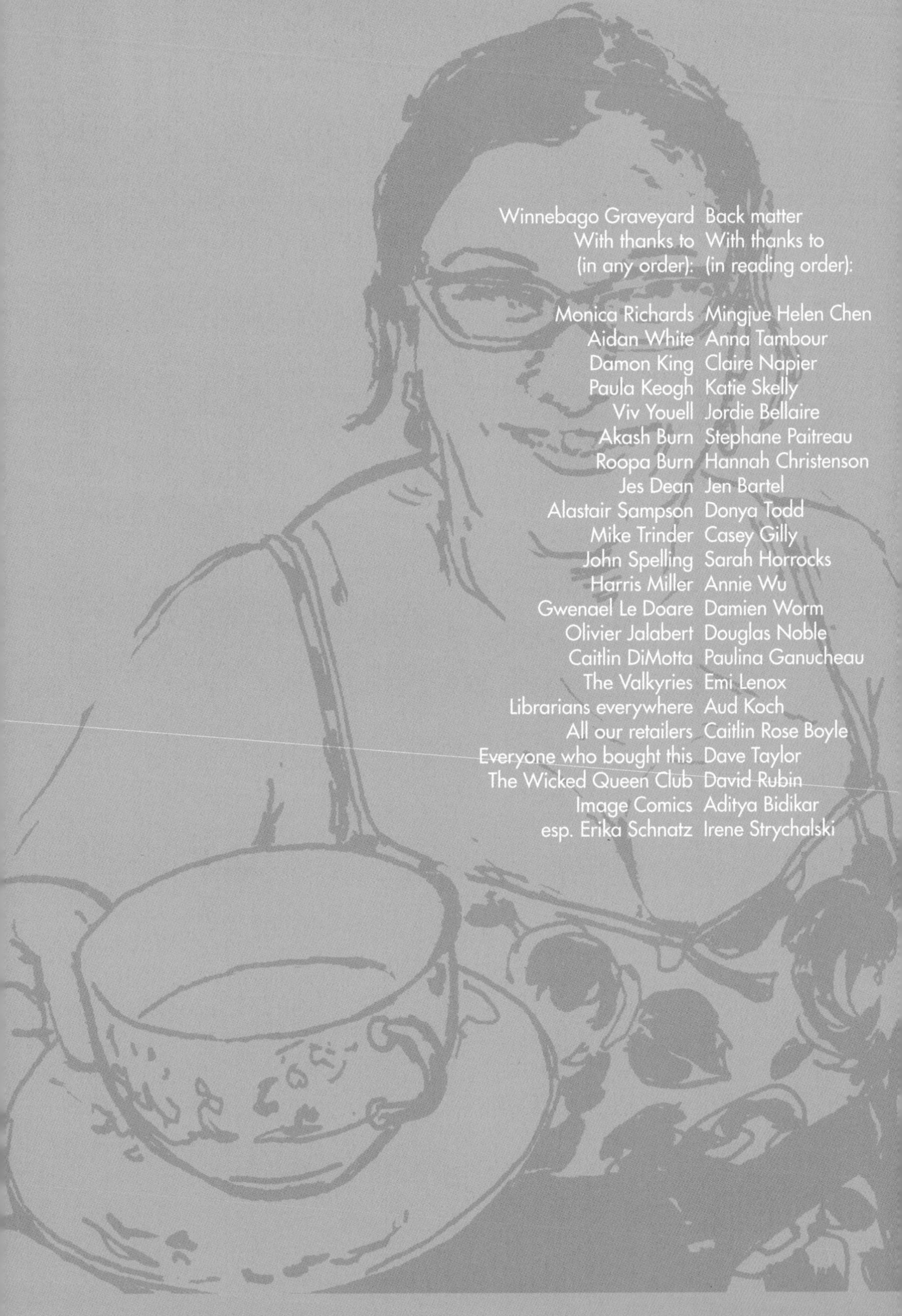

Winnebago Graveyard With thanks to (in any order):	Back matter With thanks to (in reading order):
Monica Richards	Mingjue Helen Chen
Aidan White	Anna Tambour
Damon King	Claire Napier
Paula Keogh	Katie Skelly
Viv Youell	Jordie Bellaire
Akash Burn	Stephane Paitreau
Roopa Burn	Hannah Christenson
Jes Dean	Jen Bartel
Alastair Sampson	Donya Todd
Mike Trinder	Casey Gilly
John Spelling	Sarah Horrocks
Harris Miller	Annie Wu
Gwenael Le Doare	Damien Worm
Olivier Jalabert	Douglas Noble
Caitlin DiMotta	Paulina Ganucheau
The Valkyries	Emi Lenox
Librarians everywhere	Aud Koch
All our retailers	Caitlin Rose Boyle
Everyone who bought this	Dave Taylor
The Wicked Queen Club	David Rubin
Image Comics	Aditya Bidikar
esp. Erika Schnatz	Irene Strychalski

Calling all horror afficionados--

Winnebago Graveyard is horror most normal, the most frightening and true of all. The people and settings are alive as nightmares, with nothing generic in them. But it's not as if it's just happening to them. You don't get off that easy, just being a passive onlooker. It's all those places you have felt irrational fear to stop at, or you've moved without a reason why. It's all the people who might look at you, and you look at, and you just want to flee from. Or you see it in their eyes--they feel that way about you. It's the fear of the law and the fear of no law. It's everybody needing to protect themselves from everyone. And it's you--age thirteen, when you know for sure how lame your parents are, how useless they'd be if something really freaky happened.

It isn't the evil here that is the most frightening, just as it isn't that lusciously splashed gore. The real creepout is here is space. Perspective here is terrifying, whether it's wide-open or claustrophobically close. Every picture seems to be taken from a position of fear, colored by it, as if each panel is what we in the picture are seeing, wanting to flee, hide, cower from. So it's the most banal non-active scenes that I find the most chilling. The extremely versatile artist/ architect Alison Sampson has called her graphic art 'architectural', but if so, she could design houses that could give people heart attacks in empty rooms as well as cluttered living rooms.

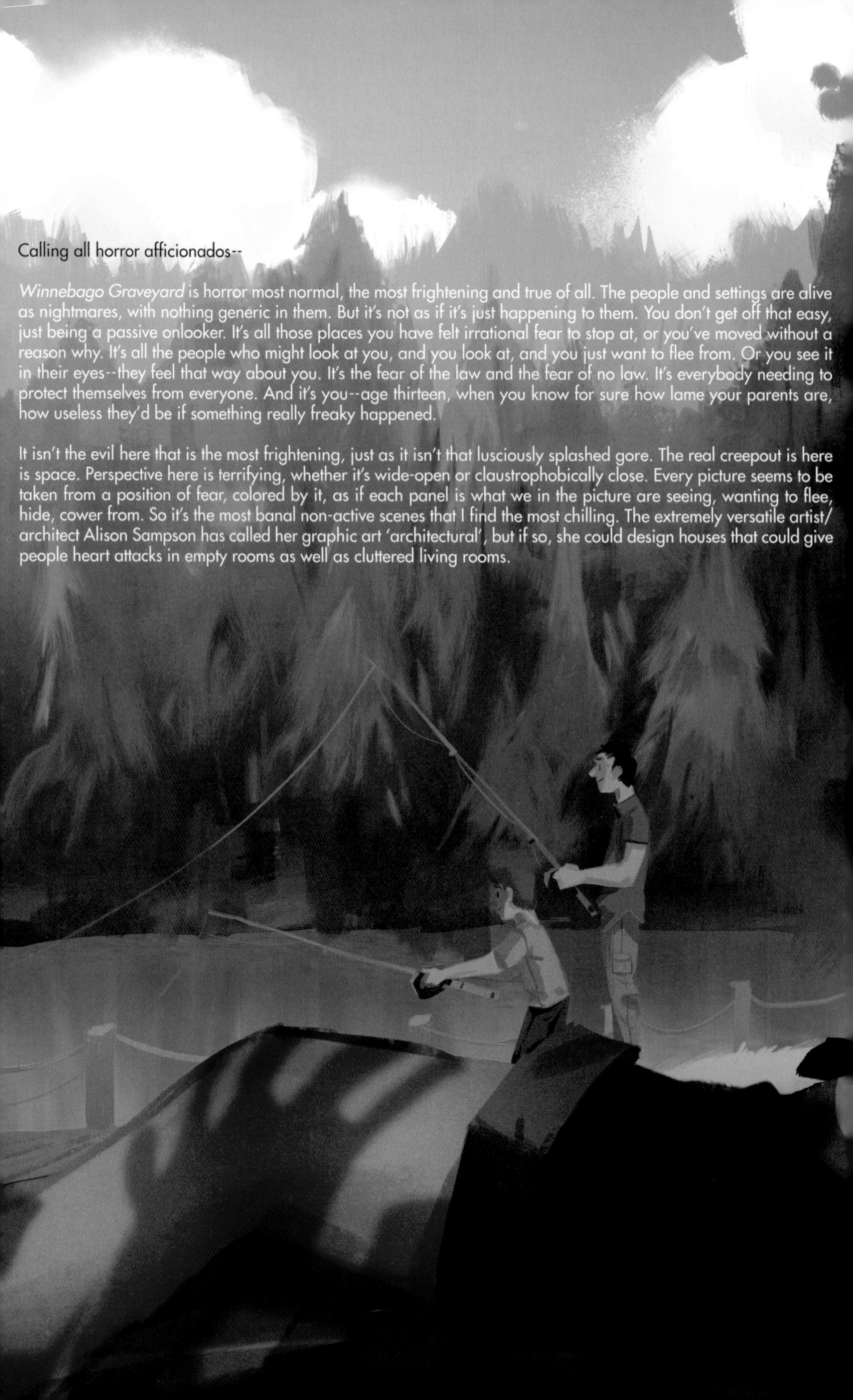

It's the little things, often, in these pictures, that catch like a burred spoon. Settings and people are wholly ungeneric, and dripping with character. Perfectly complementing the art is the outstanding coloration, by Stéphane Paitreau. Just as micrography can be ruined or made into spectacular art, the horror here needed and got, a colorist who could teach skies how to create mood.

In contrast, the script by Steve Niles, in its understated way, heightens the tension that is not only quite real, but had me thinking back to times I travelled just such roads, not in a Winnebago, but an old car we called 'the lady', whose wrinkled rubber window gaskets sang like drugged screams once she hit fifty. I had to travel, but there were some days when no place looked safe enough to stop, when the night closed in as it does here, and every little broken-down collection of abandoned cars and run-down houses looked to house people with bad intentions, drifters worried about drifters...

-- Anna Tambour

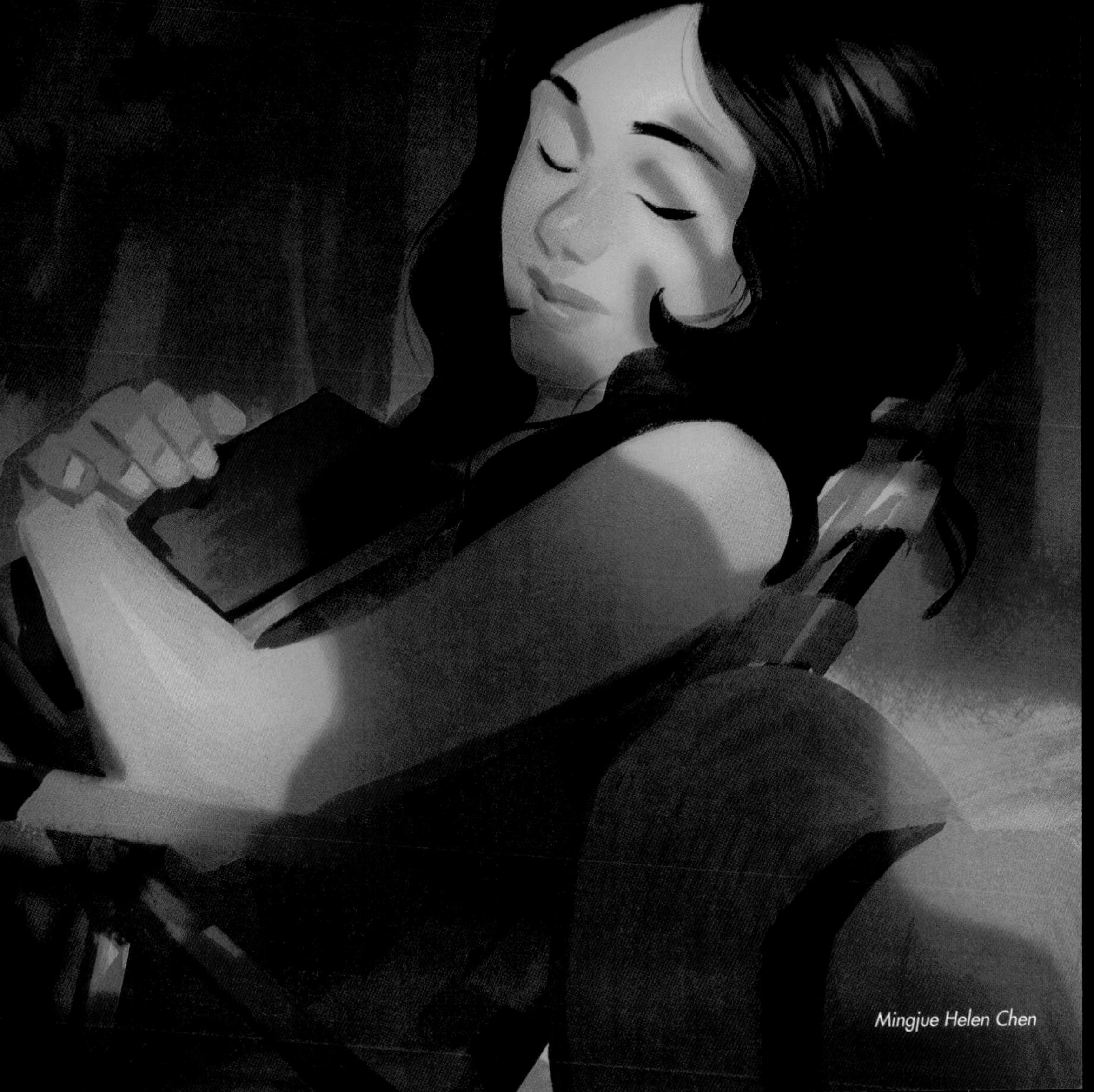

Mingjue Helen Chen

I have these two formative horror fiction memories.

In November 1994, when I was seven years old, an episode of *Mighty Max* called *Clown Without Pity* aired. Sometime around September 1995, by which time I was eight, I picked up the first *Goosebumps* novel *Welcome to Dead House.* Both of these were horror stories designed, made and marketed for children–both of them scared the piss out of me. I loved them. I treasured them.

Mighty Max was a North American cartoon based on a British line of horror toys; *Goosebumps* was an American novel line. My British childhood was steeped in an American perspective on the frightening. Honestly, that element of cultural uncertainty probably helped these two stories loom large in my mind: "I don't feel secure, what is happening" is a part of both narratives, an integral part of horror fiction (and the human emotional response "horror"). The kids in *Dead House* have just moved into a new, small community. They're alien to their new surroundings. Max is visiting a funfair (definitively a place of altered state–"fun" is something one is generally supposed to be a response to an experience, not a baseline status informed by boundaries of geography) and the theme of *Clown Without Pity* is how ostracisation can allow a soul to warp.

I introduce myself to you this way, through these specifics, because I don't know how else to talk around how on-pitch *Winnebago Graveyard* felt to me. Americans moving their domicile to a place where only murderers and monsters live and being frightened by a funfair–that's what horror is. This is my oldest language of scare. And, frankly, there is nothing in this book definitively worse than what there is in *Mighty Max* or *Goosebumps*. I re-read the *Welcome to Dead House* passage below… how many times? Countless. How awful. What a thrill.

"And then her eyeballs rolled out of their sockets, and she opened her toothless mouth, and she cried, "Thank you, Amanda! Thank you!" and collapsed."

It's funny to me (funny ha-ha, not funny strange) that funfairs and circuses loom so large in the aesthetic language of horror. I can understand an argument that it's because the subversive can enhance the horrific (that unfamiliarity buzz again) but personally I think it's something different. What I think it is is something that really tickles me, because adults seem to find it so hard to believe in real life but offer it so readily in fiction: I think that clowns and funfairs and circuses and, even, Father Christmasses are used in horror so much not because it's ironic but because to children they are alarming. In Playgroup and in Primary School I could sit with my friends and read books about witches and vampires quite happily because they did not scare me one bit.

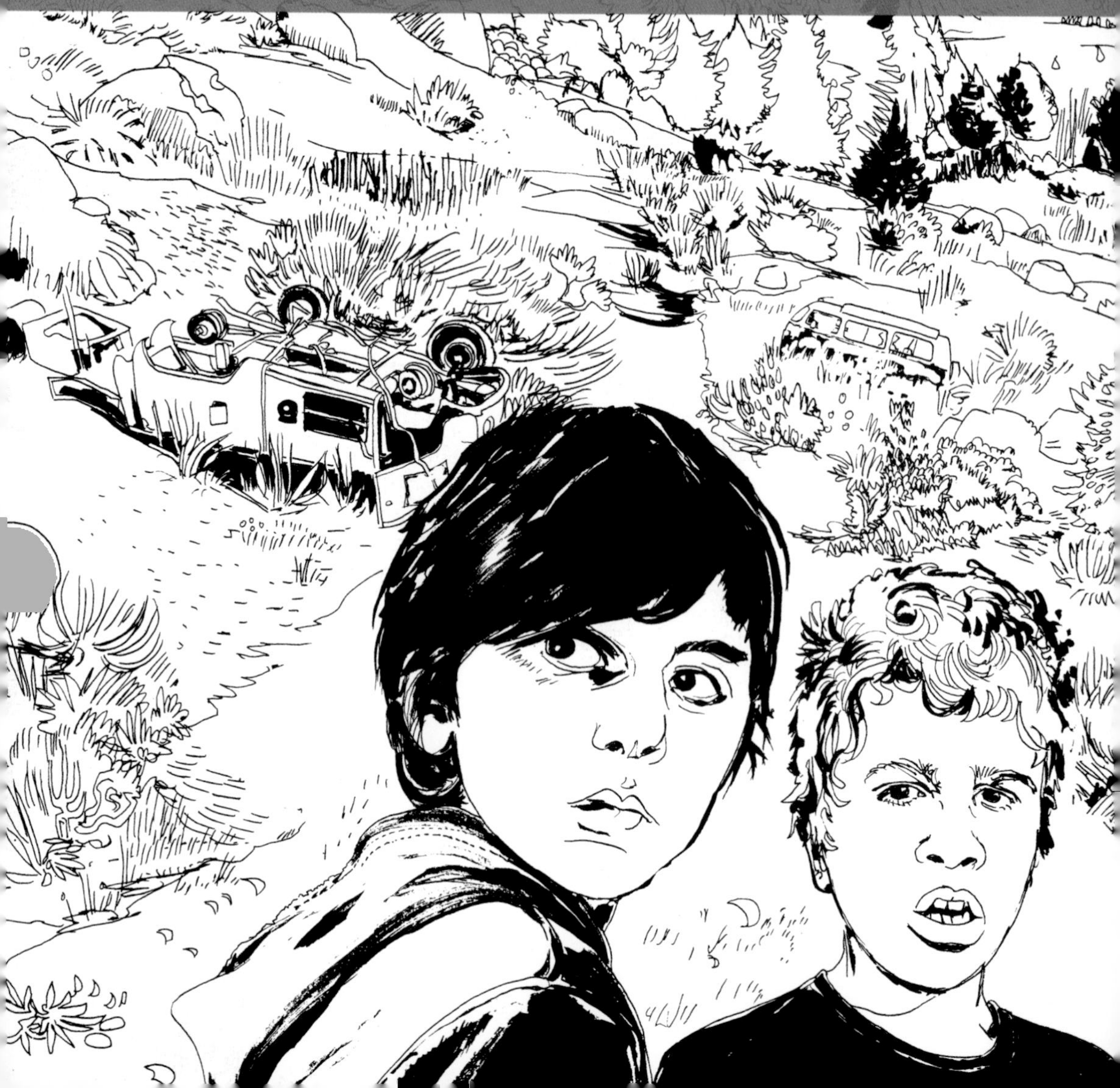

But come back a week later and there I'd be: sat with those same friends, and a good half of us shifty and nervous because someone dressed up in something performative had been invited down to "entertain" us. Funfairs are symbols of unease not because occasionally the person dressing up or running the stall is a molester– only the unluckiest children are aware of what a molester is and this fear or discomfort is more widespread. It's because people dressed up are faking it, which means that as they engage you they aren't reassuring you based on any true fact. A clown in his clown uniform is purposefully unfamiliar; you don't see a clown just walking around buying biscuits and shampoo because a clown isn't supposed to be not-a-clown. Mister Normal the Office Guy wearing a big floss beard and painted on rosy cheeks to play Santa is telling you he is something he isn't. The nature of the horrific, that "something is not right," is innate to these agents of lies. Plus, often, they shout.

In any feminist discussion of horror there will be acknowledgement of the school of thought which argues women seek out horror because horror takes (women's) anxiety and danger quite seriously. Horror does not deny predation, or the forcefulness of misogyny. Women, the theory goes, like horror because we recognise it as true, and by defining it as horror it is framed and controlled. We become the observer where we are used to being the observed.

And I think this runs in parallel to why even children who have not been sexually victimised dine so gleefully on the scary.

Children are small and have no real social power. Children are inexperienced. Children get shouted at and told what to do, and the grown-up people they need don't remember what it's like to need people in that way. For the very young, unfamiliarity is the name of a very familiar game.

A child who has been to the circus and been, whether they also enjoyed it or not, overwhelmed by the volume of the experience may look at a horror story set in a circus and compute, subconsciously, You see? I knew it! I told you! That place was too much! It was far out! When we are older, we remember how our basest fears were validated by something that was fun, by some scary cartoon... that was also about a kid getting the better of evil and being a good, cool person. And that makes safe fear something we want to reproduce and re-experience. Fear of these specific unfamiliarities feels familiar. So these motifs–scary kid-targeted entertainment, moving house without controlling your destination–stick around. The horror comic *Winnebago Graveyard* has a funfair and a home in motion for the same reason that it has a monster and a maiming: without these, it wouldn't be.

This essay on horror and the circus, from a child's point of view, is by Claire Napier

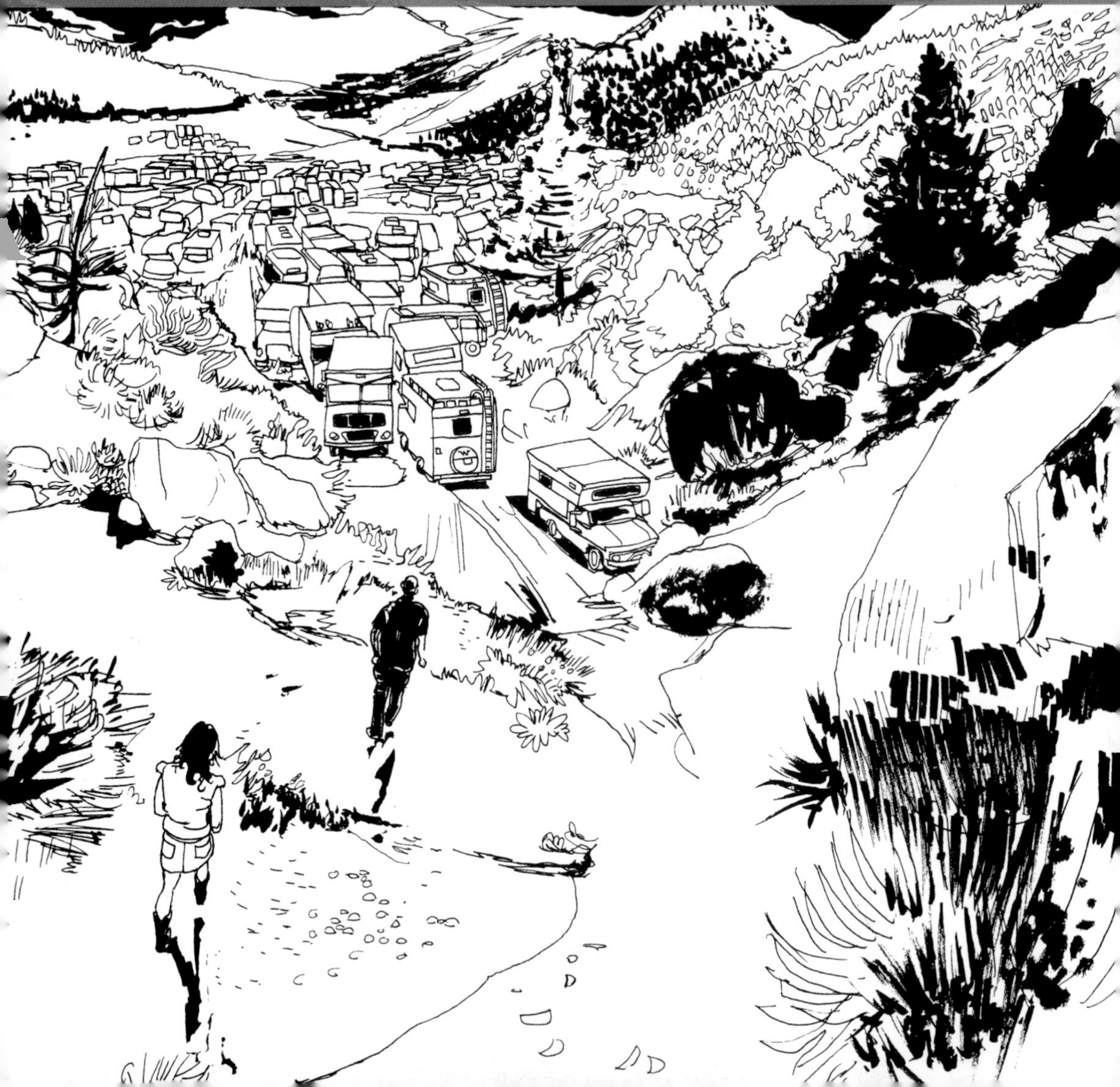

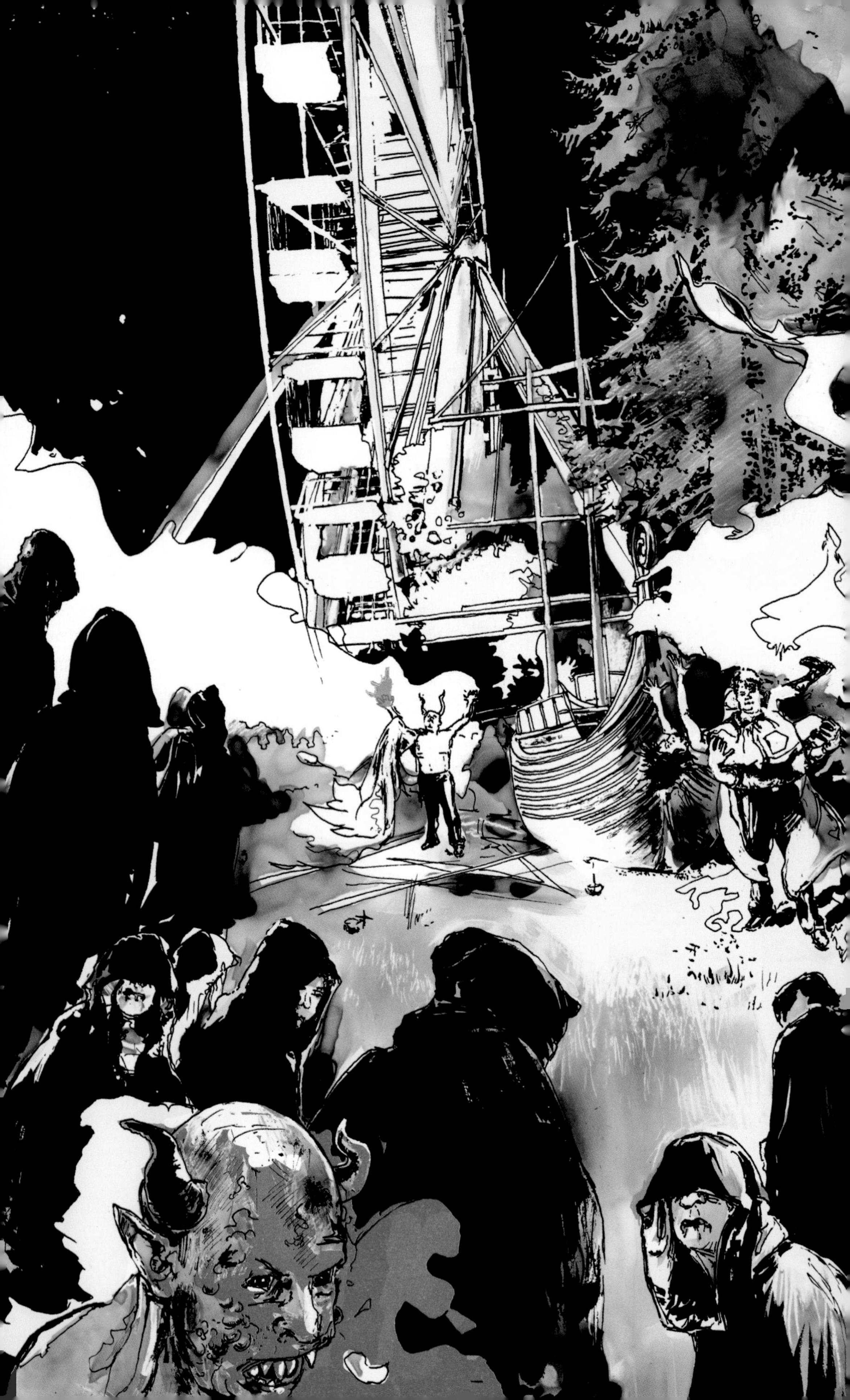

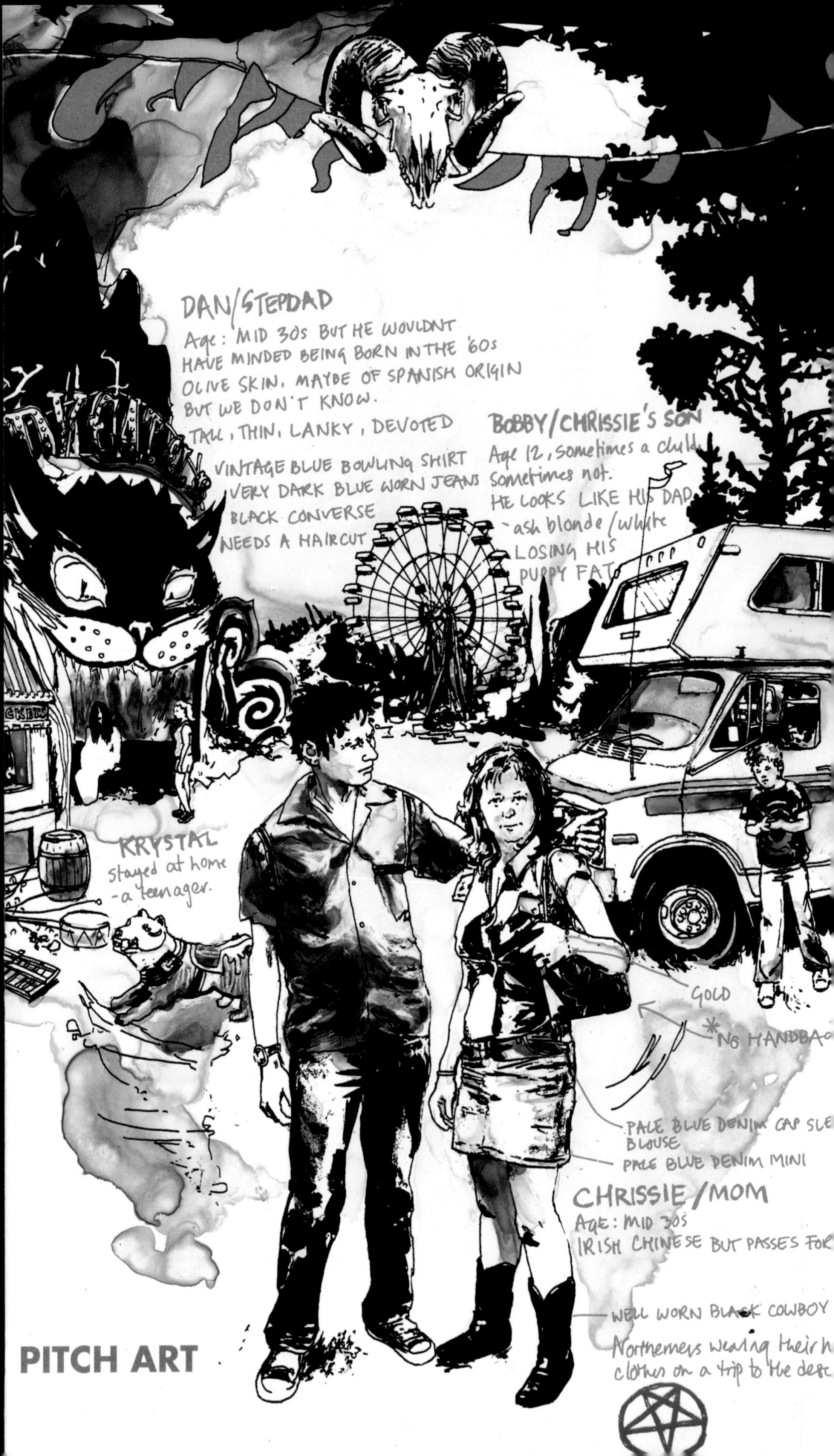

DAN/STEPDAD
Age: MID 30s BUT HE WOULDNT HAVE MINDED BEING BORN IN THE '60s
OLIVE SKIN, MAYBE OF SPANISH ORIGIN BUT WE DON'T KNOW.
TALL, THIN, LANKY, DEVOTED
VINTAGE BLUE BOWLING SHIRT
VERY DARK BLUE WORN JEANS
BLACK CONVERSE
NEEDS A HAIRCUT
BOBBY/CHRISSIE'S SON
Age 12, sometimes a child sometimes not.
HE LOOKS LIKE HIS DAD
- ash blonde/white
- LOSING HIS PUPPY FAT
KRYSTAL
stayed at home - a teenager.
GOLD
* NO HANDBA
PALE BLUE DENIM CAP SLE BLOUSE
PALE BLUE DENIM MINI
CHRISSIE/MOM
Age: MID 30s
IRISH CHINESE BUT PASSES FOR
WELL WORN BLACK COWBOY
Northerners wearing their h clothes on a trip to the dese

PITCH ART

As a kid I was terrified of horror movies. I'd watch them compulsively and then pay for it at night when the nightmares came. My parents wound up forbidding me to watch them but I would still sneak and watch Creature Features every Saturday night. Then one day everything I was scared of became an obsession. I started devouring horror movies, comics and books. I've never really understood the switch but I'm glad it happened.

I really loved the 70s satanic cult movies like *Devil's Rain* and *Race the Devil.* Also classics like *The Devil Rides Out.* That's a great one with a fantastic Richard Matheson screenplay. I find it very creepy following characters out into something totally unknown to them, that kind of civilization vs. the "wild" but with a really dark spin. It's something that can still make the blood in your veins run cold when they're on their own looking for help in a strange place.

I started with the title, *Winnebago Graveyard.* It really struck me. I mean, you know exactly what you're getting into with a title like that, right? I first began developing the story around *Winnebago Graveyard* when I was briefly living in Texas, but when I moved to the desert outside of Los Angeles, the story started to come together. I'd always lived in cities so moving to a remote small town had an effect. You don't have to drive far to find yourself alone in the rural desert outside the city and there are some creepy areas out here just waiting for a good spooky story.

I saw Alison's art the first time when it was shown to me by a friend and immediately fell in love with her style. I could see she would be perfect for a horror comic. When I pitched her the *WG* idea it was clear she knew the kind of story I wanted to create and started running with it. Seeing the art come together has changed the way I approached the rest of the story. That doesn't happen much but Alison's art is so striking, it changed the whole direction. The detail she puts into her work is incredible and inspiring. She really made the story come to life. You can't ask for more than that.

-- Steve

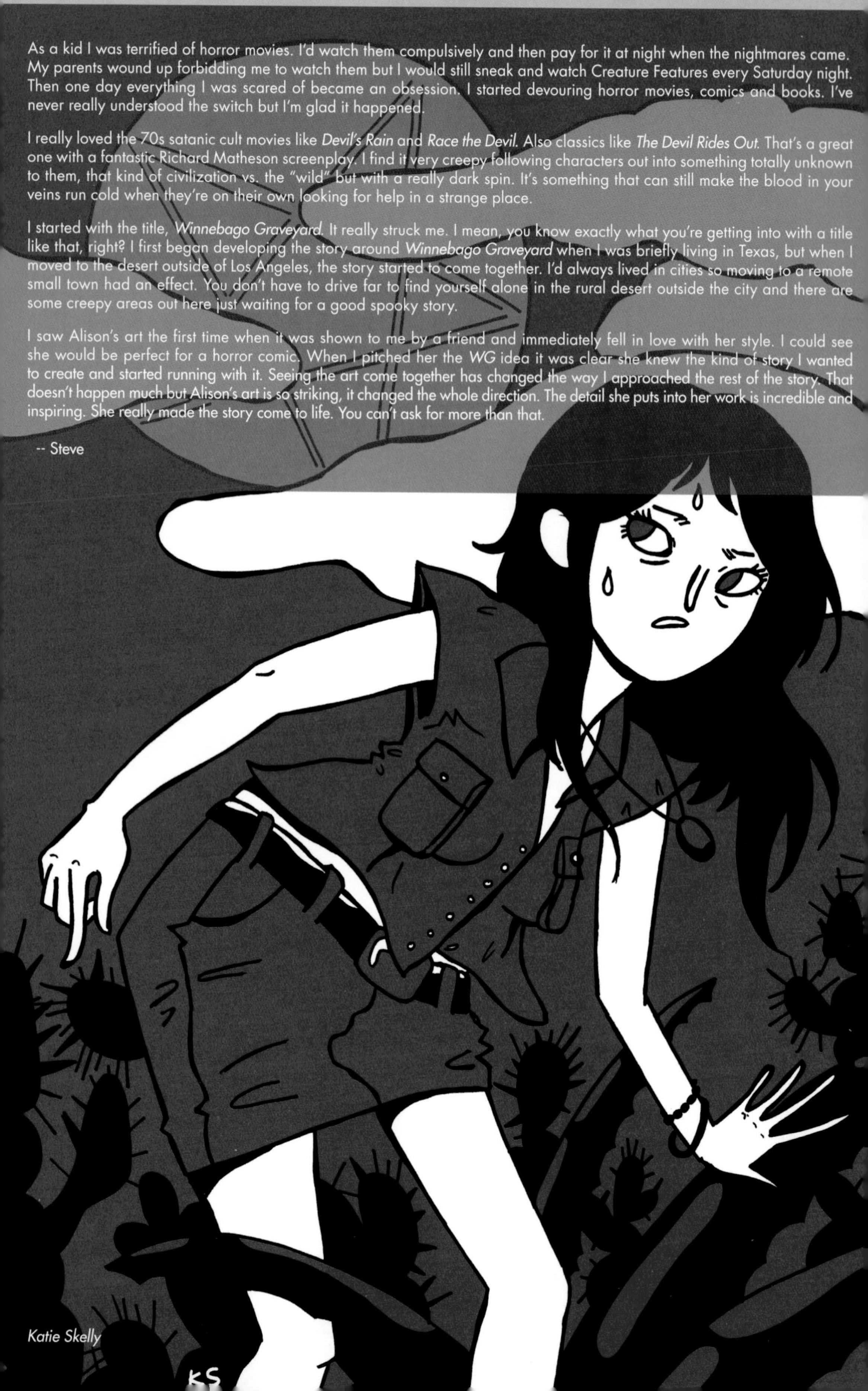
KS

Katie Skelly

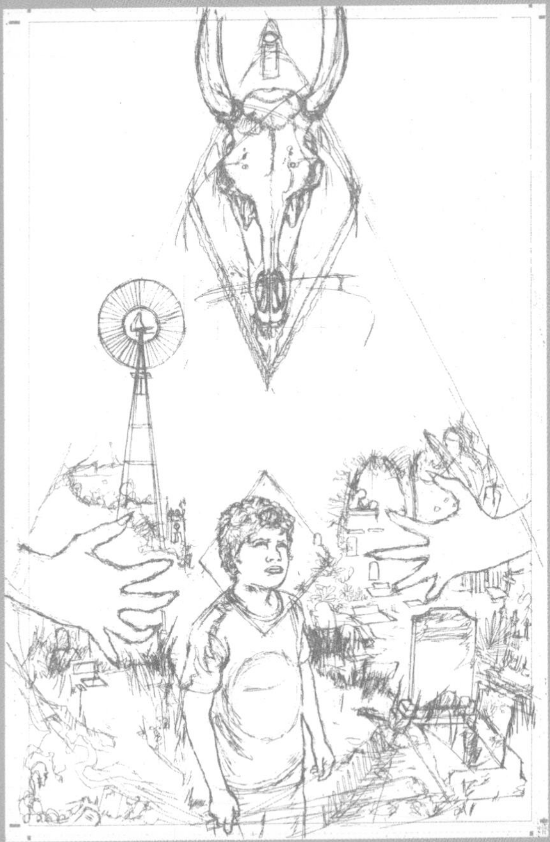

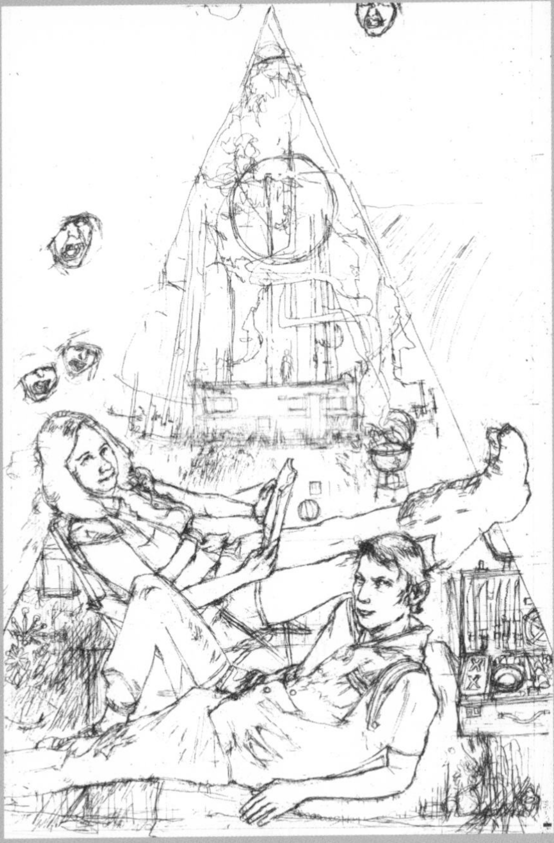

Top left and clockwise: Pencils for cover #1 (The Pyramid of Death); Pencils for cover #2; "Inks" for cover #1

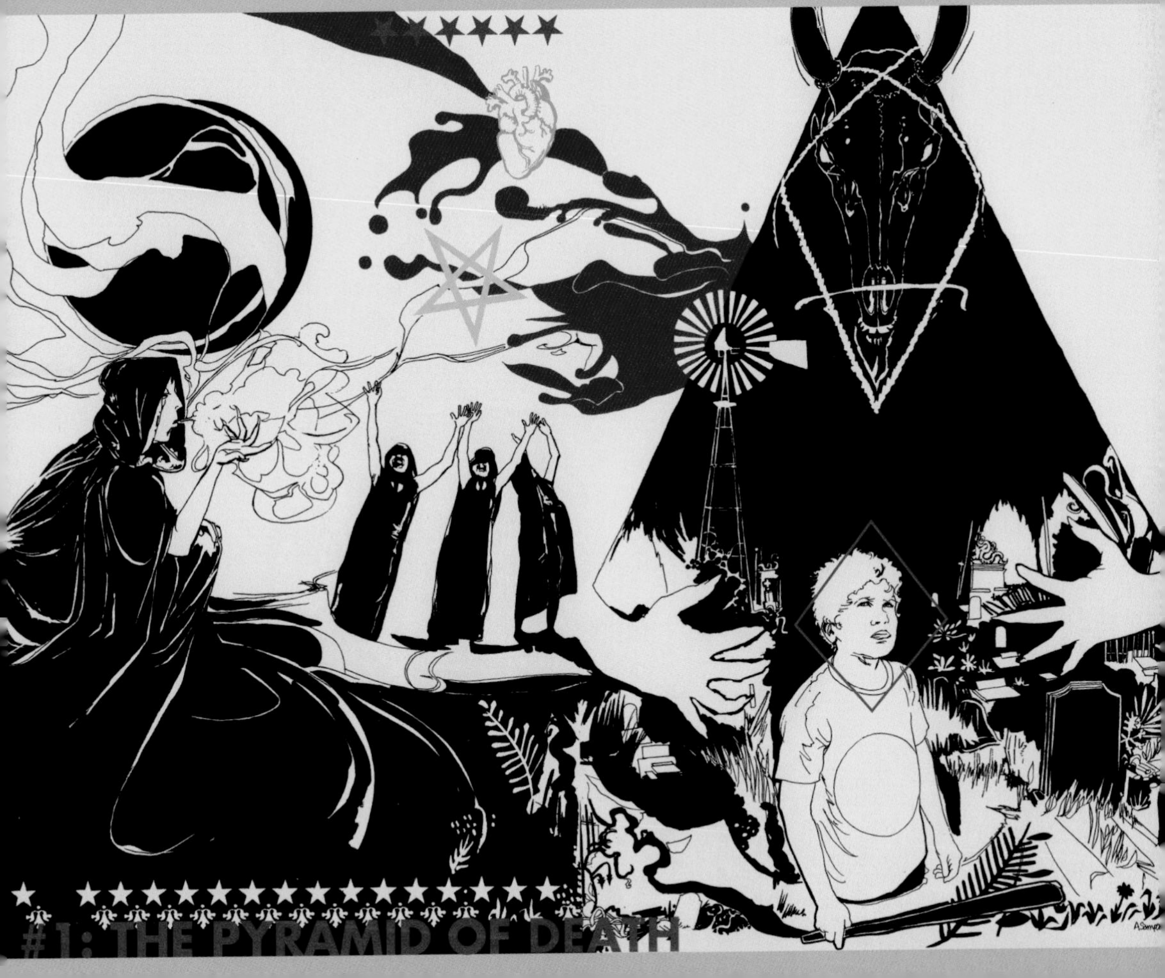
#1: THE PYRAMID OF DEATH

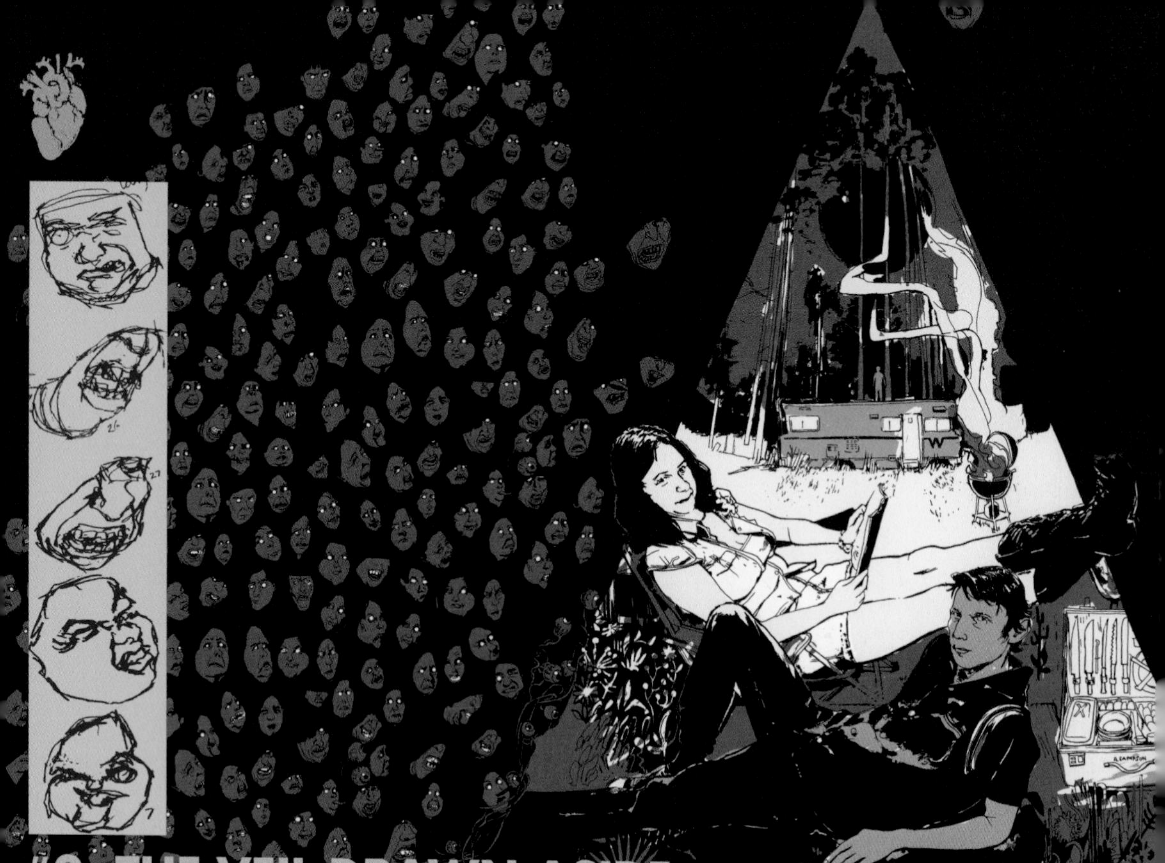

#2: THE VEIL DRAWN ASIDE

Top: Inks for cover #2: From the point of view of the Other, the veil of Death is pulled aside, and our world is seen as a point of light
Bottom: Inks for cover #3: Here the flag bearing, torch carrying, unspecified Other takes prime position, Death moves to the right

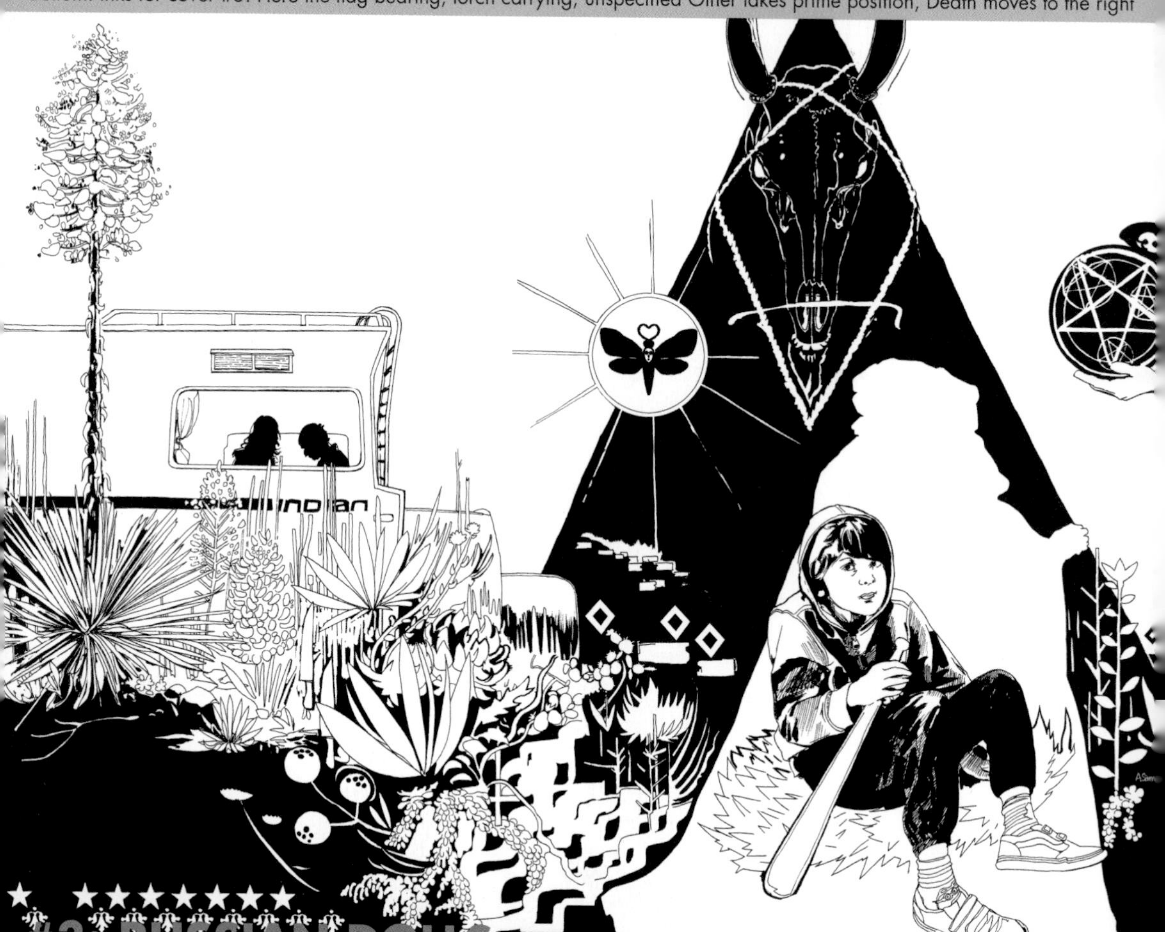
indian

#3: RUSSIAN DOLLS

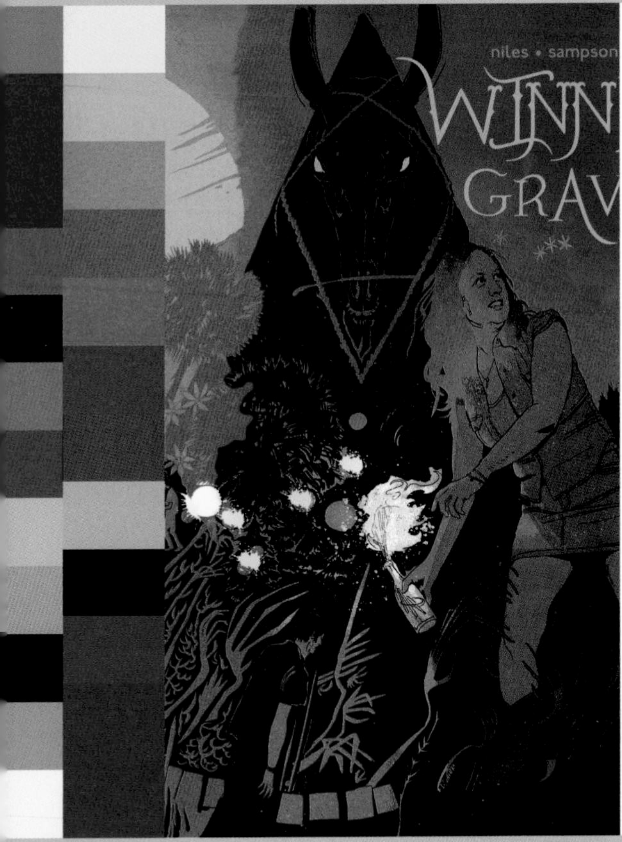
niles • sampson
WINN
GRAV

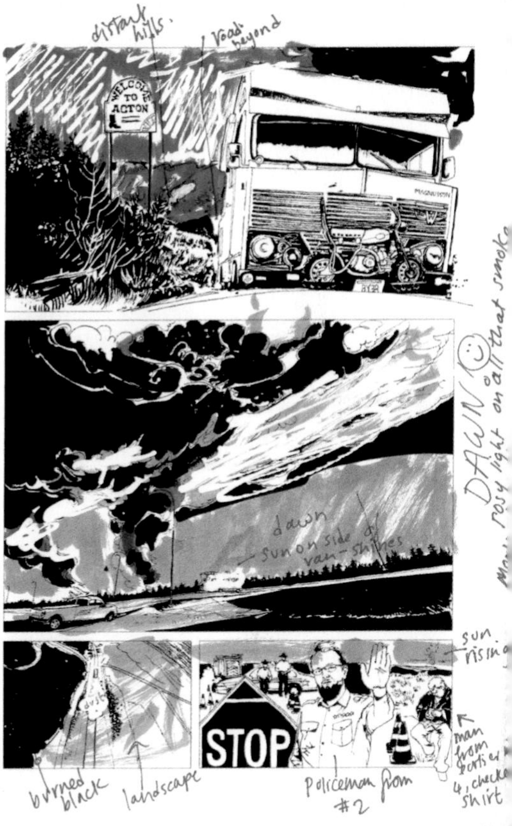
distant hills.
road beyond
WELCOME TO ACTON
dawn
sun on side of van
DAWN
rosy light on all that smoke
sun rising
STOP
burned black
landscape
Policeman from #2
man from earlier 4, checked shirt

Top left to right: Alison's suggestion for color (Arrow Books' Solaris book cover, 1973), compared to Jordie's final palette (right); Art direction from Alison to Stephane, story page 21; Below: Alison's final inks for the cover to #4, for Jordie/David Cooper

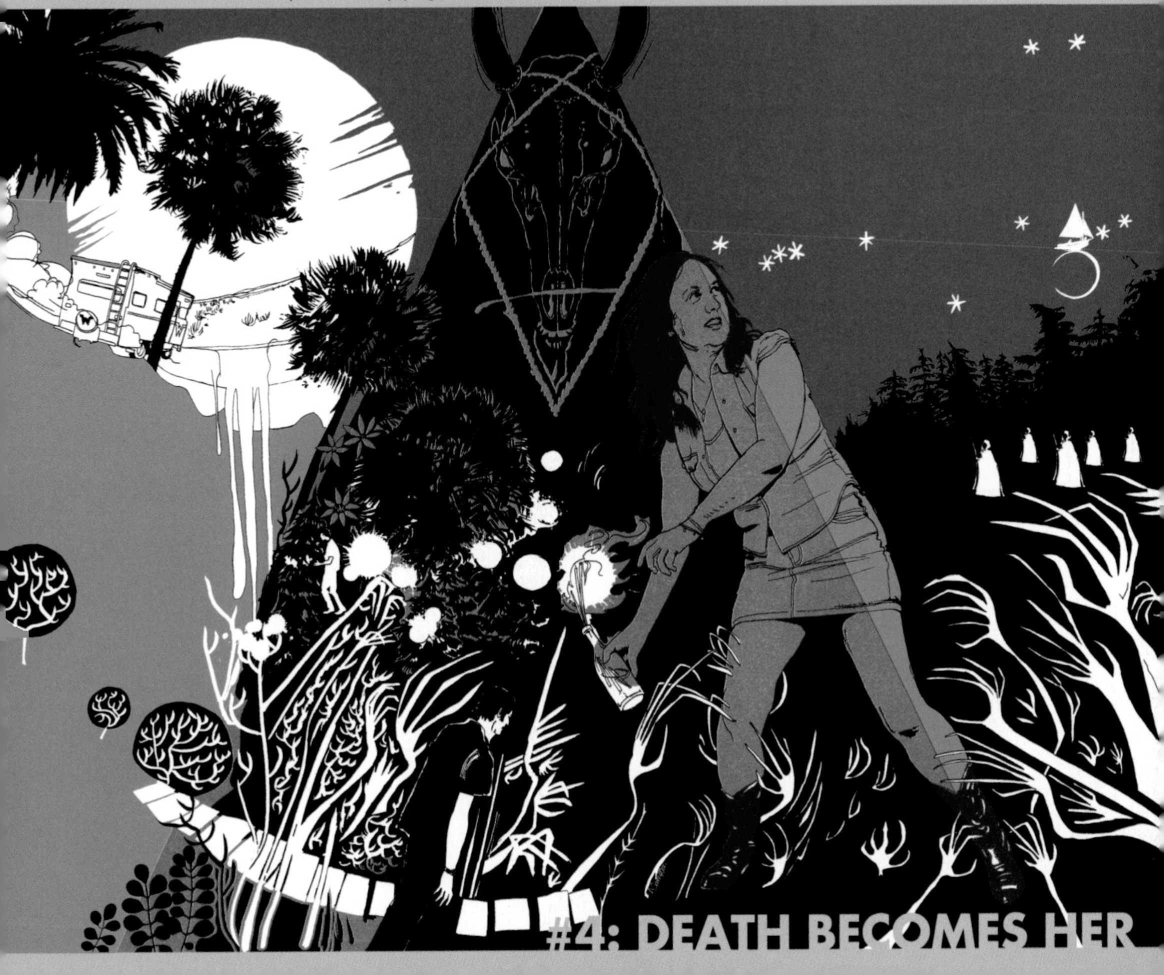
#4: DEATH BECOMES HER

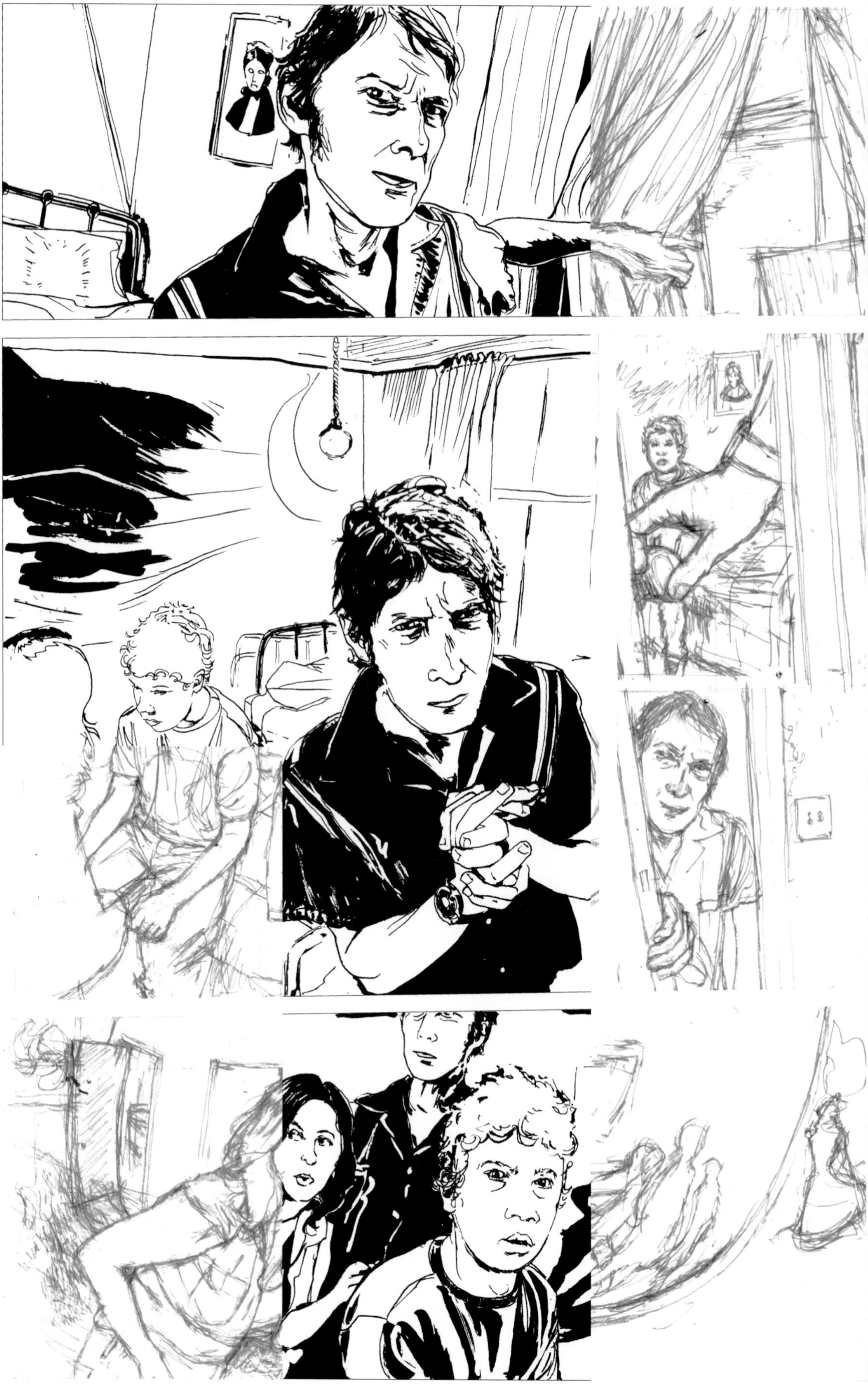

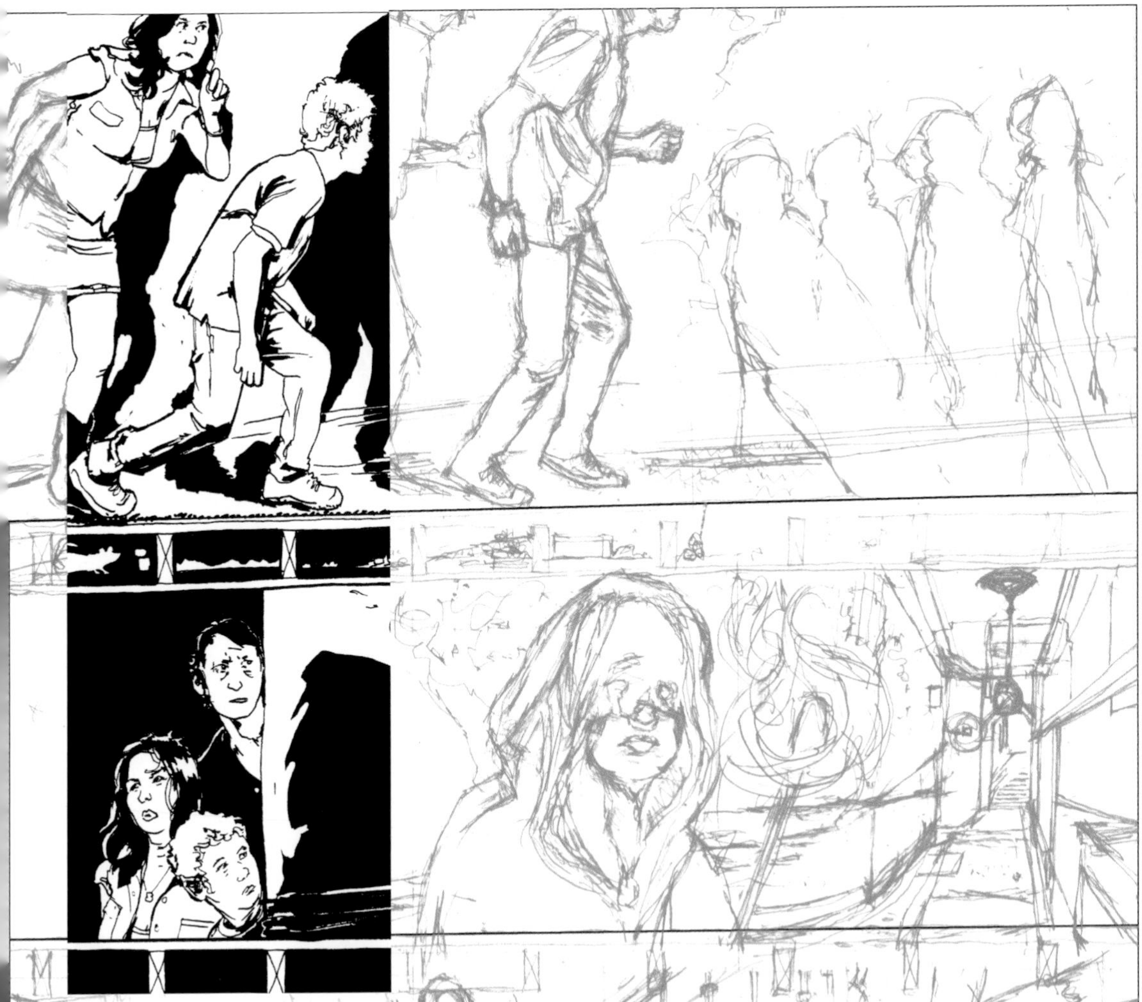

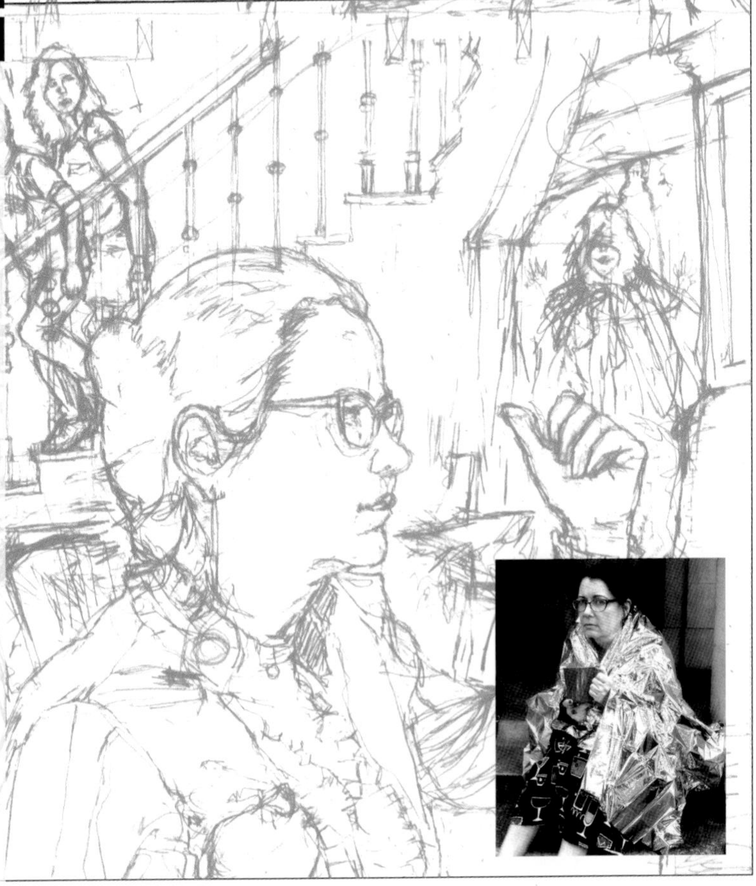

PAGE TEN
Panel 1: Inside the room Dan pushes the curtain closed in a panic.

DAN
Get away from the window!

Panel 2: Dan and Christie are panicking. Bobby seems confused.

CHRISTIE
Who are they? What do they want?

DAN
We have to get out of here NOW.

Panel 3: Dan opens the room door to the hallway...

Panel 4: ...and peers out, down the hallway.

Panel 5: Then ushers the family to go.

DAN
It's clear. Let's go.

PAGE ELEVEN
Panel 1: Dan leads, holding hands with Bobby who holds hands with his mother as they slowly, cautiously move down the hallway.

Panel 2: They stop as a FIGURE appears at the end of the hall.

Panel 3: They run into the hall

Panel 4: ...but the old lady is pointing them out to a cloaked figure.

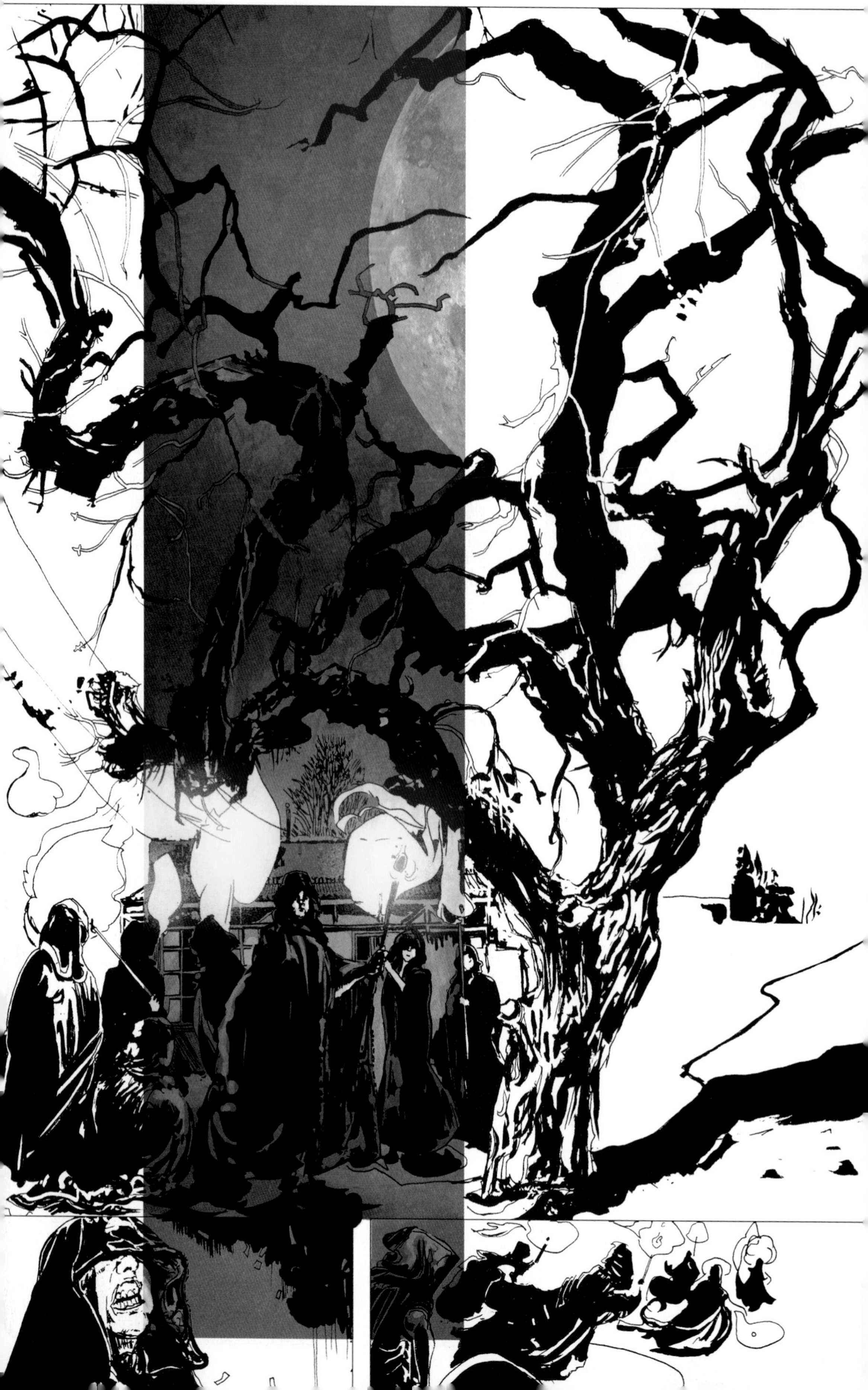

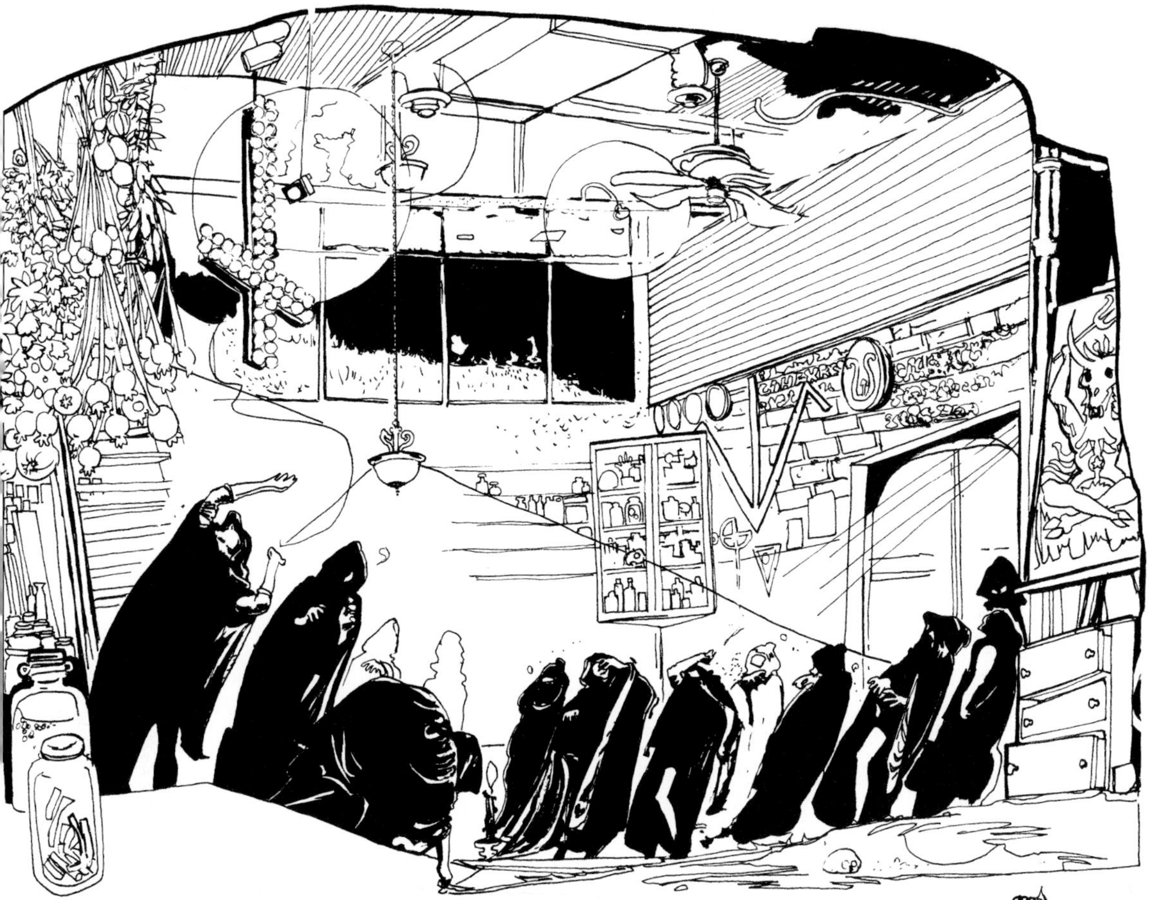

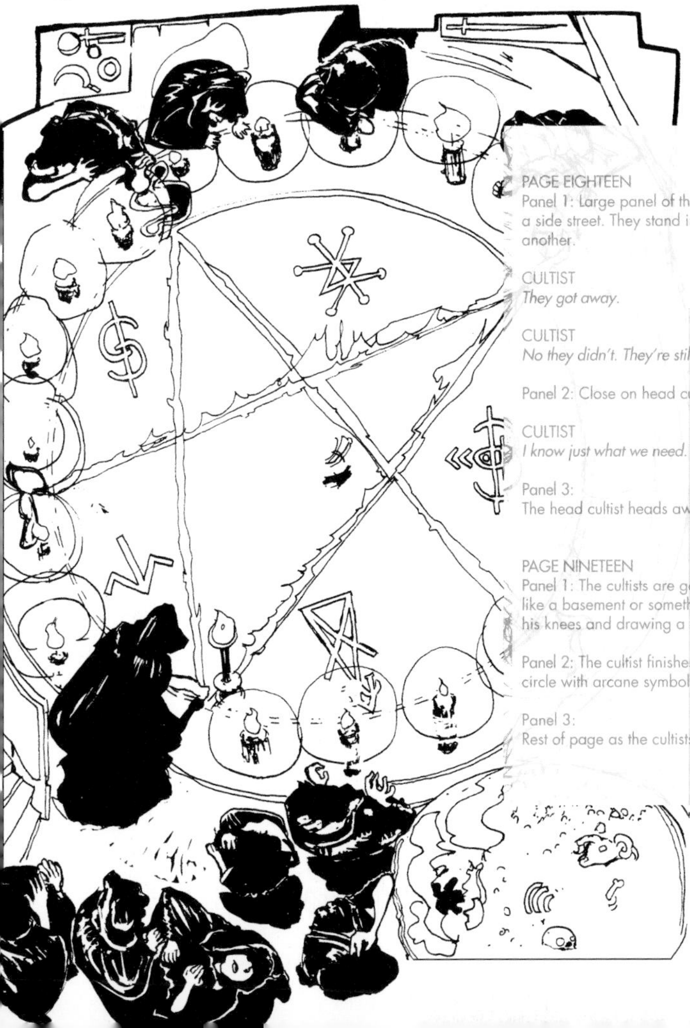

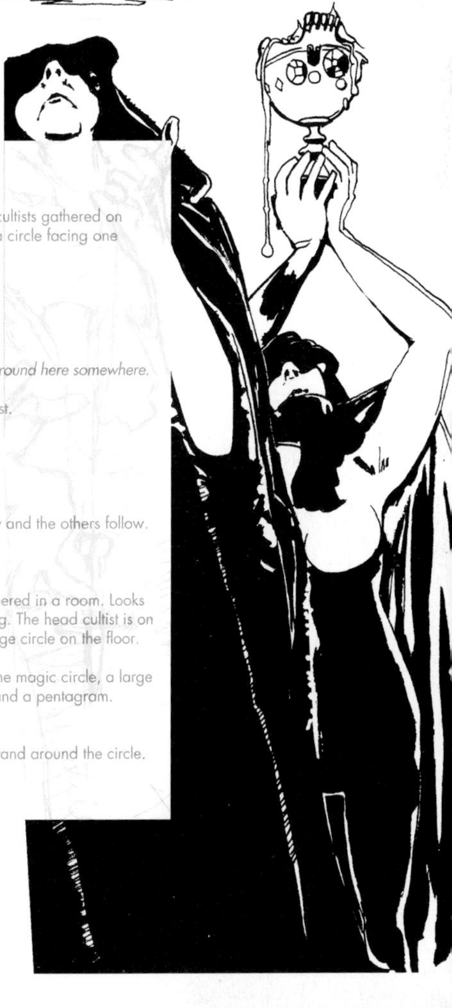

PAGE EIGHTEEN
Panel 1: Large panel of the cultists gathered on a side street. They stand in a circle facing one another.

CULTIST
They got away.

CULTIST
No they didn't. They're still around here somewhere.

Panel 2: Close on head cultist.

CULTIST
I know just what we need.

Panel 3:
The head cultist heads away and the others follow.

PAGE NINETEEN
Panel 1: The cultists are gathered in a room. Looks like a basement or something. The head cultist is on his knees and drawing a large circle on the floor.

Panel 2: The cultist finishes the magic circle, a large circle with arcane symbols and a pentagram.

Panel 3:
Rest of page as the cultists stand around the circle.

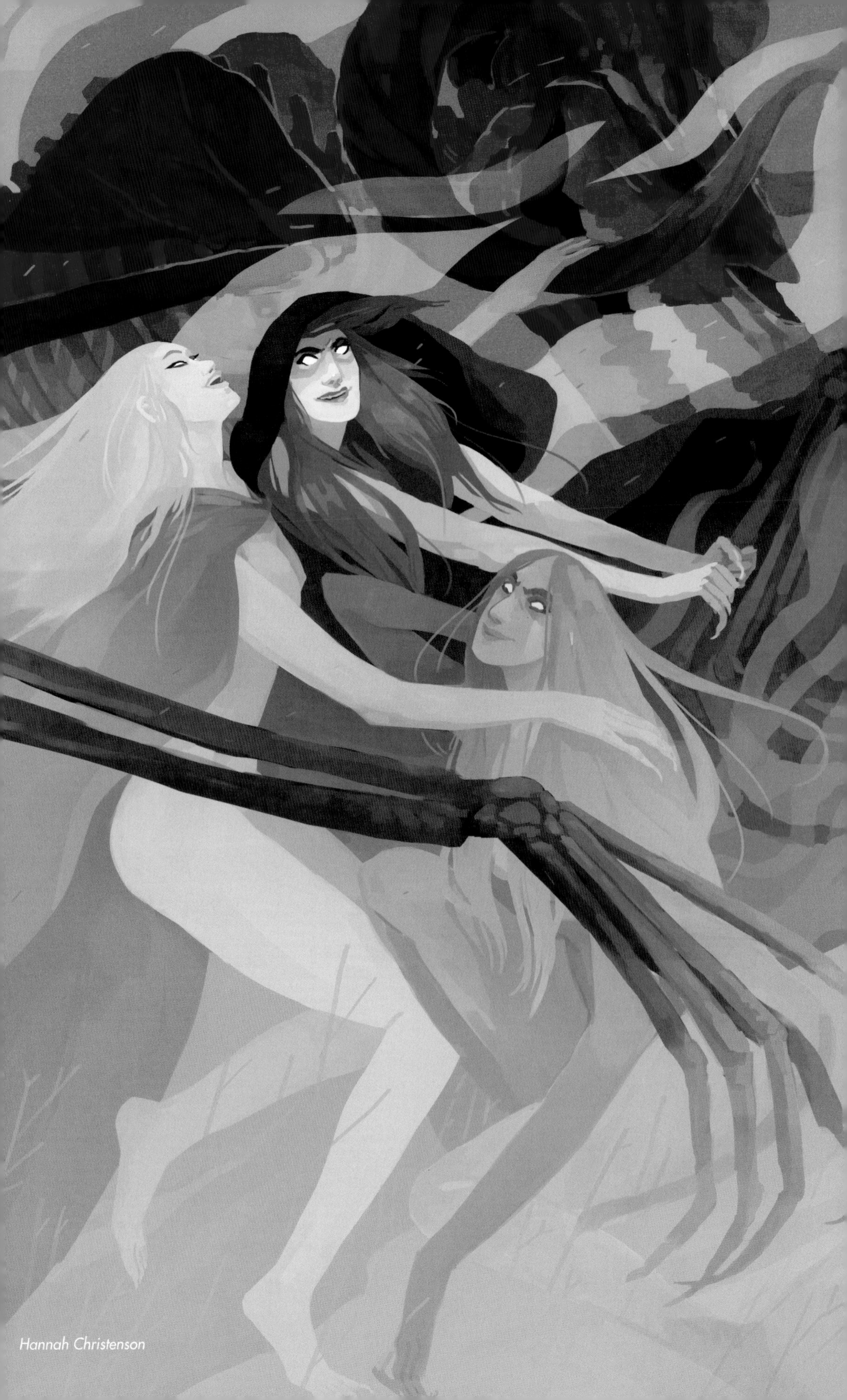
Hannah Christenson

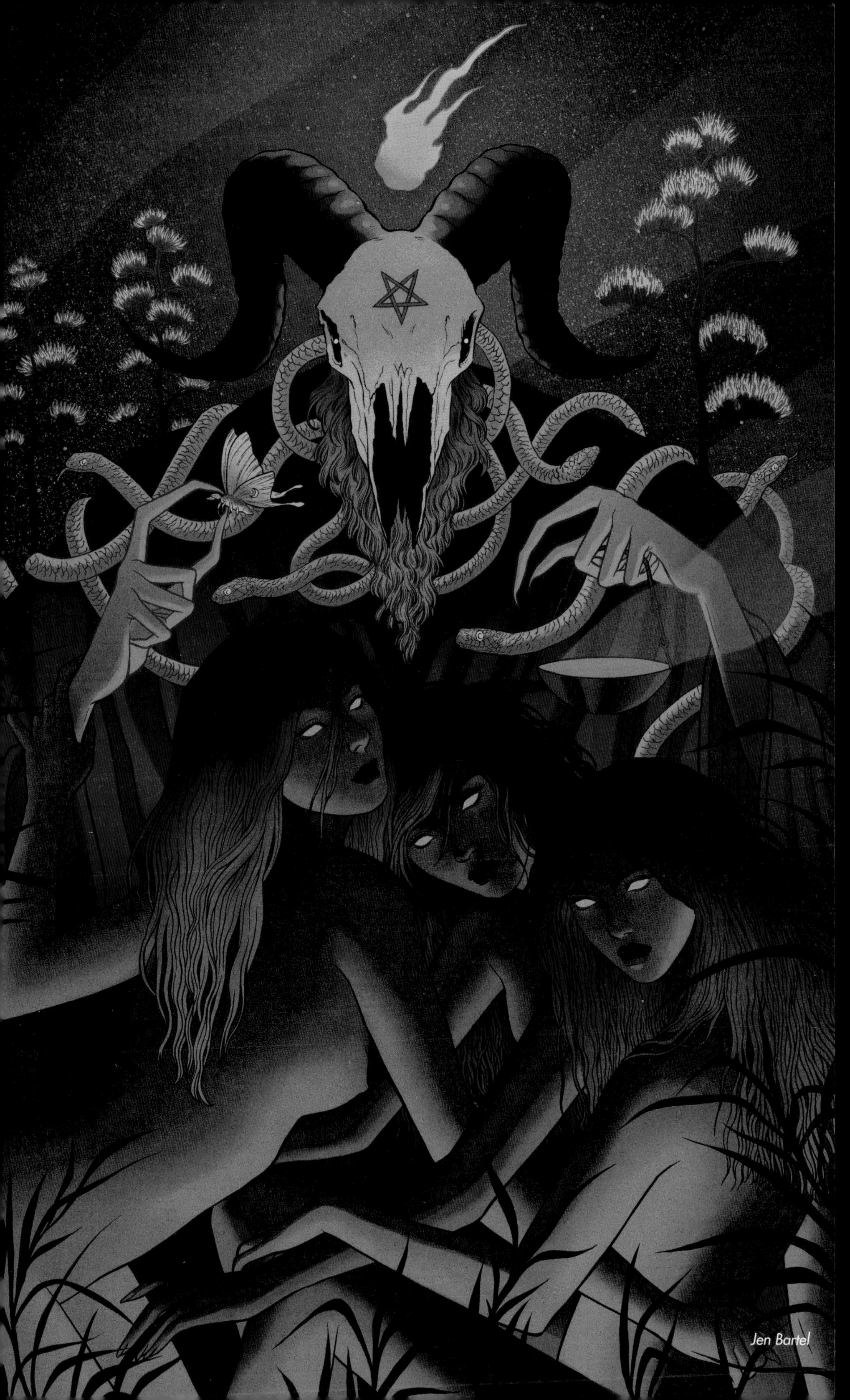

Jen Bartel

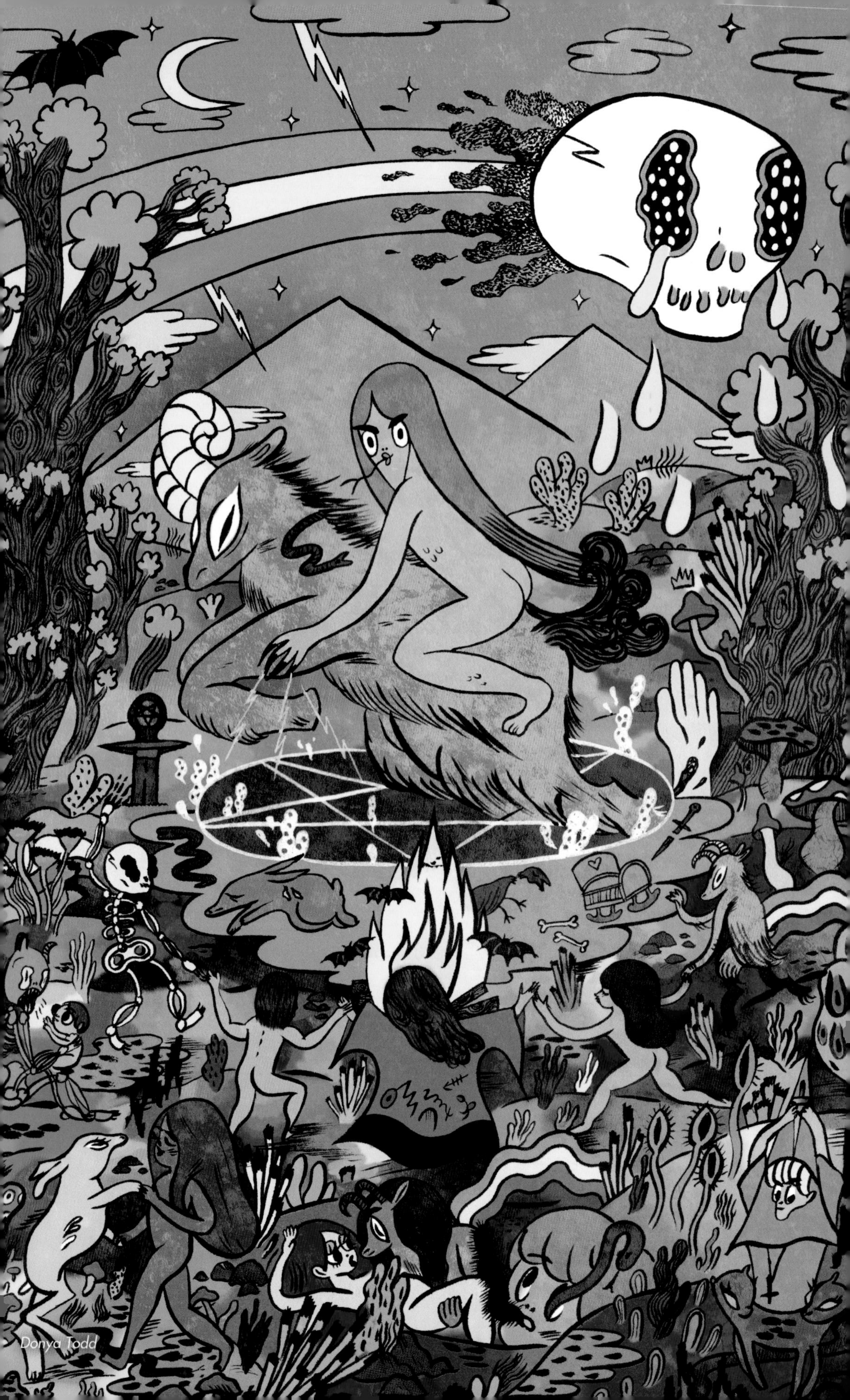
Donya Todd

In dark times, it's natural to seek comfort. To reach for a light in the shadows, to seize a flame in the night. And for some, it's even more natural to become blacker than the darkness, to absorb fear and transform it into a twisted power. That power is seduction–a warm forbidden caress, awakening sensations repressed by obligations, standards, and ideals. This is the oldest story ever told, and one, for some reason, we never tire of hearing. This is the story of how true evil, and even copycat carapaces of evil, can lure in the innocent.

In the 1960s, the city of San Francisco was emerging as a beacon of light in turbulent times. Filled with flower children, free love, and thousands of young people standing in opposition to the Vietnam War, it embodied innocence, passion, and a return to Bohemian lifestyles. Rejecting the conformist consumerism of the government, hippies gathered in communes to create art, discuss philosophy, and indulge in psychedelic explorations of body and mind. For some, it was a paradise, and for others, it was an opportunity to exploit the genuine desire for community and grounded fears in the future. For one man in particular, it was a platform for rebirth.

On April 30th, 1966, almost exactly a year before the infamous Summer of Love, Anton LaVey founded The Church of Satan, headquartered in The Black House, his inky Victorian home, and site of the church's rituals. For LaVey, this was a coming out of sorts, after spending the previous ten years holding lectures and hosting esoteric gatherings out of his home. The birth of the Church of Satan was held on Beltane, a Gaelic holiday and Wiccan Sabbat, welcoming the birth of spring. The name Beltane means "bright fire," and it is a celebration of fertility honoring the blessings of abundance. For witches, it's a time of year to embrace the vitality and passion of the goddess and to rejoice in the warming of the earth for literal and metaphorical growth. For LaVey, it was a time to simply grow his power, and maybe align his newly founded church with pre-existing ideas of witchcraft, meanwhile distorting one of its major holidays. He called this day the first year of the "Age of Satan."

With his shaved head, priest's robes, and flair for the dramatic, LaVey fully utilized the power of esoteric outer mysteries–appropriating the myths, images, and aesthetic appeal of dark religions–to attract beguiled followers interested in commanding that sort of presence. He understood that under the youthful hunger for peace and love was an equally fervent need for control, for justice, for self-centered fulfillment. And that is precisely what he founded his church on. Indulgence, moral ambiguity, vengeance, and selective compassion represent the ideals of LaVeyan Satanism, which he outlined in The Satanic Bible. On the surface, Satanism is simply a focus on self instead of community, a way to avoid the dogma of sin and live by one's own rules instead of societal expectations. In fact, according to LaVey, Satan is just a metaphor–so what could possibly go wrong?

The idea of outer and inner mysteries is what makes Satanism both frightening and lurid. Like other mystery religions, Satanism cultivates and encourages mysteries that serve to protect their true agenda, while attracting devotees. The concept of Mystery Religions dates back to the late Roman Empire. Acceptance in these religions was based on initiation, ritual participation, and devout secrecy. Perhaps inspired by the esoteric and occultism of then-popular Mystery Religions such as paganism and Wicca, LaVey adopted their philosophies of private and public image control. The outer mysteries are like a costume shown to outsiders, a way of projecting a specifically designed aesthetic, which is perhaps contrary or incomplete in its view. The inner mysteries of Satanism are known only to its followers at the heart of the religion, protecting the inner workings of its faith.

We all have a picture in our heads of what a Satanist looks like–a lithe, sexual alpha, draped in black and positively exuding dangerous pheromones, with a tongue sharper than a ritual dagger and clandestine intentions, hopefully including plenty of candlelit seduction. And it's that exact superficial icon that exists within and outside of the church, summoning people with all kinds of different...motivations. Look at the story you read today and ask yourself, what is Christie seeing? Are these truly evil people, or are they simply angry, displaced outsiders, seeking to chase away the unfamiliar by using the shorthand of Satanic guise? Go back and read the issue again, considering why the outer mysteries of Satanism might appeal to people, especially if those people want to protect something far more sinister. Could their actions, and the actions of similarly minded others, be what gives Satanism a bad name?

Or is it all just a bunch of nonsense?

This essay by Casey Gilly is the first of a series, exploring Satanism in the real world.

THE BLACK HOUSE

The Manson Family (2003) is a movie directed by Jim Van Bebber which retells the infamous mythology of the feared 1960s clan through a phantasmagoric melange of blood, violence, and demonic imagery. The film uses the framing device of a Manson documentary producer reviewing footage of clan interviews, interweaving with re-enactments of key Manson family lore. Exterior to this is a young group of Manson fan-obsessives who are preparing to murder the aforementioned producer to service their iconoclastic sense of preservation of their particular idea of Charles Manson.

Van Bebber's film is the yowly splatter horror culmination of the themes that have built throughout his career to that point. He has always had a powerful sense of space and here he uses the desert as a forge through which to hellmouth a demonic worldview that is less a moralistic fairy tale warning of the dangers of falling out of more an anarchic inferno writ large like a sneering nihilist fist into the sky spit high into the night sky. His film shreds the Manson story of its "flower child gone wrong" pretensions, and instead presents it as an orgiastic parade to the culture of the young violently cannibalizing the old.

The bulk of the film takes place at Spahn Ranch, which was also the setting for Old Hollywood TV shows like Bonanza (1959-63), Zorro (1957), and The Lone Ranger (1949-57). There's no small irony that it was the Manson family's relationship with Hollywood at the time, that enabled much of the delusions Manson was able to offer up to his followers—whether it was partying with a Beach Boy, or choosing the Tate residence for their murder—part of the horror of Manson was not only the terror of children turning on their parents—it was the sensationalism of it all being so very Hollywood. The versatility of the ranch for those purposes largely resided in its mixture of idyllic flora and fauna, and old western death plains—elements which also served as the perfect backdrop for both Manson's messianic pretensions, and geographically linked him with the LA music scene that he wanted to ascend through. For Manson, the landscape and geography was very much a significant aspect of his ability to control the family—arguably just as important as the LSD. But it was also this landscape that most likely shaped the dark turn the family took. The lack of resources meant that they had to deal, deal drugs, steal from drug dealers—and the isolation meant that once the killing started given the number of people there, and the isolation, there was no way to do anything but go along with it. But there was also a symbolic side to the way the land played with Charlie's message—it was this symbolic quality between Eden and exile that Van Bebber uses as the baseline for his film—jarring an edenic hippie facade against the nightmarish void of a desert crawling with demonic invocation.

The family entered the desert as wide-eyed flower children following a mysterious guru who promised them a greater authority in their lives, those desert nights made sure that they left as blood crazed disciples of demonic possession. It was the crucible of the desert that shaped these creatures in Van Bebber's film. The isolation from society, mixed with the ecstasy of drugs and sex, partnered with the scarcity of resources fashioned wolves out of human skins. The Manson family would then creepy crawl their way back from that desert night, into the infamous spree of murders that would create their legacy. In Bebber's film, once the night starts, it elongates infinitely, casting its shadow through time.

Van Bebber juxtaposes all of this against the latest generation of Charlie's kids, patrolling a corollary wasteland divorced of anything but the joy of violence and upheaval. They have no illusions and they pledge openly to the glory of bloodshed. This chronal distortion of the film creates the sense that these demons are beyond time, and that their actions are happening all of these years apart, but simultaneously.

Van Bebber repeatedly intercuts the modern group in with the footage of the original family. The true legacy of the Manson family wasn't the fall of hippie idealism, but the infamy of violence, and the appeal of that violence to the disillusioned and disenfranchised. In these children, they are the simulacrum of the legendary Manson family—and like all copies, they are harder, more direct, but less soulful—trading originality for extremity—in their reproduction they are natural born killers. The distortions of the copy both reflect and project—reflect the original qualities of the original, but project the distortion of the logical extremes of the stresses that reproduction introduces through time.

There's a brilliant section in the middle of the film, where the family are holding a fiery black mass, replete with blood sacrifices, bonfires, orgies, and Charlie nailed to a cross—in this jitter of time, blood, void, and slogans, a spell casts itself into a kind of Kenneth Anger version of Antonioni's Zabriskie Point (1970) as transmuted through Van Bebber's extreme blood splatter cinema of degradation. That Van Bebber is able to do all of this without affectation, and solely for its visceral impact is remarkable given the self-awareness that tends to overshadow this kind of work. The aesthetic appeal of Van Bebber, even going back to Deadbeat at Dawn (1988), is his ability to depict a kind of gutter sludging of the human form, devolved into supernatural mythos in the service of blood and ejaculate. His violence is unique in cinema, not only in the singular elements: the abrupt cuts, the yelling, the montage, and always this kind of watery secondhand blood that sits somewhere between Argento and Fulci like a boiling bright red sewer paint cut a little too thin—it is the sum of these numbers that produces Van Bebber's magic.

The Tate-Labianca murders are this exhausting sensory overload of over-the-top scissoring of knife hitting meat, mixed with screams, grain, and music. Wojciech Frykowski crawls across the black void backdrop, dragging a deranged Tex Watson, who is just pounding with his knife into Frykowski's flesh over and over and over again to the soundtrack of squealing pigs—and you watch and hear as the knife sound deteriorates into this human mush squish sound as Frykowski's body breaks down from the mutilation. It is a singular experience. Van Bebber's film asserts, if anything, that the lesson of Manson wasn't the evil that men do, but that the celebrity of extreme iconoclastic violence that the Manson mythos helped create—and the satanic celebrity that he and his followers enjoy—speaks to a particular kind of fetishism born out of disconnect with the wider horror of the world around us. Van Bebber's Manson Family is something of a culmination from the themes in Deadbeat at Dawn, Roadkill: The Last Days of John Martin (1994), and My Sweet Satan (1994). It is the heavy metal extremity of excess—his films are not provocation, there's never a sense he is doing anything with his films that are for the feelings of others—but rather these films are an expression of sex, of violence, of the ways that polite society does not serve the appetites of communication fully, and an experience that is not always linguistic in its manifestations. Language organizes the visual world, but it does not express it. And the strength of Van Bebber is in the fluids, in the bodies, that there are words is only that they are ineffectual—Manson's own words are all lies, he is Satan after all. But the violence he creates in others is truth, and their expression is at the limit of language's utility. This is about how if you howl into the desert, no God can hear you. These films are from hell, from exile.

This essay on the film The Manson Family, *by Sarah Horrocks, is the final part of her, otherwise singles-exclusive, series. Sarah's comic Goro series began in September 2017. For fans of trashy melodrama in the vein of Dynasty or La Usurpadora, Goro tells the story of an assassin hired to kill an evil matriarch. For more information go to: https://mercurialblonde.squarespace.com*

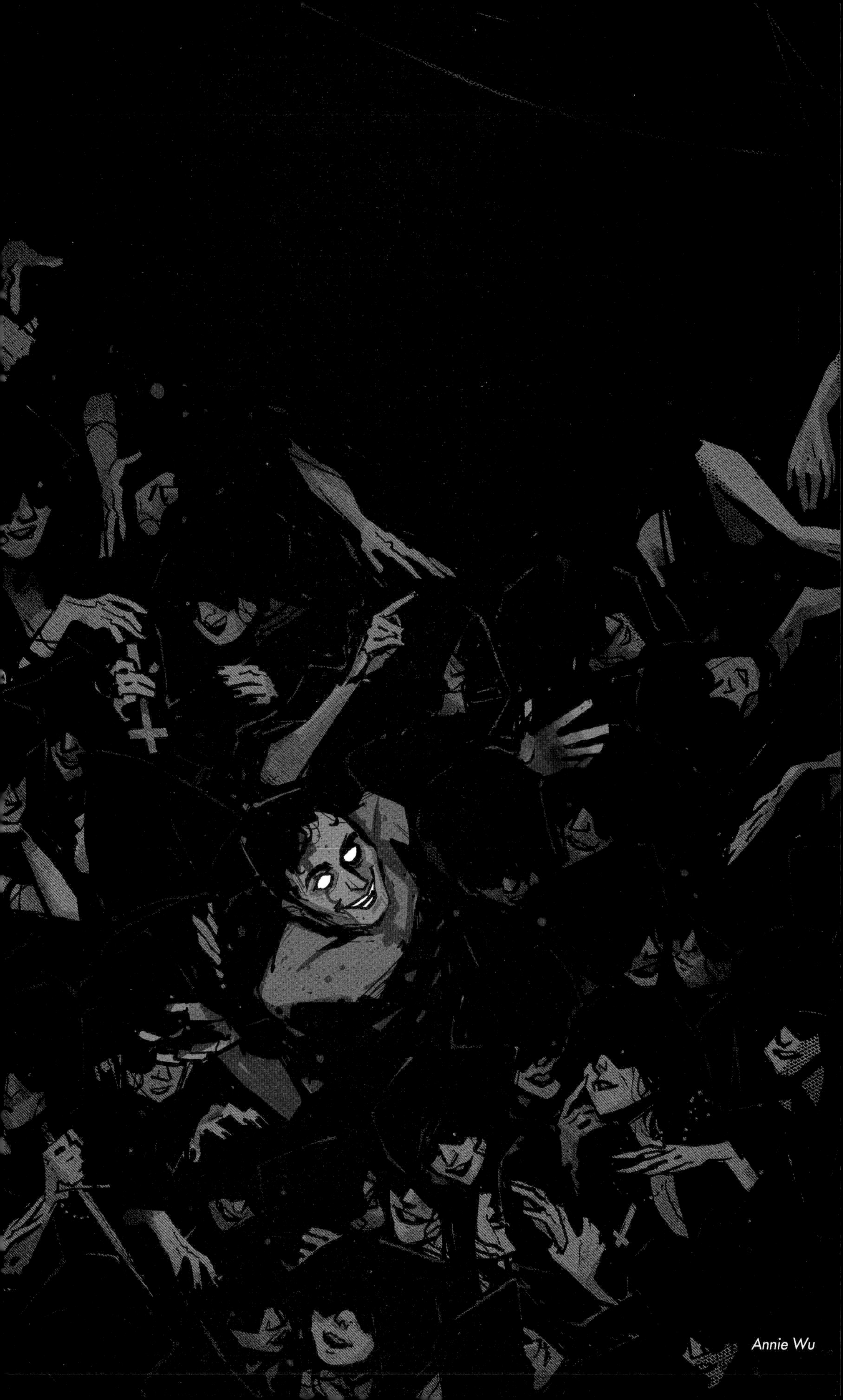

Annie Wu

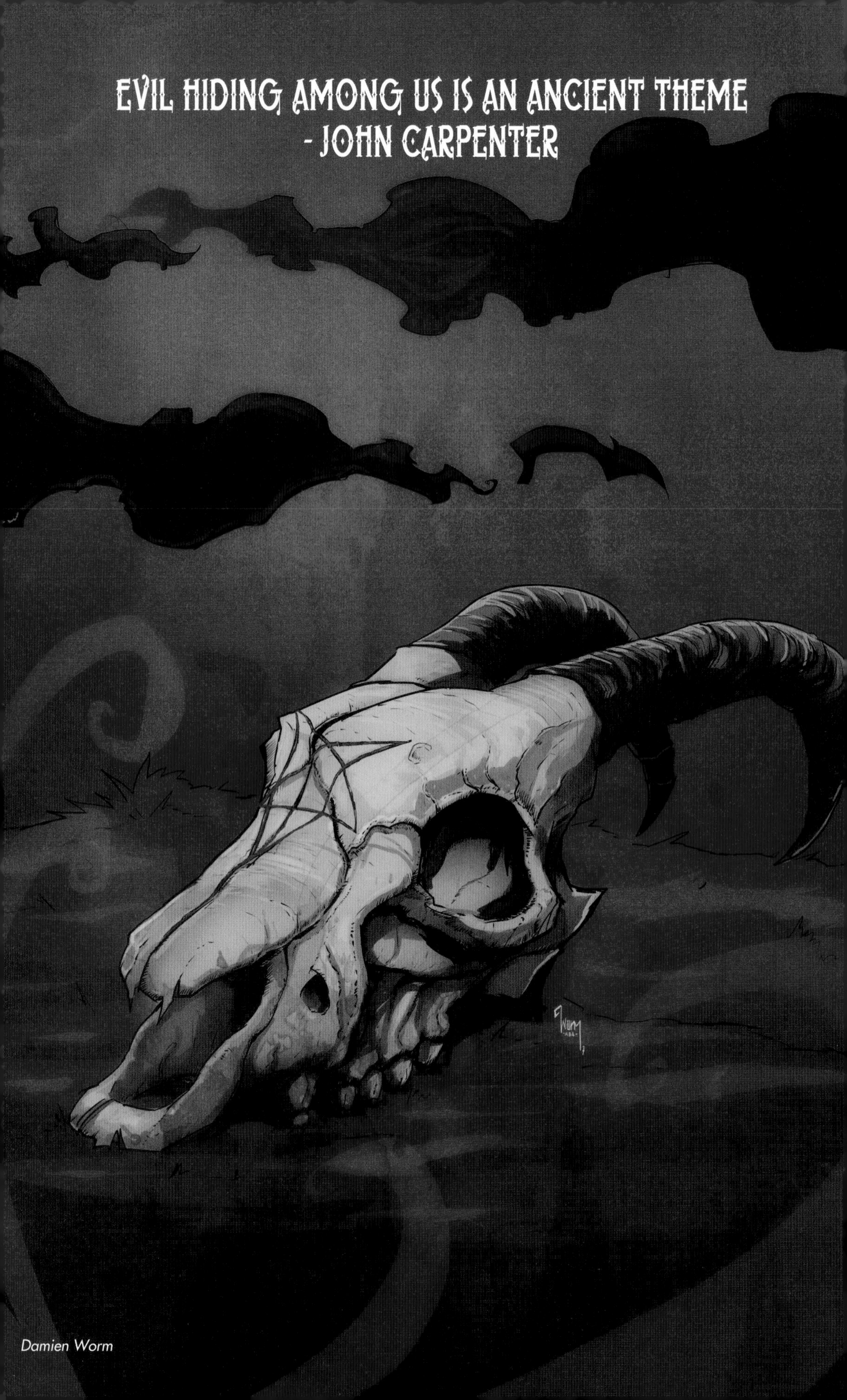
EVIL HIDING AMONG US IS AN ANCIENT THEME
- JOHN CARPENTER

Damien Worm

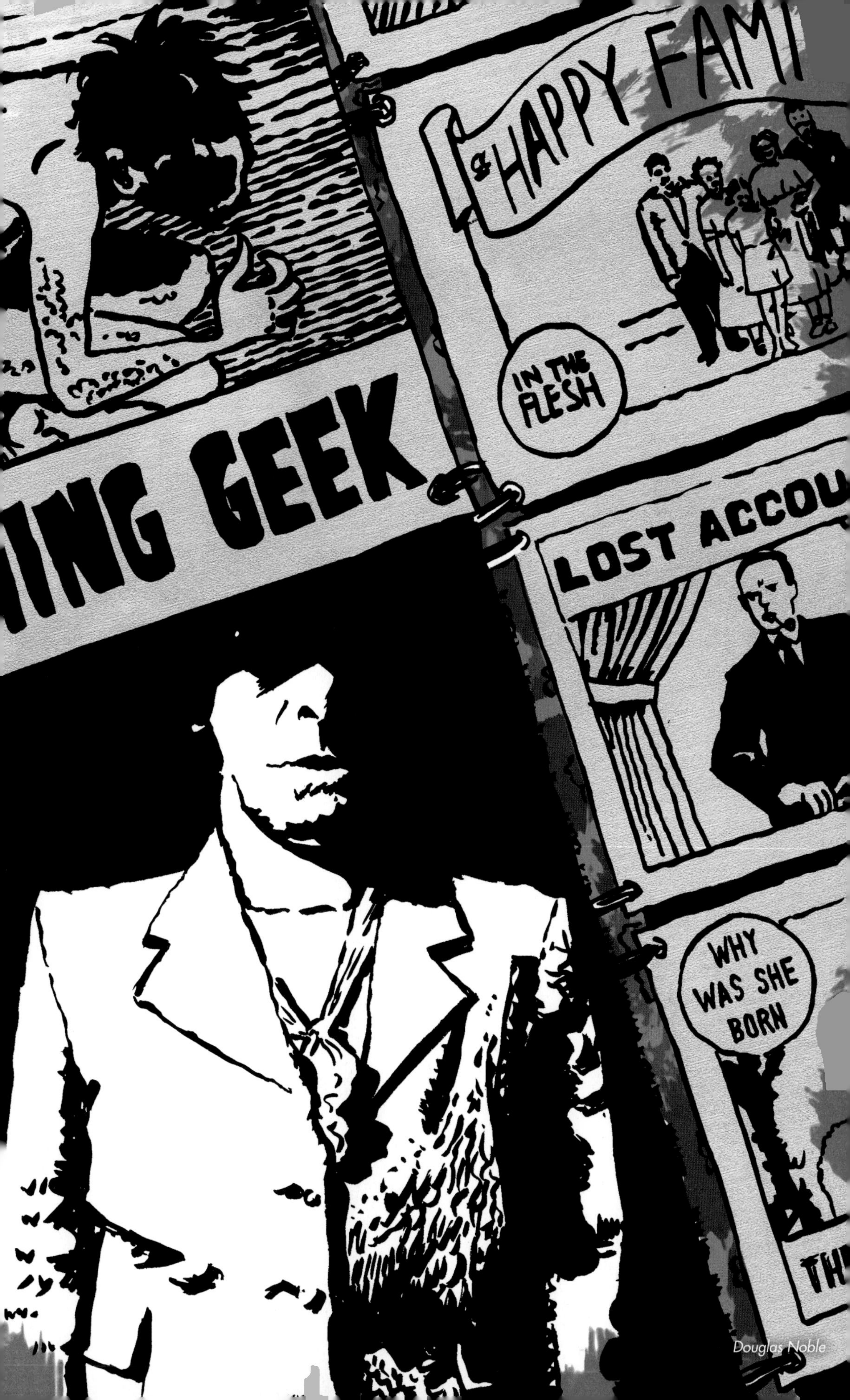
ING GEEK
& HAPPY FAMI
IN THE FLESH
LOST ACCOU
WHY WAS SHE BORN
TH
Douglas Noble

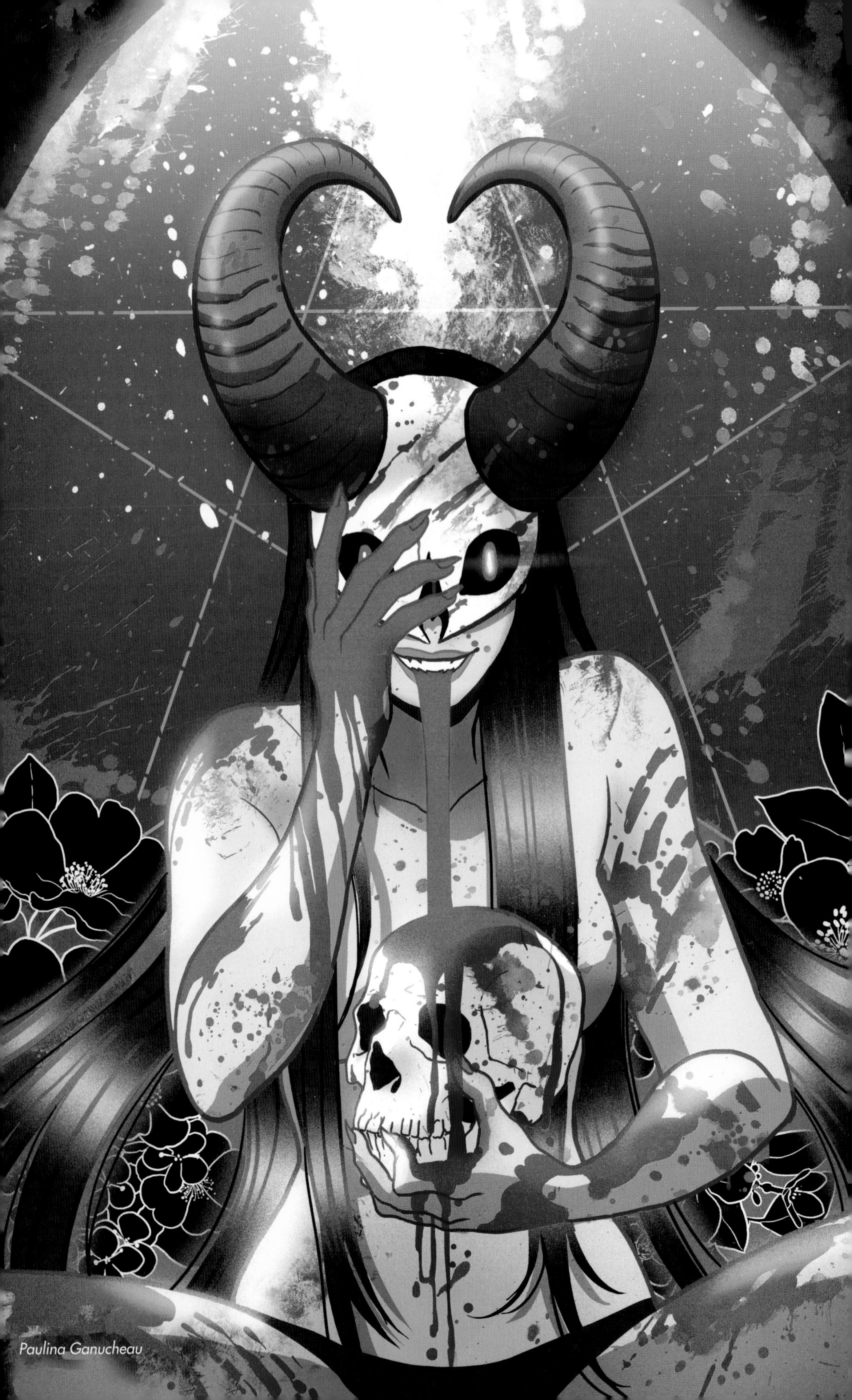
Paulina Ganucheau

sacrifices have long been known to please a diverse pantheon of gods. From burnt offerings for Christian and Pagan deities to animal sacrifices compelling the Orisa for healing in Santeria to a prehistory littered with human sacrifices, it seems that blood has always been the pathway to the divine. But why has it held this power? What kinds of gods crave the life force of their creation? And who could bring themselves to carry out such things?

In ancient times, blood offerings and human sacrifice were thought of as both a way to bring prosperity and to unite a community for a common purpose. By giving up a small piece of themselves, they thought to secure safety for the greater good. Perhaps it was considered an altruistic practice at the time, and perhaps some victims were as willing as one could be under such circumstances, but there is no evidence of what was gained. There is only the evidence of what was lost, in the forms of bones and mass graves. Many sacrificial practices became symbolic in nature as the world quickly evolved, but the ideas remained: blood spilled is power gained. So while the killing faded into grisly obscurity, the lingering whispers of liquid offerings still seduce certain devotees even today.

Within certain spiritual walks, blood rituals are used to forge a relationship with a God, or to strengthen the power of intent, or as a form of payment for services granted. Giving a little of ourselves to gain a little more of favor seems simple enough, but what kind of ties might it forge? What sort of unknown variables might be waiting in the shadows to steal a few drops? The consensual spilling of one's own blood might not seem like a big deal, but how do you really know what you're in for? Both scientifically and spiritually, the power of blood makes an impact. By cutting ourselves in the name of ritual, we open a sacred space for anything we choose to invite in…potentially including foreign presences, some we never wanted to host.

We come into this world in a wave of blood, anointed with the life force of our mothers, slick little crimson mermaids taking our first breaths of air. Blood sustains our bodies, carries our oxygen, keeps us healthy, and fills our beating hearts. Women and men who have periods go through a moon-based cycle monthly, where our bodies store and shed blood in preparation to receive life. When our wombs are empty, the blood is spilled in what could be considered either an act of praise or sorrow, depending on how badly you want children. That ritual, menstruation, is almost a biological confirmation of the power of blood. When we leave the world it's often bloody, or at least it will be during embalming. It's not hard to understand why the fluid is considered so powerful when it symbolizes the very acts of birth, death, and possibly rebirth. From blood comes creation, and from creation comes a new existence—maybe even for a creature we don't recognize.

In *Winnebago Graveyard*, we saw a haunting and primal blood offering. Do you think it worked? What

do you think the coil summoned? And why? Do you think the hooded figures were men or women--and does it matter? Does the blood of the practitioner influence the nature of what is conjured? And do you think they are able to exercise power over it? Or do the expected rules of creation follow, meaning that just because we've brought something to life doesn't mean we get to control it...?

This essay by Casey Gilly is the second of a series, exploring Satanism in the real world.

WHO MADE THIS?

Steve Niles
Writer Steve Niles is best known for *30 Days of Night, Criminal Macabre, Simon Dark, Mystery Society, Frankenstein Alive Alive, Monster & Madman* and *Batman: Gotham County Line*. Niles works for comic publishers including Black Mask, IDW, Image and Dark Horse. Steve is currently writing *The October Faction* for IDW and has written a number of titles for Image Comics, including creator-owned *Heroes, Strange Cases, Spawn* and *Chin Music.*

30 Days of Night was released in 2007 as a major motion picture. Other comics by Niles, including *Remains, Aleister Arcane* and *Freaks of the Heartland* have been optioned for film and TV.

website: www.steveniles.com

Alison Sampson
An award-winning architect and illustrator, Alison's work has been widely published, including by Marvel (*Jessica Jones in Civil War II*), DC/Vertigo, Dark Horse (*Creepy*), IDW, Boom Studios, The BBC, The Guardian newspaper, and in various Kickstarter-based books, including, most recently *Femme Magnifique*, with Shelly Bond and Hi-fi Color. She previously worked on the graphic novella *Genesis* for Image Comics with Nathan Edmondson, and has contributed to various other books at Image, including *The Wicked + The Divine*. Aside from her illustration work, much of Alison's output can be seen in built form on the streets of her native London. This is her first mini-series.

website: www.alisonsampson.com

Stéphane Paitreau
Based in France, comics and animation colorist Stéphane Paitreau mainly works for Soleil on titles including "Samurai Legends" "Samurai Origins", the long-running "La Geste des Chevaliers Dragons" / "tales of the dragons guards" "Durango" and many others. Most recently he completed colors on *Espace Vital*, for Glénat. This is his first work for Image Comics.

website: www.spaitreau.deviantart.com

Aditya Bidikar
Apart from *Winnebago Graveyard*, Aditya is currently lettering *Drifter, Motor Crush* and *Black Cloud* for Image Comics, *Night's Dominion* for Oni Press, Grant Morrison's *18 Days* and *Avatarex* for Graphic India, and the *Femme Magnifique* anthology, among others.

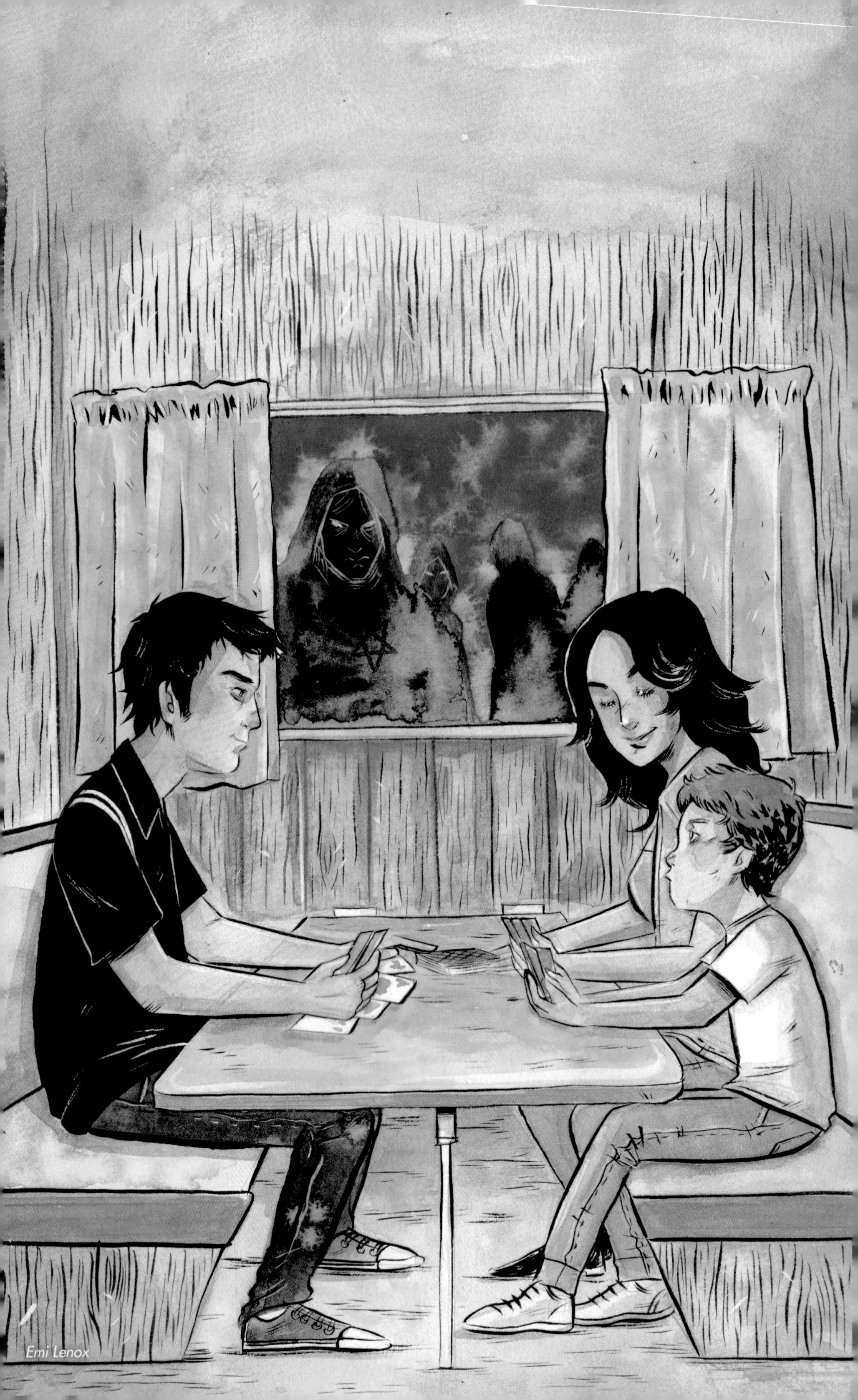
Emi Lenox

What makes a stranger so dangerous?

What is it about the unknown that sets our minds speculating? In *Winnebago Graveyard*, we've seen most of our main characters react to their unusual surroundings with a mixture of curiosity, judgment, disbelief, and violence. But what do they really have to fear? What if they've just misunderstood these new people, leading to false assumptions about the intentions of others? Would you blame the cloaked figures for fighting back if they felt threatened by uninformed outsiders?

It certainly wouldn't be the first time fear of the other lead to outrageous accusations.

Only four decades ago, we saw the rise of what is now known as Satanic Panic, a phenomenon rooted in fear over the alleged presence of Satanic people and activities in various communities. From pre-school teachers to lesbians to misfit teens, innocent people were accused of and held accountable for sinister activities in the name of a dark agenda. It gripped the 1970s and 1980s in its clutches, confusing social change, rising feminism and progressive restructuring of the American family for acts of evil. The hysteria influenced court cases, talk shows, and literature, sparking a media frenzy over what was essentially misinformation–but with dire consequences.

In 1983, a family-owned daycare in Manhattan Beach, CA, became one of the first cases of Satanic Panic leading to legal proceedings. Family members of The McMartin Pre-School were accused of ritualistic abuse, including molestation, exposure to sexual encounters with animals, and physical violence. Instead of exercising discretion, police sent form letters to parents of current and former students, outlining allegations of abuse and asking for additional witnesses to come forward. Which they did. After suggestive interviewing techniques with unsupervised, highly suggestible children, the list of accusations grew from concerning to truly bizarre. The McMartins went to trial, which lasted eleven years yet resulted in no convictions. If you're asking yourself how this happened, consider the times–women were prevalent in the workforce, shifting traditional expectations of childcare and parenting. The prevalent Christian family model was disrupted by a budding feminist agenda, where children were cared for outside the family. The guilt and anxiety of challenging long-standing family values were easily warped by dogmatic beliefs, leading parents to readily accept the presence of even the most ridiculous influences: Satanic cults in a pre-school.

Unfortunately, not everyone wrongly accused under the hysteria of Satanic Panic avoided conviction. In San Antonio, TX, in 1994 four women–Elizabeth Ramirez, Kristie Mayhugh, Cassandra River, and Anna Vazquez–were accused of molesting two young girls. All four women were lesbians and their sexuality strongly influenced investigators, including Doctor Nancy Kellog, a child abuse expert who examined the victims. Kellog testified against the women, stating that a female perpetrator, and especially more than one perpetrator, was an excellent reason to suspect Satanic abuse, although Kellog also admitted she'd never personally seen observed such a case. Even though this testimony wasn't allowed before the jury, prosecutors took the lead on infusing the trial with connections to Satanic abuse. Between rampant homophobia and fear of unfounded occult influences, Ramirez was sentenced to 37.5 years in prison and the remaining three were sentenced to 25 years. Luckily, logic prevailed 15 years later in the form of the Innocence Project of Texas who took on the case and were able to free and exonerate the women in 2016. But nothing can return the years of their life, stolen by ignorance and intolerance.

Ultimately, who is to blame? Perhaps cases such as these say more about what lives inside each of us. Our paranoias, prejudices, and possibly our desires influence what we project onto others. Maybe we are the ones who want to wield all of the power, maybe we're all monsters inside our own heads. Maybe what we fear most is what we know we're capable of: oppressing those who are different, attacking that which confuses us, and compelling others to share our world view. What if our terror of the other will always be more powerful than compassion? And what if that is the truest of evils after all?

This essay on Satanic Panic, by Casey Gilly, is the third of a series, exploring Satanism in the real world.

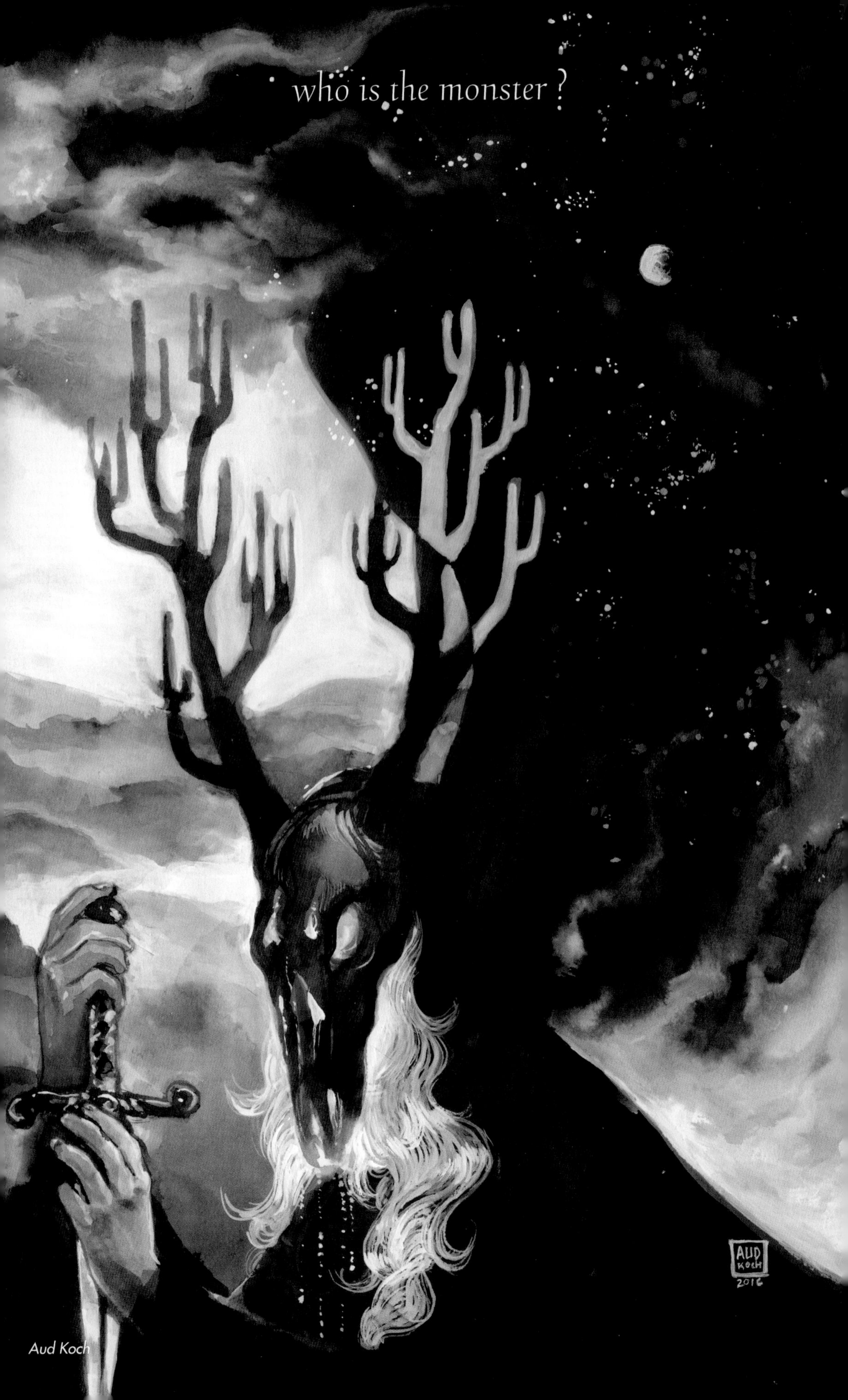
who is the monster?
AUD KOCH 2016
Aud Koch

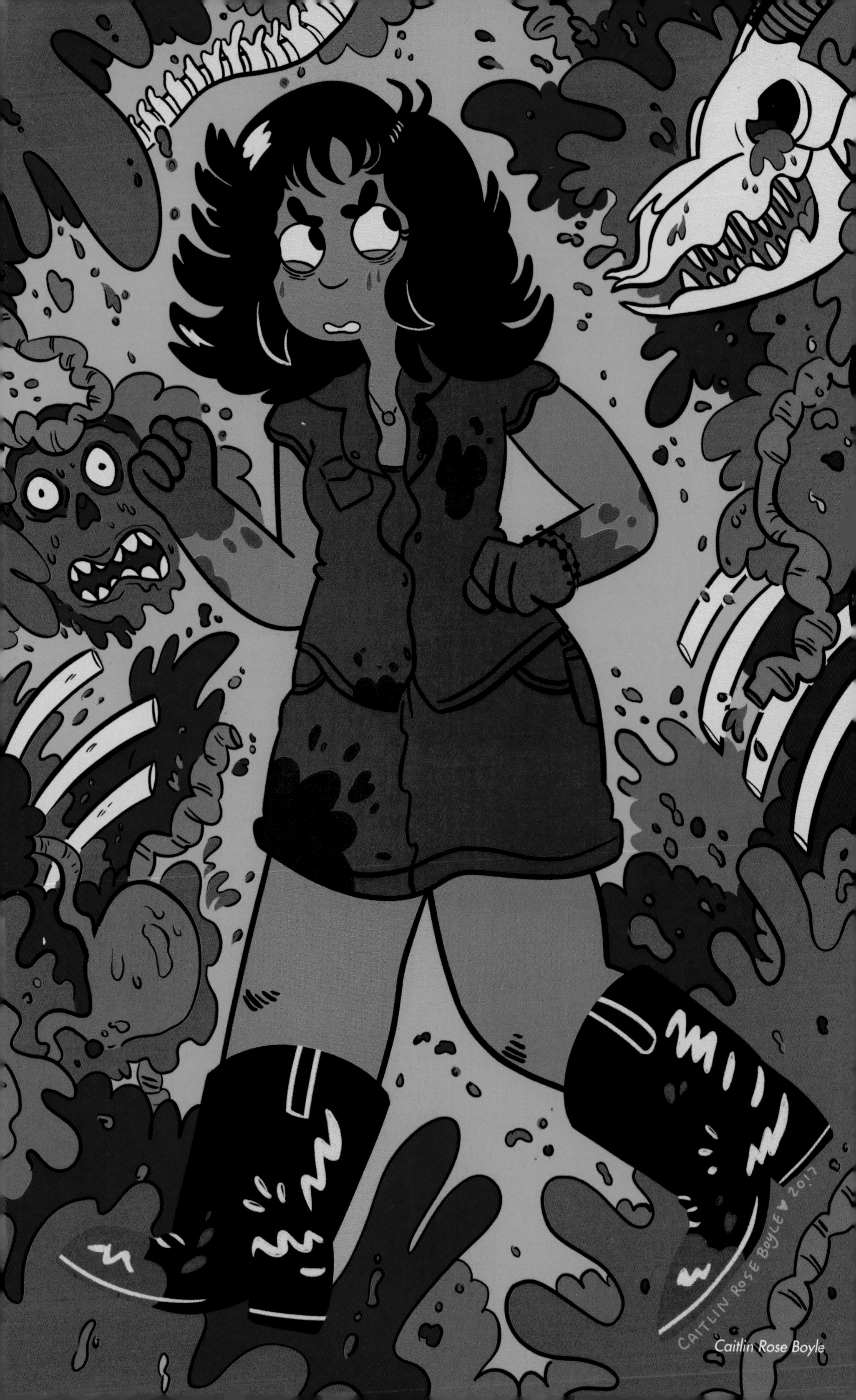
CAITLIN ROSE BOYLE 2017

Caitlin Rose Boyle

As *Winnebago Graveyard* draws to a close, we see a family's journey in a frightening and unpredictable world reach its end. In spite of their best efforts, even with their honest intent, was anyone able to avoid danger? Was anyone ever truly safe?

Are any of us?

In our day to day lives, we encounter evil far more than we might imagine. In fact, the average American meets an unapprehended murderer around 10 times in their life. Sometimes it's not quite as specific. Sometimes evil brushes up against us, sending a blind chill up our spines. Or perhaps it sits next to us on the bus, provoking us to exit sooner than intended. Sometimes it looks us in the eye and wishes us a good morning. Sometimes it stalks us, creeping ever closer only to be banished at the last minute by a savior of chance. We will likely never know how close we've come to dark fates, just by a stroke of good luck.

Or is it something more than luck?

For true evil to exist in the world, it makes sense that there must also be good. For every hooded figure devoted to chaos and bloodshed, is there a counterpart devoted to benevolence? And how are we to decide what the actions of each side should look like? How are we to know if something that appears violent and cruel might be working toward honorable means? Our own interpretations of unfamiliar ways, unexamined belief systems, and unknown agendas certainly shapes our responses, and perhaps leads us into harm's way more often than it protects us.

Why do we have any faith in ourselves to determine who the real monsters are?

Making judgment calls about our own safety can be daunting, and so we turn to generalizations. We assume we can identify risks by their appearance, by reputation, by misalignment with our own beliefs. We assume evil always wears the same face. We turn away from the darkness, distracting ourselves with perhaps reckless self-indulgence. We have our own rituals of safety, just as the hooded figures from this book have theirs, and in the end, people are going to do whatever it takes to protect themselves...even if it means taking on something loathsome.

In the past few essays, we've examined Satanism from several angles: the historical, the practical, and the dogmatic. Like any set of spiritual beliefs, it can be practiced by wonderful people who lead healthy, sane lives. Or it can be twisted as a means of justifying hostility, violence, and even murder. The same could be said of any religion, though, couldn't it?

Any belief system could be taken to dangerous extremes. Our belief in a stable world, in a steady hand guiding us, in an underlying order charting our course can inspire us to be our best selves and, sometimes, can blind us to our own excesses. When my beliefs and your contrasting beliefs brush up against each other, the ontological friction can create earth-rending conflict, and when we part it's possible that nothing will be the same for either of us.

In this way, the story of *Winnebago Graveyard* could be the story of any of us, of all of us. The story of our world. Will the voice we hear inside our selves, the one that creates the very foundation of our reality, lead us up into the light? Or further in the darkness? And–the piece that should give all of us pause–when that voice gets loud enough, will we even know the difference?

This essay on Satanic Panic, by Casey Gilly, is the fourth of a series, exploring Satanism in the real world. This book is for her son, who was born between this piece being written and its publication.

Guest art for Winnebago Graveyard *by Dave Taylor*

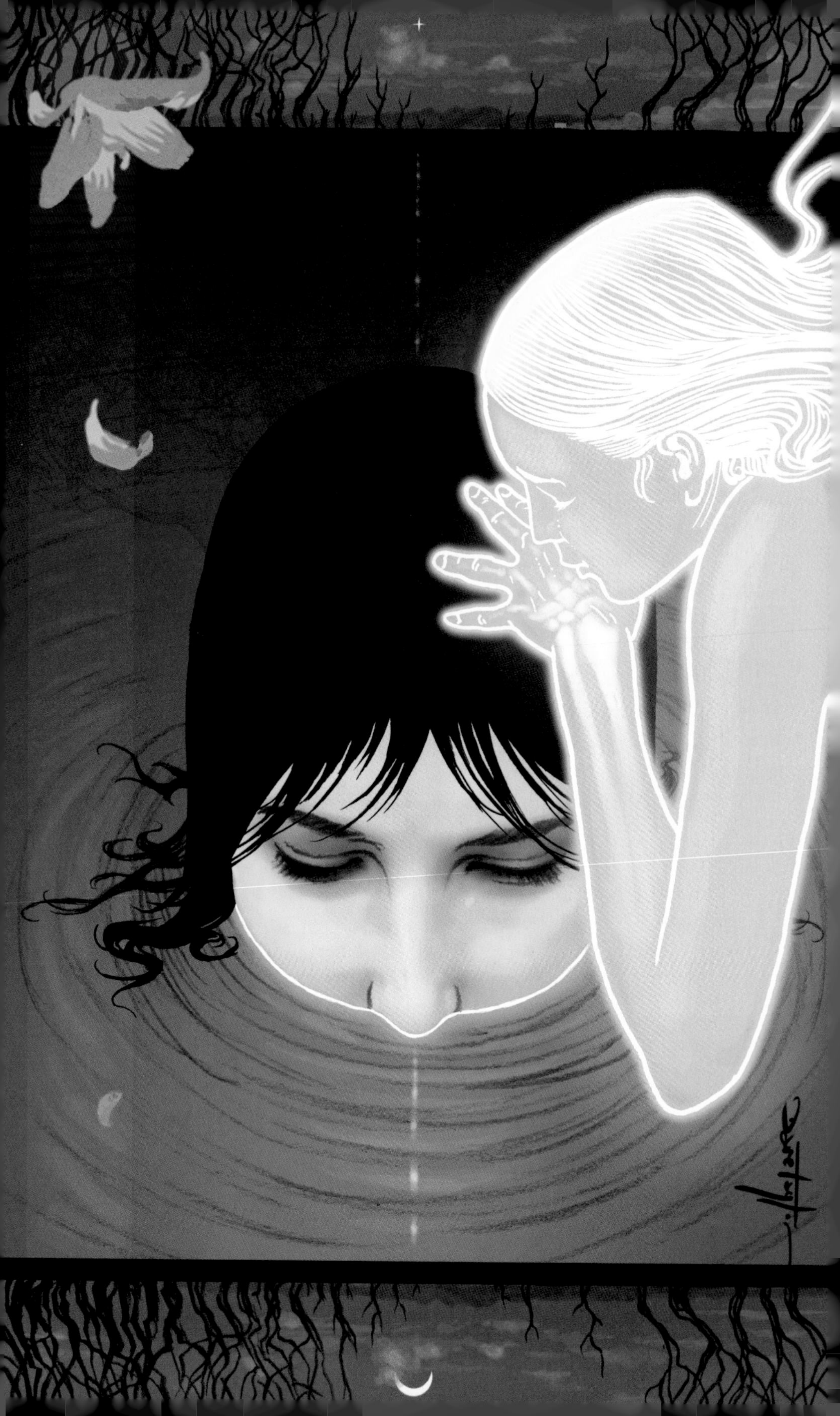

**The art is beautiful.
The story perfect.
This is my favorite comic of the last few years already.
I LOVE THIS BOOK!**

- MARK MILLAR

**I really loved *Winnebago Graveyard*.
Smart and creepy horror by Steve Niles
and eerie art by Alison Sampson.
Niles at his horrific best.**

- RICK REMENDER

Everything about this book gives me the willies.

- GAIL SIMONE

**Its like a hallucinogenic nightmare
and it is damn impressive!**

- TERRY MOORE

**Beautiful, grotesque and scary
a must read for horror fans.**

- RILEY ROSSMO

**If Ray Bradbury went for grindhouse thrills,
I think we'd get a story like this.**

- CULLEN BUNN

**Amazing, beautifully drawn,
wicked fun.**

- CHELSEA CAIN

**Moody, unsettling and beautifully drawn...
Everything in this book strikes a perfect tone...
A distinct and compelling vision,
brought to life expertly.**

- KURT BUSIEK